LUTHER M. SILER

THE
SANCTUM
OF THE
SPHERE

THE BENEVOLENCE
ARCHIVES: OMNIBUS
EDITION

PROSTETNIC
PUBLICATIONS

THE SANCTUM OF THE SPHERE: THE BENEVOLENCE ARCHIVES, OMNIBUS EDITION

ISBN-13: 978-0-9906253-4-6
ISBN-10: 0990625346

First Printing: April 2015

THE SANCTUM OF THE SPHERE is dedicated to Brian K. Vaughan, who has never heard of me, but who is nonetheless still responsible for my stupid little book's existence.

Thanks for the inspiration, Brian.

TABLE OF CONTENTS

FOREWORD

Welcome to *The Sanctum of the Sphere*, the second volume of *The Benevolence Archives!* Well, most of you, at least. If you're reading this on some sort of magic rectangle, welcome to the second volume of *The Benevolence Archives*. Are you holding a book, made of actual paper? Welcome to *The Benevolence Archives*. The print edition contains *both* volumes that have been released to date, since *BA Vol. 1* is short. Too short to print on its own, in fact, so I just stuck both of 'em inside the same set of covers.

If this is your first visit to the *BA* universe, worry not! I've done my best to make this accessible to new folks, and you will find if you are skilled with the Google that you can get the first volume at minimal cost anyway.

Minimal cost. Less than that, even. I won't pay you to read it, but the next best thing.

Some thank-yous, and then I'll let you get on with the story. First, *The Sanctum of the Sphere* would not have been possible had a certain charitable organization not noticed me and funded me to do nothing for a summer but sit and write. For various reasons I'm not going to name them here, but they know who they are and I'm very grateful. I'd like to thank my alpha/beta readers: Holly Bland, Scott Brown, L.S. Engler, Molly Enrick, Lauriel Masson-Oakden and Thomas Weaver. Their commentary and feedback was invaluable, and many of them will be able to point to specific scenes in the book and take credit for fixing them. I'd also like to thank Gene'O Gordon,

Natacha Guyot, Winter Bayne and Adam Dreece for their help with publicity, marketing, and just generally keeping me sane.

Finally, I'd like to thank my wife Becky, who lost a fair amount of sleep staying up at night to beat the manuscript into shape and argue with me about em-dashes and ellipses. I love you, babe. I'll get the next one right, I promise.

The next installment in the *Benevolence Archives* universe will be another short story collection, believe it or not. There are a lot of little corners I'd like to shine some light into before the next novel-length effort. In the meantime, check out the back of the book (or the end of the file) for a look at something else you might enjoy.

Thanks for reading.

Luther M. Siler
Somewhere in northern Indiana
April 10, 2015

"THE PLANET IT'S FARTHEST FROM"

I have a bad feeling about this, the gnome thought.

The saloon had a bad reputation, but precious little on this backwards shithole of a planet was thought of highly. The only thing that Kratuul was known to export was exotic fevers and several deep-space-capable varieties of mold; there was indigenous life that had been rumored to have reached sentience, but having met several of the locals he was unconvinced.

The saloon was located at the ass-end of a wide patch that had been hacked out of Kratuul's ubiquitous jungle. It was one of six in a tiny trading depot barely worth the name; the gnome couldn't think of a single thing he might want enough to travel to Kratuul in order to get it.

Well, one thing. It was inside the saloon. He'd have to go inside to get it.

I bet it smells terrible in there. Gnomes were blessed with an especially keen sense of smell, something that felt like less of an adaptation when it couldn't be turned off in malodorous places. He smoothed his fur and adjusted his clothing, making sure his assortment of weapons were all in the right places-- easy enough to reach, less easy to detect in a quick pat-down-- and strode toward the door.

The door was rather bigger than he'd expected it to be.

Oh, hell, he thought. This was not a good sign.

He put his shoulder into the door, pushing it open slowly. The gnome was large for his species, but that still put him at barely over one and a quarter meters tall, even with the lifts he'd had installed in his boots. The door was clearly built for a species much larger than he was.

Always do your own research, you idiot, he thought. He hadn't been prepared for an ogre bar. *Someone* had failed to let him know that he was going to be looking for his target in an ogre bar. The only question was who to choose to blame.

The saloon, unsurprisingly, stank of ogre-- an odd mix of sweat, lubricant, and a spice the gnome had never managed to identify. It was surprisingly full; apparently it was happy hour, or whatever ogres called that. *Glower hour,* he thought, hating himself a little bit for the thought. The clientele was about what he'd expected: overheated, mostly male, sweaty, and mostly twice his size. Ogres were by far the largest of the recognized Galactic Types; they ranged from two meters at the small end to nearly three meters tall, and were generally as musclebound as they were oversized. Most of the patrons had legs thicker around than he was. And most of them were staring at him, scattered pairs of red eyes glowing in the darkened room. Several were openly laughing.

He looked around, giving his eyes a moment to adjust, and spotted an empty stool at the bar. The halfogre sitting next to the empty stool looked just as unfriendly as the others but was noticeably less massive than the rest of the clientele. He also hadn't turned around yet. Stride, he thought, and did his short-legged best to not look like he was waddling as he walked to the stool.

Which was taller than he was. He cursed under his breath. *Always do your own research.* He climbed up into the stool, which lifted him just high enough to see over the top of the bar-- which, surprisingly, gleamed; it was the one thing in the saloon that looked like it had any attention paid to keeping it clean. He cursed again and stood on the seat, pounding on the bar a few times to attract the barkeep's attention.

The barkeep did not appear to appreciate the gesture.

"We don't serve your kind here," he snarled. "I don't even have cups in goblin size. You see a kiddy table around here?"

"I'm a gnome," the gnome responded, sighing theatrically. "Not a goblin. Look at me. I'm wearing *clothes*."

"Unless they make you taller, I don't *fucking care*," the barkeep retorted, pulling his lips back and raising his voice a bit. His teeth were filed. "I ain't gonna repeat myself, neither."

"My money spends," the gnome said, trying not to notice that the saloon was getting noticeably quieter than it had been when he'd entered. "How about we start with me buying my friend here a drink?" He gestured toward the halfogre next to him, hoping that his neighbor was in a reasonable mood.

The halfogre pulled a knife from a sheath and slammed it into the bar, burying the tip of the blade three inches deep in the wood. *Not so much, then.*

"Why did you even bring that with you?" the gnome had time to squeak, and then all hell broke loose. The bartender, roaring, swung a bottle at the halfogre's head-- a bottle that was snatched from his hand and hurled across the saloon so quickly and easily that it almost looked practiced. The bottle struck a mirrored wall and shattered, spraying something foul-smelling and thick over a table of four sitting underneath it. Three of the four, all females, shrieked. The fourth, a male, who had been directly under where the bottle struck the wall, was completely drenched.

He stood up and tossed the table out of his way. The gnome took this in and then looked back at the bartender and his former seatmate, not sure which direction to bolt.

"*Run,*" the bartender growled, settling the issue. The halfogre pushed his sleeves back, revealing arms covered in tattoos and a pair of wicked gladiator's gloves on his hands.

Right, then, the gnome thought. This was not going as he had expected. It had been a while since he had been in a bar fight. It had been longer since he'd been in one where the furniture was all bigger than he was. He leapt from his stool, hitting the floor hard and rolling underneath a table. The fight was already spreading, a pair of ogres having taken unkindly to having had a table thrown at them and a few others apparently joining in for the sheer joy of it.

A hand clamped down on his ankle. And most of his shin; it was a large hand. The gnome was dragged unceremoniously from underneath the table and shaken in the air. It was the seatmate, who *grinned* at him and hurled him bodily at the drink-soaked ogre across the saloon. The gnome flew through the air, hitting Wet Ogre in the chest and clinging for dear life to his clothes, digging his hands into the ogre's vest and holding on.

"Save me!" he shrieked. "I have money!" He climbed up Wet Ogre's chest, swinging himself over his head and clinging to him like a backpack. The other responded by whirling, trying to knock him off. He leapt instead, landing behind the bar and fleeing through a nearby door.

As it turned out, it smelled even *worse* in the kitchen, but at least it was empty. The sounds of combat intensified behind him, the first telltale whines of laser blasts joining the melee.

Window. It was higher than it should have been, of course, but at least it was open. The gnome leapt onto a countertop and from there to the window, clambering through and dropping to the ground outside, losing a few buttons off his shirt in the process. He fled, retreating to a darkened alleyway a few blocks away. In the distance, he heard sirens. The local constabulary was actually responding; surprising for a place like this. As fast as the saloon had dissolved into chaos, bar fights had to be a common occurrence. He waited, watching back toward the saloon, not willing to trust the open streets just yet. The planet was in unclaimed territory, far from gnomespace, and he was probably the only gnome in the settlement. It was likely that the constables would be looking for him soon, and probably not to see if he'd had medical attention.

A few more minutes of noisy chaos, and a shadow detached itself from the wall ahead of him. An uncomfortably large shadow. *No way.*

"Brazel."

The gnome breathed a sigh of relief. "Grond?"

"You should hope so," the halfogre said, shaking blood from one of his gladiator gloves. "Everybody else back there is busy blaming the fight on you. Did you get it?"

"*Did I get it?* Of course I got it," Brazel said, insulted. He held up a data chip. "I got the chip, his money, a shiv, and two different data pads to go with it. I'd have lifted his gun, too, if he hadn't spun around so fast. You care to explain why you didn't mention we were going to a *fucking ogre bar?*"

"Did I forget to mention that?" Grond said, sounding confused. "I can't imagine why. Sometimes I forget how short you are, you know. Was there something wrong with the plan?"

"Ass," Brazel retorted. "The plan was that you'd create a distraction and I'd lift the chip. In and out, easy. I was expecting you to *bump into him* or something, not to get chucked at him like a bloody throwing knife."

"Exciting, wasn't it?" Grond said, chuckling. "Can we go now, or do you want to yell at me for a bit longer?" He cocked his head, listening to the sirens, which were growing louder. "I bet I can convince the authorities I've captured you. We could charge more if we have to break you out of jail before we bring the chip back."

"I'm taking two thirds of the take," Brazel said. "It's the least I deserve for being used as a projectile." But Grond was right; it was time to get back to the ship. Revenge could come later.

⋊⊂⊃⋉

"THE CLOSET"

"Found us something to do," the gnome said.

"Details," the halfogre responded, not bothering to look up from his book. Brazel could be longwinded, and it was better to let him do the explaining than to ask questions.

"It's actually pretty straightforward," the gnome said. "Somebody owes Prescott some money. He wants it back."

Grond waited. Brazel didn't add any details. "He happen to say how?"

"It's up to us, apparently," the gnome replied, grinning. "We can steal it back, convince the fellow to hand it over voluntarily, or just beat it out of him. Complete discretion. I asked Rhundi how pissed Prescott seemed about it. She said it sounded pretty routine."

It was never *routine* to owe Prescott money, Grond thought. Prescott handing off carte blanche on getting his money back to a couple of freelancers was a little bit on the unusual side, but they'd worked for him before. He'd normally have handled something like that himself; maybe it really just wasn't a big enough deal for him to bother.

"Here's the dossier," Brazel said, tossing a datapad in Grond's direction. Grond caught the thing one-handed, carefully setting his book aside and putting his reading glasses on top of it. The glasses were an affectation; he only wore them when he was reading something that was actually on paper. They helped pull him deeper into his reading, somehow.

The target's name was Arrakin Darl. The dossier listed an address in a rough neighborhood in a large city on a basic terrestrial planet relatively nearby, on the border zone between gnomish and dwarven territory. The pictures included were of a human male, 22 years old, of slight build. He looked like a junkie. Grond raised a scarred eyebrow at the amount he owed.

"How'd this kid get into Prescott for thirty thousand?" he asked. "He doesn't look like he's seen half that in his entire lifetime." Prescott was rich enough that he could have written off the debt with little trouble, but this amount of debt hardly seemed *routine.*

"No details," Brazel said. "I'd have told you already. For all I know he borrowed five and the rest is interest."

It would take about a day to get there, Grond considered. Maybe another two or three days to find the kid and scope the place out; another day to get back. Assuming there were no complications.

He didn't have anything he needed to do in the next five days.

"Usual rate?"

"Plus ten percent," Brazel said. "He's still being nice to us after the bullshit we got into last time."

Grond nodded, chuckling. Brazel had burned off a third of his fur the last time they'd done a job for Prescott. Their usual rate now included a grooming rider.

"Gimme an hour," he said. "I'll meet you at the dock."

Three days later, they'd found the kid and had had him under near-constant 'bot surveillance for a day and a half. Brazel had spent the time watching him while Grond and Rhundi checked every source they had for information about him. Other than owing unsavory people money, the kid was boring. He was a *student,* if you could believe that, spending most of his time commuting back and forth to class or in the library. The apartment was in a rougher part of town, but the kid seemed to live there mostly because the rents were cheap. Brazel and

Grond hadn't seen him do a single thing that rated as dangerous, much less interesting, the entire time. The junkie look appeared to be just that; a look. The kid was just skinny.

"You'll be the scariest thing he's ever seen," Brazel said. "How do you want to handle this?"

"You stay with the ship," Grond said. "Stay nearby in case I end up throwing him out of a window or something; I may need you to catch him. The building's sized for bigs, so I'll go get the money. Or his head. I'll play it by ear."

"My ears, I hope," Brazel said. Grond's were mostly either scar tissue or missing.

"Joke away, pipsqueak," Grond growled. "Only one of us gets to be pretty."

Grond didn't pass a single person on the way into the apartment block and rode an empty hoverlift to the kid's place on the 114th floor. He wasn't home, which they knew; they'd watched him leave an hour before, and Brazel was keeping an eye on him. The first option was to toss his place and see if there was anything to steal, but Grond could tell seconds after breaking in that that wasn't going to be the case. The only thing in the apartment that looked expensive was a desk console that rivaled the one in Rhundi's office, but even for Grond something like that was too big to be portable. *The kid doesn't have much money,* Grond thought, *but he has priorities. He spends it on things he needs.* The fabber in the corner had come standard with the apartment, the furniture was secondhand. The desk console was handprint-locked. Hackable, certainly, but electronics were generally Brazel's thing. He certainly wasn't going to be able to convince the console that his hands were human. He spent a few minutes rummaging through cabinets and the bedroom's one closet; no luck.

He almost missed the false door. It only took him a minute to pick the lock.

His eyes widened when he saw what was behind it.

He opened a comm channel to Brazel. "Braze, we gotta pull out of this. There's a—"

"Too late," Brazel said. "He just got home. Was about to tell you. He should be upstairs in a couple of minutes. Alone. What's wrong?"

Shit.

"Just be ready for me to need to go fast," Grond said.

The second the kid opened the door, Grond hit him in the head. The kid collapsed instantly, bouncing off a wall on the way down. *Huh,* Grond thought. He'd expected a fight. Instead, he'd knocked the kid out cold with a single punch. *Is he even still breathing?*

He was. Grond shrugged, tying him to a chair, stuffing a rag into his mouth and blindfolding him.

"Brazel."

"You sound less concerned than you did a few minutes ago," the gnome responded.

"Yeah, well... there's a full fuckin' suit of Benevolence armor hidden in a closet in the room. Four expensive-assed rifles, too. I figured the hardware was his. Looks like it isn't."

"Shit. He's dead, isn't he."

"Nah, but I hit him like I was hitting Benevolence, not like I was hitting a half-sized human with tissue paper for muscles. He'll be out for a few minutes. How do you wanna play this? The suit and the rifles are worth the debt right there."

"I wanna know where he got 'em, I think."

"So do I. Stay where you are. I'll wake him up once I'm sure there aren't any more surprises in the apartment somewhere. We missed something."

The kid was still out, so Grond took a harder look around the apartment, taking careful note of how thick the walls were and looking carefully for anything that might hide a secret compartment. He shoved the furniture around, checking underneath the bed and moving rugs. Nothing. The apartment's only secret seemed to be the hidden space in the closet, and

Grond had that cleaned out in minutes, piling the suit of armor and the guns in front of the kid. *Anything else he's hiding is going to be software in the desk,* he thought.

"Braze, see if you can remotely hack into the desk console. Pull everything you can off it. We can steal it if we have to but getting it out of here is going to be hell."

"On it," the gnome answered. And then, a moment later: "You, uh, may want to turn the thing on."

Grond activated the desk's startup sequence. It displayed a hand outline on its surface, along with the text CONFIRM VOICE AND HAND MATCH. He didn't speak, waiting patiently for Brazel. It didn't take long before the display started flickering.

"Nothing other than standard security programs, Grond. Namey'll have the ice cracked in five. Go ahead and wake him up if you haven't already."

Grond glanced over at the kid, whose head slumped down as he turned around. *Awake already, and he had the sense to stay quiet. He's not an idiot.*

"Shake your head if you hear me, boy."

The kid's shoulders tightened up reflexively, then he shook his head.

Grond lowered his voice, speaking directly into the kid's ear. "In a second I'm going to take the blinders off of you and pull that rag out of your mouth. I need you to understand something, son: if I get the idea even for a second that you're lying to me or even *imagining* using a spell on me, I'm going to start solving that problem by ripping your jaw off. I know people who can get the information I need from you straight out of your living brain. The rest of you does not have to be attached. Shake your head if you understand me."

I didn't say piss yourself, Grond thought, as the kid shook his head, his pants darkening.

He walked back around in front of the kid again and took his blindfold off. The tears were already rolling down his cheeks, the bruise where Grond had hit him already livid and angry-looking.

Good. But we need a little bit more.

He didn't touch the rag in his mouth, leaning forward and staring directly into the kid's eyes. His eyes brightened, losing their usual dark brown color and brightening to a fiery, glowing red. Full ogres could do this with little effort. It had taken Grond months of practice.

"Look carefully. Think about what you've gotten yourself into."

Grond was dressed inconspicuously, wearing a heavy duster coat. When he'd entered the apartment building, he'd been wearing a hat. He stood up and shrugged the coat off.

Underneath, he wore his gladiator clothes: two bandoliers, crossed over his chest, both bristling with ammunition and bladed things of all descriptions. A breechclout. Well-used gladiator's gloves on both hands, bristling with spikes and blades. Next to nothing else.

Not that you could really tell. Grond's natural skin color was a pale yellow. Other than his hands and his head, though, virtually none of his original skin tone was even visible any longer. His entire torso, legs, and arms were covered in scar tissue and fantastically elaborate tattoos. Grond had spent his entire youth and a good chunk of his adult life enslaved and working as a pit fighter. The scars and tattoos were all trophies. Occasionally he'd thought about having his skin rejuvenated. He never did, precisely for moments like this.

The kid started screaming into the rag, absurdly trying to get away. The chair shook. He wasn't going anywhere, though.

One more thing.

Grond picked his bow up from the floor next to the kid's chair. Snapped his wrist, unlocking the limbs, the bow's energy string shimmering into existence.

"You know what this is?"

The kid sat still, his eyes wide, still crying. Didn't shake his head yes or no.

"This is an Iklis sniper's longbow. Her name's Angela. Say hello."

The kid didn't do anything.

Grond smiled, showing his front teeth.

"I said fucking SAY HELLO," he said, putting every ounce of bass he could muster into his voice and tripling the volume.

The kid screamed again, making sounds that would probably be *hello* and quite possibly *please god no help me anyone* in the bargain.

"I can kill you with Angela from two klicks away with my eyes closed. If I have them open it'll be three. Go ahead and run around corners. I'll hit you anyway. That's what I can do *if*, somehow, you get out of the room. Which has me in between you and the exit. And you don't know how many of my buddies are out there, either. Ready for me to take the gag out?"

The kid nodded.

Grond pulled out the gag. The kid sobbed, gasping for air; it looked like he'd shoved it into his throat a little farther than he'd intended to. Or he'd sucked part of it into his airpipe, what with all the screaming and pleading he'd been doing.

"You owe someone I know a whole goddamn lot of money."

The kid blinked. "You work for Jarekh?"

Ha. "Prescott."

If anything, the name made him look even more panicked. "I paid Prescott back! I swear I did!"

"He doesn't think so. He thinks you're into him for thirty thousand."

"I only borrowed twelve!"

Hell, Brazel was right.

"Let's make this conversation shorter. I don't care how much you borrowed or why you borrowed it or whether you paid Prescott back already or who the hell this Jarekh is. I care that I got hired to get Prescott's money back from what looked like a spike junkie and instead I found a closet full of Benevolence hardware behind a *fucking fake wall*. Which you will now explain to me, so that I can decide whether I'm gonna kill you or not."

"B ... Benevolence? What?"

Grond moved out of the way, showing the kid the pile of armor and guns. He screamed again.

"It's not mine! None of it! I've never seen any of that shit before! Fuck, I gamble! I owe a couple of bookies some money! You think I'm stupid enough to fuck with the Benevolence? Are you crazy?"

Timed perfectly, straight into his ear, Brazel spoke up. *"Grond. I think he's telling the truth. There's nothing but sports schedules and research data on city planning on that console. The kid's in engineering school. We didn't miss anything when we looked at him. The hardware's a goddamned coincidence."*

"I don't like coincidences," Grond muttered.

He grabbed the chair the kid was tied to, lifted him three feet off the floor, and ripped the chair in half, tossing the wreckage into the corners of the room. The kid hit the floor hard, kicking feebly with his legs and screaming. Grond grabbed him by the face, lifting him back off the floor again.

"C'mere, you lucky asshole."

He dragged him across the apartment, shoving him into the false room in the back of his closet.

"You telling me you live here and you never knew about any of this?"

"I moved in a month ago! Fuck, I'm never even here! I spend all my time at school! Hell no, I've never seen this!"

He's telling the truth. Grond had never seen anybody so obviously scared shitless; he didn't have enough brainpower left to construct a lie.

"Count to a thousand," he told him. "You should be able to break out before you starve to death in there. I'm taking all your shit and giving it to Prescott. That'll get him off your back. Lemme make a suggestion: don't ever gamble again. I see you, I'm gonna kill you." Not waiting for an answer, he slammed the kid into the back of the hidden space and closed and locked both the doors.

"Pickup. Now," he said over the comm. "I'm tossing his couch out the window in thirty seconds. Meet me there with the cargo door open. I want to be outside the atmosphere in five minutes."

"Coming," Brazel said. "Rhundi will be so pleased when she finds out she gets to move Benevolence gear."

"We're keeping the difference, too," Grond said. "Think we ought to mention it to Prescott?"

"Yes," Brazel said. "He's adding twenty percent to our usual fee next time."

"YANK"

Getting yanked out of tunnelspace at velocity hurt. And it hurt uniquely; every cell of your body felt like it got shoved about a centimeter away from where it was, except no two cells went in the same direction, and it took a second for your body to convince itself that, yes, it was still all put together the right way, and nothing had fallen off, and perhaps the contents of your stomach should stay where they were, and didn't belong on the floor. Or in your lungs.

Getting yanked out of tunnelspace at velocity counted as one of Brazel's absolute least favorite things. Getting yanked out of tunnelspace at velocity to discover your happy little smuggler's boat surrounded by half-a-dozen Mal pirate skiffs and an obviously stolen Benevolence blockship was *worse*.

THEY'RE POWERING UP WEAPONS, the boat's AI said into Brazel's ear.

"No way," Brazel said. "I could never have guessed. I figured they just detunneled us to show off a new *paint job*. GROND!" Brazel was the *Nameless'* pilot; the cockpit wasn't really sized for bigs, although Grond had rigged up a copilot's chair in his quarters that would let him fly the ship virtually if he needed to. Mostly, though, it was used for the guns, so Brazel really needed his partner to be sitting in his chair right now.

"Already in position," the halfogre growled, and Brazel's viewscreen lit up with combat diagnostics. The blockship that had detunneled them was pulling back behind the skiffs; it would be lightly armed, if at all. Benevolence would have had the thing surrounded by twenty times the hardware that the pirates had. Brazel wondered how they had managed to steal it.

SHIELDS TO FULL, Namey squawked. BEGIN PRETARGETING?

"They're not shooting," Grond said. "Why aren't they shooting?"

RECEIVING A COMMUNICATION FROM THE BLOCKSHIP, Namey said. SHALL I TELL THEM TO FUCK OFF? I LOVE DOING THAT.

"Not when they outnumber us, dear," Brazel responded, making a mental note to speak with his partner about the personality he'd selected for the AI. "Gimme the holo."

A dwarven face shimmered into existence in front of Brazel. He figured it was probably female; it was usually hard to tell.

Wait. *No.* He knew this one, and it was definitely female.

"Shocksie," he said. "That was awfully rude of you."

"My name is Shocks-the-Mountains, Brazel, and you're under arrest," she said. "So's Grond. Let us board, or we'll blow you to bits."

"That is even ruder," Brazel responded, wrinkling his snout at her and signaling Grond to hold off on violence. "And last I checked, Mal pirates aren't government. Care to explain how I'm under arrest?"

She glared. Mal pirates weren't especially fond of being called that; the name was pejorative—they didn't actually call themselves the Malevolence; it was just a natural consequence of opposing a group that called themselves the Benevolence. "You're under arrest because we control this avenue of space right now and I say so. And I have six ships and you only have one. Stand down."

"Charges?" Brazel asked. *Any chance of outrunning them?* he subvocalized to the ship.

UNLIKELY, Namey spouted back in his ear. WE'RE FASTER THAN THEY ARE BUT THERE ARE SIX OF THEM AND THEY'LL BE SHOOTING. NOTHING TO HIDE BEHIND EXCEPT THE BLOCKSHIP. I WANNA FIGHT! LET'S FIGHT!

We're not fighting yet, he subvoced.

"Quit chirping to your ship," Shocks-the-Mountains boomed over the holo channel. "Kidnapping. Theft. Murder. Destruction of property. Shall I continue?"

"KIDNAPPING?" Grond roared. He wasn't on the holo channel; Brazel figured Shocksie probably heard him anyway.

"It's not kidnapping if the client is the person you're kidnapping. The word for that is *rescue*," Brazel corrected.

"It's kidnapping if it's my *son*, you wretch," the enraged dwarf bellowed back. "No dwarven male of my line gets to *ask* for rescue. He is *mine*."

Dwarven society was highly matriarchal. Brazel chose not to press the topic any longer, slowly backing the *Nameless* away from the skiffs.

"Well, I don't feel like being arrested today," Brazel said, "and Namey would be awfully upset if you dismantled him. So if you don't mind, turn off the blockship and I'll just—"

Laser fire erupted from four of the six skiffs and the *Nameless* at the same time. Flashes from the shields popped, darkening the viewscreen and forcing Brazel to navigate by the display. He threw the ship into a spin and accelerated directly toward the blockship.

"Is that a good idea?" Grond said over the comm.

"It makes 'em pay for it if they miss," Brazel said. "Namey, the thing's shielded, right?"

QUITE, the AI replied.

"Well, it makes 'em pay for it a little, then," he said, swooping around the ship. One of the skiffs disappeared off his viewscreen, replaced with a cartoony X.

"Got one," Grond said.

"Start using explosives, chaff, whatever we've got," Brazel said, partly talking to the AI and partly to Grond. He was struggling to remember the last time he'd had to upgrade the ship's armory; the *Nameless* wasn't exactly built for extended combat operations. The shields were upgraded to hell—and a near miss from *something* boomy rocked him in his seat, making him freshly pleased with that fact—but they didn't have much that was going to get through the shielding that blockship probably had.

Another skiff blinked off the viewscreen. Grond chortled over the comm.

There were four skiffs left, and they were doing their best to keep the *Nameless* surrounded, with his ship in between them and the blockship. Brazel picked one at random, highlighting it on the viewscreen, still doing his damnedest to dodge laser fire.

"Grond. I'm heading straight for—"

The ship went spinning as a massive explosion overtook their shields and tossed them away from the blockship. *What in the—*

BLOCKSHIP   DESTROYED.   TUNNELSPACE   IS AVAILABLE AGAIN.

"Grond, did you do that?"

"I didn't," the halfogre said. "Did you?"

BENEVOLENCE FORCES DETECTED. RECOMMEND SPEEDY EXIT.

Oh, shit. The Benevolence had detected the tunnel pull somehow. And they'd found their missing ship that quickly.

"Go," Brazel told the AI. "Somewhere. Anywhere. Go go go go *now.*" His viewscreen was starting to fill up with Benevolence ID codes, what looked like an entire *fleet* of ships.

THIS IS IMPRESSIVELY BAD LUCK, Namey said. IT APPEARS THAT THE BLOCKSHIP MANAGED TO PULL A BENEVOLENCE SHIP OUT OF TUNNELSPACE BY ACCIDENT. THE REST OF THEM FOLLOWED.

"So fucking *take advantage!*" Brazel said. "Get us the hell out of here before they notice us." The Benevolence spiderships had already blown two of the four skiffs into flaming powder. The other two were fleeing in opposite directions. No one was after them yet.

THEY'RE SCANNING FOR ID CODES. YOU WANT ME TO LIE, RIGHT?

"Yes!" Brazel said, hoping that his own ship was screwing with him, and punched the ship into tunnelspace, hoping the Benevolence didn't have another blockship with them. The *Nameless* shuddered a bit and jumped, his viewscreen fading to black.

"That was close," Grond said.

"Poor Shocksie," Brazel said. "I kinda liked her. Should we tell Walks-the-Waves what happened?"

"Maybe leave the part where she was shooting at us out of it?"

"I think so," Brazel said. And after that, he would work on how the Mals had managed to get ahold of a blockship. That sounded like something that Rhundi would want to know. *Nothing's ever easy,* he thought to himself.

"REMEMBER"

They were halfway home from a successful job when the message came through.

Well, not a message, precisely. A set of coordinates, a timestamp, and a single word. The timestamp was two standard days away. So were the coordinates. The word was REMEMBER.

"Grond," Brazel said over the shipwide comm. "You may wanna come look at this."

A moment later, the halfogre was there, leaning forward into the cockpit, which was much too small for him. "What? I was reading."

"That," Brazel said, pointing at the screen.

He heard Grond mumble something under his breath.

"You know anything about this?" the gnome asked. "That's in the Queris system. Hell if I've ever even *been* to the Queris system. I certainly don't remember pissing anyone off there."

"I've been there," Grond said. "But not for a very long time." He stared at the coordinates. "Pull up a map. Let's see this a little closer up."

Brazel manipulated the map. The coordinates were ... nowhere. The Queris system was four planets, around an utterly average-looking star; the one named planet was nearly exactly opposite in its orbit from where they were being sent. There was nowhere terrestrial, much less inhabited, anywhere near it.

"And I suppose that two days from now there isn't going to be anything there either," Brazel said. "There's no way Queris orbits that fast, is there?"

"It doesn't," Grond muttered. "Remember. There's ... ah, *shit.*"

"We're going to die, aren't we," the gnome said. "How's it going to happen?"

The halfogre chuckled. "*Remember.* It's not a suggestion, Brazel. We're idiots. It's a fucking *name.* Lady Remember's called us. It's a *job.*"

Several expressions-- annoyance, surprise, shame, and more than a touch of fear-- crawled across Brazel's face all at once.

"*The* Remember?" Brazel spluttered, his fur involuntarily standing up. "*That* Remember? Remember needs something from *us?* When did we get so important?"

"Oh, we aren't. We're still going to die," Grond rumbled. "She probably just needs someone for a suicide mission. Or cannon fodder of some kind. I'm still guessing we're not about to ignore Remember asking us to drop by."

"We are not," Brazel said. "Not on this life am I gonna ignore Remember telling me to do something. You wanna comm Rhundi and let her know that we're not coming straight back?"

The halfogre grinned. "How come I have to do it? You're about to miss something, aren't you?"

"Birthdays," the gnome grunted. "Three of 'em, in the same week. I don't know how--"

"Yes, you do," Grond corrected. "Think about when *your* birthday is."

"Shut up and make the call," Brazel said. "We've got just enough fuel to get to her. I hope there's a supply cache we can raid somewhere before we do whatever she's calling us about."

"I suspect she does," the halfogre replied, heading to his quarters to comm Brazel's wife.

><co}<

No one was quite sure what Remember was.

She had an elf's lifespan, or she'd figured out how to magic her way into it. Just the stories Brazel had heard about her were too much for one regular-breed human to have accomplished, and there were doubtless plenty that Brazel had never heard. He could remember his parents and grandparents telling him stories about Remember, too; to the class of people likely to end up as a smuggler, the way Brazel had, the woman was a combination of a living legend and a demon.

It was Remember's job to know things. There were any number of organizations, both legit and otherwise, that would have gleefully sacrificed the population of entire planets in order to gain access to her sea of contacts and informers. People went to Remember— sometimes paying large sums of money to dishonest "friends" of hers to arrange a meeting— when they needed to know things. Sometimes she required payment. Sometimes she refused it. On rare occasions, she would summon people to her or-- more rarely-- seek someone out in order to pass on a piece of information. Her motivations for doing so were rarely clear. Some people insisted that she didn't ever *have* reasons-- that she'd just set things in motion on a lark. Brazel was sure she was playing some sort of long game. It just wasn't clear what.

And she wanted Brazel and his partner for a job.

The coordinates in the Queris system were nearly exactly two days of tunnelspace away-- which was a bit alarming. It implied that Remember not only knew how to directly comm the *Nameless*, she knew its *exact location* when she did, and had timed the meeting to ensure that Brazel and Grond came directly to her-- no time to get back home for a refuel and resupply or, critically, to pick up any passengers or extra muscle. Not that they often needed extra muscle with a halfogre on board, but still. If nothing else, Rhundi had proven herself to be more than capable in a firefight-- possibly more capable than Brazel, who preferred to talk his way out of trouble rather than fight.

Of course, Brazel didn't *know* that Remember wanted them for a job. It was possible that they'd crossed her somehow and she was bringing them in to have them killed. That felt like Remember's style; there was no reason to hire expensive thugs to hunt the two of them down when she could just summon them to their own deaths and have them pay for their own fuel.

There was little else to do on the way to the meet other than discuss Remember's motives, and since they didn't have any real idea what those were, Brazel and Grond spent most of the trip arguing. Rhundi was no help; she wasn't foolish enough to suggest that the two insult Remember but in her mind that was no reason to be nice about it.

"I've got thirteen kids," Brazel said, after attending the birthday party of his fourth-youngest via comm. "I don't need this shit."

"Fourteen," Grond corrected.

"Whatever," the gnome groused. "This had better be worth it."

It surprised neither of them that when they reached the rendezvous point there was nothing there. Remember would almost certainly have some sort of remote or 'bot in the area scanning for their ship; they were going to wait for her, not the other way around-- although Brazel was certain that their punctuality was still expected.

"Scan ... hell, scan everything," Brazel told the ship. "If there's anything out there bigger than two carbon molecules jammed together, I want to know about it."

MY SENSORS DO NOT OPERATE AT THAT RESOLUTION, Namey responded. ALSO THAT WOULD BE TERRIBLY BORING.

"One of these days I'm reprogramming you into something subservient," the gnome grumbled. This was unlikely; the ship had been a lippy bastard for as long as he'd owned it and he had made that threat any number of times.

NOTHING WITHIN RANGE AT ALL, the ship blipped. NO RESIDUAL ENERGY SIGNATURES, EITHER. THERE HAS BEEN NO SHIP OR PROBE HERE WITHIN THE PAST THREE STANDARD DAYS.

Right about then was when the proximity alarms started.

The ship-- no, it was too big for a ship, the *moon*-- filled the viewscreen entirely, and appeared to be no more than a few klicks away from the *Nameless*. If it hadn't popped into view they'd have plowed into it in seconds. As it was, Brazel had to nearly tear the yoke off to pull the ship back, running parallel with the ... with *whatever the hell it was* instead of directly toward it.

"The shit is that?" Grond said over the ship's comm. The halfogre was in place in his copilot's chair in his quarters; he had access to a projected view of Brazel's viewscreen. "Is that a *ship?*"

Namey had lost his smugness all the sudden. THE OBJECT IS FOUR KILOMETERS IN DIAMETER, he said. IT DID NOT JUST EXIT TUNNELSPACE. IT WAS ALREADY THERE. IT APPEARS TO BE ENTIRELY ARTIFICIAL IN NATURE.

"Hail it," Brazel commanded.

THOUGHT OF THAT ALREADY, the ship responded. NO RESPONSE. THERE APPEARS TO BE A DOCKING PORT ON THE OBJECT'S FAR SIDE. NO SIGN OF SHIELDS OR WEAPONS POWERING UP.

"There was no sign of the *entire goddamn thing* two minutes ago," Brazel said. "I don't trust your sensors anymore."

WE HAVE NOT BEEN DESTROYED. I DO NOT BELIEVE MY SHIELDS WOULD HOLD UP LONG AGAINST ANY WEAPON SYSTEMS THAT OBJECT POSSESSES.

"Ship's right," Grond said. "Let's go take a look at that port."

It took only a few minutes to circle the object. It showed no sign of life; no ships emerged from it and no apparent weapon or scanning systems tracked them as they flew around it. The docking port was big enough to fly a capital ship through and was unshielded.

"Scan it for everything," Brazel said again.

THE OBJECT IS MOSTLY HOLLOW, Namey reported. AND THERE IS SOMETHING INSIDE THAT IS EITHER GENERATING OR UTILIZING AN ENORMOUS AMOUNT OF POWER. WE HAVE NOT BEEN HAILED AND I HAVE BEEN PROVIDED WITH NO SCHEMATICS. WE ARE FLYING BLIND.

"That's Remember for ya," Grond said. "She's screwing with us."

"I'd think I'd have *heard about it* if she lived in a spaceship the size of a small moon, though, wouldn't you?"

"One would think," Grond agreed. "Maybe it's new?"

"And required an entire shipyard for two years, plus the GDP of an entire planetary system to build?" Brazel asked. But there was no denying the object; it was too big to be a hologram and, besides, had fooled Namey. The thing was real. "Is this fucker that rich?"

"I suggest we find out," Grond said. "Perhaps she shares."

"Screw it," Brazel said. "In we go."

He activated the ship's external lights as well as all its sensors and flew in through the docking port. The port itself opened into what was effectively a smooth corridor, if an absurdly big one; the floor looked flat enough to land Namey virtually anywhere but Brazel decided to continue on until he spotted something that looked more like a designated landing area. There were no other ships and nothing moving, living or artificial.

The corridor continued until they'd penetrated about a kilometer into the station, at which point the walls fell away to emptiness and the floor continued on underneath them, a gangway now instead of a corridor, continuing into the center of the object. Namey's external lights were no longer sufficient to penetrate into the darkness; the hollow area was simply too big.

"Namey, get me a map," Brazel asked the ship, and then the lights came on, and the entire interior of the object blazed into view.

There wasn't much to see.

They were in the inside of the sphere, and the walls fell away on either side of them and curved back together at the other end, just over two kilometers away. The place clearly had gravity of some sort; there was a landing pad able to accommodate a ship three times the *Nameless'* size just ahead of them, and then a narrow walkway— perhaps wide enough for four or five bigs to walk abreast, or seven or eight gnomes— that led to a structure in the center of the sphere. The structure was supported by a spire, with thick cabling coming off it in every direction heading out to various points on the inside of the sphere.

"What am I looking at, boat?" Brazel asked.

UNCLEAR, Namey responded.   BUT THE OBJECT APPEARS TO BE BEGINNING TO POWER ITSELF UP. READING ENERGY DISCHARGES THROUGHOUT THE STRUCTURE.   WHATEVER IS IN THE CENTER OF THE

SPHERE REQUIRES AN ASTONISHING AMOUNT OF POWER.

"Sounds dandy. Land," the gnome ordered. "Grond, suit up. Grab everything you own that can be used to break something. Let's go see what's in there. Namey, is there—"

THE SPHERE IS ESTABLISHING AN ATMOSPHERE, AND THE DOCKING PORT HAS CLOSED, the ship responded. INTERIOR TEMPERATURE IS CLIMBING. I PROJECT THAT THE INTERIOR WILL BE SURVIVABLE IN TEN MINUTES AND COMFORTABLE IN THIRTY.

"Let's be ready in fifteen," Brazel said, heading off to his quarters to change. If he was going to be meeting Lady Remember, he was certainly going to do it in nicer clothes.

Grond was armed and ready in five minutes; it took Brazel twenty, as the gnome rejected three different outfits before settling on something that was an acceptable mix of stylish enough to meet with one of the galaxy's most powerful people and utilitarian enough to be able to conceal a number of small weapons and useful tools underneath. The gnome suspected he would be searched; he had several items that he assumed or hoped would be found and a few, more carefully hidden, that even a scan ought not to locate. The halfogre was not dressed for subtlety at all; he wore his gladiator's gear: two bandoliers, weighted down with ammunition and weaponry, crossed over his chest; spiked gloves on his hands, and minimalistic protective gauntlets on his forearms and greaves on his calves. His Iklis sniper's longbow, lovingly named Angela, was slung over his back, and two heavy guns hung at his waist. The only other thing he was wearing was a multicolored, ragged-edged thermal utilicloak; the thing looked a horror to Brazel, but it provided a few dozen places to hide additional useful sharp things and could even produce its own heat for low-temperature environments. He'd found the time to treat his skin with something, too; his tattoos glittered in the low light of the *Nameless'* cargo hold.

"Good day to die?" Grond asked. The gnome nodded once, grinning, and they exited the ship into the sphere.

Nothing happened as they followed the walkway to the structure in the center of the sphere. There was a low electrical hum, almost too low for Brazel's ears to pick it up, as the machinery of the sphere continued to power up, and a slight breeze from the newly created atmosphere tickled his fur. The gnome stayed directly in the center of the walkway; the manufacturers had neglected to include guardrails on either side and he wanted room to roll if he needed to without falling off. Grond paced him, following a few steps behind, not quite openly carrying weaponry yet but clearly itching to.

The structure ahead was dome-shaped, perhaps ten meters high in the center, with a single door and no windows anywhere. It was the same steel-grey color that the rest of the sphere was. *There hasn't been a single word or direction or sign written anywhere on this thing*, Brazel thought. No decoration or ornamentation or even any color anywhere. It had to have cost more money than Brazel and Grond would clear in several lifetimes to build the thing; the owner hadn't bothered to invest in *paint*. Strange.

The doorway noiselessly slid open as the pair approached. The space inside was dark.

"We going in there?" Brazel asked.

"I imagine we are," Grond replied. "Otherwise you got all dressed up for nothin'." The ogre muttered something Brazel couldn't hear, subvocalizing a command to the ship. "Namey says that he's figured out at least a little bit of what's going on around here, but he doesn't like it. The entire damn place is a power plant. And everything it's generating is getting funneled into this room. Whatever's in there is pulling enough energy to run a mid-sized city for a month."

Brazel tried to run the credits in his head again and gave up.

"Also, there's a scanner just inside the door," Grond said.

Brazel shrugged. "Not like she doesn't know we're here," he said, and walked inside. He actually *felt* the body scan; his fur rippled and he felt prickles on his skin even through the layers of fur and clothes on top of it. Remember wasn't bothering to be subtle; she wanted them to know this was happening. The lights came on.

The room was empty. It was also much smaller on the inside than it looked from outside-- the dome had been maybe ten meters high, but the interior space was a rounded cube perhaps four or five meters to a side. Other than the doorway, Brazel couldn't see a mark or a seam anywhere. The ceiling, walls and floor were covered in some sort of material he didn't recognize; a black matte color, textured like very soft rubber, spongy to the touch.

As soon as Grond stepped inside, the door slid closed behind him. As Brazel watched, the black material flowed over the doorway. Five seconds later the way out was all but invisible.

"I have a bad feeling about this," Grond said. The halfogre stood perfectly still, hands on his guns, waiting for something to happen.

A moment later *everything* happened. Brazel felt, rather than heard, the immense energies the sphere was generating slamming into the dome they were standing in, and a sound like a sun exploding assaulted his ears, the vibration going straight into his bones. He felt movement, and the material on the walls abruptly expanded, trapping him inside, immobile, blind, and suddenly blessedly deaf.

Everything went away.

Brazel awoke on the floor, some time later, his head pounding and his teeth feeling oddly loose. He shook his head, clearing the cobwebs, and forced his eyes open. He was still in the room, with nothing apparently changed. He located Grond, a few feet away, also sprawled on the floor.

Wait. One thing had changed. The halfogre was stark naked.

Brazel looked down. He was naked too. He sat up, pulling himself into a crouch, scanning the room. Other than the two of them, it was empty.

The ship. His comm link with the *Nameless* was mostly subcutaneous, hooked into the bones of his ears. It was still there. He tried to reach the ship. Nothing.

Grond staggered to his feet, growling, a deep bass rumble that Brazel could feel in his chest. The halfogre's eyes glowed a dim red even in the bright light of the room.

"The fuck happened?" he grumbled.

"I think she disintegrated our stuff or something," Brazel said. He fluffed his fur, looking and smelling for singed parts. Everything looked and smelled fine. *How the hell did she pull that off?*

With a noxious slurping noise, the black material pulled back away from the doorway. The door clicked and slid partially open.

"Me first," the halfogre said, flexing his muscles and clenching his fists. "First thing I see, I'm gonna beat it to death. Just so's you know." The gnome nodded.

They had entered the structure from the hollow interior of an enormous spacecraft. The doorway opened into what looked for all the world like a lobby in a pricey resort. There was expensive-looking furniture scattered about the room, artworks from various cultures adorning the walls, thick plush carpeting at their feet. The ceiling, six or seven meters high at least, was painted a deep blue, scattered with hundreds of twinkling lights, imitating a starlit sky. In the middle of the room was an enormous, free-standing firepit, where some sort of scented wood blazed away merrily; a grand staircase in the back of the room led to both higher and lower floors. A few feet in front of them sat an ornate square table made of some sort of elaborately carved hardwood, two paper-wrapped packages sitting atop it. The packages were wrapped with festive ribbons.

"You might beat the hell out of an end table, I suppose," Brazel volunteered. There was no one but the two of them in the room.

"This ain't right," Grond said. "Hologram? Hard-light? What do you think?"

"No idea." Brazel picked up the packages. His name was on the smaller one. He shook it; whatever was inside slid around like it was made of cloth. He locked eyes with Grond for a moment, who shrugged. Brazel tossed Grond the other package and opened his.

There was a robe inside, made of the softest cloth Brazel had ever laid hands on-- and the gnome had always had very expensive tastes in fabric. He put it on; it was sized perfectly. He tucked the ribbon into a pocket and glanced at Grond; the halfogre's package had included a robe as well.

"Now what?" he asked.

As if in answer, a panel slid aside in the ceiling and a 'bot flew into the room. It was a simple model, an oblong-shaped levitator with a couple of manipulator arms and a battery of sensors. The 'bot flew toward the pair, pausing a few meters in front of Grond, hovering at his eye level.

"Greetings," it intoned, in a softly feminine human voice. "You are--"

Grond hurled the table their robes had been on directly at the 'bot. The heavy table knocked the thing out of the air and then landed on it, crushing it to scrap metal. The 'bot squawked once in alarm and then quieted.

"Did that make you feel better?" Brazel asked.

"The next one had better have Angela with it," the halfogre muttered, his eyes still glowing dangerously.

The next one did not have Angela with it. It did have two impressive-looking projectile cannons on it, however, one trained on Brazel and the other on Grond.

"Greetings," it spoke, in the same voice. "You are in no danger. Please follow me."

"Those guns don't say *in no danger* to me," Brazel muttered. The 'bot made no response, but hovered backward toward the staircase, keeping its guns aimed carefully the entire time. The 'bot led them up the staircase, down a corridor in a far corner of the room and eventually down another stairwell, ignoring a number of other rooms and side paths along the way. *This place is huge*, Brazel thought. *What the hell's going on? How long were we unconscious?* It finally stopped outside a set of double doors, which swung open.

"The mistress will be with you shortly," the 'bot said. "Please wait inside."

Brazel glanced over at Grond. The halfogre had lost all of the red in his eyes, which were wide and staring. They were being led into a *library*. And, judging from the smell, most of the books were printed on actual paper, and not the thin polymer sheets that most of the physical books still available were created from. The shelves were stuffed full, running from the floor to the ceiling, with a half-dozen or so freestanding shelves scattered around the room as well. There were *thousands* of books.

"Uh ... Grond?" Brazel said. "Stay with me, buddy. We still don't actually know what's going on here, right?"

"Don't care anymore," Grond said. He picked a book off the shelf and leafed through it, leaning in and inhaling the scent of the pages. "She can kill us both so long as she gives me a couple of hours in here first. She can kill *you* whenever, actually." The halfogre looked around, spotting a lounge chair his size on the other side of the room, near yet another fireplace. There was a second chair next to it, this one not sized for bigs.

How much time did Remember have to customize her furniture for us? Brazel thought. If they were actually in Remember's home, it would make sense for most of her furniture to be sized for humans, or ... well, human-*sized* people, at least, which Remember supposedly was. Grond's chair barely creaked as he settled his nearly two-and-a-half meter frame into it; the thing *had* to be reinforced. It wasn't human furniture. Seeing no better alternative, Brazel sat down in his chair and watched the fire.

"We have a game plan here?" he asked.

"We don't," Grond said. "I assume you've tried to contact the ship already. Either our comms are blocked or the ship is destroyed, near as I can tell. We're unarmed. I wrecked one of her robots and she sent a bigger one with *guns*. I don't see that we've got much of a choice but to sit here and see what she wants. Meanwhile..."

He waved the book, which looked positively dainty in his hands. "May as well relax until we find out why we're here."

"You're here because I have a task for you to perform," the fire said.

Grond and Brazel both sat up straight in their seats.

The fire shaped itself into a person.

That's impressive, Brazel thought.

As he watched, the fire-person's appearance refined, becoming something more like a holographic projection than a manipulation of the flame. It was a woman; a bit less than two meters tall, slightly above average for a human female, with long hair twisted into a topknot and then flowing down her back to below her waist. She appeared to be dressed in a loose, flowing robe, much like what had been provided for the two of them. Her hands were clasped behind his back.

Brazel and Grond waited. The fire-woman made no movement.

"Courtesy dictates that you explain the task. And perhaps introduce yourself," Brazel said.

"I am Remember," the fire-woman said. Her voice was surprisingly low, raspy. "My apologies for not meeting with you more ... personally."

"And the part where you destroyed all our stuff," said Grond, his eyes glittering red again. He had the book in his lap, holding it in such a way as to make Brazel think he planned to throw it. The gnome noticed the ribbon from their robe package marking a page. *He's not throwing that book*, Brazel thought. The chair would go first. Neither seemed terribly useful against a hologram made of *fire*, though.

"Your things are where you left them," Remember said.

"You knocked us out dressed and armed and we woke up naked," Brazel said. "I didn't *leave* my clothes anywhere. I rarely meet with business contacts naked. Tends to make me a trifle more difficult to take seriously."

"As I said, where you left them," Remember said. "*You* are not where you were when you were dressed and armed." She gestured and the room darkened, a star chart popping into existence in the middle of the library. Two stars glowed green.

"That's Queris," Brazel said, looking at one of the green dots. "And the other?"

"Is you," Remember said.

Brazel and Grond both laughed. The two points were halfway across the galaxy from each other; they had to be fifteen or twenty *parsecs* apart.

"That's a month. In tunnelspace," Brazel said. "You didn't have us unconscious for a month."

"You were unconscious for twelve seconds," Remember said.

Grond actually dropped his book.

"That's impossible," the halfogre said. "Teleportation?"

"It requires a ... moderate expenditure of power," Remember said. "I chose not to bring your possessions along with you. One of you might have chosen to bring something ... *unwise.*" She stared at Brazel as she said that last word, making it clear that she knew exactly how many *unwise somethings* Brazel had tried to bring with him. Grond carried all of his tools openly; the halfogre felt that concealing weaponry was pointless. An easy belief, when you were as large as he was.

"Okay, so, we're impressed," Brazel said. *And you're lying,* he thought. There was no way Remember had *teleported* them. "You have access to a technology that as far as we know exists nowhere else in the galaxy and you've used it to move the two of us halfway across that galaxy so that you could *mysterious* at us out of a fireplace. Let's talk about the *job,* Remember."

Brazel wasn't sure, but he thought the fire-face grinned. "A relatively simple task, actually; I will be monitoring to see how well you follow your instructions, and there will be more complicated jobs for you in the future if you perform well. There is a certain package; I wish it to be delivered to a certain place. Twenty-five days later, I wish for you to retrieve it."

"We're not messing with Benevolence," Brazel said.

"The location I wish the package delivered to is not within Benevolence space," Remember responded.

"How much?" Grond asked.

Remember named a figure. An *enormous* figure.

"We're in," Brazel said. He signaled to Grond, a brief gesture that meant *not now— we'll discuss this later.*

"I am glad to hear it," Remember said. "Grond may keep the books, as well, if he wishes."

The halfogre's eyes cleared immediately. "B.... *books*? Plural?"

Remember's hologram smiled again, and bowed. The shape dissolved back into the fire.

Grond found a few boxes neatly stacked outside the library and insisted on spending an hour carefully going through everything in Remember's library, an hour during which he was lost in literary bliss and the gnome did his best to avoid going out of his mind from impatience. He refused to help transport the boxes back to the teleporter; Grond laughed at the notion.

"They're heavier than you," he said. "I think I can handle it."

The 'bot waiting for them when they finally left the library was an identical copy of the one Grond had crushed; Brazel noticed it seemed to be trying to keep its distance. It led them back to the lobby and the door to the teleporter slid open. There was a small table just inside with two glasses of blue liquid on it.

"Drink," it said. "And when you get inside, lie down. The fluid and lying prone will help with the teleportation. You will find all of your effects waiting for you when you arrive. We will send the books in ten minutes, along with the lady Remember's package. The package will give you the coordinates for the delivery. And you will find, by the way, that your ship has been refueled."

Grond shrugged and downed his drink. Brazel inspected his before drinking; other than the oddly bright color there was nothing unusual looking about it. It tasted like a combination of especially strong tea and finely ground, blueberry-flavored gravel.

I've paid for worse, he thought as he finished. He'd learned, over the years, to never let his partner pick the drinks.

Teleporting while conscious was somewhat more pleasant than the alternative; the black material holding him still for only a few seconds, the teleportation itself loud but otherwise painless. Brazel had thought he'd be able to pinpoint the exact moment at which they jumped, but if he really was jumping parsecs across the galaxy he certainly couldn't feel it happening.

True to the 'bot's word, their gear, Angela included, was waiting for them and the boxes of books came through precisely ten minutes after they arrived. Remember's package was a metallic case, perhaps a meter square by just under two meters long. There was a blank screen in the middle of the top of the case and a single button; handles were built into the side. Grond stacked his books on top of the case and crouched to pick it up.

And grunted, exhaling explosively. The box didn't move.

"No way," the halfogre muttered, and moved the books, trying the case by itself. He couldn't budge it. He moved to one end, gripping the handle and trying to lift from the end. Brazel watched, half-amused, as veins stood out on the halfogre's neck and arms and his legs strained to try and budge the box.

"You're gonna pull something," the gnome said. "Or ... well, not, maybe."

"You fucking pick it up then," Grond said, letting go of the handle and straightening up. Brazel looked over the case carefully, then pushed the button. The screen lit up with what were clearly coordinates-- one set indicating their current location in the Queris system, and a second that Brazel didn't immediately recognize. A soft buzz came from inside and it lifted a few feet off the ground. Brazel poked it with a finger and it slid toward the door. He waved a hand underneath the box. There was nothing happening underneath to indicate how it was being lifted.

He risked making eye contact with his partner, who snorted and made a rude gesture.

"Teleportation and portable antigrav," he said. "What the hell's she need us for?" Antigravity rigs weren't uncommon, necessarily; lots of ships used them and certain larger 'bots, but they were generally expensive and much, *much* bulkier than whatever was inside this box had to be.

With a brief burst of static, his comm reestablished contact with the *Nameless*.

YOU'RE BACK, the ship said.

"We are," Brazel said. "How long were we gone?" He pushed the antigrav rig out of the teleportation room, Grond following him with the books.

I LOST COMMUNICATION WITH YOU ONE HOUR AND FORTY-SEVEN MINUTES AGO, the ship responded. FIFTEEN MINUTES AGO THE SPHERE BEGAN POWERING BACK UP AGAIN. I SURMISED THAT WHATEVER PROCESS HAD CAUSED US TO LOSE CONTACT WAS ABOUT TO BE REVERSED.

"Teleporter," Brazel said. "We were on the other side of the galaxy."

IMPRESSIVE, Namey responded. THE AMOUNT OF POWER GENERATED BY THE SPHERE IS LIKELY SUFFICIENT TO HAVE TRANSPORTED THE TWO OF YOU, PROVIDED THAT THE TECHNOLOGY TO DO SO WAS AVAILABLE. I WAS NOT AWARE THAT THAT WAS THE CASE.

"Apparently so," Brazel said. "Get the cargo hold open; we'll be there in a minute."

✦◁▭▷✦

As soon as they had their new cargo safely stowed, Brazel and Grond checked the coordinates that they were to deliver the package to. They identified a planet in a relatively unpopulated area of gnomespace, not far from home and more or less along their way.

"See what you can find out about that planet," Brazel told Namey. "And turn the dampers on in this room for the next ten minutes." The AI signed off noiselessly, and Brazel waited a moment for the communication dampers in the room to kick in.

"So. What's her game?"

"The books are bugged, aren't they?" Grond asked.

"Probably," Brazel responded. "Although it's not like she doesn't know where we're going, and it's not like the package itself isn't a giant homing beacon screaming HERE WE ARE halfway across the galaxy. But, yeah, I'd bet there's nanotrackers in a bunch of those books. Where'd you put them?"

"In the cargo hold," Grond said. "I'll have Namey scan the hell out of them before they go anywhere else in the ship, though. Maybe I accidentally throw them into an EMP field at some point. By *accident.* And maybe once we land they don't go anywhere else after that."

"Probably best," Brazel said. "What do you think's in the box?"

"I've been thinking about that," Grond said. "No idea. I halfway wonder if there's actually anything in there in the first place. This whole thing scans like some sort of elaborate test, and I can't figure her angle. We're small-time; there's no reason for Remember to have noticed us unless we screwed her first. And bringing us to her to talk for ten minutes then send us back and put us on an overpaid courier job makes me think maybe she needs an accountant. We could buy a whole new ship to move that box in for what she's paying us. It's insane."

"We're not *that* small-time," Brazel complained. Grond shrugged.

"We can have Namey scan the box, too," Brazel added, "Remember didn't say anything about not opening it or anything like that; she just said *take it here* and then *go back and get it*. She didn't seem too concerned about what we did with it in the meantime."

"He won't find anything," Grond said. "We know this, right?"

"We do," Brazel agreed. "I don't like this job, though. I don't like it at all. We're being paid too much to do too simple of a job, and both of those things scream it's a trap to me. And it's not even a good trap; if she'd wanted us dead, I'm sure that 'bot wasn't the only dangerous thing she could have turned loose on us."

"Look on the bright side," Grond said. "Twenty-five days from now we're either dead, which means no more worrying about it, or we're very, very rich. I figure I can live with either of those."

"I don't need to tell you to keep your eyes peeled, I assume," Brazel said.

"I always do," the halfogre rumbled, chuckling. "Unlike you, I can see over the furniture, so I sort of have to be the one looking out for everything."

>{∞}<

A series of scans and a thorough electromagnetic decontamination later, Grond's books were pronounced safe and they were no closer to determining the contents of Remember's case. Brazel and Grond mutually decided to not worry about it. They were three days away from the system, which was called Gallireen, after the largest planet of the system, a jumble of mid-sized terrestrials mostly too close to the star to be terribly hospitable for life and a handful of gas giants. The exact location was on a moon of one of the inner gas planets, which according to Namey's databases, housed a few hardscrabble settlements and some minor green areas but was mostly desert and stone, pulling enough heat and light to survive from the huge planet it orbited. Namey called it Gallireen 12A; the locals no doubt had some other name for it.

"Looks like ... huh," Brazel said, paging through the database. Grond raised an eyebrow.

"Mostly *human* settlements," he continued. "Even though the planet's in gnomespace. Not a lot of native humans in gnomespace. That tell you anything?"

"Smugglers," Grond responded. "Or outcasts. Or both. Outcasts who became smugglers. Also means I might actually be able to sit at the bar, if we find one."

"Don't get your hopes up," Brazel responded. "I doubt we'll be there long enough for a drink. I want this job over and done with as quick as we can; if we're on this rock for more than an hour it'll mean something's gone wrong."

Grond just grinned.

"Okay, fine, and I refuse to use a booster seat in my own damn neck of the galaxy;" Brazel snapped. "Plus, hell, I'd like to get home sooner or later. That way you can be the wrong size for all the furniture for once."

He cued up the coordinates and the *Nameless* fell into tunnelspace.

The trip passed uneventfully; Grond had already worked his way through three of his new books by the time the *Nameless* emerged from tunnelspace a few hundred thousand kilometers from their destination.

INSTRUCTIONS FOR APPROACH? Namey asked.

"Any reason we need to be particularly careful with this one?"

NONE, the AI responded. NO NOTICEABLE MILITARY PRESENCE AND NO BENEVOLENCE SIGNALS OR STANDARD CODE FREQUENCIES IN USE.

"One of the more common identities, then," Brazel responded. "Just pick one."

There was a moment of silence as the *Nameless* negotiated with Gallireen 12A for permission to dock.

GRANTED. THERE IS COMMERCIAL DOCKING SPACE AVAILABLE WITHIN EASY REACH OF OUR DESTINATION.

Brazel breathed a sigh of relief. He'd been concerned about that; his maps of Gallireen 12A were not especially detailed and he'd been concerned that the nearest docking facilities that could handle the *Nameless* were going to be on the wrong side of the planet from wherever they were supposed to drop off Remember's package— which meant two round-trips on planet, since they'd have to recover the box as well. The *Nameless* could land on rough terrain in a pinch, but if anything the gnome was pickier about his ship than he was his clothes; he didn't like risking the ship to substandard landing conditions unless the job absolutely demanded it.

"Bring us in," he said. "Who are we, by the way?"

THE *HAMSTRINGER*, OUT OF THE OKRASTER SYSTEM, the ship responded. ON PLANET ON BUSINESS. LENGTH OF STAY, TWO STANDARD WEEKS. NO ONE ASKED YOUR NAMES; CALL YOURSELVES WHATEVER YOU WANT.

"Works for me. Where's the box going?"

THE BASEMENT OF A COMMERCIAL BUILDING WITHIN EASY WALKING DISTANCE OF THE SPACEPORT.

"We're couriers, then," Brazel said. "You get the feeling anyone's paying attention to the spaceport?"

THEY ARE BEING EXCEPTIONALLY SUBTLE ABOUT IT IF THEY ARE, the ship responded. THE PORT AI WAS BORED. I DIDN'T THINK ARTIFICIAL INTELLIGENCES GOT BORED.

"I didn't think they used contractions."

EVERY SO OFTEN I LIKE TO SHAKE THINGS UP.

"Wake up the halfogre, then. He's got recon to do."

Brazel had never understood how it was possible that his partner— his former gladiator, heavily tattooed, scarred, two-point-four-meters-tall halfogre *partner*— was so much better at going unnoticed than he was. Grond had walked through rooms full of gnomish children more than once without any of them noticing he was even there. He had the uncanny ability to blend in *anywhere*, right up to the point where he *wanted* to attract attention— and few were better than he was at *that*, either. Grond walked off the ship dressed in well-worn laborer's clothes, Angela folded up and concealed under a jacket and no more than seven or eight knives concealed on his person.

He was back within an hour.

"This really is the easiest job ever," he said. "There's a back door into the building straight into a stairwell, and get this— only the two top floors of the building are even *occupied*; some kind of medical research company— and there aren't even any windows facing the back. There's an alley in between it and another building and neither of them have any windows facing each other. And the two of them are the two tallest structures in the neighborhood. I coulda had the case dropped off already if I'd thought to bring it with me. I like this place; everybody minds their own business."

"I'm still going with you for the drop," the gnome said.

"May as well," Grond said. "You hang back, though; I'm gonna look like I'm carrying the box. Nobody anywhere is gonna believe that a halfogre needs help from a gnome to move something heavy."

Brazel nodded. "I'll watch your back," he said.

Grond had been right— the trip to the drop spot took no more than a fifteen-minute walk and neither Grond nor Brazel attracted anything more than a stray glance or two along the way. The alley between the buildings was slightly narrower and *much* higher than Brazel liked— they were trapped if for some reason they had to fight their way out of the building— but Grond cracked the lock in moments and they were inside the building quickly. The back door opened into a stairwell.

"Downstairs," Brazel said. "Coordinates are a bit underground."

"You think we're supposed to hide the thing, or…?" Grond asked.

"We're supposed to leave it here for 25 days," Brazel responded. "Stands to reason we probably ought to make sure nobody moves it before then. Let's see if there's a storeroom or something down there."

A few minutes of searching produced a likely spot; the lower levels of the building were clearly disused and the pair quickly found a lockable closet in a part of the floor that felt out of the way.

"That work for you?"

"Yeah," Brazel said. "Let's get out of here."

Neither of them heard the device begin to hum as they closed the door behind them.

Being paid to laze about on Arradon, Brazel found, was very much to his liking. With nothing in particular to do during Remember's specified 25 days, and unlimited access to the resort his wife owned a partial stake in, he found himself taking a lot of long baths and spending a lot of time relaxing and playing with his children.

The peace and quiet lasted precisely ten days.

"We have a problem," Rhundi said.

"I don't have a problem yet," Brazel responded. He was neck-deep in a hot scented bath and very much not in a temper where "problems" were possible things for him. *"I* only have a problem if you give me one." *Please do not give me a problem,* he thought.

"What was the name of the planet you dropped Remember's box off at?" she asked.

Brazel thought about it. "One of the Gallireens, I think. 11A? 12B? I don't remember. Ask the boat."

"12A, right?"

"Sure," he replied. *This can't be good.*

"It isn't," she said, reading his mind. Rhundi and Brazel had been married for *quite* a long time and had had conversations very much like this many times.

"And it's not a problem I can fix from the bath, is it?" he asked, sighing. It never was.

"Plague," she said.

He got out of the bath.

"First cases were reported seven days ago," she said. Brazel had made himself dry, dressed and presentable in record time, and Rhundi was reading reports from her desk console in her office. "And as of right now it's spread over a third of the moon. They've estimated something like four thousand cases on a rock that only

has a population of about twenty times that many people. Most of them are in the neighborhood of a city called Rua'ta."

She paused for a moment. "Two guesses where you dropped off the package."

"I never even found out the name of the town," Brazel said. "We were just following the coordinates. Fuck, I knew there was gonna be a catch."

"It gets worse," she said. "The plague is a technovirus. It's internally networked. The victims are flocking, like birds, and they're actively seeking out new victims to infect. That's how it moves so fast. If the Benevolence finds out there's going to be an interdiction."

"They'll wipe out the entire fucking moon," Brazel said.

"Likely," she responded. "The virus doesn't seem to be smart enough right now to animate its victims to do much more than seek out other people to infect. But we don't know what will happen if it continues to infect more people. If the thing ends up being a distributed AI, and if it gets smarter as it gets more widespread..."

"It eventually figures out how to make someone pilot a boat, it packs as many infected as it can into the holds, and it heads somewhere with a lot more people," Brazel said.

"Thus the interdiction," Rhundi said. "Death sentence for the entire planet. And everything on it. I told you this job was a bad idea."

"You did not," Brazel responded. "I specifically remember never asking you."

"You knew I thought it," she snapped. "Remember's bad news, and we never should have gotten into business with her."

"Do we know it's the box?"

"The first cases were *three days* after you dropped off the box, in the *same city* you dropped the box off in," Rhundi responded. "You do the math."

"Never liked math much," Brazel said. "Ask Grond."

"Grond agrees," the halfogre said, lowering his head to get through the door. There was a single chair in Rhundi's office sized for him, and he collapsed into it. "You don't like math much, *and* this is our fault. We never shoulda taken this job, Braze."

"Right, because you were totally arguing against it," the gnome said, disgusted. "How is this suddenly my fault?"

"It's not," Rhundi said, laying her hand on her husband's arm and smoothing his fur. "But we're going to do something about it."

"What?" Brazel asked. "Seriously, what can we do about it? Slip back onto the planet before the Benevolence find out and blow it to pieces and then deactivate the box or something?"

Grond grinned.

"*Stop grinning.* That is not a plan," Brazel said. "That is fucking madness and you know it. How the hell do we even get close to the thing without getting infected ourselves?"

"That we should be able to handle," Rhundi said. "I can get ahold of some gear. Just... try not to bleed. Or breathe too much."

Brazel glared at his wife.

"Eighty thousand people, Brazel," Rhundi said. "I can't have that on my conscience. Neither can Grond. And even if you won't admit it, neither can you."

"We could just tell the Benevolence where the case is," he said.

"Which would let them know where *we* are," she retorted, "and wouldn't you *love* to explain to the Benevolence how you *know* where the source of a technovirus is? Or that you knew there was a source in the first place? You're delicate, Brazel. You wouldn't last half a day under Benevolence interrogation."

"Okay, that was stupid," Brazel said. "I admit it. But ... really. You want us to, what, blow the box apart? Will that kill the virus? Or just stop it from replicating?"

"I don't know," Rhundi said. "Yet. But I've got my people working on it already. We'll have something for you in a day or so. Right now, start prepping the *Nameless*. You two have work to do."

Brazel and Grond both stood up.

"Oh, and Brazel?"

"Yeah?"

"Shuni's birthday is next week. You may want to spend some time with her before you leave."

"I *knew* that," Brazel said. "I've even got a gift picked out."

"Good. Also, Grond?"

"I know," the halfogre rumbled. "Bring him back alive."

Rhundi nodded, a smile barely touching her eyes, and went back to work at her console.

"I feel compelled to point out that we *still* do not have a plan," Brazel said a day later as the *Nameless* dropped into tunnelspace.

"We're making some assumptions," Grond said agreeably.

"We're making nothing *but* assumptions," Brazel responded. "We're assuming that we had anything to do with this. We're assuming that destroying the box or getting it off-planet will do anything other than *spread the virus further* if we're right about it being our fault. We're assuming that we can do this before the Benevolence show up and ruin our day and everyone else's. And we're assuming that we can slip into a technovirus-infected planet that is presumably full of violent nanobot-driven innocent people and do *all of this* without getting infected *ourselves.*"

"Sounds like a tall order, when ya put it that way," Grond said.

"Don't you get all folksy with me," Brazel snapped.

The comm chirped. It was Rhundi.

"Good news," she said. "Well, mostly good news. My engineers think they can find a way to turn the virus off. All you have to do is get them a sample of it." Brazel spent a moment reflecting on the phrase *my engineers.* His wife's business dealings had always been well beyond him; she had been every bit the smuggler he was when they'd met but was almost entirely legitimate now. He'd not realized that she'd gotten into anything that involved employing *engineers.*

"You say that as if *get them a sample of it* and *all you have to do* belong in the same sentence. Tell me *exactly* what that means," Brazel said.

"Grab one of the infected people, get a blood sample, drop it into the nanoanalytics unit I had installed on the *Nameless* before you left, comm us the results," she said. "Try not to kill the infected person while you're getting blood from them. Also, try not to let them bleed on you. Or on the ship. There's not enough news coming off the planet to let us be sure exactly how the virus transmits itself. Also, don't breathe unless you're wearing a respirator. Those are on the ship too. Hopefully my gals get back to you with a kill signal before your position becomes inconvenient."

"Easy," Grond rumbled.

"And blow the box along the way," she said. "We're figuring that if Grond couldn't lift the thing without the antigrav pads on, it's not too likely that he's going to be able to move it now unless it wants to be moved. My people figure it's manufacturing the virus and pumping it into the air. If we cut off the source and then shut down everything that's in the wild, we'll have saved the planet."

"Another understatement," Brazel said. "Any word on Benevolence?"

"No movement yet," she said. "The planet's out of the way and a lot closer to us than it is to them. You won't have a ton of time once they find out and take action, though; the first thing they'll do is drop a blockship into the neighborhood to keep travelers from entering tunnelspace and the next step is to blow up anything that tries to leave the planet or get too close to it. It won't be pretty. Then... boom. We're monitoring, though."

"Okay," he said. "Anything else?"

"You've also got a few cases of stun ammo. Try to use that instead of anything lethal unless you don't have a choice. And seriously, don't die," she said. "I'm too busy for dating right now and replacing you would be a pain."

"You remain the light of my existence, dear," Brazel said and signed off.

✦{⊞}✦

They spent most of the trip modifying their weaponry to use Rhundi's stun ammunition. This was a simple process for a single gun, but Grond tended to carry a lot of guns on the ship and insisted on modifying virtually everything before they arrived. "Never know what tool you'll need," he said when Brazel called him out on it. "Don't really wanna kill someone on account of being too lazy to reset my guns on the way."

"What if you *do* need to kill someone?"

Grond pointed at a wall full of bladed weapons. "I do it up close," he said. "And I can switch Angela over in a coupla seconds; those Iklis weapons are built to be versatile. We'll be fine."

"If you say so," Brazel said.

APPROACHING THE GALLIREEN SYSTEM, Namey announced. DOCKING FACILITIES PLANETWIDE ON GALLIREEN 12A ARE BROADCASTING LOOPED EMERGENCY MESSAGES. WE ARE INSTRUCTED THAT WE ARE NOT TO LAND UNDER ANY CIRCUMSTANCES.

"Do it anyway," Brazel said. "Or at least get in close. Let's do a flyover of Rua'ta and see what it looks like down there."

Namey clicked an acknowledgement and the *Nameless* closed in on the moon.

"She was right, it's like watching birds," Grond said. The *Nameless* was hovering a klick or so above Rua'ta, and even from that distance, viewing a holoprojection, it was easy to tell that something was terribly wrong in the city. It had looked sparsely populated on their first visit; this time, nearly everyone was *outside*. From above the patterns were clear; there were knots of people standing virtually still, while others roved in large groups of perhaps thirty or forty, moving together in what almost looked like purposeful formation. Every so often one of the still groups would all move at once, relocating— at what looked like top speed— to some other location, then freezing in place again.

"There's the office building." Grond tapped the image once and the building they'd left the box in lit up. "That's... uh, that's not good."

"How many do you think there are?" Brazel asked.

I ESTIMATE FOUR HUNDRED, Namey added helpfully.

The building was completely surrounded with people, who didn't appear to be doing anything other than endlessly circling it in a manner that reminded Brazel less of birds and more of insects in a death spiral. There was clearly no way to approach the place from the ground.

"Namey, any way to estimate the number of people who aren't infected down there?"

ONLY INDIRECTLY, the ship responded. THERE ARE THREE THOUSAND SEVEN HUNDRED AND THREE STANDARD-TYPE LIFE FORMS OUTDOORS WITHIN TWO KILOMETERS OF OUR COORDINATES RIGHT NOW. THE

POPULATION OF RUA'TA WAS ROUGHLY SIX
THOUSAND A MONTH AGO.

"So two thousand people uninfected, *maybe*, assuming all the
plague victims are in the flocks outdoors," Brazel murmured.
"That's ... an awful lot of people."

THIS ASSUMES NO CASUALTIES AS WELL. THE
TECHNOVIRUS IS DESIGNED TO SPREAD ITSELF, NOT TO
KILL, BUT SURELY THE UNINFECTED WOULD HAVE
FOUGHT BACK. THE ROVING GROUPS APPEAR TO BE
PATROLLING; THEY MAY HAVE CLEARED UNINFECTED
FROM THE AREA AROUND THE BOX ALREADY. THERE
ARE SCATTERED POCKETS OF LIFE FORMS INSIDE SOME
STRUCTURES AROUND RUA'TA BUT I HAVE NO WAY TO
DETERMINE THEIR STATUS AS INFECTED OR
UNINFECTED.

"Still a lot of people," Brazel said. "Now would be the time to
hear about your plan, Grond."

"Drop me on a roof nearby," Grond said. "Then come get me
when I need you to."

"You're *kidding*," Brazel said.

"Not a bit," Grond said. "Somebody's gotta fly the ship;
you're a better pilot than I am. And it's nuts to try to get there on
the ground. That leaves the windows or the roof."

"And *when* they see us and come into the building to find
you?"

"So distract them," Grond said. "Namey's got external
loudspeakers. Make the loudest most obnoxious sound you can
and then fly a few blocks away. See if you can get them to follow
you. If not, I'll manage."

"Or we could just *bomb the building*. That seems a trifle
safer."

"For us. There's a few hundred people that are gonna get
landed on if you do that. And the box is in the basement. No
guarantee that dropping the rest of the place on top of it is even
going to do any good. We're not Benevolence. We're not killing
four hundred people today even if we think it saves more than
that."

"Tell me you're at least suiting up."

"Completely," Grond said, holding up an envirosuit. "Rhundi had this thing custom-made. There's even *holsters* built into it. She's thoughtful, that wife of yours. You oughtta treat her nicer."

"*You* treat her nicer," Brazel grumbled. The halfogre was right, though. He had a much better chance of getting in and out than Brazel did, and both of them leaving the ship was crazy.

COMPLICATION, Namey said.

"Of course there is," Brazel answered.

THERE ARE ALREADY LIFE FORMS IN THE TARGET BUILDING, the ship responded. ALL ON THE TOP FLOORS. MOST BUILDINGS IN THE AREA ARE ABANDONED.

"I thought you said they'd cleared everything?"

CONJECTURE. THEY MAY HAVE MISSED SURVIVORS IN THE BUILDING OR THESE MAY BE INFECTED.

"Are there less than four hundred of them?" Grond said.

THERE ARE LESS THAN A DOZEN.

"I'll survive," the halfogre said, pulling on his envirosuit. "Braze, get me near that building across the alley. Do a nice slow pass and I'll jump out; if we get lucky they won't even realize that anyone left the boat. Then make a bunch of noise and fly off somewhere else. Maybe they'll follow you, maybe they won't; either way if they're not looking at the roof I ought to be able to get across and into the building. Wait for me to comm you back and come get me. Easy."

"Famous last words," the gnome said.

"Nah. My last words are probably gonna be *much* more profane than that. I've always figured 'Oh, *fuck!*' would be the last thing I ever said," Grond responded.

"Quit telling jokes and head for the cargo hold," Brazel said. "I hope your timing's good. You're not going to enjoy the fall if you miss your jump."

Grond slung his longbow over his back and grinned.

"I won't miss if you can fly straight," he said.

Grond didn't miss, and the halfogre fell into a forward roll as soon as he hit the rooftop, stopping his momentum before running into anything solid. He rolled to his feet, a heavy projectile pistol loaded with stun darts in one hand and a heavy knife in the other. He looked around. There was nothing alive anywhere near him. He flinched as the wall of sound from the *Nameless* hit him; Brazel seemed to be playing every audio file on the boat at once at the highest volume Namey's external speakers could handle. Hopefully it would draw some attention.

He took a moment to be briefly grateful that the two buildings were the same height. The gap between them was about eight feet wide; in the alley below, the mass of plague victims was already starting to separate and clear. None of them appeared to be looking up. He took a running start and cleared it easily.

Need a way in. There was an access door in the northwest corner of the building, right over the door they'd used to get in from the alley. The stairwell, presumably, would go all the way down to the basement. Convenient. He spent a moment thinking about the best way to get the door open quietly and then laughed at himself; the *Nameless* was still making so much noise that nothing short of explosives would made a difference.

Also, it was unlocked, as he discovered when he tested the handle. He opened the door slowly anyway, widening the gap just far enough to squeeze his huge frame inside the doorway. *Good thing the planet's sized for bigs*, he thought. It was too dark to see inside; he felt his way down the stairs to the top floor and then waited, listening carefully. Namey had said there were less than a dozen people inside. That meant he'd assume twenty.

He couldn't hear a thing.

It was too easy the first time, he thought. Maybe he'd get lucky again. He gave his eyes another minute or two to adjust to the darkness, adjusted his respirator over his mouth and nose, then started making his way downstairs.

He made it almost an entire floor before all hell broke loose.

Something exploded on the floor beneath him, blowing the door on the landing beneath him off its hinges and into the stairwell. A small form stumbled through the doorway, coughing and wiping its eyes— a human female, it looked like— and then shook her head as if to clear the cobwebs and fled down the stairs. A moment later a scrum of other humans flowed through the doorway and down the stairs after her. "Flowed" was the only word for it— at the speed they were moving, they should have been running into and stumbling over each other, but not one of them made contact with anyone else as they came out and headed down. There were glowing blue lines tracing over their exposed hands and faces; their features were distressingly calm. Not one of them made a sound. And not one of them noticed Grond as he shrank back into the upper floor.

Shit. He had enough to do without adding a rescue. At least they were headed the right way. He heard a scream from below, thumbed Angela into stun mode and hurled himself through the smoke and down the stairs.

The woman was fighting for her life against a crowd of infected, a short stun baton in one hand and a crackling electroblade in the other. Grond dropped two of them with two shots in the back before they noticed he was there, their bodies slumping harmlessly to the floor. One turned its head to look his way and then, moving as one, the *entire group* disengaged itself from the first fight to focus on him.

"You've gotta be fucking kidding me," he said, retreating and shooting two more. The woman, meanwhile, turned and fled back down the stairs without a word to Grond.

"HEY!" he shouted, assessing his situation. They'd be on him in a moment; he wouldn't be able to shoot fast enough.

Nonlethal methods be damned; it was time for blades. He threw Angela onto his back and drew two of them; either would be a sword in Brazel's hands but looked like long daggers in his. He didn't have the room for anything bigger. The victims were unarmed, but there were a lot of them and he needed to keep his envirosuit undamaged. The woman hadn't been wearing one; he wondered if she was infected yet or not.

Circumstances aside, though, one armed and skilled halfogre against what turned out to be nine unarmed humans did not end up being a long fight. Their motions were coordinated but it was clear that none were warriors and Grond was able to put all of them down in a couple of minutes of intense fighting. *Pretty sure a few of them aren't even dead,* he thought. A few would need to learn occupations that didn't involve having two arms, though.

Back down the stairs. This time he made it three floors down before the woman barreled into him, coming *back up again* and around the corner. She swung the stun baton at him and he grabbed her wrist, the baton flying out of her hand and bouncing harmlessly off the wall.

"Who the hell *are* you?" he asked.

"No time," she said. "They're coming."

Pain exploded in Grond's right forearm, and he looked down to see a ten-inch gash torn through his suit and his arm as well. There were more of them coming— *lots* of them— and one had just thrown something sharp at him.

Shit. Networked. The ones outside found out about the fight inside. No amount of noise Brazel was going to make would distract them now. The woman wriggled out of his grasp and headed up the stairs. Grond grabbed the first infected to get close to him and hurled it at the rest of them, knocking a dozen or so people back down the stairs in a writhing, silent mass.

There was no way he was getting into the basement without killing his way through all of them, and he wasn't equipped for it. And his suit was compromised. The wound on his arm looked bad.

GROND, Brazel commed into his ear. UPSTAIRS. NOW. WE'RE ABORTING.

What?

"I was about to tell *you* that," Grond muttered, turning and fleeing. "What's *your* reason?"

THERE'S BENEVOLENCE ON THE OUTSKIRTS OF THE SYSTEM, Brazel responded. NAMEY SAYS WE'VE GOT FIVE MINUTES TO GET CLEAR BEFORE THE BLOCKSHIP GETS CLOSE ENOUGH TO KEEP US HERE.

The halfogre didn't need to hear anything else, making his way back to the roof in a matter of moments and locking the door behind him. The woman was still up there, eyeing the gap between the two buildings as if trying to decide if she was going to be able to jump it.

"Need a ride?" Grond asked. "One chance. Benevolence is coming; we're all dead in a few minutes."

"I've got a ride," she said.

"Unless it's fucking *invisible*, no, you don't," Grond said. He heard the wail of the *Nameless'* engines as Brazel brought the ship around, opening the cargo door and giving him room to jump in.

RIGHT NOW, GROND.

The two of them wasted no time with more words, turning and sprinting for the ship. Grond leapt, landing and rolling to safety in the cargo bay first. He heard and felt the woman land next to him.

The cargo bay door groaned closed as Brazel streaked out of the moon's atmosphere.

"Stay here," he told the woman, locking the cargo hold behind himself and heading for his copilot's chair in his quarters. He threw himself into his chair, activated the holographic screens, and commed Brazel.

"You noticed we picked up a stray," he said.

"Tell me later," Brazel responded. "She look smart enough to figure out to hold on to something for the next couple of minutes?"

"She heard me say *Benevolence*," he responded. "I hope so."

"We're heading for the other side of the star," he said. "Namey doesn't think they've noticed us yet. Cross every finger you have that they don't or they'll probably come after us too."

His arm was still bleeding badly. *No time for that right now.* If the Benevolence sent spiderships after them they'd need him handling the guns, not in the closet that passed for the ship's medical bay. The long-range sensors showed two blockships and a sub-*Testament* class capital ship; they were definitely planning on an interdiction.

"How far?" he said.

"Just a couple minutes," Brazel responded. "We're not trying for tunnelspace if we can hide; they might notice the jump."

Grond waited. Watched the capital ship move into position near Gallireen 12A. Watched, as a sequence of energy blasts from the ship scorched the surface of the moon into flaming cinders, the sheer violence of the blasts tumbling it from orbit. The massive explosion when it inevitably fell into the planet would be visible from lightyears away.

They had failed.

They waited for hours on the other side of the sun, waiting for the Benevolence to leave the system, and then for a few more hours after that, just to make certain they were really gone. Grond sat, staring, the bleeding from the wound on his arm eventually slowing on its own, uncared for. Brazel wandered the ship, taking care of little maintenance jobs here and there that he'd not found time for but that suddenly seemed terribly important. They let the ship take care of their guest for a while, Brazel eventually bringing her some food himself just to have someone to talk to.

"She's asking for you, you know," Brazel said, braving his partner's quarters. Grond was sitting on his bunk, his arm still unbound, staring at a thin, lightweight shiv that he had balanced on one finger. It was the narrowest blade he owned, nearly useless for combat but perfectly balanced and easier than most to conceal. He could actually toss it from one finger to another without dropping it on a good day.

Grond said nothing.

"You're probably not infected," the gnome continued. "We'd know by now. Rhundi wants you to use the nanoanalyzer anyway. She's worried about you."

The halfogre spun the knife into his palm, reached into a drawer next to his bunk, and tossed something at Brazel. The gnome caught it, a surprised look on his face.

"It's ... a vial of blood. You have a vial of your own blood in a drawer next to your bed."

"I was gonna do it," Grond rumbled. "Just ... not ready to yet. Gimme a bit. Go run the blood; I'll be out in a few minutes. We'll talk to the girl and then decide what to do next."

"We did everything we could, Grond."

The halfogre stood up.

"Not yet," he said.

Her name was Ilana, and that was really all she had to say about anything. She was a female human, perhaps 25 years old, and amazingly slight for a human, perhaps only forty to fifty centimeters taller than Brazel. She'd willingly surrendered her electroblade and another smaller blade she'd had concealed in a boot; she said she had had a gun but had lost it in the battle before encountering Grond. She would say nothing on why she was on Gallireen, much less in the precise building that Grond and Brazel had left Remember's package in.

"So what do we do with you, then?" Grond asked, scratching at the bandage he'd finally put on his arm. "We could space you and be done with you. You're not telling us anything, which makes you hard to trust. I could *make* you tell us things. So could

Brazel. But I feel like we've hurt enough people lately. So why don't you just tell us what you need."

"Just pick somewhere with a spaceport and drop me off," she said. "I'll figure it out from there. I can take care of myself."

"You'd be *dead* if I'd let you take care of yourself," Grond said. "And *I'd* be dead if I didn't have Brazel flying a ship for me. So can the solo act. But fine, you'll get what you want."

He turned to Brazel, who was standing just behind him. "We'll set up something comfortable in one of the bigger lockable cargo bays. She can stay there until we get somewhere civilized. You okay with that?"

The gnome nodded.

He turned to her. "You okay with that?"

She nodded.

"Fine, settled. Namey, where are we going?"

THERE ARE HALF A DOZEN ACCEPTABLE PLANETS WITHIN A DAY'S TUNNELSPACE FROM OUR CURRENT POSITION, the ship replied.

"Pick one on the way back home," Grond said. He looked at the other two. "We done here?"

No one spoke.

"Fine," he said. "I'll be in my bunk." He turned on one heel and left the room.

"Enjoy your stay on the *Nameless*, I suppose," Brazel said. "I'll be back in a bit. For right now, you're staying right here. The ship won't let you get anywhere outside the cargo hold. I'll bring you some bedding and a change of clothes once we're moving."

She remained silent.

"Have it your way," he said. "The halfogre's actually a pretty remarkable guy when he hasn't just had a planet blown up in front of him. I'm the one you need to worry about. He's upset that they're dead. I couldn't be happier that we're *alive*."

She smiled at that, just a bit.

"And you?"

"Both, I guess," she said. "Thank you for saving me. I owe you. But that doesn't mean we have to be friends."

"That's fair," Brazel said. "Mercenary, even. I like that in a person. I'll come back when I know where we're going."

᚛⊡᚜

He didn't even make it to the cockpit. Years of piloting the same boat had taught him to recognize the subtle shift in his body when the *Nameless* entered tunnelspace; most flyers couldn't tell you unless they happened to be watching or paying close attention when it happened.

Coming *out* of tunnelspace was something entirely different, especially when it happened at speed. Getting torn out of tunnelspace was *exquisitely* painful. It wasn't quite as unpleasant as the unexpected teleportation had been, but it was hard to imagine anything that was that didn't kill him or leave most of his insides somewhere new.

The ship stopped dead, too fast, faster than it ought to be able to. It overcame the inertial dampers and sent him flying into a wall.

"The fuck was that?"

There was no response from the *Nameless.*

Oh, fuck. "Namey. Say something. Grond, you out there?"

"Yeah," the halfogre said, sounding dazed. "I'm ... holy shit, the AI's *rebooting* ... Oh fuck. Get to the damn cockpit. The fucking teleporter. It's *outside.*"

"What the hell do you mean it's outside?"

"I mean Remember just yanked us out of tunnelspace, which means she's got her own blockship *built into* that thing, and she's not shooting at us yet but she *might start,*" Grond yelled.

Brazel sprinted to the cockpit, ignoring pains from what seemed like half of his body. The grey facade of Remember's enormous teleporter filled the *Nameless'* viewscreen. The ship appeared to be listing to the side, drifting across the face of the sphere.

Wait. He checked their coordinates and gave the yoke an experimental twist. They weren't moving. The teleporter was *rotating.* The boat was still dead, immobile in space. He checked Namey's brainbox; Grond was right— he was rebooting. The last time the AI had had to reboot the boat had nearly been blown in *half.* And without the AI's help, he couldn't figure out why the ship couldn't move without manually checking the engines himself. He couldn't see any evidence of an inertia beam outside the ship, but that didn't necessarily mean anything.

The sphere rotated, and the docking port slowly came into view. With a jerk, the *Nameless* began moving again, pulled inexorably toward the landing bay inside the sphere.

Remember was calling them to her.

"We don't have to go, you know."

"I'm not keen on starving to death," Grond said, adjusting his bandage, which had fresh bloodstains on it. "We broke her fuckin' rules and now she's calling us to account. I don't see any way this plays out other than to *let it play out*. You think she's just gonna turn the inertia beam off and let us go? I doubt it."

"We could have Rhundi come get us."

Grond glared at him. "You know twelve reasons that won't work and I'm not going to bother explaining them to you. Only decision we actually get to make here is what we're doing with Ilana."

"May as well take her with us," Brazel said. "She'll get to tell everybody she met Remember. That's gotta be worth something."

"Assuming she doesn't take her out too," Grond said. "Another body on our conscience. All right. Go get her. Meet me outside."

Brazel made his way to the cargo hold, collecting Ilana's confiscated weapons along the way. She was pacing the hold, muttering to herself.

He tossed her the weapons. "We're stuck, and the two of us have to take a little trip. You're not going to be able to go anywhere until we get back, and for all I know we might not be coming back. So you can wait here and take your chances that eventually you'll be able to take the ship or you can come with us and see what happens. Your call."

"What the hell was that?" She had an angry bruise on the side of her face; she had clearly taken a hard hit when the ship was pulled out of tunnelspace.

"We made somebody mad. She's requested an interview, and she didn't do it in the nicest possible way. You ever heard of Lady Remember?"

A strange look crossed her face.

"Yeah. You're ... you're tangled up with Remember? And you're going to see her now?"

"Quite possibly for her to kill us, yes."

"I'm in," she said. "Always up to meet a celebrity."

"Hopefully that's not the worst mistake you ever made," he said. "If it is, it'll be your last."

Brazel filled Ilana in on the finer points of instantaneous intergalactic transport— and the distinct possibility that she would wake up naked with two relatively unfamiliar, and also naked, men— on the way into the teleporter room in the center of the sphere. "You're not going to have your guns, either, so hope that she plans on sending you back," he added. Neither of them had bothered to bring anything of any importance with them this time, assuming that the teleporter would simply leave it behind again.

There were *three* glasses of the odd blue drink sitting on the threshold of the teleporter.

"Well, okay," Brazel said, drinking his. "So much for surprising her."

A few minutes later, Ilana weaving a bit unsteadily, they were in the lobby. This time, there were two floating 'bots along with their robes, which were again neatly wrapped in ribboned packages. Both were armed.

"Please come this way," one of them said. "Lady Remember will be with you shortly."

Brazel glanced over at his partner. The teleporter had even left his bandage behind; Grond's scar was roughly stitched together. It wasn't good enough to be medbot work; he'd done it himself. Brazel winced. *That must have hurt.* He absentmindedly tucked the ribbon from the package into his pocket again.

"We go nowhere," Grond said, putting his robe on. "Remember meets with us personally, and she meets with us *here*. We're not taking another fucking step."

The two 'bots leveled their guns at Grond.

"I think Remember knows she's going to need to send more than two," Grond said offhandedly. The big halfogre didn't look the slightest bit intimidated.

"I'm not with these guys," Ilana said, casually moving away from Grond and Brazel.

There was a brief, tense moment of silence.

The 'bots folded their guns away.

"The lady Remember agrees to meet with you in person," one of them said. "But you will come with us nonetheless."

Grond and Brazel exchanged a look.

"Good enough," Grond said. "Lead the way."

They were taken a different way this time, not to the library but to a simple room, wood-paneled, with a large table with seats for half a dozen and another fireplace. Grond sat in one by the door, putting his feet up on the table. Brazel and Ilana circled around, putting themselves closer to the fire.

Remember arrived a moment later, the door swinging open without announcement and seemingly on its own. In the flesh she looked much like her flaming avatar had before. Her hair was white, tied in a loose topknot that fell to below her waist. Her clothes were loose, flowing, covering most of her flesh; only her hands and her face showed, and she still had her hands clasped behind her back. Her skin was lined, caramel-colored, papery like an old woman's, but none of an old woman's frailty showed in the rest of her. The form underneath the robes looked robust and strong.

"You did not follow your instructions," Remember said.

That was as far as she got. There was a wet, meaty *tearing* sound from the front of the room and Grond leapt at Remember, his narrow shiv in his hand, his arm freely bleeding again. The halfogre went for Remember's neck with the blade, and Remember … just suddenly *wasn't there* any more. Brazel had never seen a dodge so elegant; she had slid around Grond like she was made of smoke, forcing the halfogre to pivot and try again. Almost faster than Brazel could see, Grond took three, four, *five* swings with the blade at Remember, all of them narrowly missing their mark. Remember had a broad grin on her face, a weird silvery tint starting to take over in her eyes.

She never moved her hands from behind her back.

Brazel felt something cold and hard pressing into the back of his neck. He glanced to his right.

"Grond."

The halfogre ignored him, red-eyed and roaring now, trying his best to lay even a single *finger* on Remember and failing.

"*Grond.*"

Something in Brazel's tone got through this time, and the halfogre hesitated, holding the blade in front of him, amazingly *out of breath.* Brazel had seen the halfogre in battles hours long; seeing him winded was incredibly rare.

Ilana had a gun to the back of Brazel's head. A gun that she certainly *hadn't* had after the teleporter; there hadn't really been anywhere for her to hide one. Which meant it was either in the box with her robe or in the room, waiting for her. Which meant she was one of Remember's people.

Which meant she was fair game. Brazel had learned many years ago that most humans had no real idea how to hold a gnome at gunpoint; the height difference never worked in their favor. He dropped to the floor in a flash, simultaneously shoving her gun hand high, over his head and toward Remember. He scuttled between her legs and climbed up onto her back, yanking the ribbon from his robe out of his pocket and wrapping it twice around her neck, squeezing tightly. Ilana slumped to the floor, unable to bear his weight on her back, scrabbling at the improvised garrote and dropping her gun.

"Okay, you're a badass, and Grond can't hurt you," he said. "I can hurt *her.* Your move."

The grin on Remember's face *broadened*, if anything. She cast a sidelong glance at Grond, straightened herself up, and bowed to the two of them.

"I said you had not followed directions. I was given no opportunity to discuss my opinion of your transgressions. You may release my employee; you are in no danger."

Brazel grabbed Ilana's gun from the floor and hit her in the back of the head, knocking her unconscious.

"Only lady gets to hold me at gunpoint is my wife," he said. "I tend to take it personally."

Remember watched her fall to the floor and shrugged.

"I would appreciate it if you would put down the knife," she said.

Grond slammed the knife into the table, snapping it in half.

"You're responsible for *eighty thousand dead,*" he growled. "And you brought *us* into it."

"Untrue," Remember said. "It is not outside the realm of possibility that *she*," this with a nod at Ilana, "is partially responsible, but you are not. The disease had begun to spread before you even landed."

"So you sent us into a plague zone without any warning? That's *not* better," Brazel retorted. "I went home to my *wife and kids* after that job."

"You had no risk of infection," Remember said. "The liquid you imbibed prior to the delivery saw to that. A simple nanoinhibitor. One that could be manufactured in high quantities, given the right equipment."

"The box," Brazel said. "Is *that* what the damn thing was for? You were trying to cure the plague? But the plague took over the planet anyway."

"It didn't work," Remember said, shrugging. "I had hoped to arrest the plague, or even stop it in its tracks, but I failed. The cure worked on you, however. It is apparently more effective when ingested."

"Why the hell didn't you *tell* us?" Grond said, his eyes still shining red, although most of the aggression had gone out of his stance. "You knew this was going to happen and you sent us in anyway?"

"I told you that I would be monitoring you to see how well you followed your instructions," Remember said calmly. "I said nothing about whether I *expected you* to follow those instructions. If the cure had worked, the twenty-five day cycle would have been sufficient to clear the nanovirus from the surrounding area. If you had not returned once news of the plague became public, I would know you to be cowards; men of little conviction or moral strength. You returned to save people, against my clear instructions, with no thought to the consequences."

"*Plenty* of thought to the consequences," Brazel corrected.

Remember smiled again. "But you did it anyway."

"And the girl?"

"Insurance," Remember replied. "She was to try to arrest the disease at its source more ... directly than you were told to. She failed as well. It seems that some things ... cannot be changed, after all."

"The medical firm on the top floor," Grond said. "They set the plague loose?"

"Unwittingly, I believe," Remember said. "Intent so rarely matters, unfortunately."

"You're lying," Grond said. "Or deliberately concealing something. How the hell did you even know about the plague in time to send us there to stop it?"

"Some things I will not be sharing with you," Remember said, a hint of ice creeping into her voice. "Learn to live with ambiguity."

No one said anything for a moment.

"You have two choices before you," Remember said. "The first is to choose to believe me, or not, and accept your payment and the likelihood that I will be using your services in the future. The second is to choose to try to kill me again. You will find that this time I will not restrain myself." Her hands, Brazel noticed, had still not moved from behind her back.

Brazel looked at Grond. The halfogre shrugged, clearly still angry but accepting the inevitable.

"We'll take that payment now," he said.

"A word on that," Remember said. "I offered you a certain sum for following my instructions. You did not follow those instructions. And there is a small matter of some destroyed property as well," glancing at Grond.

"You're trying to welsh?" Brazel asked.

"I am not *trying* anything," Remember said. "I have altered the deal. You will find, however, that the end result will still be to your liking. Your wife owns a partial stake in a resort on Arradon, yes?"

Brazel nodded, feeling the blood drain out of his face. *This can't be good.*

"You will find that she now owns the *entire* resort," Remember continued. "With my compliments. Her network of informants is … impressive. Even to me."

Brazel ran the numbers in his head. Their pay had been cut by about a third, but Rhundi would be able to turn her stake in the resort into much more money in no time, and she'd been trying to buy her partners out for *years* without success.

"Grond?"

The halfogre nodded.

"Fine," Brazel said.

"I will be in touch when I require you again," Remember said, turning to leave.

"And what if we want *you?*" Grond asked.

Remember paused.

"You will find," she said, "that the two events will tend to overlap. Look for the *Memento.*"

She left the room, her robe trailing behind her. The door swung open to admit her, then closed.

"What memento does she want us to look for? Awful cryptic," Brazel said.

"It's a goddamn pun," Grond said. "It's the name of the teleporter."

Brazel thought about it for a moment. "I'm not sure I get it."

"A memento is an object," Grond said. "One that leads you to remember."

Brazel snickered.

"C'mon, let's go," he said. "I'll let you be the one who gets to tell Rhundi about her new resort, what with the old woman beating you in a fight and all."

"Bet I can hit *you,*" Grond responded.

"Let's get out of here first," Brazel said. "You can try and hit me all you want once I'm back in my own ship."

Grond gestured at Ilana, still unconscious on the floor. "Think we should just leave her there?"

"Yeah," Brazel said. "I didn't get the feeling Remember was too happy with her. And I think that's two she owes us, now."

"Works for me," Grond said, following his partner out of the room.

>{⊞}<

"THE CONTRACT"

"Explain to me exactly why this has to be my problem."
The goblin wrung her hands, stress evident on her face, her fur and ears held flat. "We can't make him go away, ma'am. He says he has a contract. He's not scared of us. Maybe you send Grond?"
Rhundi raised an eyebrow, letting her own fur raise up a bit in response. Her husband Brazel and his halfogre partner were a couple parsecs away; they were finished with their job, but she'd just told Brazel about a delivery job that had come up. They'd likely be taking care of that before they came home, which meant they were probably not going to be back for a few days at the very earliest.
Not that anyone else really needed to know that.
"You're not suggesting I can't handle this on my own."
The goblin deflated further, staring at the ground and continuing to rub her hands together. "No, ma'am. Of course not. Just that— well, you're the boss. You shouldn't have to, ma'am."
Rhundi ignored that.
"Did he show you the contract?"
"He says the contract says he doesn't have to, ma'am. He wouldn't even open the door. He doesn't anymore, unless we've brought meals, and then only after we leave."
"I own the place. He doesn't have a contract that says he doesn't have to show it to me."
The goblin cringed again, saying nothing.
Rhundi rubbed her forehead. She had only just recently assumed full control of the resort, and it had become abundantly

clear to her quickly that previous management had made frequent poor decisions regarding their treatment of the staff. "It's not your fault... what was your name again?"

"We are Corvix clan, ma'am. This one is Twelve." Goblins were strongly group-oriented; personal names were perceived as being for family only. There were thirty-seven goblins working at the resort, none of whom would divulge their personal names. She apparently had at least twelve members of the Corvix clan on staff.

Rhundi nodded. "Twelfth Corvix, you are not to blame for this. I will deal with him. You may return to work." The goblin nodded and scurried out of Rhundi's office.

She pushed a button on her desk console, opening a comm to her personal secretary.

"Gorrim."

"Yes, ma'am." Gorrim had an unusually deep voice for a gnome, and it sounded odd to hear him through the desk comm.

"Call the troll. Tell him I'm coming to see him in an hour, and tell him if he tries to lock me out this time I'm going to take the door down. If he says a single thing about a contract, tell him I'm bringing Grond with me."

"He's not going to like that, ma'am."

"I'm not going to like it either. Do it anyway."

She cut the connection.

Rhundi's resort— she was renaming the place, now that she owned it, but hadn't come up with a suitably grand name for it yet— was, at the most, a mid-level tourist attraction on the planet of Arradon, a smallish rock in one of the more out-of-the-way tentacles of gnomespace. Owing to some quirks of planetary geography and location, the entire planet was regarded as a tourist destination by most of the galaxy, so she had her work cut out for her if she intended to make a name for herself in legitimate work. She'd started off as a jack-of-all-trades, much like her husband— it sounded nicer than "smuggler" or "fence," which were a bit more accurate— but she'd been trying to steadily increase the amount of capital their family was able to accumulate from more legitimate work. She'd owned a third of the resort only a few months ago; both of her business partners had abruptly sold their shares to her on very little notice and vacated the planet altogether. She had her suspicions as to their reasons but had been too busy to look into them. There was too much to do.

The troll on the fifth level was one of the problems she'd managed to inherit. Large portions of the resort were subterranean; she wanted to expand, and she was going to have to demolish the suite of rooms he occupied in order to do it. He had occupied them for nearly fifteen years.

And he was not terribly interested in moving.

In general, the resort did not cater to long-term stays; most of their guests were on-planet for no more than a few weeks. The troll's rent had been changed any number of times without complaint; he appeared to be independently wealthy and, apparently, working from home, as he rarely left his rooms, having his meals— the same meals, every day— brought to him by the staff. He hadn't been difficult, really; in fact, he had made her an awful lot of money over the years. But he was in the way of her making more money, and that meant he needed to move.

There were any number of ways to handle the situation; all of the gentle ones short of her showing up had been used. The next step after a personal conference would involve lawyers, subterfuge, or force, none of which she was terribly interested in at the moment. No, she'd have to visit him herself.

She walked to the troll's suite. There were lifts and personal transports that could have gotten her there faster; she wanted the time to think, and it was good for her employees to see her out and about in the resort instead of stuck in her office. She noted fourteen things that needed her attention along the way, memorizing a mental list as she walked. The entryway to the troll's suite was the fifteenth; you could tell you were underground while walking down the final corridor to his door. It was damp and cold, as if the climate balancers weren't reaching it properly, and the approach lacked artistry as well. He was in one of her larger suites; the bare, straight corridor to his door was not up to the degree of decor and class that she expected from what was now her own establishment.

She stood in front of the door, letting the suite security scan her. Every resident had the right to set rules for who could bother them; the door was soundproofed enough that knocking would do no good. If the guest was interested enough in privacy it would take a small explosion outside their rooms for them to notice it inside. She had an override, of course, as did most of the staff, and the suite would be telling the troll that she was standing outside in moments. If he didn't let her in, she'd let herself in.

She gave him three minutes, counting the heartbeats.

Nothing happened.

"Open," she said. "Authorize override Rhundi Tavh're'muil. Password *Darsi*." Darsi was her and Brazel's firstborn. It wasn't the most secure password in existence, but the voiceprint and bioscan were proof enough of her identity without it.

Nothing continued to happen.

"You've *got* to be fucking kidding," she said. The damn troll had hacked her security software. Well, he hadn't replaced the door. She'd brought a gun. She pulled it out and aimed it at the latch.

Wait.

She reached out and put her hand on the door; gave it an experimental push. The door didn't give at all. Almost all of the standard doors across the resort were hollow-core but filled with soundproofing gel. There should have been just the tiniest amount of give when she shoved on it.

"You *have* replaced the door, you clever bastard," she said.

She took a moment to think.

"Sirrys ban Irtuus bon Alaamac," she said, using the troll's threefold, formal name. "I know you are inside and I know you do not wish visitors. I also know that you can hear me. I intend to get inside your room. It is best for both of us if this happens peacefully. If I must force my way inside it will not go well for you." She was going to have to figure out how to get a tunnel 'bot into this corridor anyway to widen it; she couldn't imagine a single thing the troll could have rigged inside his suite that would keep that out. The things were designed for digging through bedrock, and the widened access would be considerably broader than his doorway anyway.

"You have three minutes," she said, counting heartbeats again.

She heard the door click unlocked in two minutes and fifty-six seconds.

Smug bastard, she thought. He hadn't bothered to actually open the thing; he'd just unlocked it. She opened the door herself and stepped through.

It was immediately apparent that the troll hadn't let housekeeping in in a very, very long time. The smell of poorly-washed troll, as well as rotten odors of old food and some sort of weird chemical and ozone mix, was so thick it was nearly physically crawling into her snout— and gnomes had exceptionally acute senses of smell— an evolutionary perk that she found herself regretting.

She ignored it. The room was going to be demolished; the smell didn't matter.

Sirrys ban Irtuus bon Alaamac stood before her. Well, slightly *below* her, technically; trolls had a remarkably malleable physiology and could go from shorter than a gnome but broader than a dwarf to cadaverously thin but taller than an ogre in a matter of seconds. This troll was scarcely a meter tall at the moment but was actually wider than he was tall; his bluish skin sagged off his body and gathered into rolls at his joints and hips. He had a long, narrow nose and a pointed chin that contrasted sharply with his saggy voluminosity everywhere else, and a shock of stiff straw-colored hair that spread from the top of his head down his back and over his shoulders. In troll style, he wore a loose lower garment gathered at his waist and nothing else on his upper body. It was difficult to design clothing that elongated and contracted with a troll's upper body, so they often didn't bother. Pants were simply easier.

"I have a *contract*," the troll whined.

"It honors me that you do not pretend you don't know why I'm here," Rhundi replied. "Your contract is not with me. It is not even with the owners immediately prior to me. And you've never actually shown it to me."

"It is not to be shown to you," the troll said, this time in a slightly less plaintive tone of voice.

"I have no idea what that means, Sirrys ban Irtuus—"

"Call me Irtuus-bon," the troll said, his mood— and his size— shifting abruptly. "Come." He turned on a heel and stalked off, his body lengthening as he walked. Rhundi took a moment to look around. She'd entered into a sitting room; the lights had been switched out for something darker; the troll's eyes likely worked on a slightly different set of wavelengths from hers. The room looked nearly unused; there was dust on the furniture and the floor, but a clean path from the door to the room that Irtuus-bon— now at his full height— had disappeared into. She spent a moment considering the possibility that the troll had lived in this suite for fifteen years and had never once sat down in the front room.

That possibility became a certainty the moment she followed him. The troll led her into one of the bedrooms. These were generally all furnished in similar fashion; one oversized or two smaller beds, a couple of desks, a couple of dressers, a large mirror, and one to three seats of varying degrees of softness for sitting or reclining. There was a cot in a corner of the room. The rest of it was dedicated to computer equipment; an entire wall had been given over to an enormous monitor displaying several dozen data readouts and a handful of maps, simultaneously.

Her first thought, ridiculously, was *how did we not notice the power drain?*

Her second thought was to wonder where the enormous hole in the wall opposite her led to. It wasn't supposed to be there, and the troll had never bothered to finish his renovations. There was simply a large hole dug through the wall and into what was supposed to be bedrock behind it. The damn troll had *expanded his living space.* Her partners had either never known about it or simply hadn't bothered to inform her of it.

Mental note: deal with extreme rage issues later.

She followed the troll into his hole, going down a half-flight of stairs into the cavern he'd somehow managed to open behind his apartment. It looked as if at least part of it was natural, but over the years he'd reinforced the roof and managed to power and light the entire thing. There were more computer consoles and wall monitors all around the space, which was roughly circular and perhaps ten meters wide, with a five-meter ceiling, more than high enough for an ogre or a troll at his tallest to feel perfectly comfortable. A hollow in the wall led to yet another cavern beyond theirs.

Irtuus-bon stood in the center of the room, next to a holomap that had to have cost a sizeable portion of Rhundi's annual income. He pushed a button and the thing burst into live, spreading a map of what looked like most of known space across the room. Bits of it were shaded red, glowing. Benevolence space.

"What do you know of the Benevolence?" he asked.

Rhundi went cold. This couldn't be a setup. He'd been there far too long for that to be possible, living right under her nose. It *couldn't* be a setup.

"Only what everyone knows," she said. "They don't bother us out here, so we get along fine."

"Sssss ..." the troll answered. "A most ... *political* response. You are cautious. This is good. I know what you are, Rhundi Tavh're'muil, and I know what your husband and his most interesting halfogre partner are as well. I have known for ... a long time ... and I have not betrayed you yet. I will not be starting tonight. But, as you can see, I cannot acquiesce to your desire that I relocate, either."

She took a moment to take this all in. Brazel and Grond's activities were hardly a carefully guarded secret but she hadn't thought they'd ever been clear to the tenants before.

Focus on the important parts, she thought. *Figure out the rest later.*

"What have you been doing here?" she asked.

"This way," he beckoned, and disappeared into the hollow.

Rhundi adjusted her gun and followed.

The chamber the troll led her into was even larger than the one they'd left. Again, it looked as if Irtuus-bon had enlarged and reinforced a natural cavity in the rock. This one, however, contained no technology beyond that needed to light the room. This room contained artifacts. Hundreds of them, on shelves built into the wall and freestanding shelves and tables scattered around. Some of the objects were stone or wood or bone; others were made of materials harder to recognize. Many of them bore clear symbols or sigils etched or painted on them. One caught Rhundi's eye; there was a section near her devoted to dozens of symbols that bore a faint resemblance to an insect, an eight-legged monstrosity with one central eye.

"Do you recognize these?" the troll said.

Rhundi looked around, trying to find anything familiar.

"I do not," she said.

He brought her a ruined, broken piece of alloy; whatever the material was they made the outer hulls of ships from.. The spider symbol was painted on it-- hurriedly, it seemed, as it had dripped in places before it dried.

"This, perhaps?"

"It's a piece of metal," she said. "Wreckage, or salvage. It could have come from anything."

"From a ship, in fact," he said. "A ship you knew very well."

Rhundi let her lip curl derisively.

"You can't possibly be serious." It was part of a ship, and the paint job, though pitted and scratched, was the right color, but--

"Ah, so you do know it," the troll replied.

"This is not a piece of the *Incandescent*," Rhundi insisted calmly. "That ship was blown to bits half a lifetime ago, practically on the other side of the galaxy. Just because it's the right goddamn color doesn't make it the same ship. You're not fooling me, Irtuus-bon." Her hand drifted toward her gun again. What was his game? Just to rattle her? This was too stupid to work. She was better at that than the troll was. She'd rattled with the best of them.

"I collect things," the troll said, ignoring her. "Sometimes people bring me interesting things, or send them to me, and sometimes I hear of events and I make requests. You know the Benevolence; better than you have admitted to me. You know of them better than most do, in fact. But not better than I; no, not at all. I know the Benevolence, and I know their magic, and I know their *gods*, Rhundi Tavh're'muil. Each of these artifacts is a story; some of death, some of rebirth, some of stranger things. Your ship was not destroyed by accident. It was cursed. This symbol is the proof."

"Anyone could have painted that on the wreckage afterwards. And I'm far from convinced that it's even a piece of my ship."

"Believe what you will," the troll said. "I say this to you: the Benevolence do believe. And their beliefs have been known to ... change things."

She blinked. *I've let him change the subject*, she thought.

"You haven't actually answered me," she said. "Although I appreciate the attempt to distract me with superstitious nonsense. I'll not ask a third time, Irtuus-bon: what are you doing at my resort?"

His mood changed again, and he lost half of his height in an eyeblink. He cackled. "Clever, you are, so clever. Sirrys ban Irtuus bon Alaamac is proud. Shall I give you the truth, this time?"

"I believe you have given me some of the truth already," she said. "But not enough."

"More, then," he said.

"More. My patience is growing short. I would not like this to end impolitely."

He cackled again, staring at her. She returned the stare, impassive. He turned away, stomping out of the room. She followed to find him rummaging through a pile of data pads. He produced one for her. It looked as if he had had it for some time.

"My contract," he said.

She powered it on and scrolled through. It didn't take long; it wasn't especially complicated.

"This entitles you to a long-term lease;" she said. "There is no mention of this particular suite, no mention of any conditions that prevent me from entering, and-- rather importantly-- absolutely nothing that entitles you to carve holes in my walls or run an unauthorized ... whatever all *this* is."

"Old owners never looked," he said. "Fooled them."

"I think I want Irtuus-bon back," she said. "I liked him more."

The troll blinked a couple of times, shrugged, and grew.

"Your other incarnations are rather childish," Rhundi said.

"As must they be," Irtuus-bon replied. "My people contain multitudes."

"My people are somewhat more straightforward. You will reveal to me in simple language what you have been doing in this room for all these years, with no subterfuge or misdirection, and you will do it now, or I will forcibly evict you and turn these things you're harboring over to the Benevolence."

The troll's eyes narrowed. "Sss. Overplaying your hand, I think. You would not... willingly draw the attention of Benevolence, not out here. There are very good reasons I chose your planet to do my work; the disinclination of the Benevolence to come anywhere near it is a large portion of those reasons."

Rhundi reached for her gun, and the troll raised a hand, continuing. "I do, however, believe the threat of force. I am a researcher and a collector and a historian. I watch the Benevolence, Rhundi Tavh're'muil. I collect their scraps when they come into my possession and I collect knowledge of their movements from ... well, everywhere I can. Trolls, as it turns out, are exceptionally good at this sort of thing. It may be that we are not taken as seriously by the Benevolence as perhaps we should."

"Tell me something I don't know."

"Would the current location of the *Testament* be sufficient?"

Oh my. The *Testament* was the Benevolence's flagship. There were any number of reasons why having a handle on its location might be useful.

"It would, if you could prove it."

Irtuus-bon sighed. "Well, you could go to it and see, but by then it would likely be elsewhere."

"Try again, then."

"You have in your possession a suit of Benevolence armor and some of their weaponry, yes?"

No use denying it. "I do." She'd thought about trying to move the items, but had held on to them instead. You never knew when something like that might come in handy.

"And you have had no luck in getting their weapons to fire."

"Also correct." Grond had gotten curious one day and had taken one of the rifles out for some target practice. He'd come back frustrated, the rifle nearly entirely disassembled, with no clue what was preventing it from firing. "These are, however, things that I know. I believe I specified the opposite."

"I am about to hand you a weapon. Do not panic." The troll stretched to his full height, reaching behind one of the displays mounted on the wall. He revealed a Benevolence rifle, a near-identical model to the ones that Grond and Brazel had brought back to her.

"I would ask that you not fire this in my room," he said, "but you should be able to verify that it will. Use ... a light touch on the trigger." He held out the weapon to her, butt-first, taking care to never point the business end of the thing at her. In fact, he was keeping it pointed at his own chest.

Rhundi stifled back a snort. She'd been handling weapons since before she could swim; she wasn't about to accidentally fire any Benevolence hardware in her own place no matter how much she wanted to renovate. She applied the barest touch of pressure to the trigger and felt the gun warm up to her touch. Benevolence weaponry, like most weapons that fired energy instead of projectiles, generated ammunition as the trigger was pulled. She could feel the subtle vibrations of the thing starting to warm up and could smell the tell-tale, burnt-ozone scent that it produced. The gun would work. Grond hadn't even been able to get his trigger to move.

"How?"

"A combination of a number of things," the troll replied, "all of which I will be happy to share with you once the matter of my rooms is settled. Needless to say, I can convert most of their weaponry to general use, at least in theory. Actual working examples to test are ... sss ... as you might imagine, somewhat difficult to come by."

"I cannot allow you to remain here," Rhundi replied. "That is not negotiable. You are moving."

A sudden movement on his part, as the troll tried to snatch the rifle away and reverse it. He counted on his greater strength to help him. It proved less than useful, as Rhundi simply let her feet leave the ground and let the troll's own movement pull her off the ground and into his body. She wrapped a hand around his neck-- which was, at the moment, thin-- and scrambled onto his back, her gun pressed firmly against his temple.

"That was foolish," she said. "If your neck starts feeling too thick for me to break easily, you can expect me to start shooting. Get on your knees. Now."

Irtuus-bon complied.

"Drop the rifle. In fact, toss it across the room."

He followed those instructions as well.

"Now stretch out on the floor, hands over your head and flat on the ground."

A moment of shuffling on the troll's part left her perched on his back with him flat on the ground and his hands in a safe position. Her gun remained at the back of his head.

"You said I overreached earlier, Irtuus-bon. You were probably right. But understand that I am *not* bluffing now. I am, in fact, offering you a *deal*. You can accept it, you can leave my property *right now*, forever, with none of your belongings, or you can make anything *remotely* like a sudden movement and I can blow your head clear off of your shoulders. Tap your finger on the ground *once* if you would like to hear my proposal or *twice* if you would like to leave under armed escort. Anything else, including three taps, and I start shooting. And I *assure you* I am faster than you are."

He hesitated for a moment, then tapped a long finger once on the floor.

"You *are* moving. I want this space for expansion, and now that you've gone to the trouble of locating a cave network down here that will make my expansion *easier*, there's no way I'm backing off on those plans. That doesn't mean that you are *leaving*. In fact, I plan to relocate you somewhere *better*. Closer to me, in fact, where you won't have to run illicit power lines and I can keep an eye on you. Whatever you're currently stealing from me to run your operation, I'll provide. And your rent? Consider your living expenses your *pay* now. But everything you discover and everything you know? Is *mine* in exchange."

She paused for a moment, letting him take this in.

"That's your deal, Irtuus-bon. You give up your gross, dusty hole in the ground and your bootleg, cobbled-together equipment for a dedicated power source and the best stuff I can buy. And your days as a freelancer are over. It's that, homelessness, or a hole in the one part of your body that you can't *shrink*. You have ten seconds to think about it. Tap once if you agree."

She let thirty seconds go by before giving a slight nudge to the back of the troll's head with the gun.

He tapped once. She let herself breathe.

"I'm going to back up now. So are you. You are going to do *nothing stupid* and you are not going to stand up any shorter or more obnoxious than you are right now."

She took a few steps back, toward the rifle, keeping herself in between it and Irtuus-bon. The troll slowly pulled himself to his feet, stretching his joints. He had, surprisingly, a gleam in his eyes that almost looked like happiness.

"I'm keeping the rifle," she said. "Anything else dangerous in here that I should know about?"

"Some of the artifacts could be *incredibly* so," he replied.

She considered this. "Anything in there you can shoot me with?"

"Not that kind of dangerous," he admitted.

"I'll be back in a day," she said. "In between now and then, I want you to make me a wish list. Let me know what you need and how much you think it will cost. I'll let you know after I see it how much of it I think you're going to *get*. Do we have a deal?"

"We ... sss ... have a *deal*," the troll responded. Yes, that was definitely happiness, no matter how much he was trying to hide it.

"Good," she said, pivoting on one heel and walking out of the room. "And that door had better let me in the next time I come back, too."

She let the door shut behind her as she left, wrinkling her nose again at the damp smell in the outer corridor. No wonder; there were unventilated cave systems attached directly to the room. It was a wonder she hadn't had mold problems.

At least I didn't need any lawyers, she thought. *It could have gone worse.*

"SIGIL"

"There's a job," Brazel said.

"We're on a job right now," Grond replied. "There can't be another job until the first job is finished."

"Technically, we're on our way *back* from a job," Brazel answered, nonchalantly smoothing his fur. "The job itself is finished. The only bits left are delivery and receiving of payment, and we've got a solid week before deadline. That's plenty of time for a side trip."

Grond pointed at his ear. Both of his ears were masses of scar tissue under the best of circumstances, but one of them looked rather more singed than usual.

"That'll heal," Brazel said.

"It'll heal with time," Grond growled, "and some time is exactly what I was looking forward to just now. Time, and a book. Maybe a cold compress or two."

"Speaking of that," Brazel said, making sure he was comfortably out of his halfogre partner's rather long reach. "Keeping it cold won't be hard."

Grond's eyes flashed red.

"No," he said.

"It's a *little* ice planet," Brazel said.

"NO," Grond said again, putting a bit more bass into his voice this time. "No ice planets. I told you no ice planets. You know this."

"They're not that bad," Brazel whined.

"You are a *gnome*. You have *fur*," Grond said. "I do not. You're fucking adapted to living on an ice planet. Ogres live on planets with jungles and deserts. Not on damned iceballs."

"There's a penalty rider in the contract," Brazel said. "We get an extra twenty percent if the temperature goes under fifty below." He spent most of the next thirty seconds dodging, as Grond threw a few convenient heavy objects at him.

"I'm taking sixty percent of the fee," Grond said. "You know I hate ice planets."

"I worked that into the bargaining," Brazel answered. This was not precisely true; his wife Rhundi had done all of the legwork on this contract, but she knew Grond's preferences as well as Brazel did, and had pushed hard to make the job worth the pay. "It's a milk run anyway. The planet's in dwarfspace. We pick up a package from somebody and we deliver it to-- get this-- anywhere outside of dwarfspace. And then we get paid."

This was unexpected. Grond paused for a moment, thinking.

"You know what the package is, right?" he said.

"Person in a box, obviously," Brazel answered. "I'm guessing a dwarfcicle of some sort who's trying to flee, so probably a male." It would not be the first time they'd been asked to quietly spirit someone out of dwarfspace; in fact, it nearly counted as a full-blown side racket for them.

"Why not hide it a little bit?" Grond said. "What other possible reason would we have to just deliver outside of dwarfspace? There's really not even a planet or a system to take it to? Just 'anywhere'?"

"Anywhere," Brazel said. "And that means that our contract is probably with the dwarf himself. Rhundi said the job came through a whole complicated network of fronts; she hadn't sorted through everything yet but had a feeling it was legit."

"You're sending me to an ice planet to pick up what is probably a dwarfcicle in a box based on a *feeling* that it's not going to get us killed," the halfogre said. "Do you think that makes me any happier than I was before?"

Brazel said a number. The halfogre's eyes lost their red sheen and widened slightly.

"Now *that* makes me feel better," Grond said. "But you'd better not bitch about it the next time I send you to Kratuul."

The gnome shrugged. They could have that argument later.

"The planet's only half a day off," he said. "Barely even counts as a course correction. We'll be in and out in no time."

"Find a way to make it quicker," the halfogre said. "And there had damn well better be some cold-weather gear stowed on this boat someplace."

The planet, in true dwarven fashion, was named only with numbers; the dwarves called it 00901213. It was, as Grond had feared, an ice planet, far enough from its star that it would only barely register as a sun from the planet's surface. It was tiny, too, but despite being smaller than many actual moons that Grond and Brazel had walked upon, it had two of its own: captured nickel-iron asteroids, from the look of them, each about a dozen or so kilometers wide, that whirled around the planet in a day or two each.

"We shall call it *Shithole,*" Grond said, looking at a holo of the planet.

"Do the moons get names?" Brazel asked.

"Nah. Fuck 'em for not choosing a better planet to orbit," Grond said. "How much do we need to know about this place?"

Brazel shrugged.   "No major population centers; the package is at what appears to be either a hermitage or a small research station. There's some mining, but it's on the opposite side of the rock from where we're going; basically a few pockets of heavy industry among a whole lot of nothing. Shithole's too small to have much of an atmosphere, so we'll need envirosuits with a supply until we can get into somewhere pressurized."

"We needed envirosuits anyway," Grond said.

"Right, I completely forgot it was cold on account of you hadn't whined about it in ten minutes," Brazel retorted. "Point is, you won't be able to breathe enough useful air into your lungs to complain during the couple of minutes it'll take you to freeze to death. Our target is actually mostly underground, not a domed hab like most of the surface structures-- it's apparently actually accessed through the side of a mountain, believe it or not."

"Do they know we're coming?"

"Apparently," the gnome said. "Which doesn't quite square with the dwarfcicle idea. But there's a place to land almost on top of the doorway, so we won't have to travel too much to get where we're going. You'll barely be outside at all. And even if they weren't, Namey hasn't spotted anything that looks like planetary defenses. The rock's harmless." Namey was Brazel's nickname for their ship, the *Nameless*. He and Grond had argued for months about what to name the boat when they bought it, and had never settled on an acceptable answer.

"Dwarven research station, I assume."

"Yeah, so probably not sized for bigs. But we won't be there long."

Grond shrugged. At 2.4 meters tall, he was nearly twice his partner's size, but he had spent most of his adult life in the company of gnomes, and was well used to existing in places that didn't cater to beings his size. So long as the ceilings were manageable-- and dwarves were taller than gnomes, so they ought to be-- he would be fine.

"So long as there's no complications," Grond said.

"I wish you hadn't said that," Brazel responded.

NO ANSWER TO OUR HAIL, Namey chirped in.

"That's your fault," Brazel said.

Grond just glared.

"I told you I hate ice planets," he said.

An argument ensued, and by the time it was resolved that they were going to land and check out the station, Namey had, without consulting either of them about it, landed himself on a strip of level ground half a klick away from their target. It really was built into the side of a mountain— a towering, jagged set of frozen peaks that jutted high from a level plain of ice. Unexpectedly, the mountain was located next to a shallow lake, filled with a mirror-sheened white liquid of unclear composition.

"Any sign of anybody home, Namey?" Brazel asked.

THE BASE IS POWERED, the ship responded. NO LIFE SIGNS, BUT MY SENSORS WILL NOT PENETRATE FAR INTO THE ICE. IF THE BASE IS MOSTLY SUBTERRANEAN THE LACK OF LIFE SIGNS WOULD NOT BE SURPRISING.

"Plays merry hell with the idea that they know we're coming, though," Grond said.

THERE CONTINUES TO BE NO RESPONSE TO HAILING FREQUENCIES, Namey continued.   I HAVE TRIED A VARIETY OF COMMON DWARVEN, GNOMIC AND HUMAN FREQUENCIES AS WELL AS A NUMBER TYPICALLY USED BY BENEVOLENCE.   THERE APPEARS TO BE NO ONE LOOKING.

"Discouraging," the gnome muttered.   "We're going in anyway."

"We're arming ourselves a bit more heavily than we'd planned, though," Grond said.   He was already pulling on an envirosuit, to which he had strapped a few energy weapons-- the thin atmosphere made projectile weapons unreliable-- as well as his usual complement of sharp things and Angela, his prized Iklis sniper's longbow.

"You're bringing Angie?" Brazel asked.   "We'll be indoors. Not much use for a long-range weapon even if we do end up in trouble."

"I don't trust a single thing about this," said Grond, "and I'm not leaving tools behind on the ship.   Plus, she's scary.   I like scary."

Brazel nodded.

"Also, if you call her Angie again, I'll throw you in the lake," the halfogre added.   "Try me if you think I'm kidding."

One thing was clear: they were going to earn the penalty rider for the temperature.   Grond flatly refused to even speculate on what the temperature was, but Brazel put up a readout on the faceplate of his envirosuit that registered the temperature at fully ninety degrees below zero.   Luckily for both of them, Shithole's thin atmosphere meant that the wind was not a factor.   The surface was, in fact, frighteningly still.   Shithole had no indigenous life of any kind, and the quiet was almost maddening.   The system's sun was a cold white pinprick far in the distance, providing just enough light to the surface to maneuver around without assistance but not enough to see well. Overhead, one of the planet's two moons tumbled by.

"Faster we move, faster we're done," Grond said, and headed toward the station's entrance.   This was a round portal--

gratifyingly, sized for bigs-- set into a recessed part of the base of the mountain. There was a simple access panel set into the ice next to the doorway with a single button. He pushed it, and after a few moments the door obligingly glided out of the way.

"Not much on security, are they?" he said.

"Not sure why they would need to be, I guess," Brazel said. "The thing probably locks when they want it to; it's not like they're going to get a lot of drop-ins way out here." The portal opened into a long tunnel; an intercom system was set into a walled booth just inside, along with controls to re-close the door, which Grond did. Fiddling with the intercom produced no response, although the lights were on.

"Down the hallway?" Brazel asked.

"I assume so," Grond replied. They walked for a few minutes, passing through a second larger portal into what was clearly a reception area, with a long counter against the far wall and a few chairs and tables scattered around. There was no one anywhere to be seen.

"Answers the security question," Grond said, walking behind the reception counter. "They'll let you into that outside hallway to get you out of the cold, but I'm guessing there's no way through that second door unless somebody in here buzzes you through. Or-- hmm." He waved his partner over.

There was what looked like a space for door controls set into the employee side of the counter. They'd been ripped out.

"We got lucky; the door must have been unlocked when whoever wrecked the controls," Grond said. "Otherwise you'd be cutting your way in here."

"You mean we," Brazel said.

"I mean *you*," Grond said, "on account of this would have just become your nonsense side job and I'd be back on the ship waiting for you to come to your senses. Namey, you still hear us?"

I DO, the ship responded.

"Anything moves within two hundred thousand kilometers and I want to know about it," he continued.

THAT INCLUDES THE ORBITS OF BOTH MOONS, the ship responded. I ASSUME YOU DO NOT INCLUDE THOSE IN YOUR REQUEST.

"I don't remember programming you to be a smarmy asshole," Grond said.

BRAZEL DID IT, the ship replied.

"I thought you picked the personality," Brazel said.

"We turn him into something more obsequious the second we get back," Grond said. "Yes, asshole boat, you may ignore the moons. Nothing else, other than the two of us. Got it?"

UNDERSTOOD, the *Nameless* replied.

"I'm going to, just this once, suggest that something has gone wrong, that it is not our business what has gone wrong, and that we should just leave without trying to figure out what it is," Grond continued. "There's no one here with a package, no one answered our hails, and the entire station looks to be abandoned, and abandoned with at least a little bit of prejudice. I think we should leave."

"That's no fun," Brazel said.

"I knew you were going to say that," Grond said.

"Like you haven't said it yourself a hundred times," Brazel retorted. "You just don't like it here because of the climate. I'm perfectly comfortable."

"Or, at least, you would be, if you could breathe the air."

Brazel snickered. "Actually, there's still atmosphere in here. It's probably safe to crack the faceplates if you want."

"I'm good," Grond said. "At least until we have some idea why we're alone."

"Only one way to find out," Brazel said.

The top level of the research station proved to be entirely abandoned-- of living things, if not of furniture and materiel. The rest of the top floor appeared to be devoted to office space, filled with midrange desk consoles and a large server room. The servers were shut down, and a few minutes of experimentation had left Brazel unsuccessful at getting them back online again. Other than the damage to the door controls at reception, there was no sign of vandalism or violence, although the two found a large loading dock that had been left open to the elements, presumably deliberately.

"Do you think anything's missing?" Brazel asked. "Maybe they evacuated or they found something really interesting somewhere and went out to look at it. They're scientists, after all; scientists get curious."

"Doesn't look like it," Grond responded. The dock had a number of six-wheeled ground transports parked in it, but they were prominently numbered and the numbers were consecutive. "I gotta imagine that it'd take a few of these to get everybody out, and if it was some sort of discovery they'd still have left someone behind. And this has been here for at least a couple of days, I think." He dragged a foot across the floor, disturbing some of the dust and snow that had blown in from the open entryway.

"Wait a minute," he said. "Something on the floor."

The two of them spent a few moments sweeping away dust and snow to reveal a large symbol on the floor of the dock. It was black in color, perhaps three meters wide, and more or less in the exact center of the room: an oval shape, with a circle centered inside it, and four curved lines-- two long, two short-- protruding out from each side.

"That look like a spidership to you?"

Brazel squinted. "A little, maybe? It's awfully stylized if it is." Spiderships were the Benevolence's short-range, single-pilot fighter ships. They were basically a metal oval with a viewport in front and eight arms on the sides, which could be used for propulsion, manipulating objects, or precise aiming for weapons. Spiderships' ability to shoot in virtually any direction made them deadly in larger numbers, although the more of their arms they devoted to combat the less maneuverable they became. A typical Benevolence capital ship would have dozens on board, if not more.

Grond squatted, scraping at the symbol with his fingers. "It looks like it's just been painted on, and more hastily than I'd expect from dwarves. It's too sloppy. What's it doing here?"

"No idea. This isn't Benevolence space. And I can't imagine a bunch of dwarven scientists being real big on attracting their attention, either."

"Okay, gnome, you got me. Now I'm curious."

"Oh, sure," Brazel said. "We just found a suggestion that Benevolence are involved with whatever's going on, which means that this thing just went from weird-but-passive to actively dangerous, and now you get interested."

"Let's find an elevator," Grond said. "See how deep this station goes. There have got to be dorms somewhere, at least. If we don't find anything useful, interesting, or expensive in an hour, we'll give up and split."

"Deal," Brazel said.

It didn't take long to locate the lift-- it was in the back of the loading dock, just past where the transports were parked. There was only one other floor for it to go to, and the descent took several minutes. The basement floor was clearly deep below the surface.

The lift glided to a stop. Grond pulled Angela off his back and snapped his wrist, popping her limbs into position, the string crackling with energy. Brazel took a step back, his hand on a gun at his waist.

Nothing happened.

Grond nodded at Brazel, who moved forward to pull the door open. Grond was the better shot and Angela by far a deadlier weapon, so it made more sense for him to have his hands free. Brazel grunted, the heavy doors at first refusing to separate, then catching and sliding apart smoothly.

The doors opened into what was obviously the laboratory/work space of the station. When the station was operational, this would have been bustling with activity; there was equipment and tech everywhere in a large open room, with doors leading to smaller rooms or other labs around the outside.

The station was clearly no longer operational. The entire room had been torn to bits; furniture overturned, equipment smashed, the ashy evidence of small fires everywhere. Most of the lights had been shattered; the few that remained shed a shaky glow over the room. Half of the doors had been torn from their hinges and the remainder were blocked off with rubble and wreckage.

"Bodies?" Brazel asked.

"Don't see any," Grond said.

"Five minutes. Mark."

The two separated quickly, picking their way separately through the room and searching for anyone, living or dead, who could shed some light on what had happened. Grond threw a few larger pieces of equipment out of his way, looking to see if anyone had been buried. Five minutes later, they met in the center of the lab.

"Not a thing," Grond said. "Not a drop of blood, either."

"And somebody did this on purpose," Brazel said. "This isn't an earthquake or a natural disaster. The walls are still standing, everything upstairs is fine. Somebody-- or a bunch of somebodies-- came down here and did this intentionally."

"Our package?"

"I doubt it, if we were even right about the package being a person. Can you imagine a dwarven male pulling off something like this on his own? It's generally all they can do to summon the willpower and the luck they'd need just to get away from the clans. I've never even heard of one using violence, much less anything on this scale. No, this wasn't dwarves, unless it was a separate clan entirely, and they'd have killed somebody along the way. Where do you think the dorms are?"

"Only two ways to go," Grond said. "Back there through all the shit they've piled up, which will take longer than I like, or back through one of those halls there." He pointed back toward the lift; there were halls stretching in either direction out of the near corners of the larger lab.

"Let's check 'em out," Brazel said.

Grond nodded, taking the lead. The hallway did indeed lead to living space; and living space for the females, at that, judging from the luxury of the furnishings. The hall opened up into what was obviously a common area, with a bar, comfortable chairs and couches and tables, and even a small stage tucked into a corner. A traditional dwarven hearth sat in the middle of the room, directly underneath a ventilation duct to keep smoke and gases from the fire from filling the space. Another corridor to individual rooms continued on past the common room.

The individual dorms were occupied. The pair checked the first three rooms they reached. Each room had either one or two beds, and each bed had a single dwarven female in it. All were either dead or deeply unconscious.

Brazel pulled off a glove and checked for a pulse. "I think she's gone, but it's hard to tell. She's clammy, but ... shit, this could be suspended animation." He pivoted back the faceplate of his helmet and wrinkled his snout, taking a deep sniff of the room. "She doesn't smell dead. I don't smell rot at all, but I don't know if I would in a place like this. There wasn't anything alive on this rock other than the dwarves; I don't know if there's even really enough bacteria around to decompose them properly."

"Look at her hands," Grond said.

The dwarf's knuckles were bloody and bruised. Her clothing was filthy, too, with small rips and tears everywhere.

"Go check a couple more of them," Brazel said, and Grond slipped out of the room silently. The other dwarf in the room was much the same; no clear pulse or signs of life, with the only signs of violence being damage to her hands.

Grond was back in two minutes. "Four more, same stuff. One's got a nice gash on the side of her head but she might have just gotten hit by something while they were ripping their lab apart. And I found this on the floor in one of the rooms." He held out a club that had once been a table leg; it had clearly been ripped from the table and used to pound on things for a while. The business end of the thing was beaten to pieces but there was no blood on it anywhere.

"So they wrecked their own lab," Brazel said. "And they were frenzied enough about it that most of them did it with their bare hands. And then they just came back in here and laid down quietly and died. That's ... ominous." He suddenly felt a strong need to have his envirosuit completely back on, pulling his glove back on, closing his face mask, and double-checking all of his seals; breathing the local air seemed like an incredibly bad idea at the moment.

"I told you I hated ice planets," Grond said.

"You know we've got to check on the males now," Brazel responded.

"Yeah. We do," Grond said.

They abandoned the female wing of the dorms and moved to the males' wing. This was much smaller: rather than an opulent common room, the hallway opened into a barracks, with plain bunks stacked three high set along one wall and simple cubbies along the other for the dwarves' sparse belongings.

There was a pile of bodies in the middle of the room. All had been strangled with identical lengths of black wire.

Neither spoke, moving to the pile and carefully pulling the bodies out, looking for survivors. There were eighteen bodies in all; each one of them was rather unambiguously dead.

Under the pile was a second symbol. This one, rather than having been quickly painted, looked to have been roughly scratched into the floor with something sharp.

"Time to go?" Grond asked.

"Time to go," Brazel confirmed.

The lift was still settled at their floor, and it was all Brazel and Grond could do to keep from running to get back to it. The ride back up felt incredibly slow.

GROND, said the boat.

"We're on our way back," the halfogre responded. "Get warmed up to leave as soon as we get there."

WE HAVE A PROBLEM.

"I do not want to hear about a problem right now."

YOU SAID NOT TO TELL YOU IF THE MOONS WERE MOVING.

"That's right."

I FEEL COMPELLED TO IGNORE THAT ORDER.

"I fucking know the moons are moving, Namey," Grond snapped. "They're orbiting. That's moving. That's what moons do."

I WOULD NOT CHOOSE THE WORD "ORBITING" TO DESCRIBE THE MOTION OF THIS MOON.

Brazel and Grond looked at each other.

"What word would you use?" Brazel asked.

CRASHING.

"Crashing."

CRASHING. THE MOON IS MOVING TOWARD OUR POSITION AT A RATHER ASTONISHING RATE OF SPEED. I CALCULATE WE HAVE TEN MINUTES UNTIL IMPACT.

"Crashing on us?" Grond said. "How the fuck is it crashing on us?"

I HAVE NO IDEA, the *Nameless* responded. THE MOON ABRUPTLY DREW TO A STOP IN THE SKY AND THEN JUST AS ABRUPTLY CHANGED DIRECTION AND BEGAN HURTLING TOWARD US. IT IS ACCELERATING.

"This elevator needs to go fucking faster," Grond said.

I HAVE ALREADY BEGUN TAKEOFF PROCEDURES, Namey said. PLEASE HURRY. THE MOON WILL OBLITERATE   EVERYTHING   FOR   SEVERAL KILOMETERS IN EVERY DIRECTION WHEN IT IMPACTS THE PLANET. IT WOULD BE AN EXTINCTION-LEVEL EVENT WERE THERE ANY PREEXISTING LIFE ON THE PLANET.

"Shit. The miners." Brazel said. "See if you can get any communication with the settlement on the other side of this rock and let them know what's coming." *As if they'll believe it,* he thought. *Maybe if they made sure they were underground in time...*

I THOUGHT OF THAT ALREADY, Namey replied. I HAVE RECEIVED NO COMMUNICATION FROM THAT SETTLEMENT EITHER. I HAVE BEGUN RUNNING DIAGNOSTICS ON MY COMMUNICATIONS MODULES.

The two exchanged a look again. Had whatever happened to the research station happened on the other side of the planet as well?

A million years later, the lift finally slid into position on the top floor. Grond wasted no time, slamming the doors open. They fled for the front door.

Only to be stopped by the closed airlock door in the reception area.

"Oh, *fuck*," Grond said. He threw himself at the door, muscles straining, putting everything he had into shoving the door open. To no avail. The door was simply too big, even for him.

I ESTIMATE FIVE MINUTES, the *Nameless* said.

"Get your ass around to the back of the building!" Grond shouted. "There's a loading dock! Meet us outside! Fucking now!"

ON MY WAY.

Grond had much longer legs than Brazel, and was in much better shape than the gnome was. There was no time to wait for him, and no time to be polite about it. He snatched Brazel up from the ground and tucked him under one arm, running through the station at top speed back toward the loading dock, hoping he remembered the way. He saw the silhouette of the *Nameless* as it landed beyond the entryway, and sped out to the ship.

And then he looked up at the sky.

He had thought that the sight of one of Shithole's moons careening toward him would be the most terrifying thing he was going to see that day. It was not. The thing that had thrown the moon was.

He stood, jaws hanging open, until his partner punched him in the ribs.

"Go," Brazel choked. "Shockwave alone will kill us before it even hits. Keep running."

Grond tore his eyes away from the thing in the sky and sprinted toward the *Nameless*, which was several feet off the ground, engines roaring, before he even reached it. He leapt for the hatch, hitting the floor and rolling, then bellowing for the ship to move as he spun back to his feet.

"What the fuck is that thing?" he said.

WHAT THING? Namey asked. Grond felt the ship accelerating under his feet.

"Just head the fuck away from the fucking moon!" he shouted, heading for his room. The cockpit was Brazel's, and sized for gnomes; Grond had a copilot's chair in his quarters that allowed him to see anything Brazel could see from the pilot's seat.

"What the fuck is that?" he said again.

He heard a strangled gasp from his partner and realized that Brazel was only now seeing the thing-- he'd been facing the ground in Grond's arms before they got aboard the ship.

The moon had been torn from space and thrown to the earth by the arms of an angry god.

It was immense; it *defied* immensity. Grond and Brazel had once encountered a deep-space teleporter that, for a brief moment, they'd mistaken for a moon. This dwarfed that object by an order of magnitude; it made the moon it had hurled look like a child's toy. It bore the faintest resemblance to a spidership; a central sphere, with dozens if not hundreds of tentacles extending from its equator. The tentacles themselves were composed of more connected spheres; Grond had the horrible feeling that if they were somehow severed from their parent, they would grow their own arms rather than die.

It hung in the sky, its arms moving, horribly alive and organic, synchronized and pulsating as if to a terrible celestial song that only it could hear.

The *Nameless* accelerated.

WE ARE AT SAFE DISTANCE, the ship reported.

"Not safe," Brazel mumbled crazily. "Never safe. Not from that. Keep going. Faster. Hit tunnelspace the second you fucking can." He'd never encountered or heard of anything living that could enter tunnelspace on its own. Could it still reach them? Those tentacles had to be dozens of kilometers long.

The moon crashed into the planet's surface, obliterating the mountain and everything beneath it, sending out a shockwave so great that it would circle the planet's surface three times before settling down. What little atmosphere 00901213 had burned. The ice sublimated, escaping the planet's gravity before refreezing in the cold of deep space. If there had been anything alive anywhere on the planet, underground or not, the earthquakes would have killed them by now.

The thing took no notice of them at all. It hung in the vacuum, watching the destruction it had wrought, and Brazel lost sight of it as his boat finally leapt into tunnelspace, heading home, heading to safety.

Neither of them spoke for a very long time.

⊰⊙⊱

THE
SANCTUM
OF THE
SPHERE

THE BENEVOLENCE
ARCHIVES: VOLUME TWO

PROLOGUE

He awoke to white light.

No, not just the light—the whole room was white, white walls curving into white walls and a white ceiling, a perfect, clean oval with no corners for darkness and shadows to collect in. The light came from everywhere, sourceless. This world was warm, soft, like a loving parent's embrace.

He looked down at himself. His body was not his own, the one he wore now much younger. There were no scars, no calluses on his hands, the nails neat, even and pink. A child's body, but genderless, dressed in a simple, soft white robe. He wanted to wrap the robe around himself and, content, sleep forever.

He opened his mouth to speak, then closed it again. He felt uneasy speaking before he was spoken to.

A symbol flashed once, burning into the back of his eyes. An oval eye, with four arms protruding from each side.

YOUR OFFER IS ACCEPTED, the voices said. There were dozens, speaking in unison. They were masculine, feminine, old, young. SHOULD YOU SUCCEED, YOU WILL BE RETURNED TO US.

"To Azamoeg," he said, quietly. His voice was weak, timid, high-pitched.

TO US.

"And after?"

THAT DOES NOT MATTER, NOW. WE AGREE TO YOUR RETURN, SHOULD YOU SUCCEED. THAT IS ALL.

"And if I fail?"

DO NOT FAIL, the voices said. WE ARE WATCHING.

The symbol flashed in his eyes again, and the white faded away. He came back to himself, to his own body, to the small, dirty room he occupied.

He stood up, stretching. His hand sat atop a statue. He removed it, working the feeling back into his fingers, running his thumb along the ring he wore.

A large shape appeared in his doorway. A very large shape.

"We in business?"

"We are," he said, feeling sudden relief to hear himself speak in his own voice. "Bring him. We have much to do."

ONE

The halfogre couldn't shake the idea that he'd made some poor decisions.

To start with, he wasn't terribly happy with where he was. The system was on the far outskirts of ogrespace, so far out that the ogres hadn't bothered to name it. The locals, gruesome insectoids that communicated with a mix of obscure gestures and directed *smells*, had some name for it in their language that he was biologically unable to pronounce. It sounded like a throat clearing, with some hand-waving, a head-bob of some kind and a strong smell of fruit. The eyes were involved somehow too, but he wasn't exactly sure how. Rhundi had spelled it "Khkk" when she'd commed about the job.

In about three minutes, a fast-moving ground transport was due to pass about five meters beneath him. It was an elongated, poly-legged mechanical monstrosity that followed a permanent pheromone trail to move cargo from one place to another. He'd heard the local name for it, but he wasn't any more able to say that than he was able to say "Khkk."

He'd decided to call it a *train*. He'd been hired to rob it.

It was fast and loud and heavily guarded at both the start and end points of its destination. Less so in between. And he was about to have to leap onto it, then find a way to break in.

It was nighttime, but the gas giant that hung overhead reflected more than enough sunlight to be able to see by. Khkk was rarely in real darkness. The local landscape was flat and dusty, dotted with occasional oversized rock formations that were the only thing that broke the monotony all around him. He'd found one that made an arch, twenty meters high, and if his map was to be believed the train was going to pass directly through it. He'd have about twenty minutes to find his package and get back off the train before getting picked up again got complicated.

He wanted to avoid "complicated" today.

He heard the train coming before he saw it, approaching from the west, the sun setting behind it. The halfogre shaded his eyes with his hand, trying to gauge the thing's speed.

Fast, he thought. But coming right where he expected it to, which was good. He was nearly two and a half meters tall, which meant that he'd only have a drop of a couple of meters if he was hanging from the underside of the arch when the train passed underneath. Even at high speeds, he ought to be able to control the fall easily enough. He adjusted the climbing gloves on his hands and scrabbled around to the underside of the arch, easily holding himself in place on the rock's rough surface despite hanging upside-down.

Which gave him a clear, if upside-down, view of the train as its path started to bend away from the arch.

"You've gotta be fucking kidding me," he muttered. The map was wrong. Of *course* the map was wrong.

Moving fast, he pulled himself back up to the top of the arch and judged the distance. It looked like the train was going to go around the arch to the north. If he measured the jump *perfectly* he just might be able to hit the top of the train. Of course, then he'd have to stop himself before sliding off the other side, a feat that wouldn't have been too tricky when he was dropping straight down sliding *along* the train, but was going to be a hell of a lot more difficult when he was leaping and sliding *across* it. Getting trampled by those stampeding feet did *not* look like an exciting way to go.

The train's path kept bending northward. He had about thirty seconds to decide. And it *really* didn't look like he was going to be able to make the jump. Which meant...

Shit.

"Okay. I can do this," he muttered again, climbing down as fast as he could.

"Sure." He hit the ground and sprinted toward the train.

"Simple." He was still in front of it, but just barely. It would be a lot easier if he could *see* the pheromone trail the train was following. He needed to get right alongside it.

He watched the legs pistoning up and down as the train came toward him. The tips of those legs were probably *really* sharp.

He just had to time it perfectly—

Ow. He leapt toward one of the legs as it slammed into the ground next to him, straining his arms a bit but scrambling to the top and hurling himself toward the body of the train before any of him got caught in a joint somewhere. The sides of the train were smooth, but his climbing gloves found some purchase in the material anyway, and he was able to drag himself onto the top within a few moments.

Now to get inside. The object he was looking for was supposedly toward the back of the train.   He could break in anywhere he wanted, but didn't want to spend any more time inside than he absolutely had to. The clock was ticking. Staying low, he moved carefully toward the back of the train until he located a hatch. He tested it carefully, hoping he would get lucky and find out it wasn't locked.

He was not lucky. *Naturally.* Not only was the hatch far too small for him to get through, but the locking mechanism looked unfamiliar. Even if he'd had time to pick it, he'd still have to widen the hole somehow. The halfogre unclipped a microtorch from his belt and thumbed it on. The flame the torch emitted was only a few centimeters long but was more than hot enough to burn a halfogre-sized hole through the train's metal skin in a couple of minutes. He grabbed the handle on the hatch, yanked the entire mechanism out of the hole he'd created, and tossed it off the side.

The interior was unlit, pitch-black beyond the bit just below him.   He slid himself into the hole he'd made and froze, listening. There weren't supposed to be any guards on the train itself–no sentients, anyway–but it was always worth double-checking and he'd already been wrong once on this job as it was.

Nothing moved. He pulled a pair of night-vision goggles over his eyes and moved toward the back half of the train. The package was supposed to be marked with a dye that would glow brightly if viewed through these goggles.

Huh.

He was standing on crates. There were crates to his left and right as well, and even a few netted to the ceiling.   In fact, *everything* was held down with netting and ropes. He'd gotten lucky. They hadn't put anything directly underneath the access port he'd carved through, although he could see where he'd scorched a few boxes that were too near to his torch. There was enough room for him to move around, but not much more. He'd been expecting an actual floor to walk on.

And about every fifth or sixth package was glowing brightly. The natives on this rock apparently saw in a different visual spectrum from his in addition to communicating through pheromones.

"This just keeps getting more fun," he muttered, heading to the back of the train anyway. He activated his comm.

"Brazel."

"What?" his partner responded into his ear. "You find it already?"

"So, uh, was the package supposed to be marked in any particular way? Because half the shit down here glows."

He heard the gnome laughing over the comm.

"This isn't funny."

"It's hilarious," Brazel responded. "And as a matter of fact, yes. It's covered in warning symbols, apparently."

"*Warning* symbols."

"Yeah."

"Warning about *what?*"

"Danger, I'd guess. They're gonna be visible in the normal spectrum, too, but Rhundi figured the ones the goggles picked up would stand out a bit more. I guess not, eh?" Grond could hear his partner chuckling on the other side of the comm. "The crate it's in is about a half-meter square by two meters long, if that helps any."

"Knew that," Grond said.

That was *something*, at least, since none of the crates were consistently sized. He moved toward a section that seemed to be mostly smaller boxes. Most of the crates that were glowing were either covered in whatever paint or dye was showing up in his goggles or were covered in writing. One of the boxes, about the right size, was painted in wide stripes and had a variety of scary-looking symbols all over it. It stood out.

"I think I've got it," he said, cutting through the netting that was holding the box in place.

"I'm told it's not fragile," Brazel said. "So don't worry about being too gentle getting it out of there. I'm not far away. Tell me when you're on your way out and I'll bring the ship over."

"On it," the halfogre responded. Which was about when the floor leapt up and tossed him into the ceiling. He hit a couple of crates hard, head-first, and then hit the floor just as hard a moment later, bits of broken crate raining down on his head. Something heavy clonked off a shoulder. He looked at the floor. It was a pistol. Three more that hadn't bounced off of him on the way down to the floor lay nearby.

Weapons?

"The fuck was that?" he said.

"Trouble," Brazel responded. "Something you just ran over *exploded.*"

There was a moment of silence on the comm before Brazel came back.

"Grond, you'll love this. There's a bunch of assholes trying to rob the train."

"There's *already* a couple of assholes trying to rob the train. Be more specific," Grond grunted. He pulled himself back to his feet and pulled the crate from the shelf. It was startlingly heavy for its size. *The gnome wouldn't even be able to move it*, he thought.

"Ambush. They've got sinkholes all over the place. The bugs are just pouring out. A couple hundred."

"Hundred?"

"Dozens. I dunno. Want me to get Namey to count them?"

TWO HUNDRED AND THIRTY-SIX AND COUNTING, his boat chirped into his ear.

"That's too fucking many. Where are you?"

The train bucked again. Grond saw a few of the bugs starting to peer into the hole he'd cut into the roof.

"They didn't pay us killing wages on this one," he said.

"You don't speak their language," Brazel responded. "Good luck talking your way out."

"You'd be surprised at how persuasive I can be," Grond said, drawing a heavy pistol and firing a few shots. Crates near the hole exploded into splinters and the bugs retreated. The Khkks had clearly modeled the train on their own body shapes.

They were elongated and multi-legged too, only with harder carapaces and distinct heads. They also had longer limbs at the front of their bodies that served the function of arms.

Oh, and sharp teeth. And some of them had wings, too. It was those that had gotten to the train first. The others were likely waiting for the first bunch to get the thing stopped–

The floor *fell* out from underneath him this time, his momentum hurling him toward the front of the train as the rest of it abruptly came to a halt. It got him close enough to the boxes he'd just shot to see what was in them. *Even more guns.*

Oh, this is going to go wonderfully, Grond thought.

"Train's stopped," Brazel said. "The legs all just went flat at once, like it laid down."

"Where the fuck *are you?*" Grond shouted, firing a couple more shots at an ovipositor that had appeared in his hole. The thing turned toward him and spat something his way. It hit a box and burst into flames.

Fantastic. Apparently someone had paid the *bugs* killing wages. Hopefully whatever was in that box wasn't too terribly explosive.

"I'm about three hundred meters up," Brazel said. "Namey doesn't think we can fight the bugs off if it comes to that. Nothing on the damn boat can target anything that moves the way they do, and even if we hit something it'd be overkill." The *Nameless* wasn't a fighter to begin with, and what armament it had was mostly focused on blowing up other ships.

"That didn't sound like a suggestion, Braze." He ripped down some webbing from the wall and tossed another crate on top of the fire the bug had spat at him. Several more appendages poked their way through the hole, and more fire-sputum sped his way. He growled and ripped down more webbing, causing the cargo above him to crash down and give him some cover. He picked up his box, holding it balanced on his shoulder, and headed toward the back of the train.

There was an actual door there. It was locked. He shot the mechanism out and kicked the door open.

"Oh, *shit,*" he said, and yanked it closed again.

There were considerably more than two hundred bugs surrounding the train now. Two *thousand* might not even have been accurate. Each of them was only a fraction of his size, but there was no way he was shooting his way out.

He looked around. *Okay. Can't go up. Can't go backwards.*

More boxes came down from the ceiling, creating a second barricade between Grond and the back of the train. He started tearing through the ones underneath him, initially just throwing them out of his way and then being a bit more careful once he remembered what he'd seen in the ones he'd already broken open.

Only one direction to go.

He activated his microtorch again, burning a hole through the bottom of the train. He was lucky. Since the thing walked rather than rolled, most of the machinery was on the *sides*. He could hear the bugs coming, knocking the boxes out of the way, and he took a few shots toward the hole in the ceiling as he worked, bringing down more cover as he did.

He cut a hole big enough to fit through, lifting the metal plug out and tossing it out of his way. There was nothing but dry ground underneath him.

"Braze. You said they were coming out of holes in the ground, right?"

"Yeah. Listen, Namey thinks we ought to start strafing. Apparently there are *bigger* bugs coming ..."

"Gimme a minute. Lemme try something first."

He took a deep breath and stomped on the ground as hard as he could. And felt it *give*.

It took three more stomps before he fell into darkness.

TWO

The tunnel Grond had bashed his way into was surprisingly round and even, and painted everywhere with the same phosphorescent stuff that had been glowing on the train. It wasn't sized for him, not at all–but it was close enough. He'd lived with gnomes for most of his adult life, so having to stoop once in a while wasn't such a big deal, and the very narrowness of the tunnel meant that the bugs would be unable to swarm him.

He hoped.

"Okay, Braze, I'm underground," he said. "Have Namey keep tabs on me and let me know if I get off track. Heading toward the cliffs."

"That's crazy," his partner responded.

"Fighting ten thousand bugs is *crazy*. This is just difficult." The cliffs had been what he and Brazel had *originally* been worried about. They were no more than a couple of kilometers away from the level ground giving way to an enormous canyon–and their map of the train's path had it going straight *over* the canyon–or, perhaps, given its legs, straight *down*. They had both figured that having Grond off the train before it got there was probably best for everyone. Now he was heading directly for the canyon.

"Just keep me on track," he said, hunching over, holding the box like a spear, and hoping his direction sense held up underground. The goggles were doing a decent job of illuminating the tunnel around him. Hearing was going to be a problem, because the echoes were going to be a mess and he was making an awful lot of noise, sacrificing silence for speed. The bugs were probably able to pick up the vibrations he was setting off by moving through their tunnels. He'd let that become a problem before he wasted energy worrying about it.

His luck held for a few minutes, when the tunnel abruptly widened into a larger chamber–which let him stand up, but gave him nowhere else to go. The only way in was the way he'd come. There was nothing moving in the chamber with him.

"How close am I?" he asked.

"A hundred meters, maybe," Brazel said. "And you're farther underground than you were when you started. Not by much, but you're definitely descending. What's going on?"

"Dead end," he said. "And I didn't really see any branches in the tunnel before I got here." He could always go back–the likelihood that the tunnel that he'd stomped his way into was a single one-way tunnel with a room at one end and no other way up seemed low, but he didn't see any reason to press his luck.

"Nothing down there with you?"

"Not yet," he said.

Which was *exactly* when the clicking started.

Why do I ever talk? Grond thought. Life had been so much easier, in some ways at least, when he hadn't been allowed to.

The clicking got louder, coming from opposite sides of the chamber. A loud rumbling sound accompanied it.

Something was coming through the goddamn *walls*. On both sides of him.

Okay. He put the pistol away. He had enough room to maneuver in here, provided that it was just a couple of search parties coming after him and not the entire insect army. Maybe they hadn't bothered. He'd left them the train, after all. He set the box down on the floor between his feet.

He pulled his Iklis sniper's longbow off of his back and snapped his wrist, flipping the bow's arms into position and extending the energy string that generated his shots. The bow's name was Angela, and she was his most prized possession. And she was just about perfect for situations like this, because she killed what she hit and she didn't need to be reloaded. Which was exactly what he needed right now.

The wall to his right started coming down. He pivoted and fired three shots in rapid succession into the hole. Something keened and a gout of greenish-yellow blood exploded into the room.

The thing on the left side got into the room before he had a chance to shoot it.

"Ugh," Grond said, and shot it anyway. He wasn't exactly sure how an insect managed to adapt to chew through solid rock, but this thing *had*, and it had done so by evolving into something that was almost all *mouth*. Dozens of rows of buzzsaw-shaped teeth, attached to a body much more squat and muscular-looking than the rest of the insects possessed. He spent a split second wondering how it managed to walk without falling over, since it looked so horribly weighted toward its head and teeth, then cleared his head with a shake and focused on killing it. Two shots from Angela did the job. A dozen more took out the smaller insects behind it, but not before several of them had managed to spit their flame-goo at him. One singed a shoulder as he dodged out of the way. He swung back around to the right where the first bug had started to break through. Nothing else came through. He switched back to his pistol and picked up the box, grunting again with the weight of the thing.

Please let the tunnel go the right way. He tossed the crate through the hole and shoved his body in after it, only losing a few square centimeters of skin to the rocks along the way.

It did. It went in both directions, in fact–farther along toward the cliffs, where he wanted to go, and back toward where he'd come from. He turned right and headed for the cliff.

"Brazel, come find me," he said. "Are the bugs chasing?"

"Most of them are ransacking the train," Brazel responded. "Their numbers aren't what they were when you were back there. A lot of 'em have gone back underground. Namey can't figure a way to tell if they're headed your way. He says there's life signs *everywhere* down there."

That was comforting.

He heard scrabbling from behind him and redoubled his pace. Brazel had said he was a hundred meters or so from the face of the canyon. He *had to* have gone that far by now, right?

The tunnel abruptly bent off to the left.

In the distance, he saw something moving.

The scrabbling, clicking noise continued behind him, as the insectoids got closer.

"Solution *soon*," he said into the comm.

"You're a meter from open air," the gnome said. "Go back toward where you were a bit."

"*Back* is not the word I wanted to hear, here," he said. "There are things back there that were trying to eat me a few minutes ago."

"You heard me," Brazel said. "Back toward them. Not far. Five or ten meters."

That was the last he heard, as the bugs spotted him and charged his way. He started shooting. There was no lack of targets. Every time he killed one, the rest just pulled its body down and climbed over it. He fired a few shots into the ceiling, hoping to trigger a tunnel collapse. No luck.

Then the tunnel behind him exploded.

The blast threw him to the floor and shook the ceiling loose where he'd shot at it. A small rockslide blocked the passageway. He started to turn to look behind him, tearing his goggles off in pain from the amplified light.

Wait. Light?

A smoking hole four meters wide had been blown into the side of the tunnel. Outside, the *Nameless*. He couldn't see Brazel, but he was pretty sure that the gnome was smirking. The ship's cargo bay was pointed toward the hole, wide open.

"Jump, will ya?" the gnome asked. "We've got stuff to do."

Grond picked up the box from where he had dropped it and leapt to freedom.

"*So what do you think is in there?*" Brazel asked. The box sat on a table between them. The *Nameless* was in tunnelspace, heading out of Khkk's system. They were still waiting for Rhundi to get back to them with drop coordinates.

"We got paid to steal it and deliver it," Grond said. "Nobody said anything about not messing with it in between. You think the second raid on the train was a coincidence? Or did somebody decide to send an army to steal the same object that somebody else sent the two of us to steal?"

"They kept ransacking the train after you got off of it," Brazel said. "And they didn't really spend a lot of energy chasing you down. Then again, who knows if they even knew you were *on* there, or what you were there to do. Rhundi's got her people digging into their politics. For all we know it was just a raiding party and we got *really* unlucky. Nothing tried to follow us off-system. I'm not going to worry about it until we have to."

Grond shrugged and pulled the box over to his side of the table, then ripped the wooden lid off.

He looked inside for a moment, then glanced across the table at his partner.

"Ooh," he said, his eyes widening.

"Please don't say 'you have to,'" Brazel said. "Or any variant of that."

Grond reached into the crate and pulled out an enormous, terrifying-looking rifle. It was long enough to have filled most of the box, matte black in color and unornamented. The scope looked substantial enough to study surface features on nearby asteroids.

"Ain't *that* the purtiest thing I ever saw," Grond said. "There's *two* of 'em in here. And ammo." He pulled out a handful of magazines.

"They hired us to rob a train for a couple of guns and some ammo?"

"*Pretty* guns," Grond corrected. "Be nice. They're bigger'n you." He rummaged around in the crate a bit more.

"Oh, and these, too, I bet. In fact, *just* these, I think." He pulled out a wallet full of data chips. "Who knows what's on 'em, but I bet they're not usually kept in with the rifles. I bet those are a happy accident. And–huh–what's this?"

He removed a small, simple-looking statue, perhaps thirty centimeters high. It was a simple sphere, made of a dull, dark grey metal, on top of a hexagonal base made of wood. There were faint lines traced on the sphere, but other than that there was no ornamentation or detail of any kind.

"You still got those goggles handy?" Brazel asked. "Go put 'em on and take another look."

Grond shrugged and went to get his goggles. Brazel walked around to take a closer look at the statue, running his fingers over the lines. He paused, a confused look on his face, and set his ear against the side of the sphere. He closed his eyes, listening.

"Something I need to know about?" Grond asked, returning to the room.

Brazel blinked. "It's humming," he said. "And I'm not completely sure, but I feel like it's vibrating a little bit too. Check it out."

Grond put a hand on top of the sphere. "I don't feel anything," he said, then paused and listened carefully for a moment. "Or hear anything, either. But you've got better hearing than I do." Gnomes had excellent senses of smell and generally had better ears than ogres did. This was particularly true in Grond's case, since his ears were badly misshapen after years of keeping himself alive as a pit brawler.

"I'm not convinced," Brazel responded. "Namey, you picking up any audio from this thing?"

VERY SLIGHT, the ship responded. AND THERE IS A MINOR HARMONIC VIBRATION AS WELL. THE MATERIAL THE STATUE IS MADE OF IS INCREDIBLY DENSE. I CANNOT DETERMINE THE SOURCE OF THE SOUND OR THE VIBRATIONS.

Brazel ran an experimental fingernail over the surface of the sphere. The material was fairly hard as well.

"You can't tell if it's hollow?"

I CANNOT, the ship confirmed. PERHAPS IF YOU COULD CUT OFF A PIECE OF THE SPHERE, I COULD ANALYZE IT MORE THOROUGHLY, BUT I SUSPECT THAT MIGHT ANNOY YOUR CLIENTS.

"Probably right," the gnome agreed. "Grond, anything?"

"Take the lights down, Namey," Grond said, and the ship followed orders, plunging the room into darkness. Grond slid the goggles back on. There was no trace of the glowing ink on the statue, nor on anything else in the box other than the box itself. He picked it up and looked underneath the base. Nothing there, either.

"It's clean," he said. "Bring 'em back up."

The room re-illuminated itself.

"I'm concerned about that buzz," Brazel said. "Namey, any signals coming out of this thing? It's not some sort of beacon, is it?"

NOTHING I CAN SENSE. IF IT IS BROADCASTING IT IS WITH AN EXTRAORDINARILY NARROW ENCRYPTED POINTBEAM. WE MOVE TOO FAST IN TUNNELSPACE FOR SUCH A THING TO BE EFFECTIVE.

I NOTICED NO TRANSMISSIONS WHEN IT WAS BROUGHT ABOARD.

"Also, electronics don't generally vibrate," Grond said. "You don't need moving parts to send a signal. This has got something mechanical inside it."

Brazel ruffled his fur for a moment and shrugged. "I still don't like it. But there's still not much of a reason to worry about it."

"I'll find a new box to put everything into," Grond said. The old one had been rather beaten up in the escape from the bugs. "And I'll make sure that it's dense enough to block signals. No need to let them track us."

"Could we EMP the thing? Just to be sure?"

"Probably electronics in the guns," Grond said. "A lead-lined box ought to do the job."

INCOMING COMMUNICATION, the ship chirped. IT'S RHUNDI.

Rhundi was Brazel's wife and the mother of their fourteen children. They'd been married for longer than the gnome really cared to remember, most of the time. She'd been a fence when they met. Nowadays she considered herself a respectable businesswoman, which hadn't really made her any less of a fence. Almost all of Brazel and Grond's jobs came through her extensive network of contacts, which was exactly how Brazel liked it. She did all the legwork and negotiated the contracts, and he just executed them. She owned a resort on Arradon, out in the fancier edges of gnomespace. It had been mostly paid for with Brazel and Grond's jobs, a fact he enjoyed reminding her of from time to time.

"Good afternoon, dear," Brazel said.

"Morning, actually," Rhundi replied. "I just got into the office."

"Got anything for us?"

"Yeah," she said. "Drop coordinates. It's in dwarfspace. You're looking for 9013LV." Dwarves were notorious for being unsentimental about place names. All but the oldest of their settlements had serial numbers instead of actual names.

CALCULATING A COURSE, Namey interjected.

"Don't bother quite yet," she said. "Drop's not for two weeks for some reason. I think they thought it was going to take you guys a lot longer to steal the box. Come on home for some R&R in between. There's no point in hanging about in dwarfspace for any longer than you have to."

"Any details yet on whether we're gonna be chased down over this thing?" Grond asked.

"Nothing," Rhundi replied. "The theft made news all over the system, but because of the other bugs, not you. You literally managed to walk into the opening salvo of a minor war. Some sort of ongoing tax dispute that just exploded into something bigger. I'll send a dossier for you to read with the details."

"I'm good," Brazel said.

"I was talking to Grond," Rhundi responded. "I know you don't read."

Brazel ignored her.

"Anyway," Rhundi continued, "I think you're good and the attack was just a coincidence. But I'll have my people keep an eye on Khkk for a few more weeks just to be sure. And I'm probably going to have a word with our contact about it, too."

Brazel grinned. *Have a word with* generally meant *extort more money from* when Rhundi said it in these circumstances.

"Who are we meeting?" he asked.

"Her name's Smashes-the-Stars," Rhundi replied.

"Friendly!"

"Yeah. Anyway, she's a front–she's not the actual client– but she'll be who meets you at the drop location. It's on-planet, and I'm sending coordinates now. There won't be an exchange. I'll let you know when we've been paid and you go give them the box."

"Might have gotten a little busted in the escape, unfortunately. Grond's repackaging everything. There's a couple of guns, some datachips and a statue in there."

"I don't care if it's a dozen adorable human children, dear," Rhundi said benignly. "If you're giving it to them in something other than the crate you found it in, it had better still be *in the crate* inside of your new box. Especially if there's any kind of artwork in there. Last thing we need is them deciding you tried to forge something."

Brazel sighed theatrically. "I'll have Grond put the box back together," he said.

"Grond will put the box back together, but not because Brazel told him to," Grond replied, a smile on his face.

"Sounds like a plan," she replied. "I'll see you guys when you get home. And stay safe."

"Always," Brazel said. "Tell the kids I said hi."

"Already did," Rhundi said, and cut the connection.

THREE

If there was a better place to take a bath than the hot springs of Arradon, Brazel didn't know about it. Not that he had many opportunities to actually take baths–the facilities on the *Nameless* only included showers–but he had trouble imagining how anything would compare to what Arradon made available. A perfect example of the economic hyperspecialization that was so common in the galaxy nowadays, fully half of the planet's available surface area and nearly all of its subterranean areas were dedicated to resort areas for tourism, and the planet's combination of enormous underground freshwater lakes and a way-above-average level of volcanic activity meant that geothermally-heated bathing facilities had become the entire planet's calling card. The pool Brazel was grooming himself in was scented with a dozen spices and half a dozen more exotic oils, most of which he couldn't have named even if he bothered to try.

They made his fur soft and shiny and he smelled wonderful for a few days. It was grand. The *Nameless* stunk of ogre. Grond was here somewhere, too–the halfogre probably wasn't bathing, but there were other ways to enjoy yourself–but no matter how much money Brazel invested in air scrubbers and the latest cleaning 'bots, having a halfogre as a partner meant putting up with certain olfactory hardships. Gnomes had an especially acute sense of smell, and anything that covered up the smell of ogre tended to be overpowering in its own right. It wasn't worth the trouble.

He let himself sink deep into the bubbling water, puffing his fur out in what probably had been some sort of threat display hundreds of thousands of years before gnomes became civilized, much less took to the stars. It didn't make his not-quite-one-and-a-quarter-meters-tall-without-his-boots   frame   look   any scarier, but it certainly helped in letting the scents and oils penetrate through to his skin. He had reserved a full afternoon's access to this pool and he didn't intend to get out of it until he was clean and pleasant-smelling in places that he previously hadn't even known were there.

The gun pointed at his face when he resurfaced altered his priorities.

"Rude," he said. "I'm busy. Whatever you want, come back later." He tilted his head back, lowering himself into the water again.

The gun tapped him on the top of his head, upsetting his balance and forcing him to put his feet down. "Maybe I just wanted to see my husband," she said.

"There are security cams for that. I'm smelly. Or I *was*. You know I don't like heading straight to you when I'm smelly." He went back underwater.

The gun rapped him on the head again.

"Wives aren't supposed to hit," Brazel replied. "Especially with guns. And double-especially with *my* gun. Bother Grond."

"Husbands aren't supposed to leave weapons just lying around where anyone can get at them, either. We've got a problem, Brazel. There's Benevolence on Arradon. Not far from here. That pique your interest at all?"

Shit, he thought.

"It does," he said, and climbed out of the pool.

Rhundi was taller than Brazel was—typical for gnomish females—and her fur was a golden brown, several shades lighter than his. Most of the time she had it dyed. Today everything was tipped with a lovely green shade, matching her eyes. He'd had to hold her at gunpoint for a brief time on their first date, and she'd enjoyed getting the drop on him whenever she had the chance ever since.

He spent a few minutes in a sonic shower, blasting the excess water out of his fur, then recovered his gun and the rest of his gear and got dressed. He sighed at the condition of his flight suit—he'd planned on spending some of his time between jobs getting everything he owned carefully cleaned and retailored, a task it didn't sound like he was going to have time for. Rhundi looked impatient.

"Have you found Grond already?" he asked.

"He was playing chess," she replied. "He wasn't hard to find. You actually took a little bit longer to track down. He should be in my office already." Brazel grinned. His partner was a lot more intelligent than anyone ever gave him credit for and he'd probably been toying with his opponent. He'd seen Grond win chess matches against two opponents simultaneously on more than one occasion. Brazel didn't play, so the halfogre frequently slipped away to find a game whenever they were land-bound for more than a day or two.

"How are the kids?" Brazel asked.

"Not much different," Rhundi said, thumbing a recessed wall panel to summon the direct lift to her office. The response vaguely alarmed Brazel. Rhundi had never dispensed with their children's welfare in three words before. She was more concerned about the Benevolence than she was letting on.

The lift door slid open and the two entered Rhundi's office. She was right. Grond was there already, sitting comfortably in the only piece of furniture in the office suited for a halfogre. He was dressed in what he called his "civilian" clothes, a basic long-sleeved, belted tunic over loose, comfortable pants–which meant that he wasn't openly displaying any tattoos, scars, or anything sharp. He was also wearing his reading glasses. He had a thick book in his hands and another sitting on his lap.

"Been waiting long?" Rhundi asked.

"Not long," Grond rumbled. "But I had a few minutes. What's going on?"

Rhundi settled in behind her desk, an oversized (for a gnome, anyway) ornate wooden affair, and pushed a recessed button somewhere. The entire desk shimmered, the holographic antique look fading away and being replaced with the modern console desk that it actually was. She waved one hand at an icon on the desk surface and another at Brazel and Grond, beckoning them over. The desk surface projected a holographic image of a black-armored Benevolence agent having a conversation with an alarmed-looking clerk behind a counter somewhere.

"Just one?" Brazel said. "Maybe he's on vacation."

"There's two," Rhundi said. "The second stayed behind on their spidership. He's not left the dock since they got here—probably right around the same time you guys did. They're in a marked Benevolence ship and the agent has been moving around in full armor. I've had camera 'bots tailing him since the second they hit the ground. He either hasn't noticed them somehow or doesn't care that they're there. He's literally just traveling around bothering people, but no arrests or violence that I've heard about. No purges. I want to know what he's doing here. This video's live, so he's nearby."

"You could ask," Grond said.

"I could find out on my own, too," Rhundi replied. "And that's a lot less likely to result in getting lied to or arrested. Last I checked, Benevolence weren't generally too forthcoming with answers when gnomes got impertinent with them, and I don't have anybody who I'm willing to risk on being polite right now. So it's up to you two."

"You're sure they're alone?" Grond said.

"As sure as I can be," she replied. "He's clearly looking for something and they haven't found it yet."

"So what do we do about it?" Grond asked. "We can take care of two of them, especially if we get some help and go after them separately. But that'll bring two dozen as fast as they can get here. We have a way to find whatever they're looking for before they do?"

Brazel shrugged, wrinkling his snout in a gnomish gesture of disgust. "We need to find out what they're looking for first. Specifically. Rhundi, you have any contacts that they've actually talked to? Who's this in the holo?"

"That wasn't far from here," she said. "I don't know who he is yet, but I can find out easily enough. The 'bots are all over the place."

"Comm us an address," Brazel said, standing up. "Grond and I will pay them a visit. Keep an eye on the agents and let us know if anything changes." He waved to Grond and headed toward the lift.

"Mind if I borrow these?" Grond asked Rhundi, holding up the books.

"Just bring them back. Bring him back, too," she said. Grond nodded and followed his partner out of the office.

FOUR

Namey had the local coordinates before they even got to him, and it took no more than half an hour in atmosphere to get where they were going. The two didn't talk much on the trip. Brazel was deep in thought, Grond busy with his books. He was ready for business by the time they landed, though, wearing just enough weaponry to be able to handle a brawl but not enough that he'd be looked at twice by Arradon's rather meager security forces.

The shopkeeper the Benevolence agent had been spotted harassing owned, of all things, a jewelry shop. The vendor was a gnome, but the place was sized properly for bigs, so Grond followed Brazel inside. The walls were lined with glass cabinets, mostly displaying necklaces and rings, with a few larger pieces of artwork and statuary lining the walls and on shelving across the back of the store. Brazel fought to avoid wrinkling his snout. Most of the wares on display were far too gaudy for his tastes. There was a younger female gnome sitting behind the counter.

"Boss around?" Brazel asked.

"She's busy," she answered. "But I can help you with anything you need." She looked with alarm at Grond.

"I don't really think you can," Brazel answered.

"We already paid our binda for the month," she said, looking just a little bit more alarmed. Brazel filed this information away for later reference. He hadn't been aware that there was anybody extorting from the local businesspeople. Rhundi would certainly be interested in that information if she didn't already have it.

"What's your name, dear?"

She blinked. "Xurrin."

Brazel smiled, trying his best to look charming. "Xurrin, I'm not here about protection money, and I'm not here to hurt or threaten anybody. But I'm also not here for jewelry. Now, I'm gonna guess that you don't normally actually work behind this counter, am I right?"

Xurrin didn't answer, but her fur flattened, tight against her body.

"Okay. So I'm right. I'm also gonna guess that your mom owns the place, and that she's in the back trying to keep Dad from puking his guts out in fear. How am I doing?"

Xurrin stood up abruptly, the stool she'd been sitting on clattering to the floor.

"What do you want?"

Brazel held his hands up. "Just to talk. And to help. I promise. But you *really* want to go get your parents for us right now. And maybe you've sold your last earring for the day, while you're at it."

Grond locked the door.

Xurrin stood still for a moment, frozen with indecision.

"I promise, dear. We're harmless, at least to you guys. Go get your parents."

She turned and fled into the back of the store.

A few moments later, two adult gnomes walked back in. Both looked rather shaken.

"This is my place. What do you want?" the female asked.

"I'm Brazel," Brazel said. "This is my partner Grond. We wanted to ask you some questions."

"I think we've answered enough questions from strangers for one day," she replied.

"I gave you our names, though, so we aren't strangers," Brazel said. "We know you had a visitor earlier today. We just want to know what he wanted."

The gnomes exchanged a look.

"C'mon," Brazel said. "If we were dangerous, you left your kid running the store. We coulda snatched her first and started from there. We're just here for information."

"He was ... he was *Benevolence*," the male said.

"I know," Brazel said. "He had a cloud of my nanocameras following him the whole time. I don't have any audio, though.

We're trying to figure out what he's doing here. What was he asking you?"

"He was asking about a statue," he said. "If anybody'd tried to sell us anything lately. I told him we don't do secondhand, though. We're not that kind of shop—"

Brazel interrupted him. "A statue? What kind of statue?"

"About this big," he said, holding his hands about 30 centimeters apart. "A sphere on top of a wooden base. Sounded really simple."

"A *Benevolence* agent in *full armor* came in here to ask you if you'd bought a statue recently?"

"Yeah," he said. "Then he asked a bunch of other questions about where somebody might go if they were looking to sell artwork to somebody. I told him I didn't really know. He got upset and left."

Now it was Brazel and Grond's turn to exchange a look.

"He just left?" Brazel asked. "No threats, no promises, nothing? He leave a card or a comm address or anything like that? Say he was coming back? Anything? He just walked in and asked a bunch of polite questions about secondhand statuary and then left?"

"Nothing," he responded. "Which, now that I think about it, is kind of weird."

"Yeah, it is," Brazel said. He scribbled a comm address on a nearby receipt pad and handed it to him. "If he comes back, let us know."

The gnome nodded, still too shell-shocked to do anything other than agree.

"And maybe go ahead and take the rest of the day off," Brazel added. "Neither of you really look in shape to be negotiating with anybody right now. You get somebody clever in here they're going to rob you blind."

The two of them left.

"Rhundi," Brazel said, opening a comm channel. "You still following the agent?"

"He's still in the neighborhood," Rhundi said. "Still going around from place to place. He's visited a few stores and–get this–a *brothel.*"

"A Benevolence agent visited a brothel."

"You heard me."

"Let's make sure we're in agreement here," Brazel said. "He's not here for a bath, or as a tourist. He wouldn't be in full armor and in a Benevolence ship. That's not a *person* in that armor, it's a Benevolence agent, and he knows that there's no way he's going to relate to anyone as anything other than Benevolence while he's wearing it. If he was here for something legitimate he'd be out of uniform and on his own ship. And they're plainly not here as part of a political delegation or a legal proceeding because Benevolence love overkill for that shit. If he was security of any kind there'd be a dozen of them, not two. Which leaves only one real possibility, and I don't think I like it very much either."

"Impostor," Rhundi said.

"Impostor," Brazel echoed. "Which means he is simultaneously rather clever *and* the most dangerous kind of idiot."

"Agreed," Rhundi said. "I'd rather have actual Benevolence here than some moron impersonating one and drawing attention. And he's managed to steal a spidership? Not on my planet. Go see if you can bring him in."

"I'll keep you posted," Brazel said.

They headed to the port where the spidership was docked and waited for a few hours. Grond took to a rooftop nearby, watching the ship, and Brazel staked out the docks themselves. There was no need to be overcautious about watching for the agent, since the armor would ensure that everyone around cut him a wide berth. Brazel would probably know he was on his way well before actually spotting him. The sun was setting, so the agent would almost certainly be returning to his ship soon, if he didn't want to stay somewhere on-planet.

Grond was examining the ship through binoculars. Something about it seemed off, but he couldn't quite put his finger on what.

"Braze," he said over the comm.

"Yeah?"

"I don't think that's a spidership, man. It just doesn't look right. You ever seen one of these things actually docked?"

"I haven't," Brazel said. "And I've been too busy fleeing when we've seen them in action to take too close of a look, as I'm sure you already know."

Spiderships were the Benevolence short-range, disposable fighters. They generally carried no more than two crew. A spidership had an ovoid central unit with up to eight flexible "legs" that the pilot could point in just about any direction. The legs could be used for either propulsion or assault but not both at the same time. The advantage was that spiderships could be insanely maneuverable, or insanely destructive, in the hands of a talented pair of pilots. The disadvantage was that one generally had to be chosen over the other.

Grond finally figured out what was bothering him.

"I don't think those things *balance* on their legs, do they?" he asked. The spidership in the dock was perched on the tips of its eight legs, its central sphere held a meter or two above the ground. That would run the risk of damaging both the guns and the maneuvering jets. That seemed like a terrible engineering decision. He felt like Benevolence engineers were probably smarter than that.

"No idea, Grond," Brazel said. "'Ware the entrance. Everybody just got really agitated all the sudden."

Grond tore his gaze away from the ship and looked at the main entrance to the dock. A lone figure in full-body black armor, wearing a black cape over his shoulders, strode in. The crowd parted around him in a wave as he moved.

"There's our guy," Brazel said. He snorted. "Check out the cape."

"Did he have that on in the jewelry shop?" Grond said. "I can't imagine he did. I don't remember making fun of him. Why the fuck is he wearing a *cape?*"

"Capes automatically make you twenty percent scarier," Brazel said. "At least, they do if they're black. Capes of any other color just make you easier to trip."

"Not Benevolence. No way."

"No way," Brazel agreed. "How long we gonna wait?"

"Another hour, unless he leaves, in which case we hightail it back to the *Nameless* and chase him," Grond said. "Give him time to settle down and maybe see if we can catch him sleeping."

"I think that's the first time anybody's ever said the words *maybe we can catch him sleeping* about a Benevolence agent," Brazel said.

"I'm not talking about a Benevolence agent, though," Grond said. "I'm talking about a fucking idiot in an ill-advised party costume. I doubt the armor's even real, and I've got a couple of theories about the ship, too."

"Ooh, share," Brazel replied.

"Nah," Grond said. "I'd rather surprise you if I'm right." He watched the agent enter his ship through the binoculars. "He's in. Let's make it two hours. I want it good and dark."

"Gotcha," Brazel said. "You staying up there the whole time?"

"No reason to move," Grond said. "Unless he gives me one. I'll keep point. You go get Namey ready for a chase if we need to and meet me back here."

"On it," Brazel said.

FIVE

They ended up waiting three hours, as the spaceport stayed populated and busy later than the rest of Arradon. The spidership, luckily for them, had been parked in a private dock, with no other ships around. The gate to the dock was locked, but Brazel worked at it for a few moments and was able to convince the AI running the gate that he was an overzealous maintenance worker on a night shift. Eventually it opened the gate.

The spidership sat in the middle of the dock, with no external lights on or any other signs of life.

"It occurs to me," Brazel said, "that if we're wrong about this guy being an impostor and this ship not being Benevolence, that we have just done something incredibly stupid and are probably about to die."

"Yup," Grond said. Without another word, the halfogre pulled Angela off his back, readied her, and fired a single carefully aimed shot at the top of the ship. He hit a small round object that was affixed to the very top of the spidership's central sphere. The object exploded. A moment later, the entire spidership shimmered and disappeared, leaving behind a small two-man cruiser perched on three landing struts.

"Hardlight. You're *fucking kidding me,*" Brazel said.

"Yep. Spotted the projector from the rooftops a few hours ago. You have any idea how difficult it was to not just shoot the thing right then and there?"

The cruiser's external lights flooded on, and the engines began powering up.

"Shit," Brazel said.

"Can't have that," Grond said, and fired a few more shots. Each hit a landing strut, bending two of them and damaging the third. The ship collapsed to the ground awkwardly and the engines whined down.

"No external guns, I hope?" Brazel said.

"Good luck aiming 'em," Grond said, moving closer to the ship. The cruiser had a transparent cockpit, but there was no one in it.

"Come on out," the halfogre roared. His eyes started glowing a bright red color. This was an ogre trait. It had taken Grond months of sustained effort to teach himself how to do it, and he couldn't maintain it for nearly as long as a full-blooded ogre. But it was insanely intimidating for as long as he could keep it up.

The cruiser was flat and wedge-shaped, with prominent wings on each side and the engine taking up most of the back. There wasn't going to be much room in there for two people to coexist, especially if neither of them was actually in the cockpit.

"We sure he's there?" Brazel asked.

"He didn't *leave*," Grond said. "I was watching."

He raised his voice again. "Two choices, stranger: You come out or I come in. Or maybe I just cut your tin can open and let you fall out. Your choice. Five seconds." He reached into a pouch at his waist and held up a couple of fragmentation grenades.

"That'll make an awful lot of noise, won't it?" Brazel asked. "Weren't we being subtle?"

Grond didn't bother responding. He was starting to prime one of the grenades when a hatch opened on the side of the ship.

Brazel had to suppress a shudder as a black-armored, black-caped Benevolence agent walked down the stairs from the cruiser's exit hatch.

The agent walked a few meters away from his ship and stopped, his black cape fluttering in the slight evening breeze. He stood there, silently, staring at the two of them through the opaque visor on his helmet.

Grond snickered, took two quick steps toward him and punched his head clean off.

It took Brazel a few moments of sheer, trousers-ruining terror to come to grips with what his partner had just done. Despite first impressions, Grond hadn't quite literally decapitated the agent. What he *had* done was punch him in the chin hard enough to launch his helmet completely off of his head, sending it flying across the hangar to clatter into a corner. The agent was bounced off the side of his ship by the force of the blow, hitting the ground hard and rolling weakly onto his back.

Grond kicked him in the ribs and then sat on him, his eyes still blazing red. He cracked his knuckles, then punched him twice in the chest. The agent's black armor shattered under the force of the blows, and Grond grabbed what was left of his breastplate, tore it off him, and threw it into the corner to join the helmet.

"Lemme 'splain somethin' here," Grond growled, his face centimeters away from the panicked man's. "If you were Benevolence, that helmet would have been wired into your living brain, and ripping off your chestplate would have torn tubing out of your lungs. You'd be sitting here trying to decide whether to drown on your own blood or die gibbering like an idiot, and I'd have two *broken fucking hands* to worry about while you died. You're not Benevolence. This armor's a fucking *cheap costume*. You're gonna tell us who the fuck you are, and you're gonna tell us why you're bothering people, and you're gonna do it *now*, or *we're* gonna have a real problem."

He sat up a bit and raised his voice again. "And whoever the fuck else is on that boat had better be off of it before he finishes talking, too."

Brazel just stood by and watched, his eyes wide. Grond appeared to be in a bit of a mood.

The man opened his mouth to speak and passed out, his eyes rolling backward and a deep groan escaping from him. Grond slapped him, to no avail.

"Wonderful," he said.

"Still the other one on the ship," Brazel said. He had a pistol in his hands and was moving toward the door.

"Gimme a second," Grond said, tying the man's hands behind him. "I think he'll probably be out for a bit. That didn't look like acting. We'll both go." He smiled. "You first, though. Smaller target, and all."

"Asshole," Brazel mumbled under his breath, but he headed for the door anyway. He glared at the agent for a moment before boarding the ship.

"A fucking *cape*. Unbelievable."

It became clear quickly that anyone still on the ship was hiding. There was no exit airlock. The ship was not designed to be docked with or opened up outside of the atmosphere. The cockpit was empty, and the only other available room was a simple living/sleeping area with a few compartments for cargo. The ship was really only designed to move short distances quickly. Even the *Nameless*, which was hardly a yacht, looked expensive and spacious by comparison.

Grond pointed to the cargo compartments. One of them was closed. He and Brazel exchanged a few quick hand signals, having a brief, silent argument about which of them was going to open the door. Grond eventually moved behind the door, with Brazel standing a few meters away, his gun at the ready. The halfogre counted to three and yanked the door open, nearly tearing it off its hinges.

There was a 'bot inside the cargo compartment. Well, *most* of a 'bot. The thing looked about half-constructed, roughly human-shaped, with exposed wires and circuitry everywhere and one arm ending abruptly at the elbow. One of its "eyes" lit up and its head tilted toward Brazel.

"Oh my," it said.

Brazel shot it.

"Fucking creepy," he said. People-'bots had been popular for a few years a decade or so ago, but had quickly fallen out of fashion. Most people who needed a 'bot around needed it for some specific function, and that function almost never required the 'bot to look like a human being.

Grond put a hand on the thing's shoulder and pulled its smoking remains out of the cargo hold.

"Hey, this is interesting," he said. "You just shot the ship. That was a telepresence unit for the AI." He pointed at a couple of cables running from what was left of the 'bot's head to a port in the cargo hold.

"Surprised a ship this small even needs an AI," Brazel said. "Much less one that can walk around. This must have been what people thought was the second agent. God, can you imagine if Namey had legs? We'd have melted him into scrap years ago."

I HEARD THAT, the *Nameless* said over subcomm.

"The fact that you were even *listening* is part of the reason that you don't get a telepresence unit," Brazel said.

GROND TOLD ME TO LISTEN IN, the boat said. IN CASE YOU NEEDED A QUICK EXTRACT. THAT WAS HIS EXACT WORD. EXTRACT.

"You still don't get a telepresence unit. But get over here anyway. I think there's just enough room for you to crowd into the dock with us. We're bringing back a passenger."

Grond was rummaging around in the cockpit. Brazel heard a loud crack and some scraping sounds. He emerged with a glowing cube, a few interface cables dangling from it.

"Found the ship's brainbox," he said. "If our buddy outside bothered to put an AI into his boat, I want to know what it's been doing."

"I'm gonna shoot the 'bot again, if you don't mind," Brazel said.

"I do not," Grond said. "But let's get the hell out of here quick-like. Somebody had to have heard some of that, and even if they *do* think there are Benevolence in here their curiosity is gonna win out sooner or later."

Brazel shrugged and put his pistol away and the two of them spent a couple of enjoyable minutes tossing the small living area. They found a datapad and some of the "agent's" personal effects, which Grond tossed into a convenient knapsack. They also found a second suit of fake Benevolence armor, which they left behind.

THIRTY SECONDS, the *Nameless* announced.

The pair exited the cruiser and waited, Grond picking up the still-unconscious impostor and slinging him over his shoulder like a sack. The *Nameless* just barely managed to fit itself into the bay, bumping the cruiser just slightly on the way down. Brazel headed for his usual spot in the cockpit while Grond looked for a better way to tie up their captive.

"One of these days we're gonna install a detention cell in this thing," he said to himself. This was not the first time they'd needed to keep someone locked up, and something told him it wouldn't be the last either.

SIX

Somewhat surprisingly, their captive was still unconscious when Brazel and Grond got back to the resort, and the two quickly spirited him away to Rhundi's small detention center deep underground. Technically only usable by resort security for the occasional unruly guest, the facilities had been cleared out so that the three of them could interrogate their prisoner.

"How do we want to play this?" Rhundi asked.

"Well, I already did *crazy scary halfogre*, and he's been unconscious for an hour," Grond said. "For a guy ballsy enough to dress up as Benevolence he sure can't take a punch too well."

The three of them contemplated their prisoner. He'd been stripped of the rest of his makeshift armor, which had turned out to be made mostly of cheap polymer. The stuff would barely turn a *knife*, much less anything from a projectile gun or energy weapon. Grond was happy he hadn't hit him harder. He would have caved his chest in. As it was, the punch had knocked out a molar or two, and the bruise on his chin was intense enough that it was surprising Grond hadn't broken his jaw.

He was a human male, olive-skinned, perhaps in his late teens or early twenties, with a thin, underfed look to him. His hair was medium length, dyed blond from black, but it hadn't been retouched in a while and the roots were showing badly. He had a scraggly black beard that looked like the result of a couple of weeks without access to proper sanitary facilities. Brazel had already wrinkled his snout at the man's lack of proper grooming. He wore a simple black skintight bodysuit underneath the armor, which fit him closely. He'd had no weapons with him, apparently hoping that the armor itself would be enough to frighten Brazel and Grond away. It had worked, after all, with almost everyone he'd encountered all day long. It wasn't the worst of ideas. It was just that it was going to get him killed the very second it stopped working.

"Let's start off with reasonable," Rhundi said. "Which one of us is best at reasonable?"

"You are," Brazel said. "He's human, so he'll probably mistake you for nurturing."

Rhundi shot him a look. Brazel grinned and blew her a kiss.

"Wake him up," she said. "Do it nicely."

Grond quietly slipped out of the room, and Brazel held a small vial of smelling salts under the man's nose. He jerked away, snorted, and started coming around.

"We'll be right outside," Brazel said, and followed Grond out.

The man shook himself awake, trying to stretch his arms and then reacting with surprise to discover himself cuffed to a metal chair at his ankles and his wrists. He tried to speak, only to find himself gagged as well. Rhundi sat a couple of meters away, on a chair that lifted her to his eye level.

"You're safe," she said. "You're not in any danger right now. You *could be*, but you're not. Let's start with that. Shake your head if you understand, whether you believe me or not."

A glimmer of panic still touched the man's eyes, but he nodded.

"Okay. We're going to proceed here slowly. Nobody does anything stupid, right? Shake your head if you understand, whether you believe me or not."

His head shook. Rhundi tapped a button on her chair and the gag unlocked itself.

"Shake your head and use your tongue to push that out of your mouth. Just let it fall on the floor."

The man did as he was told.

"Good. Do you want a drink of water, or anything like that?"

He shook his head no.

"Okay. What's your name?"

"Haakoro," he said.

"Haakoro. Don't humans usually have surnames? Just Haakoro?"

He nodded. "Just Haakoro."

"What are you doing on my planet, Haakoro?"

He blinked. "Your planet?"

"Far as you're concerned, yeah," she said, smiling in what she hoped was a nurturing manner. *Stupid Brazel.*

"I'm looking for some people," he said.

"Okay. Got one right here. A couple more *people* pounded you into unconsciousness a few hours ago. You needed to fake up some Benevolence armor and hardlight yourself a spidership for *people*?"

"Only saw the one ogre," he said.

"Back to these people you're looking for. Who are they?"

"Not sure I should tell you," he said, a touch of amusement showing in his eyes. "Wouldn't want you to get mixed up with the wrong ones."

He's actually trying to protect me, she thought. *Brazel was totally right.* She hated it when Brazel was right.

"Around here I pretty much *am* the wrong people, Haakoro. Can the chivalry, okay? The faster you're honest, the faster we're done with the gags and handcuffs and things like that."

The bastard actually *winked.* "I kinda like handcuffs, actually."

"So does the halfogre. They hold you still while he's *beating you.*"

That got his attention.

"Yeah, you remember the halfogre? The guy who beat you unconscious and tore that cheap-ass fake armor off you? He's one of my people. He's right behind the door over there," she said, nodding toward the door. "But I don't really need him involved right now. Like I said, you're not in danger. Yet."

She paused, smiled, let just the barest hint of ice creep into her eyes and her voice. "But you're gonna have to stop the bullshit, and if you try to *flirt with me again* the halfogre will be the *least* of your problems."

She gave him a moment to let that sink in and let her tone go back to relaxed and conversational again.

"So let's start again, Haakoro. I imagine that your face and your teeth probably hurt. Would you like something to drink?"

This time he nodded.

Rhundi snapped her fingers, knowing that Brazel was coming anyway but wanting to look in control of the situation. The door opened and her husband walked in, two glasses of ice water on a tray held above one shoulder. *Where the hell did he get that?*

She took one of the glasses and gestured toward Haakoro. Brazel carefully let him sip some of the water, daintily dabbed at his chin and lips with a towel he'd brought with him, then set the glass and tray on the floor and retreated to a corner of the room. A back corner, Rhundi noted, where Haakoro couldn't see him.

"I hope that helped. We can get you some medication for the pain later, if your jaw is bothering you." They'd already injected Haakoro with some painkillers, but not *quite* enough to make him comfortable, just enough to make him a little loopy and worried that he might be hurting *more* soon. If they'd just left him alone, he probably wouldn't have been able to talk at all.

"One more try. You say you're here looking for some people. Tell me about them."

"That's the problem," he said. "I don't exactly know who they are. They've got something of mine."

Rhundi made brief eye contact with her husband. Brazel raised an eyebrow but didn't say anything.

"And what do they have?"

"I'm *really* not sure I should tell you," he said.

"This is the part where I remind you about the handcuffs again, then," she said. "We can come back in a few hours. Or a couple of days. Or I can just send the halfogre back in here for a couple of minutes."

He was quiet for a moment, thinking.

"Okay," he said. "I work for ... some people."

"There's that *people* again," Rhundi said.

He tried to wave a hand, forgetting that he was tied down, then chuckled a bit at himself. "Point is, I had a job to get some information about some guns. Middleman stuff. I was supposed to make sure the datachips were in a certain box on a certain train and somebody else was going to steal them. Only thing is, I got lucky. I got a *lot* more information than what I was supposed to get. But I had to burn some people to get it. And my stupid contacts *disappeared* on me. I can't get ahold of anybody anymore to tell them I've got more *stuff* for them."

Rhundi glanced at Brazel again. His ears were turned forward, eyes wide, listening carefully.

"And that leads to you being here on Arradon, wearing Benevolence armor and asking people about a statue?"

"Yes. I tossed part of what I'd found into the box with the guns and chips that were supposed to be in there. A statue. It's, like, a *beacon* or something. Sends out a weird signal. I couldn't find my contacts to talk to *them,* and I didn't know who my contacts were reporting back to, so I figured I'd follow the *signal* and then sort of work my way back up the chain until I found somebody to pay me for the new stuff."

"And the signal led you here," Rhundi said levelly.

"It disappeared pretty quickly. But whoever they were, they were on a trajectory toward this system. It's kinda out in the middle of nowhere and Arradon's the most populated planet. I was hoping I'd get lucky."

"And the armor?"

"It's a scam, you know that. I've had it for years. I was hoping that if the thieves found the statue they'd realize it wasn't part of what they were supposed to steal and try to move it on their own. Find that, find them. The armor scares the hell out of people. It looks just real enough that they don't look any closer."

Rhundi rubbed her forehead. "So you went door-to-door, on a random planet in a system that a signal was sorta pointed at, looking for a statue that you were hoping some thieves had noticed and tried to sell, assuming that the *buyers* would be able to lead you back to the *thieves?* That's the *worst plan I've ever heard,"* Rhundi said.

Haakoro shrugged. "I guess I didn't think it through too much. What can I say, I tend to get lucky," he said. "Always have. Dunno why. Stuff just tends to work out for me."

Rhundi gestured to Brazel. "We'll be back. If we're not back in an hour I'll have somebody bring you some food. Maybe they'll even uncuff you to feed it to you."

Haakoro let his head fall back against the back of his chair. "I'll just ... sit here with my thoughts, I guess."

"Works for me," Rhundi said, and left the room, Brazel just behind her.

>{⊞}<

"Explain," she said.

"It's like he said," Brazel said. "He's the luckiest son of a bitch alive. And you didn't want us to open the box. That thing could have been sending a signal the entire time."

"Namey said tunnelspace would screw that up," Grond said.

"Either way, when we came out it would have started up again," Brazel said. "We stopped the signal. He found us anyway."

"You guys are gonna start doing some twists and turns on your way back from jobs from now on," Rhundi said. "What do you want to do with him?"

"Get the rest of his info and then dump him off at a port with enough money to get somewhere else," Grond said. "Possibly with copious threats should he ever attempt to locate us again."

"I think we probably ought to get rid of him," Brazel said. "He's just gonna find a way to follow us. That's his find on the ship, isn't it?"

"We're not killing him," Rhundi said, making the decision. "And we're gonna split the difference on the new intel. Give everything to Irtuus-bon. Let him search through everything and figure out what the guy's got. Haakoro stays here in one of the cheaper suites under *very* close supervision until we get back to our people. If they want to get back in touch with him, that's on them."

Irtuus-bon was a troll. One of his incarnations was one of the finest researchers that Rhundi had ever met, and he had a special interest in research connected to the Benevolence. Finding a way to remove Benevolence data encryption would be right up his alley, if it wasn't just something he could already spout off about from the top of his head. He'd surprised her like that before.

Brazel rolled his eyes. "Or it could all be *our* money. We still like money, don't we?"

"They aren't paying us killing wages," Grond said. "So we're not killing anybody we don't have to."

"You guys never let me have any fun," Brazel grumped.

"There was a datapad on his boat," Grond said. "And we've got his ship's brainbox. We tossed the rest of the thing before we left. If he was holding on to any information, we've already got it from him."

"Okay. Send that to Irtuus-bon. And Brazel, get somebody over to the spaceport. I want his ship over here and I want it gone over carefully. Put some of the girls from engineering on it or do it yourself. I don't care. But if we've missed anything on the ship, I want to know about it."

"What about him?" Grond asked.

"Let him sit for a few hours anyway," she said. "Then I'll send security to put him somewhere more comfortable and give him a doc to clean his face up. If he doesn't do anything stupid, this will work out just fine for everybody. And whatever we do, let's keep that damn statue in the lead box."

The three of them split up.

SEVEN

That evening, Rhundi went to see Haakoro in his new apartment. She knocked before entering, but let herself in, not waiting for him to get to the door.

"I own the place," she said to his look of surprise. "I get to do that."

"I suppose," he said. "So, am I a prisoner, or what?"

"Consider yourself a guest," she said. "You'll have the run of the facilities. Go take a swim, eat yourself sick, fix your hair, and get somebody to shave that mess off your face. Play some sports if you want. You just can't leave. You're on camera everywhere you go, and most of the time there's gonna be at least a couple of guards following you around. And if you happen to get outside the resort, you don't have a ship, and we'll just pick you back up again."

"I could just steal one," he said.

"You could try," Rhundi replied. "I'd recommend against it. We might blow you out of the sky instead of recapturing you. I wouldn't risk it. You got anywhere to sleep more comfortable than that bed? You don't look like you're rolling in cash. Setting up gun grabs for the Malevolence doesn't scream *independently wealthy* to me."

He started. "How'd you know I was working with Mals?"

"I didn't," she said. "At least, not until just now." *Dumbass*, she thought. This guy was either seriously not very bright or dangerously clever and *trying* to look dumb. She'd have to figure out a way to be sure which it was.

The Malevolence weren't technically named that, but the name had stuck better than the *Noble Opposition*, which was what they called themselves. Most of the rest of the galaxy thought the name far too pompous. They opposed the Benevolence and were the closest thing there was to a formal opposition army to the Benevolence's goals of galactic domination. It made the nickname a natural fit.

What they really were, most of the time, was *pirates*. They were pirates who occasionally stuck their heads out and gave the Benevolence a chance to smash them, but they seemed to spend an awful lot of time hassling people who were just as interested in avoiding Benevolence as they were. Like her and Brazel and Grond, for example. She'd suspected the theft was for them, but hadn't been able to confirm it officially. *That increases the pay*, she thought, calculating how much more she'd be trying to shake out of her contacts once she nailed down exactly what she was selling them.

"I thought I'd fill you in on the status of your ... find," she said.

The room had a bed and a couple of comfortable chairs in it. He started to sit on the bed and then moved to one of the chairs.

"Go ahead," he said.

"My technicians have your datapad and most of your stuff. I have someone recovering your ship. We already have the brainbox, we're going through that too. Are the data on any of those things encrypted?"

"Brainbox is, obviously. But there's nothing on there you'd want. My shipboard AI's pretty standard. She's called the *Serendipity*."

"I'm not too worried about that," she said. Every shipboard AI's brainbox was encrypted, but most of them weren't encrypted *well*. Nothing that would hold Irtuus-bon for long. "How about the datapad?"

"Stuff was encrypted when I got it," he said. "I haven't cracked it yet."

"What kind of encryption?"

"Benevolence. High-level, too."

How the hell? That might be a little bit trickier. Irtuus-bon had all sorts of skills, but she wasn't sure he had any way to break Benevolence encryption. This data could be either priceless or worthless depending on whether her pet troll could break through the encryption.

"You were supposed to mark a box full of guns for my people, and you stumbled onto high-level Benevolence intelligence?"

"I couldn't believe it either," he said. "Literally had somebody approach me and volunteer to sell the stuff."

"Tell me about this *somebody.*"

"I don't know her," he said. "Halfogre. Didn't give her name."

"A female halfogre."

"Yeah."

"You're sure. The only thing you know about the person who sold you this encrypted intel that you haven't cracked through yet is that she was a *female halfogre.*"

"I've got no reason to lie to you," he said. "She said it would be worth the money and that I could resell it for way more but didn't say exactly what it was. She didn't give me a name. I could describe her for you if you want."

"Write it down," she said. "Maybe draw me a picture. I'll come talk to you later. If you need me for some reason, just tell the room. It'll let me know."

Haakoro nodded. Rhundi left, the door locking behind her as it closed.

>{⊂}<

EIGHT

A few days later, Brazel and Grond left for the drop. They were headed to a dwarf planet called 9013LV, a standard terrestrial-mix rock just inside independent dwarfspace. It was just far enough from its sun and just big enough to support a variety of different biospheres and a fair amount of liquid water, with a few dozen major population centers scattered around the surface and the typical dwarven subterranean spaces connecting most of them. They were to meet their target at a spaceport just outside one of the city centers. Receiving landing clearance was straightforward, the docking AI passing through one of their more common IDs without comment. The planet had no substantial military presence to speak of and, more importantly, no trace of Benevolence influence.

"We've got about three hours until the pickup," Brazel said, "and we'll still be on nightside when that rolls around. Not sure if I should play along and keep our bay dark or have Namey light up the place like the surface of a star. Who meets in the middle of the night in a spaceport?"

"Well, *criminals*, obviously. Light up," Grond said, "but don't be too obvious about it. No reason to piss anybody off."

The boat lit up his exterior lights, bathing the dock. Most of this port catered to travelers rather than larger transports or industrial vehicles, and they had a private bay. The *Nameless* felt a bit out of place, but not enough that anyone would look at it for too long.

They had decided to go ahead and hand over the statue along with the guns and datachips, but to stay quiet on the extra intel until they knew what it was. Haakoro had been cooperating, mostly staying in his room while Irtuus-bon researched a way to crack the encrypted files on his datapad. True to his word, the brainbox hadn't contained anything tremendously useful other than a record of Haakoro's travels over the lifetime of the ship, but they had been able to confirm that he was telling the truth about having been on Khkk for a while.

Brazel and Grond took very different approaches to meeting with clients they'd not met yet. Brazel dressed like a businessman, his fur carefully groomed and styled, a long maroon coat over flawlessly fitted and pressed pants and shirt, and not a single trace of visible weaponry. Occasionally he'd go so far as to sport jewelry–an earring or two, perhaps, or a pendant–but not this time. Grond knew his partner was armed– was, in fact, probably carrying just as many weapons as Grond was–but Brazel always preferred to look like the civilized, nonviolent member of the duo whenever he could, and preferred weaponry that was easily concealed.

Grond was the precise opposite. He wore his weapons openly and obviously–Angela attached to his back, heavy projectile pistols hanging on both hips, and a nasty-looking blade strapped to each of his forearms, plus well-used spiked gladiator's gloves on each of his hands. He wore a breechclout and a thermal utilicloak with the hood up and next to nothing else, displaying his neck-to-toe tattoos and the majority of his scars. His skin glistened with oils and a quick-healing agent that would work on minor cuts and abrasions and keep larger wounds from getting infected too quickly.

Brazel's clothes said *come, talk with us, we are reasonable people*. Grond's said *don't piss us off, and if you do, don't bother trying to run*. The halfogre held the box under one arm, eventually setting it at his feet to keep both his hands free.

"How long?" Grond said.

"Ten minutes, if they're on time," Brazel responded. "Namey, go on alert."

The ship chirped an acknowledgment and shifted to full active-sensor status. Brazel and Grond both wore contact lenses that let the ship display information to them when they needed it, and their fields of vision both filled with data, as the *Nameless* identified a number of sentients within a few hundred meters and indicated them.

There were five people striding toward their docking bay. Four were dwarves. The fifth was an elf.

Brazel and Grond exchanged a look, and Grond pulled Angela off his back, snapping the bow into attack position. *An elf?* Elves were bad news. The vast majority of them were Benevolence, and those that weren't were generally *trouble*.

"Arm every piece of exterior weaponry you have, Namey," Grond subvocalized to the boat. "And prep the engines to get the hell out of here quick if we need to." Namey, uncharacteristically quiet, sent a simple acknowledgment. Grond heard and felt the engines and guns power up behind him.

"Steady," Brazel said. "This is just a drop. Nobody panic."

"I don't panic," Grond said. "But I don't fuck around either."

A tone sounded, indicating someone trying to enter their docking bay. Grond approved the request and the gate slid open, revealing their visitors. Two of the four dwarves were female, one obviously the boss and the other just as obviously hired muscle. The other two were male porters, their beards trimmed nearly to nonexistence, dressed in long tunics and carrying no weapons. The elf was slender, sharp-pointed ears framing a bald scalp, wearing some sort of synthetic armor and carrying an electroblade and a shock stick. Xe had two long knives on xir forearms and a long rifle strapped to xir back as well.

Mercenary? Grond thought. Yeah, this was gonna be trouble. The elf looked familiar, somehow, but he couldn't place xir right away. Elves tended to look alike a lot of the time anyway, although the shaved scalp was certainly distinctive.

"You're Brazel and Grond," the boss dwarf said. Her voice sounded like half a parsec of asteroids.

"We are," Brazel said. "And you're Smashes-the-Stars, I take it."

The dwarf nodded. "This is Whisper-on-the-Waters," she said, indicating the other female dwarf. It was unsurprising that she hadn't bothered to introduce the males, but her lack of mentioning the elf was curious. "You have something that belongs to us?"

"We have something *for* you," Brazel corrected. "I don't know that it's your property yet."

"Semantics," the dwarf said, shaking her head. "Do you have it?"

"Here," Brazel said, gesturing at the box. Grond shoved it with his foot and the males moved to pick it up, grunting at the effort.

Both the dwarves instantly looked suspicious. The elf looked bored.

"What?" Brazel asked.

"What sort of shit is this?" Smashes-the-Stars said. She gestured angrily at the males, who put the crate back on the ground, then pulled Grond's lid off.

"That's your package," Brazel said. "The crate got a bit banged up in transit. You may have heard already that you dumped us into a *war zone.*"

"Did the war zone make the *box heavier?*" the dwarf snapped. "There's supposed to be some data chips and a couple of guns in here. Nothing that should make two grown male dwarves *grunt* when they pick it up. What are you two trying to pull?"

Fuck, Grond thought. He adjusted his stance slightly, trying to decide who to shoot first. The two dwarves who counted were visibly angry. The males were obviously looking for somewhere to hide. The elf still looked unconcerned.

"Look a little bit more closely. The guns and chips are in there. Plus one more thing. Everything in the box is what was in there when we robbed the train," Brazel said. "It was painted with a bunch of warnings, just like you said. It was the right size. We just got hired to steal the thing and bring it to you."

"That sounds like an excuse to me," Whisper-on-the-Waters said. Her hands were getting alarmingly close to her guns.

"You don't want to touch those," Grond growled. The elf, reacting for the first time, made eye contact with him, xir lips drawing back slightly. Xir teeth were prominent, ivory-white, and sharpened.

Grond decided to shoot the elf first ... and possibly second and third as well. "Let's keep this friendly," he said.

Smashes-the-Stars reached into her coat, producing a pair of goggles much like the ones Grond had worn. She put them on and stared at the ruins of the box.

"Ah, damn," she said. "They're not lying." She pulled the statue out of the box. "This is twice as heavy as it ought to be. What the hell's it doing in here?"

"I don't like it," said Whisper-on-the-Waters. "No reason for that to be in there. Could mean that they're on to us."

"*Who's* on to us, and who is *us?*" Brazel asked.

"They're Malevolence," Grond said.

"We are the *Noble Opposition,*" Smashes-the-Stars said. "But ... yes, we are. Any idea what this thing is?"

"No idea," Brazel said. "We were wondering the same thing."

"So you admit opening the box," the dwarf said.

"We just *said* that. We admit the box being *busted,*" Brazel snapped. "I told you that. But what you're seeing there is *everything* that was in it."

The elf took the statue from the box, peering at it carefully. Xe ignored the guns and the datachips altogether.

"Do you know what that is?" said Smashes-the-Stars.

The elf shook xir head, then pointed at Brazel and Grond, turning xir hand in a circle at the wrist and then pointing at the sky.

"What? No," Smashes-the-Stars said. "That wasn't the plan."

The elf turned and stared, repeating the gesture. "We go. Now." Xir voice was deep, almost as rough as the dwarf's.

Smashes-the-Stars spent a few moments staring at Brazel. The gnome stood his ground, not breaking eye contact.

"Well, if the elf says you're coming with us, you're coming with us. We have to go."

"Not without paying us," Brazel said.

"I wasn't paying you anyway," Smashes-the-Stars said. "That's happening through a third party. You should have known that already."

Right, Brazel thought.

"But I'm not authorizing payment right now anyway, because this isn't what we hired you to steal," she continued.

"Fuck that," Brazel said. "You said to steal a *marked wooden crate*. That marked wooden crate is in pieces all over the ground in front of you. That was our end of the deal. There was nothing anywhere about verifying the contents. There's something extra in there. So *what?*"

The dwarf waved one hand, dismissing Brazel's arguments, tugging on her beard with the other in what looked like an unconscious stress gesture.

"We don't have time for this. When I said *we* had to go I meant *all* of us. The job didn't go like it was supposed to and the agent never told us something had gone wrong, so we have to assume this entire job is blown. You want to get paid? You need to come along until we figure out what happened."

Brazel glanced at Grond, reading his partner's mind. This *was* what they'd wanted, technically. It was just more of the dwarves' idea than they'd wanted it to be. Meeting higher-ups in the Malevolence hierarchy was probably going to mean more jobs and more money, at least if it didn't involve being immediately killed.

"I'm not leaving my ship," Brazel said.

The dwarf opened his mouth to protest and closed it again when the elf laid a hand on her shoulder. The two shared a long look, with neither speaking. She shook her head. "Fine. But the elf's going with you. Xe knows where to go."

Brazel and Grond exchanged a glance. Grond's look said *I don't like this at all*. Brazel's said *I like this even less than that*.

"Elf have a name?" Brazel said.

"No," Smashes-the-Stars said. "At least not that you get to hear yet. You can just call xir the elf until you earn a name."

The elf crouched over the statue, brushing it with one hand. Xe started murmuring under xir breath, and a bright blue glow extended from xir hand, encompassing the statue entirely.

Grond took two steps back and drew Angela's bowstring. Brazel suddenly had guns in both hands: One trained on the elf, the other on Whisper-on-the-Waters. Grond could hear Namey's external guns whirring into position.

"The elf's Benevolence," Brazel said. "Xe just cast a *fucking spell.*"

"Calm the *fuck down*," Smashes-the-Stars said. "Yeah. Xe cast a spell. Not on *you*. Xe just put that fucking thing you brought us into *stasis*. If it's sending a signal–even if it's somehow sending one you can't detect–it can hardly keep doing it when the entire device is *frozen*, now, can it?"

This was a little difficult to argue with, given that the statue *was* actually sending out a signal.

"Braze, can you still hear it?"

Brazel's ears swiveled toward the statue. Obligingly, a deep silence fell over the spaceport.

"Not a thing," he said. "The elf stays in a berth in the cargo bay. *Locked*."

The elf stood up. "You don't really think a locked door will hold me."

"Probably not," Brazel said. "But you're going to stay in there anyway. And no more fucking magic."

The elf nodded, picking the statue up. Xe nodded at the males, who scurried to pick up everything else.

"We should go now," Smashes-the-Stars said. "The elf will give you coordinates once we're both a few hours of tunnelspace away. Pick a direction, but I wouldn't travel back toward home."

"Comforting," Brazel said.

The elf strode onto the *Nameless* as if xe owned it, the statue balanced on one hip as xe walked.

"We'll explain later," Smashes-the-Stars said, backing toward the bay exit. "Right now we need to leave." She turned on one heel and all but ran out of the bay, Whisper-on-the-Waters following. The male dwarves scurried to pick up the crate and hurried after her.

"I guess we're done here, then," Grond said.

"Sounds like," Brazel said. "Why isn't anything ever easy?"

"Because you'd be bored to death if it was," Grond answered. "Let's take their advice and get the hell out of here. I feel the need to be standing on something with a proper name."

⊁⦉⊡⦊⊰

INTERLUDE 1

Then

He was awakened by the sound of his mother's voice. The words were indistinct—hushed, and on the other side of a wall—but the tone came through clearly. Pain, with no small amount of anger behind it, poorly controlled. The young ogre rolled out of bed, stretching his arm underneath the frame to recover his spear. The weapon had been his since he'd been large enough to hold it and he had been punished more than once for allowing it to be out of his immediate sight.

He stretched, working the kinks of the night's sleep out of his muscles, listening intently to the conversation in the other room. He heard his father's voice, and a third who he did not recognize. It was not, he realized, the voice of an ogre. There was a musicality to the voice, a cultured affectation that was entirely unlike any of the adults his family shared a housing complex with on Tromaxis. There was a deep chill to the air, and he fought off the urge to bury himself among the pile of rags and furs he used as bedding again. *The heaters got knocked offline again*, he thought. Tromaxis was barely above freezing on its warmest day, being too far from its sun to gain any real benefit from it. And it was not summer. His breath was visible, if just barely. He would have to help his father with repairs again. He did not look forward to the chore.

But he was an ogre, and while he was far from coming into his growth, standing barely taller than a gnome, he was to be a warrior. Ogre warriors did not complain about cold no matter how much their skin pebbled in the temperature. He looked around his room, noting that his brothers and sisters were gone. He had slept through their morning movements, somehow. He was surprised he had been allowed to stay in bed.

He left his room, entering their common room. His parents and his siblings were all there already, along with one person he didn't recognize. A human or an elf, he thought. He had never seen anyone of either species. This person looked like an elf, but he was ... well, he was a *he*, and elves were supposed to be genderless. The stranger looked wealthy, wearing fine clothes and with glittering beads worked into his hair. He saw the boy as he entered the room, and raised an eyebrow, looking at him like one might look at livestock.

The young ogre rapped his spear once on the floor, letting his family know he had entered the room. He had not yet reached his nameday and as such was not supposed to speak in the presence of strangers. Everyone turned to look at him. One of his sisters choked back a sob.

His father had his guns with him, a pair of antique pistols. *What is happening?*

"Twenty-seven," the elf said. "He is less robust than you'd described."

The look of sudden rage on his father's face was unmistakable, and several sets of eyes in the room began to glow red. The elf was unperturbed.

"There are other families," he said. "Families with fewer mouths to feed, and better reasons to leave this frozen wasteland behind. The decision is yours to make, but make it now. Twenty-seven."

His father and mother exchanged a look. Everyone else in the room stared at their feet.

"Come, boy," his father rumbled. The red was gone from his eyes. He reached out a large hand, taking the spear from the confused youth.

And with two swift movements, broke it twice over his knee.

There were gasps from his brothers and sisters. The young ogre made no sound, his eyes wide and shocked.

"This is Bountiful," his father said. "You are his now. We reject you."

Bountiful gestured.

"Time to go, boy," he said. And then, to his parents: "What is his name?"

"He has no name," his father said. "He has not reached his nameday yet. And now he never will. You may name him yourself, if you like."

The door opened, and another ogre entered the room. This one was clearly a warrior, his body slabs of hard muscle held together by sinews and scars. He was in the prime of his might, and was larger even than the boy's father. He carried a gun at his hip and an enormous sword on his back.

"K'Shorr," Bountiful said. "Our negotiation is concluded. Pay these ... *people* their agreed-upon price, and bring the boy with you. He will need a name." The elf swept from the room, his clothes flowing around him.

"How much?" K'Shorr said.

"Thirty," his father said.

Without a word, K'Shorr drew his gun and shot him in the knee. The ogre fell heavily to the floor, screaming from the pain. The boy, numb, made no move.

If I still had my spear, I could fight.

His brothers and sisters leapt to their feet, roaring, and his mother rushed to his father's side.

No.

None of these people were his family any more. He had been *sold*.

K'Shorr grabbed one of his brothers, twisting his arm painfully behind his back and throwing him into a corner of the room. He managed to do it without taking his gun off the boy's father.

"Nothing stupid, now," he said. "Papa just tried to lie to me, so he earned that. I was *just outside the room*, you morons. Be glad I left him a fucking leg."

He held up a pouch, shaking it to show it was full of coin. He dropped it on the floor. It landed with a thud.

"C'mon, kid," he said. "Don't make me take you. Your family just put me into a bad mood."

The boy walked to K'Shorr's side. He spoke no word to his former family. Ogres before their nameday were not to speak in the presence of strangers, and he had nothing but strangers left in the world any longer.

"Pleasure doing business," the ogre said. He took both of his father's guns and then ushered the boy out of the room.

Bountiful remained in the hallway.

"I had hoped you would not have to injure anyone," the elf said placidly. He turned to leave, walking swiftly through the corridor outside the private apartments.

"These icecube-dwellers don't know what's good for them," K'Shorr answered. "One of them made bad decisions."

"And you paid them every cent of what they were owed, as I told you," Bountiful said.

"Sure," K'Shorr said. "Less an ammo fee, maybe. And the guns were just a bonus."

Bountiful sighed heavily.

"How long until his nameday?"

K'Shorr looked him over carefully. "Dunno. He looks pretty close."

"Name him, then," the elf said. "I have little patience with these ogrish rituals, and we have acquired too many today to call him *the boy*."

K'Shorr stopped, grabbing him by the chin and staring into his eyes.

"You're a tough one, aren't you? Or you're gonna be. Not a tear from you in there, even when I shot your dad. You did better than your brothers and sisters. You need a warrior's name. Something short."

The young ogre did not speak. This person was not family.

K'Shorr looked at Bountiful.

"Call him Grond," he said.

⊁⟨⊞⟩⊀

NINE

The elf had already ensconced xirself in a berth, sitting cross-legged on the floor with xir eyes closed. The door to the berth was wide open, the contents inside rearranged to provide room to sit. The door had been locked when they'd walked off the ship.

Xe had maybe a minute or two, Grond thought. Whoever the elf was, xe was impressive.

"Namey, head ... hell, head *somewhere*. Head for ogrespace, but nowhere in particular," Brazel said.

"What about Kratuul?" Grond suggested.

Brazel groaned. Kratuul was a humid jungle toilet of a planet and one of his least favorite places.

"Kratuul's on the border," Brazel said. "Too close to gnomespace. I want something more central."

COURSE SET, Namey said, and Brazel felt the *Nameless* lifting off from the port.

"Do your best to avoid anything else that flies, too," Brazel said. "Don't be too obvious about it, but keep your distance from everybody."

UNDERSTOOD, the boat replied. FLY CASUAL. ANY INSTRUCTIONS ABOUT OUR PASSENGER?

"None that aren't obvious," Brazel said. "I suspect the elf's going to do what xe wants–I'm locking xir back in the berth anyway. If anything at all happens out of the ordinary, let us know." The gnome paused for a moment, thinking. "I'm going to get some sleep. Smashes-the-Stars as much as told us we had four or five hours of inactivity headed our way. May as well take advantage of it."

"May want to let Rhundi know the schedule's changed," Grond said.

"That too," the gnome agreed, heading to his quarters.

"So how bad is it?" was how his wife started the conversation.

"Complicated," Brazel said. "The short version: We've got a passenger on board. An elf. Who locked xirself in one of the cargo holds without being asked to. Cast a spell on that statue, so xe may be Benevolence. Or, and this is a weird position to be in, we could *hope* xe's Malevolence. And Namey's headed to ogrespace right now, but that's not our final destination. Go ahead, ask me what our final destination is."

"You don't know what your final destination is, do you?"

"Your keen insight is the reason I married you," Brazel said.

"Also, pregnant," Rhundi added.

"We didn't know that yet," Brazel said.

"I did."

"*I* didn't, which means *we* didn't. Shuddup."

"You may as well start with what happened."

"Right." Brazel filled Rhundi in on the events of the last several hours.

"I'm not terribly happy about any of that," she said.

"Neither are we," Brazel said, "but if you can see where we had a better choice, I'd love to hear it."

"You didn't," she said. "Well, okay, I can probably count on the two of you and the ship to have won a firefight against two dwarves, a couple of porters and the elf, but that burns some contacts I don't really want burned and the choice you made is probably better."

"I didn't even bother arguing about it," Brazel said. "Any updates on your end at all?"

"Not much," Rhundi said. "Irtuus-bon is throwing everything he can at the data. So far, no luck. And Haakoro's behaving. He went out and got himself cleaned up but other than that he's holed up in his room watching videos and listening to music and ordering a lot of food." She paused, and Brazel could hear a smile in her voice. "A *lot* of food. He should be three times his size."

"So nothing's changed."

"Well, I do have *something* interesting for you. I talked with him a bit about where he got the encrypted data and the statue from. You won't believe the story he told me."

"Do tell," Brazel said.

"Well, apparently he was approached by a female halfogre who sold him the statue and the data. She didn't tell him what either of them were, but said that they'd be well worth his money once everything was decrypted. He doesn't know what either of them are, though. And he's still insisting he's lost contact with his handlers."

Brazel raised an eye.

"That's what he said? Really?"

"That's what he said," Rhundi confirmed.

"I have some issues with that story," Brazel said.

"As do I," Rhundi said. "So right now we really don't know what we're dealing with. Go ahead and leave the statue where it was and see how the Mals react. But don't mention the extra data without a good reason unless Irtuus-bon gets back to me with something."

"Got it," Brazel said.

"You know what clan the elf's with?"

"I'm guessing unaffiliated," he responded. "Renegade, probably. Xe knows at least a little bit of magic and clearly wants to be thought of as extremely dangerous. Don't really know anything, though. Right now xe's said a grand total of maybe one sentence to us. We don't even have a *name*, so clan information isn't gonna be forthcoming anytime soon. Nobody disagreed when Grond said they were Mals. I haven't had much dealing with them since that thing with Shocks-the-Mountains, but none of them survived that. I don't see any reason why they'd be mad at us."

"I'll get Irtuus-bon digging into the elf," Rhundi said. "You never know, xe might be a known associate of somebody or another. Keep me posted if you're able to find out anything else."

"Always," Brazel said. "Tell the kids I remember all their names." He cut the connection.

Grond considered returning to his quarters, then decided not to, remaining in the bay with the elf instead. He couldn't shake the feeling that he knew xir from somewhere, and he had not known many elves in his life. Placing this one should not have been that complicated.

"You were very young, when last I saw you," the elf said.

"Mind-reading, too?"

The elf opened xir eyes, staring at him. "Intuition. You presumably have many things you could be doing, and the gnome told you that you were facing several hours of down time. Yet you stand here, staring at me, instead of attending to your tasks. Sexual attraction seems unlikely, given who we are. I can only believe you are struggling to recall where you have met me."

Grond nodded, conceding the truth of what the elf was saying. "How young?"

"Early adolescent," xe said. "I was present for some of your training. If I remember correctly, your master tried to sell you to me."

"And you remember me from that?"

"I forget very little," xe said. "But I might not have remembered you, were it not for some of the scars. K'Shorr's brand remains on your shoulder, and I saw you receive the wound across your right collarbone."

"K'Shorr was always strict about keeping my guard up," Grond said, running a finger over the scar. The scar was actually one of his less prominent ones. It had been inflicted with a tiny blade, but the blade had been treated with a substance that slowed healing. K'Shorr had always liked for his trainees to remember their mistakes. "He didn't own me, though. That was Barren. He just hired K'Shorr to do the training. Barren never was much of a fighter."

The elf raised an eyebrow. "Barren is an elvish name."

"Yeah. And, yeah, *he*. Not *xe*." Gender was looked upon with distaste by most elves, almost as if it were a birth defect.

"He ... uh ... wasn't thought of well by elf society for most of the time I knew him. There was a reason he was working the pits and the slave markets, I guess. What were *you* doing there?"

"I was in training myself," the elf said. "I'd been sent to kill K'Shorr."

"But you didn't," Grond said. "And you lived through failing to kill him, which makes me doubt the entire story."

"I was being trained to think for myself," xe replied. "I determined that K'Shorr did not need killing and did not kill him. As it turned out, that was the correct decision for me to make. Had I attempted to kill K'Shorr, there would have been consequences."

"Consequences."

"He would likely have killed me in the attempt, and my own masters would have finished the job if he had been unsuccessful."

"K'Shorr was a pretty tough son of a bitch," Grond said. "*Is*, I guess. I assume he's still alive."

"How did you come to escape them? I do not imagine K'Shorr would have been interested in freeing you."

"You'd be surprised," Grond said. "Point is I don't have to deal with him anymore."

"And here we are," the elf said.

"Here we are," Grond agreed.

The elf rose to xir feet in a single liquid motion.

"Let us see how well you were trained," xe said.

"Excuse me?" Grond said.

"I want to spar," xe replied. "I have just as much time to fill as you do, and sparring is a better use of my time than meditation. You may set the rules. Hand-to-hand only, or shall we use weapons?"

"Who says I even want to?"

"The look on your face says so," the elf said. "And you had decided to shoot me first during the standoff, despite the fact that I had drawn no weapon at all. Do not bother to deny it. Your body language was clear enough. Let us see how you would have done." Xe crouched, opening the door to the berth.

"Weapons seem unfair," he said. "I've already got enough of a reach advantage as is, and I don't want to have to clean blood out of Namey's cargo bay."

"Bravado," the elf responded. "Back it up." And xe leapt at Grond without another word. He ducked, the elf sailing over his head and landing lightly on xir feet. He unclipped the cloak at his neck, dropping it to the floor, then put his weapons down next to it. The elf had left all of xir visible weapons in the berth. He rolled his head around his shoulders, loosening his muscles.

"More bravado," the elf said.

"Worked in the pits just fine," Grond responded. The two paced around each other, looking for an opening. Grond could tell in moments that he had his work cut out for him. Whoever this elf was, xe was faster than him, smaller, and well-trained. Grond had never been wonderful at sparring as a practice. He'd been trained to kill and kill quickly in a fight and had never forgotten that lesson. It made dialing back to fight in a nonlethal manner more difficult than it should have been.

The elf charged in, feinting at his face then swinging a leg low to try to sweep Grond off his feet. Grond let xir do it. The foot glanced off his shin without budging him. He swiped at xir ankle with a hand but the elf danced out of the way.

"I'm not easy to knock down," he said.

"I see that," xe said, and dove for his face again. He slid out of the way, landing a blow on the elf's abdomen as xe flew past him. Xe rolled to xir feet this time, once again charging in swinging. The next few moments were a flurry of blows from both of them, Grond being struck by as many swings as he managed to block and only getting one good hit on his opponent. The elf was *fast*. And those punches *hurt*, especially for someone xir size. Grond probably had a 70 centimeter height advantage and was quite possibly *three times* xir weight. It didn't seem to matter much.

Use the height. He stopped focusing on blocking attacks and trapped one of the elf's arms against his body instead, landing a solid hit into xir ribs and then wrapping a hand around a knee and lifting the elf entirely off the ground. He hurled xir against the nearest wall. Amazingly, the elf twisted in midair and managed to hit the wall feet-first, launching xirself back at Grond even faster.

It was the wrong move. Grond had been leapt at enough times during the fight, and he was ready this time. He caught the elf around the neck with both hands, slamming xir into the ground.

"Dead," he said. "That's a broken neck if we're fighting for real."

The elf only grinned. Grond felt something at both his kidneys. He looked down. Xe had daggers in each hand, one positioned on each side of him.

"Cheater," he said, standing up.

"Being righteous would not have kept you alive," xe said.

"K'Shorr always did think I should cheat more often. But who knows if the fight would even have lasted *that* long if it was for real," Grond said. "I don't spar very often."

The elf bowed. "Perhaps next time we will try blades. Dulled, of course. I think I will return to my meditation now. I will alert your partner when it is time to head to our rendezvous point."

Grond nodded, not saying anything. This was not at all how he had expected his day to go. And, worse, he had the distinct suspicion that the elf had been holding back. Then again, so had he.

TEN

Namey woke Brazel up a few hours later. THE ELF IS ASKING FOR YOU, he said. DEMANDING, ACTUALLY.

"I think that's kind of xir style," he said, rubbing sleep from his eyes. "I'm guessing we're about to be on our way." He stood up and stretched, his fur rippling. An experimental sniff revealed that he probably needed a shower, something he didn't have time or facilities for at the moment. *I should be back at Arradon in a hot bath by now*, he thought.

"Tell *the elf* I'll be there in a few minutes," he said. "Xe's perfectly free to just tell you the coordinates we're traveling to. They don't need to be relayed through me."

ACKNOWLEDGED.

Brazel blinked. The *Nameless* was being surprisingly polite lately. He and Grond threatened to reprogram Namey at least once every few days. He was comfortable with the ship being a sarcastic, lippy asshole at times but he didn't remember ever authorizing *moody*.

COORDINATES RECEIVED. WE ARE RETURNING TO DWARFSPACE, NEARER TO BENEVOLENCE-CONTROLLED SPACE THAN YOU ARE GENERALLY COMFORTABLE WITH. SHALL I ENGAGE?

"Don't see that we have much of a choice," Brazel said. "But be careful."

I WILL DO MY BEST TO NOT BE BLOWN TO PIECES.

There's my boat, he thought. He thought about his clothes for a few minutes, eventually choosing comfort over tactical usefulness. He was pretty sure he wasn't going to have to shoot anything anytime soon, so there was no reason to dress in clothing he could conceal guns in. *If the elf was going to start trouble we would have it already,* he thought.

A few minutes later he found the elf in the cargo bay.

"I felt the ship shift into tunnelspace, so you gave up the coordinates. Was there something else you needed to talk to me about?"

The elf nodded. "There was. But I will wait for your partner. I dislike repeating myself."

"I'm here," Grond said, entering the bay. He was wearing his glasses, an affectation that meant he'd been reading in his quarters. Brazel had never been sure where Grond had managed to *find* halfogre-sized dumbglasses. Every pair he'd ever seen was live in some way or another. Grond's were actual glass in polymer frames.

"You said that you thought I was Malevolence. Why?"

"It's not obvious?" Grond asked.

"Magic is not a sign of the Noble Opposition," the elf said.

"No, it's a sign of *Benevolence,* and since we haven't been tracked and killed yet, it means you're probably a renegade. Which means you'd have headed straight *to* the Malevolence if you have any sense at all. I've never met or heard of a renegade magic user. They're *all* connected to Benevolence one way or another. If you were never Benevolence, whoever taught you was."

"There are other ways," the elf replied, "but I will not speak of them now. Especially since, regardless of your reasons, you are *correct.* We are en route to a ... *Malevolence* headquarters, a spaceport called Roashan. You need to understand: its location is a closely guarded secret. Roashan's *existence* is a closely guarded secret. You will never leave if it is determined that your discretion cannot be counted upon."

"I appreciate you feeding the coordinates into my ship *before* telling me that, then," Brazel said. "But yeah, you're safe. I have no plan to inform the Benevolence where you are and no reason to discuss your existence *at all* with anyone else. The three of us have gotten exceptionally good at keeping our secrets to ourselves over the years."

The elf raised an eyebrow.

"I include my wife Rhundi, who no doubt already knows where we're headed. This is what happens when you don't bother telling me that something is supposed to be a secret."

"I see," the elf said. Xir face was unreadable. "I will assume your word binds her as well."

Brazel and Grond both burst into laughter. The elf merely raised an eyebrow.

"You have *clearly* not met my wife," Brazel said. "My word very much does *not* bind her. But she will agree on her own terms. I have no doubt of that."

The elf nodded. "That will have to be acceptable, then." Xe returned to xir berth, dropping into a cross-legged position and shutting xir eyes.

"Guess we're done, then?" Grond said.

"Guess so," Brazel said.

The coordinates were in the middle of nowhere, even for dwarfspace.

"There's nothing here," Brazel said. "The nearest *star* is half a light year away. Nothing orbits this far out, does it?"

THE NEAREST PLANETARY-MASS OBJECT IS A CONSIDERABLE DISTANCE FROM HERE, Namey confirmed. WE WOULD MOST LIKELY WANT TO REENTER TUNNELSPACE IN ORDER TO REACH IT.

"There had better not be another teleporter coming," Grond said from his copilot's chair in his quarters. The last time they'd been directed to mystery coordinates in the middle of nowhere, that had been what they had found, and neither of them had terribly enjoyed the experience of teleportation.

LONG-RANGE SENSORS HAVE DETECTED A SPACE STATION, Namey said. WE ARE BEING HAILED AND PROVIDED WITH DOCKING CODES ALREADY.

"A station? Out here?"

"Makes sense," Grond said. "If you're trying to hide the damn place, putting it *nowhere* is a good way to do that."

"Bringing us in, then," Brazel said. "Namey, ask the elf if there's anything we need to know."

"You may wish to disable your weapons," the elf replied, from right behind Brazel. The gnome nearly leapt out of his seat.

ELF, BRAZEL WISHES TO KNOW IF THERE IS ANYTHING THAT HE NEEDS TO KNOW. BRAZEL, THE ELF SAYS WE MAY WISH TO DISABLE OUR WEAPONS. I RECOMMEND AGAINST THIS COURSE OF ACTION.

"Shut up, boat," Brazel replied. "And do what xe says. Follow the coordinates. No sudden movements."

ACKNOWLEDGED.

Within a few moments, the space station was visible on the holoscreen. Calling it a "space station" seemed somehow inadequate–Roashan appeared to be several different stations, possibly created by several different cultures, that had all been crudely mashed, cobbled, jury-rigged and bolted together, occasionally with no regard for common gravity. The overall result was disc-shaped, mostly, and perhaps a kilometer wide. There were a fair number of other ships coming and going, and what looked like a ring network of long-range sensors extending another few kilometers outward.

The station was built around what appeared to be the largest ship drive Brazel had ever seen.

"The whole thing can handle tunnelspace," the elf said. "If you scanned as hostile it would be gone by now."

"Impressive," Brazel said. "And too big to be kept out of tunnelspace by a blockship, I'm guessing."

"Correct," xe replied. "Once it gets moving it's almost impossible for *anything* to stop it. The Benevolence found us once and brought *six* blockships with them. Not enough."

"You know that means next time they'll bring two dozen," Brazel replied. "And those two dozen will all be a generation beyond the first six they brought."

"We've upgraded since then, too," xe said.

Brazel nodded. "I hope it's good enough. What happens when we dock?"

"Land," xe said. "There's a force shield to pass through into the dock. You don't have to connect to an airlock. I'm going away for a while. You can either take temporary quarters on Roashan or wait on the *Nameless* until someone is able to meet with you and discuss what happens next."

"Refueling would be nice, too," Brazel said.

"That will be arranged."

"This is interesting," the gnome continued. "I had the idea when you first got on the ship that we were basically being kidnapped. You're acting like we're guests now."

The elf smiled, showing xir teeth, which completely ruined the gesture. "You'll find that for the next few days or so the two are more or less the same thing. I suggest thinking of yourself as a guest, as it will prove less stressful. You're not going anywhere anytime soon one way or another."

"Charming," Grond said over the comm. "We'll stay on the boat."

"As you wish," the elf said.

ELEVEN

Sirrys ban Irtuus bon Alaamac sat at the center of a digital web. He was within reach of a dozen fixed displays and four different holocomms, and was monitoring multiple streams of news, gossip, innuendo and the occasional outright lie from multiple planets and artificial habitats across the galaxy, simultaneously.

Sirrys ban Irtuus bon Alaamac was a troll.   He had an exceptionally long reach, when he wanted to.

A corner of one of the displays flashed, indicating that something had hit a keyword.   Irtuus-bon elongated an arm and brought the monitor closer, touching one of the feeds to bring it to fullscreen.   He listened for a moment, then touched an onscreen icon that recorded the entire feed for two hours in either direction.

He turned and tapped the comm on his desk console.

"This is Gorrim," a deep gnomish voice said.

"I need Rhundi," Irtuus-bon said.

"She is busy," Gorrim said.   "She said you were to leave a message if you called." He sounded bored. This was not the first time Irtuus-bon had begun a conversation with those exact three words.

"She is about to be much busier," Irtuus-bon said.   "What you have been told does not matter. It is essential that she speak with me at this time."

"You said that last time," the gnome said. "You were incorrect. Why should I assume what you want is important enough to interrupt her now?"

"You shall have to trust me," the troll said. "This information is for the mistress only."

"Sorry, Irtuus-bon," Gorrim said. "I'll make sure she hears you wanted her as soon as she's available."

He cut the connection.

Irtuus-bon's body underwent a sudden radical shape change, his limbs and torso shortening, transforming him into a squat figure not much different in height from, but much wider than, an average gnome. He stared at his desk console, a mixture of upset and astonishment on his face, then shook his head as if to clear cobwebs. He stood up from his chair and reassumed his tallest shape, removing a chip from the side of the monitor and quickly striding from the room.

He had previously occupied a suite of rooms far below Rhundi's offices, but soon after discovering what he was doing with them she had had him moved. His new quarters were much more opulent and—more important to him—much more functional in his capacity as the new director of Rhundi's intelligence operation. They were located much closer to the surface but far enough away from Rhundi to discourage him from visiting in person too often. Rhundi also had quite deliberately put him in a space entirely surrounded by rooms being used for other things, a move designed to make it impossible for him to enlarge his space. When she had originally stumbled upon his surveillance operation he had tunneled through a wall and expanded into the cave system behind his original suite without telling anyone. The rules were clear now: if he needed more room, he was to discuss it with Rhundi, not attempt to find or take it himself.

Well, he was going to have a discussion with Rhundi one way or another, it seemed. He grew to the tallest height he could manage and still avoid scraping his head on ceilings—which were fairly high, since Rhundi's resort featured a halfogre as one of its most prominent residents and was scaled to accommodate both bigs and what the bigs called "tinies." Adopting what he hoped was a look of high aggravation (Irtuus-bon had never been great with social cues) he left his quarters and headed for Rhundi's office.

A moment later, he returned to his quarters, making certain that all of his security measures had properly engaged behind him. They had. He triple-checked them again anyway and then turned on his heel and strode off again, taking full advantage of his elongated legs and hoping a fierce scowl would keep the staff and the other guests out of his way. It worked well. It was *very* rare for Sirrys ban Irtuus bon Alaamac to actually leave his quarters. Much of the staff did not even know he was one of them and most of the guests had never seen a troll. One small gnomish child actually started crying as he fixed his gaze upon her. He spent a moment feeling bad about that and then continued on his way.

He made two wrong turns on the way to Rhundi's office. Once, embarrassed, he had to stop and ask one of the Corvix-clan goblins what the right way to go was. However, eventually he found his destination.

Rhundi's secretary Gorrim was sitting behind an oversized—for him, anyway—old-style desk in the lobby outside her office. The gnome's strawberry-colored fur rustled violently and he got to his feet. "I told you she was busy," he barked. His voice was just as deep in person.

"I told you that this was important," Irtuus-bon said.

"And I told you it didn't *matter*," Gorrim responded, putting himself in between Irtuus-bon and Rhundi's door. This was a brave, if somewhat pointless, gesture. Irtuus-bon in his current form was more than twice Gorrim's height. "You don't get to see her until she's interested in seeing you. I'm not losing my job over you getting spooked by something."

Irtuus-bon looked around the room, spotting a hook on the ceiling that a light fixture was suspended from. He unhooked the light fixture, setting it carefully on Gorrim's desk, then reached down and grabbed Gorrim by the back of his coat.

"Hey. HEY!" the gnome shrieked, losing all composure and a surprising amount of the bass in his voice. He continued to protest and try to twist out of Irtuus-bon's grip as the troll lifted him high off the ground and hooked him to the ceiling by his belt.

"I will free you when I emerge, if you have not managed to do so yourself," Irtuus-bon said, trying to sound reasonable. "I apologize for your inconvenience."

"SECURITY!" Gorrim bellowed.

Irtuus-bon winced.   He hadn't thought this through properly. Security getting involved could be troublesome, and if Rhundi's office was not properly soundproofed...

The door between the lobby and the office slammed open.

"Put. Him. The fuck down. *Now.*"

She was pointing a gun at him. It seemed like Rhundi was *always* pointing a gun at him.   The fierce look on her face contrasted oddly with the pleasant green color she'd highlighted her fur with. He unhooked the gnome from the ceiling and put him back in his chair, then reattached the light fixture. He then collapsed back into his smallest, widest size.

"Sirrys is sorry," he said. "But the gnome would not let us see you. We have news. *Important* news. And he would not listen!"

Rhundi waved the troll off, holstering the gun and walking over to her secretary.

"You're okay?"

Gorrim was trying his best to keep his fur flat and calm, and was brushing dust and ceiling plaster off of his clothes. "I'll be fine. Just embarrassed."

"Next time shoot him," Rhundi said.   "Let him in afterwards, but shoot him."

"I want that in writing," Gorrim replied, sounding somewhat incredulous.

"Pull the security footage," she said. "That's as close as you're going to get."

Gorrim's eyes widened.   "Why isn't security here yet? Shouldn't this room be full of angry strong people by now?"

Rhundi laughed. "You yell 'security' in my office, and it notifies *me*," she said. "Anything I can't handle would probably have killed you before more than a syllable of that word got out of your mouth. Hit the panic button under your desk if I'm not around, remember?"

The gnome sighed and lowered his head. "My apologies, mistress."

"You're forgiven," Rhundi responded.   "But seriously. Next time just shoot him. Anywhere but the head. He's harder to fix if you shoot him in the head."

"I don't want to be shot," Sirrys whined.

Gorrim nodded.

"You, in my office," Rhundi commanded, pointing at Sirrys. "And I want Irtuus-bon back. You'd better be a meter taller by the time I'm seated." She walked into her office in front of the troll. The troll turned to glance apologetically at Gorrim–a gesture that the gnome resolutely ignored–and stretched to his usual height upon entering the office.

"I am sure whatever this is about is very important to you," Rhundi said. "You have less than two minutes to explain why it is important to *me*."

Irtuus-bon didn't speak, holding out the chip instead. Rhundi took it, sliding it into a port on her desk console. The troll looked around the office. He had always approved of its functional design. Little was in the room that did not need to be there. There was even an overstuffed chair that had clearly been placed there for someone of his height.

He sat down in the large chair. "This footage was recorded today from one of the news sites in dwarfspace. It'll likely be everywhere soon if it's not suppressed, but I thought it should be brought to you as quickly as possible. Your ... *secretary* would not allow me to speak with you, so I brought it ... *personally*."

Rhundi nodded curtly, suddenly all business. The feed report was about the war on Khkk. It had been escalated from a minor regional conflict to a very nearly global struggle. Nearby planets were beginning to struggle with refugees which they could neither communicate with nor ethically turn away. And, most worrying: the Benevolence, generally not much of a presence in ogrespace, had announced that they were officially discussing the formation of a "delegation" to investigate and possibly quell the conflict.

"That's not good," Rhundi said. "And all of this started with a train robbery?"

"I suspect that we will discover it goes much deeper than that," Irtuus-bon said. "It may still be that ... your husband and his associate's presence at the war's flashpoint was a coincidence. But they stole an artifact, did they not? The Benevolence always have nested motives, always. We must be very careful in this."

"I need to bring them in, don't I?"

"I may wish to examine the artifact," Irtuus-bon said. "A detailed scan should be sufficient, however."

Rhundi nodded. "I think I'm glad Gorrim didn't shoot you. At least not this time. Stay up for a while. I'll get in touch with the boys and get back to you with the scan."

Irtuus-bon stood to leave, wondering why Rhundi had suggested he stay up. He almost never slept.

TWELVE

Grond grunted as he slammed the last pallet into place in the *Nameless'* cargo hold. He had felt the need for some exercise after a day of being pinned down in the ship, and the job of restocking and reorganizing the cargo bay had beckoned at him. It took longer to do it himself than it would with Brazel's help, but it was a bit more enjoyable and certainly a better workout.

WE HAVE VISITORS, Namey announced.

Grond didn't bother responding. The announcement had been over the internal speakers, not the comm, and Brazel would no doubt be asking questions himself.

DWARVES, the ship responded. ALL FEMALES. THERE ARE FIVE OF THEM. IF THEY ARE CARRYING ANY WEAPONS, THEY ARE CONCEALED. SHALL I LET THEM IN?

"Cargo bay or the front airlock?" Grond asked over the comm.

"Front airlock," Brazel responded, both to Grond and the ship. This was probably the right decision. The entrance was tighter and they had the dwarves in a bottleneck if the situation went south. Grond grabbed two of his pistols on his way to meet the dwarves, holstering them in what he hoped looked like a reasonably unthreatening manner.

Brazel met him at the front airlock. The gnome nodded at him and then opened both airlock doors.

Four of the dwarves were dressed in what looked like standard-issue guard gear. The fifth was Smashes-the-Stars. She was wearing comfortable-looking civilian clothes, much less formal than what she'd been wearing the last time they saw her. The guards remained by the outer airlock door, standing in a straight line. Smashes-the-Stars smoothed her beard and approached.

"Your presence has been requested," she said.

Brazel and Grond exchanged a look.

"By who?" Brazel asked.

"The person in charge of this place," Smashes-the-Stars said. "Concerning the artifact you found, your pay for the last job, and perhaps some additional work as well."

"Might want to discuss those things in a different order," Brazel said. Smashes-the-Stars only shrugged.

"Does the *person* in charge want us immediately or is our big date later tonight?" Brazel asked. The genderless nature of the word *person* almost guaranteed Smashes-the-Stars was talking about another elf.

"At your convenience," Smashes-the-Stars said. "But sooner is probably better, and we've detailed the guards to take you where you're going when you're ready."

"So they're just gonna stand out there until we decide to leave?" Grond said. "I might be hungry or need a shower. I might be hungry for a *long time*, actually."

"It was hoped that you would not choose to play games," Smashes-the-Stars said. "Strangers aren't generally treated well here. You will understand that we have earned the right to be a suspicious people. The guards are for your own safety."

"I think I could take the four of them in a fight," Grond said, grinning. "Not sure how well they can *keep me safe*." The guards, certainly within earshot, didn't react to the jab.

"They're also showing you where to go," Smashes-the-Stars said. "You saw what Roashan looks like from the outside. Finding your way around can be ... a bit challenging." She didn't quite smile, but something touched her eyes.

"Fine," Brazel said. "Give us fifteen minutes. I'm not dressed for *people in charge*."

"I am," Grond said. He was still dripping with sweat from working in the cargo hold.

"Go make some friends, then," Brazel said, waving toward the guards. "I'll be out in fifteen."

"Better bet on twenty," Grond responded.

For once, it only took twelve–and judging from Brazel's less-than-perfect coiffure when he emerged from the *Nameless*, Grond suspected that the delay had been mostly due to the gnome needing to arm himself properly. The dwarves, who didn't bother giving their names, left the hangar and led them through the station.

Roashan was ... *odd*. The impression that it gave from the outside–that of having been grafted together from several other stations and possibly a few vehicles as well–was not lessened by walking through it. They walked through corridors and wide-open spaces, cut through what looked to have been sleeping rooms at one point that had been rudely hacked into a hallway, and passed through a few airlocks that looked to be left permanently open. The artificial gravity switched directions at least three times during the twenty-minute walk.

This place would be absolute hell to invade, Grond thought. He was willing to bet that no floor plan of the station existed anywhere, and that the place was probably quite a bit more modular than it actually looked–invasion would have to come from several different points simultaneously, into total chaos, with small hallways and a near-infinite supply of locations for ambush.

Then again, under most circumstances the Benevolence would probably prefer to simply blow the place to bits. He knew Roashan was built to run away effectively but the elf had given no indication of how capable the place was of defending itself. *Hopefully well enough for us to get the hell away.*

The dwarves halted in front of a pair of ornate double doors that looked wildly out of place on a space station, even one as architecturally *diverse* as Roashan was. Nearly every other portal they'd passed through on the way here had been automatic and either pulled up or to the sides. These were actual mechanical doors that swung into the room and had to be opened with muscle power. Grond tried to recall the last time he'd seen them on anything that had to worry about maintaining atmospheric pressure and came up with nothing.

One of the dwarves actually *knocked* on the door.

"Weird," Brazel mumbled.

The doors swung inward. The room they led into had probably been some sort of common room in the past. It was dominated by a long table that was either covered with a convincing holo or actually made of wood. There was a portable holoprojector sitting in the middle of the table. The ceiling was transparent, featuring a view of the deep black outside and some of the traffic and satellites circling around Roashan.

There was an elf sitting at the head of the table. Xe looked elderly, with shoulder-length iron-gray hair, eyes of almost exactly the same color, and just a hint of wrinkles around xir eyes and lips. Xe wore a green robe embroidered with gold thread and a gold circlet set with a prominent green gem on xir head. There were multiple rings on both hands, with close-cut, even fingernails painted in gold and green. On either side of the elf sat a dwarf. One of the dwarves was Smashes-the-Stars. The other they didn't recognize.

The other elf–Grond was forced to think of xir as *their* elf–was standing at the first elf's shoulder.

Grond and Brazel split up, each heading to opposite sides of the table. Interestingly, the chairs they were heading for reshaped themselves as the two approached them. *Not regular wood, then,* Grond thought, settling himself into a chair that had grown more robust for him as Brazel's elongated its legs to let the gnome sit at the high table with some dignity remaining.

The statue was sitting on the table in front of the two elves. The rifles and datachips were nowhere to be seen.

"No one bothered to disarm us," Brazel said. "That is either a gesture of trust or an impressive level of arrogance. I was looking forward to seeing if you found everything."

The elf smiled, revealing ordinary, unsharpened teeth, a detail that Brazel found oddly comforting. "Consider it trust," xe said. "We do not believe you have any reason to resort to violence in this place. You have had ample opportunities to engage in it thus far and have not taken them."

Brazel nodded. Grond fought off the urge to start playing with a knife. He hadn't brought one with him, for starters, and asking to borrow one from either Brazel or one of the elves seemed a bit awkward.

"Introductions are in order, I believe," Brazel said. "You appear to have known our names for some time. We only know one of you, and that one is *not* the one who has slept on our ship."

The older elf nodded. "Smashes-the-Stars you know. The other is Smashes-the-Stars' clanmate Glow-of-Twilight. I am Overmorrow. You have already met my child, Asper. I understand that we owe you a debt of gratitude."

Brazel blinked. He had *heard* of Overmorrow. Elves frequently changed their names and this one was old enough to have done it a few times, but ...

He shook his head. If this elf was *the* Overmorrow he would worry about that later.

"You owe us a debt of *money*," Brazel said. "Gratitude is nice but doesn't spend as well."

"As you say," the elf said. "But you shall receive it anyway. We were expecting certain *specific items* to be delivered to us. This was not among them. I can only imagine how it came to be in that box and on that train." Xir voice was more pleasant than Asper's. Overmorrow almost sounded as if xe was singing rather than merely having a conversation.

"I may have some information on that," Brazel said.

"Please share," Overmorrow said.

"Your contact on Khkk–Haakoro, the young human who you hired to mark and package the weaponry for us–apparently was able to find some additional material he thought you would be interested in. Thus the statue. He claims that the statue was sold to him and that he put it in the box because he was unable to get back in touch with anyone and could not come up with another manner of reaching you."

Overmorrow grew still. "And how do *you* know this?"

"The statue emits a signal," Brazel said. "He was able to catch part of it and got incredibly lucky. We weren't expecting to be tailed back home and so we didn't take enough precautions to hide our trail. We caught him causing trouble on Arradon after following us back from Khkk. He is currently enjoying an enforced stay at my wife's resort."

"Our contact on Khkk was not a human," Overmorrow said.

Fascinating, Brazel thought.

"That's ... unexpected. I have no explanation, then," he said. "What *were* we supposed to steal for you?"

"Weaponry, and the plans for those weapons," Overmorrow said. "Which, indeed, you *have* here. The Khkk are surprisingly talented engineers. We have been aware for some time that the Benevolence were using them to produce some advanced weaponry, and wanted to know more about what was happening. At some point we lost contact with our people on Khkk. We have begun to fear that they are lost. I know nothing of this *Haakoro*. We would be very interested in speaking further with your ... *guest*."

Brazel considered various conversational options, ranging from *I'm sorry for your loss* to *I don't really care but you can pay me whenever you're done talking* and decided to simply keep his mouth shut for a bit longer. He wasn't sure exactly what game he was playing here, but the four of them clearly had something else in mind for the two of them. No use upsetting anyone just yet.

The *Nameless* chose that exact moment to subcomm into Brazel and Grond's ears. RHUNDI NEEDS YOU, he said. I WOULDN'T HAVE INTERRUPTED BUT SHE SAID IT WAS IMPORTANT. SHE SORT OF SCARES ME.

"We need a moment," Brazel said, both he and Grond standing up from the table. "Be right back."

THIRTEEN

The two returned to the conference room a few minutes later, both looking substantially more aggravated than they had been when they left.

"That thing does scans, too, right?" Grond said, pointing at the holoprojector.

"It does," confirmed Overmorrow.

"I need it," Grond said, picking up the statue and setting it atop the projector.

"And I need you guys to be able to pipe an audio comm channel into the room so that we can all hear it," Brazel said. "It's a subcomm right now. I'm not wearing any speakers."

Overmorrow nodded at Glow-of-Twilight, who left the room in a hurry.

"My wife has an employee who has some knowledge of the Benevolence," Brazel said, speaking a bit more quickly than usual. "That rock we stole this on? It's spilled into open war since we pulled off the heist. Almost planet-wide. The only parts not seeing active conflict are so geographically isolated that they probably don't really care that the rest of Khkk is even there. And the Benevolence are moving in to put down the revolution and restore order. Khkk is in ogrespace. Any of you have any idea what the Benevolence are trying to do 'restoring order' in *ogrespace?*"

The ogres were the only species who had managed to entirely resist Benevolence influence, although gnomespace was mostly free of them as well. The Benevolence had been leaving the ogres alone for generations, focusing their influence on keeping a firm grip on human- and elvenspace and on conquering–or, as they put it, "pacifying"–the dwarves. There was a reason the Malevolence was so dominated by dwarven interests.

"It can't possibly be good," Smashes-the-Stars said.

"No, it can't, and *you* got *us* involved," Brazel said. "We aren't very happy about that."

"It could still be a coincidence," Smashes-the-Stars said.

"It's not," Brazel answered. "They're going to find out we stole that thing sooner or later. The *war* might be a coincidence. Maybe. I rather doubt it, and I'm doubting it more the longer we talk about it. They're using the war as an excuse to pacify the place and get a toehold in ogrespace, and that statue has *something* to do with it."

Glow-of-Twilight reentered the room with a portable comm speaker. She placed it on the table and Brazel connected it to the subcomm in his ear.

"Go ahead, Irtuus-bon," he said.

"Look very carefully at the very top of the sphere," the troll said over the comm. "Look and see if there is a depression or perhaps a very small crack. It would be something barely large enough to get a fingernail into, if that."

"There's little lines traced all over it," said Brazel, who had climbed onto the table to get a closer look at the statue. "A few of them meet right at the top. I wouldn't call it a *crack*, but..."

"See if you can push something into the convergence," Irtuus-bon said. "Surely the halfogre has a knife with him."

Grond shrugged. "I'm empty, believe it or not. First time, I swear."

Overmorrow looked at Asper. Xe protested at the look for a moment, then removed one of the blades from xir forearm and handed it to Brazel.

"This ought to be good enough," he said. "Am I trying to split the thing open?"

"You will find that you cannot scratch it," Irtuus-bon said. "And if I am wrong, it does not matter if you do. Simply press the tip of the blade into the place where the lines intersect."

Brazel followed instructions, realizing as he did that he could hear the buzzing sound again. Asper had apparently removed the statue from stasis at some point. He carefully inserted the point of Asper's knife into the statue and applied gentle pressure.

The buzz suddenly got much louder. A seam shot out from either side of the point of his knife, and the statue split in half. Brazel took a step or two back as dozens–hundreds, perhaps–of smaller spheres of varying sizes, apparently made of the same metal as the larger one, fell out of the inside of the statue. As he watched, the statue sealed itself back up again.

The new spheres, moving on their own, rearranged themselves around the circumference of the larger sphere. The largest spheres touched the original one, with successively smaller ones attaching themselves to each of the larger spheres until the overall effect resembled tentacles. Thirteen of them, he counted.

He took another step back as he recognized the shape the statue had formed itself into.

"Ah, I was right," said Irtuus-bon, as the hologram updated itself on his end of the conversation. "I rather wish ... that I had *not* been."

FOURTEEN

Kri was looking forward to getting to sleep. He had been serving the lady Majesty-of-Nature for close to twenty-one hours before she noticed he was starting to fall asleep on his feet and had ordered him to go to his rest and send her a replacement. He only hoped that there was room in one of the beds in the common room he shared with the rest of the males. There were eight of them and only three beds, one of which had a broken leg and could be difficult to sleep in. Someday one of them would remember to ask for the supplies to repair it. He never remembered until he was already on his way home, and the one time he had remembered while he was working for Smashes-the-Stars, the lady had been in in a terrible mood and not to be disturbed.

On the plus side, it was daylight. *Bright* daylight, well past noon. Most of his brethren should be at work. They *had* to be, didn't they?

He thumbed a button on a monitor at his ankle to signal that he had been released. Someone else would be summoned to the lady's side within minutes, possibly freeing up a spot in the very beds he was heading toward. If not, well, he'd slept curled up in a corner on the floor plenty of times before. It wasn't that bad.

Luckily, only two of his brethren were present when he got home. Unluckily, both Bna and Ler were asleep, and they'd taken the two good beds. Kri sighed and lay down in the bad bed, trying to position himself toward the three good legs so the bed didn't wobble too much. He would eat when he woke up, which hopefully would not be for several hours. He was supposed to have at least six before the monitor began buzzing and summoned him back to work again.

Less than an hour later, he was awakened. And it wasn't the monitor. It was a thunderous explosion somewhere outside. His conditioning kicked in before his common sense. He'd checked his monitor before getting out of bed every day since it had been put on, and he glanced at it almost unconsciously.

The monitor was emitting a faint hiss, and the screen, which normally would either be counting down the remaining time in his rest or displaying his next assignment, was filled with gibberish.

Had the work center been bombed? There had been a rebellion among the males on 9013LV a few generations before. The first thing they had done was destroy the work centers, a decision which had made good sense symbolically but did little for them tactically. The rebellion had been suppressed in less than two days. Kri suspected the only reason he even knew about it was because the women found it useful for the men to be aware of how poorly it had gone.

His room had no windows. He considered running outside and decided to head to the roof instead. Oddly, he was alone in the room. Apparently the rest of his brethren were already out on work detail. With eight of them sharing the room, there was usually *someone* else around.

Kri fled out the door and then up the stairs, forgetting and stumbling over the one with the bad board a few steps above his level. He was panting and out of breath by the time he reached the roof, but it would be worth it for the view. He looked toward the work center to the east. There was a huge plume of black smoke right about where it would be.

There were more plumes of black smoke to the north, and to the south, and to the west. There had been explosions *everywhere*. He'd only heard the one boom. Had they all gone off at *once?*

And then Kri looked up.

The sky was filled with black ships. Many of them were oval-shaped, with eight arms off the central oval, some of which were being used to steer and others to pour fire down upon the city. Others were angular, with actual wings instead of the tentacles, and larger. These were the bombers. There was another series of *booms* and other parts of the city went up in smoke.

This was no rebellion. This was an *invasion*.

Kri panicked. He had no training, no orders to cope with a situation like this. His ankle monitor was supposed to light up and tell him what to do and where to go at any time. In an emergency he was supposed to be summoned and given a job. He'd not been summoned before the bombs struck. He *couldn't* be summoned if the work centers were destroyed. The clans, for now at least, had no way to get ahold of him. And no way to track him. He had *no idea* what he was supposed to do.

Wait.

With a flash of euphoria, Kri realized that he was free–or, at least, freer than he'd been since he was a very small child. Anyone who might stop him would likely be busy with other tasks. If he could just manage to look like he was on an important task he might actually manage to get away from the city. And if he was caught, he could run. Who had time to chase one runaway male dwarf when they were being invaded? Surely no one.

He'd made it halfway down the stairs, in a mad rush to freedom, when Benevolence bombs blew the building into dust.

FIFTEEN

"*I am assuming that someone is about to explain,*" Overmorrow said.

"We've encountered that thing before," Brazel said. "Dwarven planet. An iceball–don't remember the name–"

"00901213," Grond chimed in.

"Whatever," Brazel said. "We got asked to come in and pick up a package, then get the package out of dwarfspace. Easy run. We figured it was a male trying to get off-planet."

There was some rumbling from the two dwarves. Overmorrow shot them a look and it stopped.

"Anyway. Research colony, I think. We got there and everybody was dead–the station was wrecked. The male dwarves were strangled and the females were just *dead*, in their beds. No marks on any of them except scuff marks and scrapes on their hands. They'd torn the station to bits with their bare hands. And there were these signs–what, Grond, three of them?"

"Two, I think."

"Two, then. Yeah–one upstairs in the hangar, one downstairs under a pile of dead males. They looked like–*that*." He pointed at the statue. The arms were waving freely, like the thing was alive. None of them had tried to touch it yet. "They were painted on the floor. And then–then this *thing* showed up."

He paused for a moment, taking a few deep breaths.

"Grond got a better look at it than I did," he said. "He was *carrying* me at the time, because the thing had ripped one of the planet's *moons* out of orbit and chucked it at the research station like it was a kids' toy. I couldn't run fast enough so he just picked me up and split."

"We heard about that," Glow-of-Twilight said. "The feeds said it was an asteroid impact. Nothing that could have been done."

"You'd think the feeds would have noticed a *missing moon*," Grond said.

"The moon was a caught asteroid anyway," Brazel said, waving the concern off. "What, you think they'd have thought *Oh, the moon must have fallen out of orbit?* More likely the records were wrong. Not like anybody important had ever been there."

"We made it off-planet," Brazel continued. "Barely. Another minute or two and we'd have still been down there. And the weirdest thing–Namey *couldn't see the thing* that threw the moon at us. When he commed us about it as far as he knew the moon had just *stopped orbiting*. He had no idea that the thing was even there."

"And this is a statue of the ... creature you saw? It was alive?"

"Yeah," Brazel said. "We were worried it was going to chase us. If anything alive could get into tunnelspace, that thing would have been able to."

"I believe I can ... shed some light, here," Irtuus-bon said.

There was a moment of silence around the table.

"Go ahead," Overmorrow said. "Everyone else may as well know exactly what we've gotten ourselves into."

"The Benevolence believe that their magic comes from the gods," Irtuus-bon said. "They are not ... worshipped, as such, they are *feared*. There are no rituals or prayers or services for this. No sacrifices. But this is Azamoeg. It is the ninth of the Benevolence's nineteen gods. The Benevolence clans are arranged around the nineteen gods."

"Their gods are *real?*" Brazel asked.

"Clearly so," Irtuus-bon said. "Seven of the nineteen–eight, including the appearance you witnessed–have made recorded appearances across the galaxy during the last two centuries, and those ... those are just the appearances I am aware of. The Benevolence have never viewed their gods as remotely metaphorical beings. *Gods* may not even be the correct word. They are beings of immense power and antiquity, but they are not creators or exemplars. They are merely power, and the source of power."

"If they don't leave a lot of witnesses behind, there might have been a lot more appearances than that," Brazel said. "Namey said the moon would have created an extinction event if 00901213 actually had any indigenous life."

"A true point," Irtuus-bon agreed. "Azamoeg himself would not have left many witnesses. He is the Scouring God, the destroyer. He is said to be the simplest to summon. Azamoeg will come if he is properly called regardless of the caller. If he finds the caller unworthy, however, they will not survive the summoning."

"Asper just cast a spell a couple of days ago," Grond said, pointing at the elf. "You didn't know about these Benevolence gods?"

"You carry weapons," Asper responded. "Do you know how they work?"

"Stab with the pointy end," Grond answered. Asper rolled xir eyes.

"Belief–or even understanding–are not necessary to use their magic," Irtuus-bon said. "Much like knowledge of metallurgy or chemistry is not necessary to use a sword or a gun, or physics to use an energy weapon."

"I still wanna know how xe knows Benevolence magic," Grond said.

"I taught xir," Overmorrow said. "The Benevolence are not the *only* users of magic in the galaxy, even if they would prefer everyone believe them to be. And their gods are not the gods of *all* of the elves."

"And how did you learn?" Grond asked.

"Elven memories are long," Overmorrow answered. "And while the Noble Opposition may have been a creation of the dwarves, even at the beginning there were elves who resisted the Benevolence. These skills were ours before they were theirs."

Brazel shook his head. This entire conversation was a distraction.

"So we have, what? A cultic object? Did the symbols on the floor at that research station *summon* Azamoeg? Or was there one of these statues buried in the rubble somewhere and we never found it? Or did the summoner just get off the planet before Azamoeg showed up?" He turned to Overmorrow. "Asper took *one look* at that thing and wanted all of us off-planet and got xirself onto my ship. Most of what Irtuus-bon just said wasn't news to you, I think."

"That is correct," Overmorrow said. "I had my suspicions that this was, as you put it, a cultic object. As did Asper. The weight and the material are the clues. Benevolence cult statues are always fashioned in this way. The signal is another. It is passive, but the statues form a network. The device can be used for communication over long distances, much like a comm signal, but more specific. The Benevolence knew that this was on Khkk. They sent it there. It very likely was a reward or a sign of trust for the beings they contracted with. And if we leave it here long enough, it will bring them *here* as well."

Asper began mumbling again, and the blue glow reappeared around the statue. The tentacles stopped moving.

"Irtuus-bon, Rhundi, you two still listening?" Brazel asked.

"We are," Irtuus-bon confirmed.

"I think it's probably about time to let them know about the other stuff, too," Brazel said.

"We don't even really *have* any 'other stuff' yet, Brazel," Rhundi said. "We haven't cracked it yet. But go ahead."

"The person who brought us the statue–who we now have multiple reasons to believe is a liar–also passed on some files that he claimed came from the same source that produced the statue. He doesn't know the contents, but they're encrypted with Benevolence tech. Irtuus-bon is working on decrypting them now."

"But you do not know their contents," Overmorrow said.

"Not yet," Brazel said.

"I think perhaps we need to interview Haakoro a bit more closely," Rhundi said.

"Clearly," Overmorrow said. "And I believe I have another job for the two of you as well."

"What would that be?" said Brazel. "Go looking for your people on Khkk? Because we kinda started a war the last time we were there. I don't think I like it there very much."

"I definitely don't," Grond said.

"Not as yet," Overmorrow responded. "We have a rather more important job in mind. It concerns the proper disposal of the artifact in front of us. We need you to transport it to someone."

"Why us?"

Overmorrow smiled. "Are you not available for work? We had the idea that you were freelancers. And the job we have in mind for you is *entirely* legal, which may be a welcome change of pace for you. Furthermore, we have reason to believe that the individual we wish you to transport this to may be more welcoming of your company than that of others."

"Oh, hell," Brazel said. "You're talking about Remember."

Overmorrow nodded. "Remember."

The Lady Remember had used them for a job in the past, a job that ended up with an entire populated moon scorched clean of any life and hurled into its planet by Benevolence forces. She had paid them by ensuring Rhundi's sole ownership of her resort on Arradon, an act that had gone a long way toward Rhundi's more-or-less legitimacy as an honest businesswoman. She had also said that she would be in touch with them in the future, a promise that she had–as of yet–failed to follow through on.

"We don't exactly have Remember's comm address," Brazel said. "She got in touch with us once and that was it."

"Remember will be contacting you herself in the next few days," Overmorrow said. "You will bring her the artifact and that will end your association with us, if that is what you wish."

"How the hell do you know *that?*" Brazel said, incredulously.

"You have *met* the Lady Remember, have you not?" Overmorrow said. "And you doubt her capability to know when she is needed?"

"She basically *said* that that was how it was going to work," Grond said.

"If I may interrupt," Irtuus-bon said. "My resources, at least in this specific domain, likely rival Remember's. Perhaps if the artifact could be brought to me, I could..."

"My *kids* are on Arradon," Brazel interrupted. "This goes *nowhere near you.*"

Irtuus-bon did not respond. Brazel imagined the look he was probably getting from Rhundi and smiled.

"This doesn't tell us what to do in the meantime," Brazel said. "If you think Remember's going to find us, we probably ought to find someplace to put this thing in between now and then."

"You guys figure that out," Rhundi said. "I'm going to go find Haakoro." There was a click as the signal died.

"Any ideas?" Brazel asked. "It's not–"

There was a frantic pounding at the door. Grond opened it, and a handful of dwarves spilled into the room, nearly tripping over each other.

"What is this?" Overmorrow asked.

"We got an emergency comm," one of them said. "9013LV's being bombed. Our agents there are busy liquidating our safehouses. They're on to us."

Wonderful, Brazel thought.

INTERLUDE 2

Then

Grond had had better fights. The ogre was large for his age, but his sparring partner was a few years older than him, and he'd reached the peak of his growth already. Grond was spotting him nearly a third of a meter and a good thirty to forty kilograms.

That was before you factored in that the other ogre had a staff and Grond didn't. He'd lost his a moment ago, and the other ogre was between him and it.

He ducked, avoiding a high swing at his head, then spun out of the way of the staff's other end. His opponent smiled, revealing a gap-toothed grin. Grond was responsible for the gap. The other ogre, whose name was Monyx, was not one of his bigger fans. Grond feinted to his left, earning a jab in that direction, and then swiped half-heartedly at the end of the staff. Monyx jabbed again, twice, three times.

At the fourth jab, Grond pounced. He let the staff hit him in the ribs, rolling to blunt the impact, then backhanded Monyx across the face. He stomped on the bigger ogre's instep, staggering him, then punched him in the jaw, enjoying the *clack* the ogre's jaws made as they slammed together.

I think he just lost another tooth, he thought. Monyx made an attempt to back up, to get Grond back within range of the staff, but it was too late. Grond slammed an elbow into his jaw in the same place, then snatched his staff away from him, hitting a kneecap and hearing it crack. The other ogre crumpled to the ground and Grond pounced on him, beating him in the face and chest until he heard K'Shorr's command to stop.

He stared at the unconscious ogre, waiting for K'Shorr to declare him the winner of the fight.

And a blow to the back of his head sent him to the floor, seeing stars.

"Monyx wins," K'Shorr said. He had a staff of his own.

"F ... fuck he does," Grond mumbled.

"You lost track of an enemy," K'Shorr said. "If I'd hit you just a little harder I'd have caved your skull in. He wins."

"You ... you weren't part of the fight!" Grond sputtered, slamming a fist into the ground.

"One," K'Shorr said, bashing Grond in the ribs with the staff, "I never said it was one-on-one. Two, even if I *had*, I was *lying*. You assumed you'd won and dropped your guard. And then you *lost*."

"To the guy who's still unconscious," Grond said.

"Yeah. He climbs the ranks. You stay where you are until you learn to *cheat*."

"I could kill him now," Grond said. "He's out. He can't stop me."

"You won't," K'Shorr said.

"You sure about that?"

"Don't get the idea that because I let you talk again that I want to hear a bunch of it," K'Shorr said. "And yeah. Wanna know how I know? You're *talking* about killing him, not *killing him*."

"Fine," Grond said, snatching his staff from the ground.

"Don't touch him," a voice commanded. Grond dropped the staff again and climbed to one knee, his eyes fixed on the ground.

"He wasn't gonna," K'Shorr said. Bountiful's wealth and influence had only expanded since he had purchased Grond, and the elf's clothing now reached a level of opulence that verged on absurd. He glittered as he moved, the muddy yellow light in the filthy training pit still managing to reflect beautifully off the bits of gemstone and spun gold woven into his robes.

"Is he ready?" Bountiful asked.

"No," K'Shorr said. "But he's readier than anybody else you've got. He beat this poor shit unarmed, and Monyx is the best stickfighter I've got."

I thought you said I lost, Grond thought, but he did not speak in the presence of his master.

Bountiful sighed heavily. "He will have to do. Have him prepared within the hour."

Prepared for what?

"Explain yourself," the elf said.

"A gift," Bountiful said. "He is well trained in the militant arts. Young. Strong. And not belligerent or troublesome. Use him as a bodyguard, if you like." Grond was on one knee again, head down, fists pressed into the ground near his feet. He was being presented to another elf, whose simple white robe contrasted with Bountiful's gaudy pomposity. Bountiful had not bothered to introduce the elf to him. K'Shorr, silent, stood somewhere behind him.

"You bring me a *person,*" the elf said, palpable disgust in xir tone.

"An ogre, at least," Bountiful said, taking no notice and striding grandly about the room. "Does he not please you? I have others. An elf, perhaps, would be more to your liking? Or a human?"

"You misunderstand," the elf said. Grond dared to lift his eyes, hearing Bountiful moving behind him. The other elf reached under xir robe, extracting a silver medallion, a symbol Grond had never seen before. It looked like a spider, or some other multi-legged creature. "You wish this, do you not?"

"Most ardently," Bountiful said.

"You have badly miscalculated how to receive it," the elf replied acidly. "The gifts of Great Azamoeg are not for *purchase,* Bountiful. They are awarded to the *worthy.*"

"Am I not worthy?" Bountiful said, the other's tone finally getting through to him. "The priesthood of Azamoeg is of one of the lesser clans, is it not? My influence is wide, and grows wider each passing year. Does the Benevolence not hold slaves? Your objections make no sense to me, sibling."

"Yet another reason to deny your request ... *brother*," the elf said, and Grond's eyes snapped back to the floor, feeling rather than seeing his master's anger flare in response to the epithet. "You are a clan-kin. This I cannot deny. You are *perhaps* capable of the lesser mysteries of the Scouring God, but a priesthood? You insult your siblings and your betters with the very *request*. That you thought to improve your chances to gain it by bringing me this ... this *overgrown boy* is proof that you lack the judgment for the honor. Azamoeg *himself* scorns your bribe."

The elf did not appear to be finished talking, but Bountiful was beyond listening. His hand lashed out, striking the elf across the face and sending xir to the floor. Grond froze, indecision halting his movement. Bountiful would no doubt expect to be defended. But K'Shorr was in the room, and Grond had received no order to stand or move. He heard the big ogre putting himself in between Bountiful and the other elf.

Bountiful, for his part, did something *entirely* unexpected, as Grond heard him fall to his knees.

"Forgive," he said, panic in his voice. "Eremite, please ... I lost my temper, I never meant to–"

"*Silence*," Eremite said, and xir eyes shone like silver, and the air in the room *thickened*, somehow, and Grond knew that he had lost the chance to stand even if he desired it. He heard K'Shorr fighting against the spell, grunting and straining to move his limbs. "You are *cast out*, Bountiful. Your properties and possessions, your effects and clan-marks, are now property of the priesthood of the Scoured God. You are left a tenth of a tenth for your own survival. *All else* is forfeit." Grond watched as Bountiful was lifted into the air, unseen hands stripping him of his fine clothes, his jewelry, tearing his hair and leaving him nearly naked.

Eremite continued, and xir voice boomed like thunder as xe spoke. "I take from thee thy *light*. I take from thee thy *seals* and thy *station* and thy *gifts*. And I take from thee thy *name*."

"No," Bountiful managed to grunt. "Please."

"Bountiful you are no longer. Bountiful is *stricken* from our memories. I name thee *Barren*."

Eremite walked to Barren, pausing inches away from him.

"But we are not merciless," Eremite said. "We grant you a boon. One only."

Xe turned and pointed at Grond, still frozen on one knee.

"You may keep *that*. Perhaps he will be useful to rebuild your ... what did you call it? *Influence*." Xe practically spat the word.

Eremite left the room, the door closing behind xir.

It was nearly an hour before they could move again.

SIXTEEN

Rhundi, sitting at her desk in her office, tapped at a few icons and called up nanocam footage from Haakoro's suite. The man was sitting at the edge of his bed, one leg crossed over his knee. He reached out with his left arm and picked up a glass of water from the table next to his bed and took a drink, then put it back.

She sat in silence for a moment, watching him. The man's motives were truly a mystery. If his goal had just been to get the statue into their hands, there would have been no reason for him to follow it back to Arradon. And he'd genuinely not seemed to know what the information was on the datapad. She couldn't figure out his angle. Why lie to any of them about where it had come from? Was he actively working against them, or just working for himself? She wasn't especially fond of working blind, and she really had little idea about how to proceed with Haakoro.

He reached out with his left arm and picked up the glass of water again, took a drink, then put it back.

Rhundi leaned forward, watching the footage a bit closer.

"No way," she said.

She tapped another icon, turning on her comm link to his room, then shouted at the top of her lungs.

Haakoro didn't react.

And, a moment later, reached out with his left arm and picked up the glass of water, precisely the same way he'd done it the previous two times.

"Son of a bitch," she said, signaling her security team.

"Find Haakoro and bring him to me," she said over her comm. Every employee she had at the resort would hear the broadcast, from Gorrim to her head of security to her engineers to Irtuus-bon to the lowliest goblin pool-boy on staff. "Bring him to me *now*, and if you want to hurt him along the way, *go ahead*."

She thought for a few moments, then opened up a specific channel.

"Lock the hangar and the parking lot down, too," she said. "Quarantine conditions: nobody goes anywhere for an hour, on land or atmo, unless we find him first." *That son of a bitch*, she thought. Her employees at the other end of the comm started sputtering back, most asking for additional details. She shut the comm off and got up, intending to head there herself, when a thought struck her.

His story about finding them had been ridiculous. But he *had* found them. And if he could find them, it seemed obvious that others could too. If he'd managed to send a transmission, even if it wasn't encrypted, *anyone* could be heading her way now.

"Gorrim, go run the parking lots," she said into the comm. "I'm sending you a holo of the kid. Get Tarrysh to run security on the dock. She's enough of an asshole that nobody'll argue with her. And I want this image sent to *every single person who works here* in the next ten minutes. Find this little bastard. We clear?"

"Clear, ma'am," Gorrim said immediately. "Let me know if you need anything else."

"I need all sorts of things," she said. The first was to go find her troll.

"So, we're taking this thing with us?" Brazel said. "How long is that stasis spell going to last, anyway?"

"Not long enough," Asper said. "Which means that I'm coming with you."

Overmorrow and the dwarves stood up. "We have to assume that Roashan's location may be compromised, so we're going to be moving immediately. The Benevolence could be on their way already."

Overmorrow and Asper embraced.

"I will let you know when we stop running."

"I know," Asper said. "Good luck."

Asper picked up the statue. "I have some things I need to recover from my quarters. These dwarves–" xe indicated the ones that had burst in with the bad news–"will show the two of you back to the *Nameless*. I will be with you momentarily."

"Can we get a resupply while we're waiting?" Brazel asked. The *Nameless* wasn't likely to be screaming for fuel anytime soon, but it sounded like it might be a while before they saw a friendly port.

"Arrange for it," Asper said to the dwarves. One of them moved away and began speaking into a comm. The others left, Brazel and Grond following.

They had almost made it back to the ship when the alarms started.

The dwarves stopped dead, Grond nearly running over them.

"Those are boarding alarms," one of them said. "That's not proximity. Somebody's *already on Roashan.*"

"How the hell did that happen?" Grond asked.

"No idea," the dwarf said. "But hopefully it's just a few of them and not a few hundred."

"Benevolence?"

"Maybe. Probably not. Why would they board instead of just blowing us apart? Only if they were looking for something." The dwarf waved the others off and kept moving, Brazel and Grond continuing to follow.

"Braze, how armed are you?"

"One gun. Projectile, so not the best choice for a fight on a space station."

"Why the hell'd you bring it with you then?"

Brazel shrugged. "Wasn't thinking, I guess. It's my smallest gun. I just felt like I oughtta have *something*. You?"

"Not even that much," Grond said, cursing his decision-making. "Hey, dwarf!"

The dwarf didn't even turn around. "I got nothing for you. You just gotta hope that nobody's landed in the dock your ship's on."

They turned the corner into a hail of fire. The dwarf, riddled with shots, dropped to the floor.

"Fuck *me*," Brazel said. "Namey, what's going on?"

TWO RAIDING PARTIES, ALL HUMAN, the ship responded. THEY WERE ALLOWED TO DOCK WITHOUT INCIDENT. I ASSUME THE SHIPS ARE STOLEN.

"Mercs?" Brazel asked. "They're not Benevolence, are they?"

HIGHLY UNLIKELY. THEY LACK ANY ARMOR OR UNIFORMS. OR SENSE OF TASTE. THEY ARE NOT ATTEMPTING TO DAMAGE PROPERTY AT THE MOMENT, ONLY TO ATTACK CIVILIANS. I AM ON FULL ALERT BUT NO ONE HAS APPROACHED ME YET.

Grond peeked around the corner. He saw no one. He patted the dead dwarf down. She wasn't carrying anything more deadly than a small energy pistol.

"Better than nothing," he mumbled. "Namey, any idea how close we are to you?"

RELATIVELY, I THINK, the ship said.

"I think it's a pretty straight shot from here," Brazel said. "Trouble is, it's toward where the shooting was coming from."

"Why is it always *toward* the shooting?" Grond said.

"It isn't. We run away from shooting *all the time*," Brazel replied.

The two of them leapfrogged each other down the corridor, which split off at the end. There was also a hatch heading up to a higher level. Grond reflected on how, perhaps an hour ago, he'd wondered how easy the station would be to defend from inside. "Namey? Any ideas?"

TURN RIGHT.

"Hope you're right," Grond said, and turned. The sounds of a pitched gun battle rattled down the hallway toward him.

"If somebody breaches the station, we're fucked. There's probably atmo suits around here somewhere but who the hell knows where they are," Brazel said.

"Asper will," Grond responded. "We just gotta find xir."

"Shit, that reminds me–Namey, if the elf shows up, let xir aboard, no questions."

PILOTING AUTHORITY?

"You go nowhere without us," Brazel said. "But *shoot* whatever xe wants so long as it isn't us."

UNDERSTOOD. THE ATTACKERS ARE BEGINNING TO TAKE NOTICE OF OTHER SHIPS. MOST OF THEM DO NOT APPEAR TO BE RUN BY AIs OR THEY WOULD LIKELY BE FIRING BACK BY NOW. A GROUP OF ATTACKERS HAS HAVE BROKEN AWAY FROM THE BATTLE. THEY ARE BEGINNING TO START LOOTING.

"Kill anyone you have to," Brazel said.

ACKNOWLEDGED.

"Definitely mercs. I'm guessing Benevolence found them in the neighborhood and told them to soften the station up. No discipline, so they're looting already."

"Sounds about right," Grond said. "Problem is gonna be telling 'em from the good guys. Sometimes uniforms come in handy."

"Right," Brazel said. The sounds of battle were getting louder as they moved farther down. "That's the hangar right there. And the ship is ... of *course* it's on the other side."

Grond moved up behind him and looked into the hangar. He could see two groups of mercs, one barricaded behind crates and firing out of his field of vision toward what were likely Malevolence forces, and a second merrily breaking into any ships they could find. "They're not watching our way. Most of the battle's pointed a different direction."

"Let's go, then," Brazel said. "Stick close to the wall."

The two edged out of the door around the outside of the hangar toward their ship, Grond taking the lead and staying as low as he could. An explosion sprayed shrapnel into the wall above them. Grond shook his head and looked around. The mercenaries had dealt with the Malevolence forces by switching from energy weapons to grenades.

"Oh, they didn't," Brazel said. "No, no, nobody's *that* fucking stupid..."

The force shield holding the atmosphere inside the dock began to flicker.

"Fuck. They hit the emitter. *Fuck.* Namey, get ready to fucking go." Brazel said. He could see the ship starting to power up across the hangar.

A few blasts ricocheted off the wall near them.

"We're spotted," Grond said, hitting the floor. It looked as if the mercenaries were starting to fan out, having dealt with the first group of Malevolence forces.

"Namey, start shooting. Target priorities are *anything that isn't us or the elf.* Go."

The *Nameless* opened fire with his exterior guns. He took three of the mercenaries out immediately, but drew the attention of several more.

"Braze, you deal with the ones coming for us," Grond said. "I'm gonna go beat up the rest of them before they beat up my ship."

"On it," Brazel said. Grond turned and tossed him the gun he'd taken from the dwarf.

"You sure? Unarmed?"

"Sure," Grond said. "It'll be fun."

"Great last words," Brazel said, and fired a couple of shots.

"Don't waste those," Grond said. "I dunno how much ammo you've got."

"More than you," the gnome snapped. "Git!"

The gnome popped out of cover and began firing. Grond crouched as low as he could and sprinted for the *Nameless*. The ship was taking potshots at mercenaries whenever they presented themselves, but wasn't getting many hits.

However, being fired at by a ship proved to be *incredibly* distracting. Grond hit the first of three nearby mercenaries at full speed, lifting the man off his feet and hurling him at one of his partners. The two went down in a heap, giving Grond just enough time to snatch a rifle from the hands of the third. He smashed the stock of the weapon into the man's face, knocking him unconscious.

The force shield flickered again. Grond felt a slight breeze as some of the air inside the dock was lost to the void. He looked around for more mercenaries to shoot. There was one taking cover by a ship nearby. He fired at him and the man dropped, either hit or trying to stay clear. A handful of others were trading shots with Brazel and several more were still clustered by the emitter that had been damaged in the explosion.

Crossfire, Grond thought, and opened fire on Brazel's targets. He hit one of them in the shoulder, taking him out of the fight, and the others withdrew. The mercenary near him fired at him again, grazing his side, and Grond turned to fire back. His shots went wide, thudding into the side of the boat the man was using as cover.

Fucking cheap guns. Grond glared at the rifle and circled around the back of the *Nameless.* Within a few moments he had a clear path to the mercenary, who was still looking back at where he had been, occasionally taking a wild shot to see if he could coax the halfogre out of hiding.

Grond heard movement behind him, rolling out of the way just before the shooting started. Most of the blasts hit the floor near where he'd been crouching, but several flew past toward the mercenary he'd been stalking, who thought he was being shot at and returned fire.

Three shots from Grond's rifle sent both of them back down to the floor, and the halfogre scrambled back to his feet and charged. The first one popped out of cover a moment too late to shoot, as Grond leapt over the cargo crates he was using as cover, knocking him to the floor. Grond wrapped a hand around the mercenary's neck and slammed his head into the ground, breaking his neck with a loud *crack.* He looked around for the second mercenary, who had fled. The man was nowhere to be found.

"Braze, any idea how many more?" he subcommed.

"Half a dozen, plus the ones who are already out of the hangar? Not sure," the gnome answered. "I haven't–oh, wow."

Wow? "Wow what?"

Grond heard screams from across the hangar. The air had been full of the sounds of combat–shouts, explosions, bangs, the occasional grunt of pain–but these were actual *screams*, of men in pain or terror. He spent a moment calculating the odds and stood up to take a look.

Asper had returned. The elf was cutting a path through the mercenaries effortlessly, a blade in each hand, not bothering with ranged weapons at all. Xe was moving practically too fast for Grond to see, and every swing of xir arms took a body part from one of the mercenaries. Asper carved xir way through four of them as Grond watched, casually incinerating a fifth with a close-range energy blast when one of xir blades got stuck in a piece of cheap merc armor.

The emitter failed again, the force shield blinking for half a second or so. The loss of atmosphere this time was noticeable. Alarm klaxons began sounding.

"Get back to the ship, *right now*," Grond subcommed. Then, shouting: "ASPER! LET'S GO!"

Asper had one mercenary left. He was firing wildly, clearly panicking, and Asper was able to slide past his shots with what looked like no effort at all. Xe slammed the side of xir hand into his throat, crushing his trachea. He fell, choking. The elf looked around, spotting Grond, and sprinted toward the *Nameless*. The ship obligingly opened the front airlock, allowing the three of them inside.

"If the emitter fails again, the dock will seal itself against the atmosphere loss," Asper said.

A second alarm began sounding. This one was faster and more high-pitched than the first.

"The hell is *that?*" Grond asked.

"That's the tunnelspace alarm," Asper said. "We've got a minute to get clear of Roashan before it jumps."

"Namey, *go*," Brazel shouted.

Grond felt the ship lift off the ground. "Come with me," he told Asper, heading for his quarters. "Too bad we don't have a gunner's seat." They'd never had reason to accommodate a third crew member.

He settled into his chair just as the ship cleared the force shield and leapt into heavy acceleration, pushing him back into the gel-cushioned seat as he buckled himself in. He looked around for Asper, intending to direct xir to a crash couch, only to see the elf sitting cross-legged on the floor mumbling to xirself. The g-forces appeared to not be a problem.

'*Kay*, he thought.

"Anybody else out there for us to shoot at?" he said.

"Doesn't look like it," Brazel answered. "Namey, you said two merc groups?"

CORRECT. EACH LANDED AT A SEPARATE HANGAR. I ASSUME THE OTHER IS BEING DEALT

WITH AS WE SPEAK. The acceleration continued, the distance between the *Nameless* and Roashan increasing by the moment.

SENSORS DETECT NO OTHER HOSTILE SHIPS WITHIN RANGE, Namey said. SEVERAL OTHERS ESCAPED ROASHAN FROM OTHER HANGARS. THEY ARE ALL ALSO ACHIEVING MINIMUM SAFE DISTANCE AND NONE HAVE PAID ANY ATTENTION TO US.

"Ignore 'em," Brazel said. "Anybody starts acting funny, let us know."

SHIPS ARE RARELY FUNNY, Namey said.

"AIs even less frequently," Brazel snapped. "Just do it."

Grond swiveled his viewscreen to the *Nameless'* aft view. Roashan was already moving–luckily, away from them. As he watched, the station disappeared from view, folding itself into tunnelspace. The slight shockwave from the entrance slapped one ship aside that hadn't gotten to safe distance fast enough. He magnified the view. The ship looked to have taken minimal damage. They'd gotten lucky. Getting caught too close to a large object moving into tunnelspace could be extremely dangerous.

"We're clear," he said.

"Clear," Brazel agreed.

"So now what?" Grond asked, unbuckling himself from his chair. He looked over at Asper. *We'll have to get xir set up to subcomm with the ship*, he thought.

"We find Remember," Asper said. "Or wait for her to find us."

⊰⊱

SEVENTEEN

Rhundi pushed the buzzer for Irtuus-bon's new suite, thinking back to the first time she'd gone to visit the troll in his previous accommodations. She'd nearly had to break in. She'd made sure the new door had a manual override in case Irtuus-bon decided to try and get cute with his security settings again.

The door slid open, granting her entry. She noted with some satisfaction that the troll appeared to have actually used his sitting room for something other than a hallway or garbage dump. Some of the furniture even looked like it had been sat on recently.

The troll called out from a back room. "What do you want? I am very busy."

"You're always busy," Rhundi said, walking into his command center. "It's why I hired you."

"Which brings me back to my question," he said, his back to the door. "I am monitoring a developing war on a moon across the galaxy and attempting to break through Benevolence encryption at the same time. It is ... taxing."

"It's about to get worse," she said. "Pack."

The troll froze in position, then turned around, his form and size wobbling as he did so. Rhundi smirked. She'd never seen the troll *not sure* what size to be before.

"No. *No.* Explain yourself," Irtuus-bon said.

"First, I don't have to explain, I'm your boss," she said. "But I will. Haakoro may have escaped already, and he's certainly *trying* to. We haven't found him yet. And I have to assume that Benevolence, or at least their allies, may be on the way. Which means two things: first, I need to get my *kids* off of Arradon, and second, I need to get my *troll* off of Arradon. You're too important to let you get caught, and my kids are more important than you. So you're fleeing. Or babysitting. Take your pick."

The troll collapsed into Sirrys' short, squat shape, then without speaking made an effort and grew back to full size again.

"And everyone else?" he said. "There are many innocents here."

"The resort's about to develop a massive problem with the plumbing, I think," she said. "I don't even want to *think* about the lost revenue. But I'd rather have that than a lot of dead people. Brazel and Grond are just going to have to work harder."

"How much time do I have?" he asked.

Amazing, she thought. She had thought the troll was going to fight the idea of leaving his lair *much* harder than this.

"You get three hundred kilos of equipment," she said. "We'll figure a way to get everything set up. I'll have people by soon to help you move everything. Two hours."

The troll nodded. "I will be ready. Is anyone else accompanying us?"

"A small security contingent," she said. "But not many. I can't spare a lot, and it's best if you're on a smaller, faster ship anyway. Farther away you are when they get here, the better."

"I will be ready," Irtuus-bon repeated.

"Thank you," she said. "My kids are depending on you, Irtuus-bon. Don't fail them."

The troll turned away, arms stretching out to begin disconnecting equipment. Rhundi left.

As she exited, she opened a comm channel.

"I need Darsi in my office."

She stopped dead in the hallway.

"Yes, *now*. When have I ever asked for my daughter to be pulled out of class and *didn't* need it to be right away? She needs to be there in five minutes. Tell her to hustle."

Idiots, she thought.

Her oldest daughter was waiting for her when she returned to her office. Rhundi took a moment to look the girl over before saying anything. Darsi was nearly an adult. She looked like a slightly shorter, more slender version of her mother. She had outgrown her father a few years ago. She had several patches of fur on her arms and legs shaved to the skin, following current adolescent gnomish fashion, a development her mother had never understood. Darsi's uncovered skin was pale blue. Rhundi didn't even *know* what the color of her own skin was.

"So what's wrong with Dad?" Darsi asked.

Rhundi suppressed a smile and raised an eyebrow instead. "What makes you think your father has done anything?"

Darsi snorted. "The last time you had me pulled out of class Dad was in prison and you thought Grond was *dead*. I'm the only one here, so it can't be anything *too* awful or you'd have everyone. At least Nichol and Hazel." Nichol was their firstborn son, Hazel their second daughter.

Rhundi nodded. "Good. You're thinking. Keep it that way." She pressed a hidden catch on the wall, causing a panel to slide aside, revealing a safe. She put one hand on the biosensor and keyed in a passcode with the other and the safe opened. She took an energy pistol in a holster out of the safe and handed it to Darsi.

Her daughter's eyes widened. "This can't be good."

"Nothing's wrong with your father," Rhundi said. "Or with Grond, either, before you ask. But there may be some trouble heading our way, and I need Irtuus-bon and you guys off the planet before it gets here."

"You're leaving us with the *troll?*"

"Not quite. I'm leaving the *troll* with *you*," Rhundi said. "You're more level-headed than he is and you're *much* more reliable in a pinch than him. He thinks he's going along to protect you. I'm actually a little disappointed he agreed to do it so quickly. I was planning to cry if I needed to."

Darsi laughed. "You? He'd have seen through that."

"Irtuus-bon is brilliant in a lot of ways, but people are not one of them," she said. "He'd have been so uncomfortable that I was crying that he'd have agreed to anything to get me to stop. But that's not the point. Your dad and I may be ... *unavailable* for a while. And I need you all safe, and I need the troll *kept* safe. Let him think he's making decisions if you need to, but *you* are in charge. I'm actually going to give you a contract that says that if you need it. Irtuus-bon loves contracts. He'll accept it."

"Is ... is it just us?" she asked. "No pilot? That's a lot of responsibility."

"I'm sending a small security team with you. Gorrim's staying here to run the resort, but you'll have a pilot and a few bruisers along for ... well, hopefully for *nothing*. But you'll have them."

A sneaky grin appeared on Darsi's face. "Can Krin be on the team?"

Rhundi sighed. Krin was several years older than Darsi and the girl had had eyes for him since before she was old enough to have eyes for *anyone*. "I'll think about it," she said. "I haven't picked the team yet. Go collect everybody else and meet Irtuus-bon and I at the hangar in two hours. Pack enough clothes for a week or two. Have a few of the goblins help the little ones pack if you need to. Grab a few of the Corvix clan, they're generally trustworthy."

"Are you sure we don't have anything to worry about?" Darsi asked.

Rhundi reached out and stroked her daughter's face, then ran a hand through her fur. "We *always* have something to worry about. It's the nature of how your father and I have decided to live our lives. But this is no worse than anything else right now. Just keep your brothers and sisters safe, and keep the troll from doing anything too stupid. You can handle this."

Truth be told, Darsi would likely be full partners with her, Brazel and Grond in just a few short years. She was, at times, almost frighteningly competent for an adolescent. The girl nodded, buckling on the gun.

"Okay, Mom. We'll be fine."

Rhundi waved her off and Darsi left to start packing.

⊰⊕⊱

EIGHTEEN

"I'd like to point out that as of right now we still remain unpaid," Brazel said.

"You're not starving," Grond answered. The two of them were sitting in the *Nameless'* common room, sharing a meal and killing time while the *Nameless* idly jumped around in tunnelspace. Flying to nowhere in particular had turned out to be more complicated than they'd thought. "We've got supplies and fuel for weeks and nothing special that we need to be doing. No one has shot at us in almost an entire day. Things have been a lot worse."

"That's the life I've always wanted," Brazel said. "Enough material possessions for survival, and conditions just slightly better than the worst things have ever been."

Grond scoffed and waved his partner off. They could bait each other endlessly later.

Grond felt the tell-tale vibration as the ship decelerated out of tunnelspace.

HMMM, said the *Nameless*.

"Blockship?" he asked.

"No. That would have been faster, and hurt a lot more," Brazel reminded him. "AIs aren't supposed to *Hmmm*, Namey. What's going on?"

LOCAL DISTRESS SIGNAL, Namey responded. I WAS ESTABLISHING DRAMATIC TENSION.

"What kind of signal?" Brazel asked, heading for the cockpit. Grond headed for his quarters.

PERSONAL TRANSPORT, SHIELDED BUT UNARMED. STRANDED, BUT LIFE SUPPORT IS STILL ONLINE AND STRONG. THERE APPEARS TO BE A SINGLE LIFEFORM ON BOARD THE SHIP.

"What's wrong with the engines?"

BLOWN.

"Deliberately?"

DIFFICULT TO SAY AT THIS DISTANCE. WE ARE FIFTY THOUSAND KILOMETERS FROM THE SIGNAL. THERE IS NO INFORMATION AS TO THE CAUSE OF THE MALFUNCTION IN THE DISTRESS SIGNAL.

"The ship transmitting any ID?"

NO, Namey responded.

"Odd," Brazel murmured. Distress calls were fairly standard across species, most sentients not being terribly picky about who helped them out when they were close to dying, but generally they included at least basic identification along with the distress codes.

"Anything else in the call I need to know about right now? And don't hold anything back to make it more interesting when you tell me later."

IT IS A SURPRISINGLY LACONIC DISTRESS CALL, the boat agreed.

"You understand that we're going to be discussing your idea of *dramatic tension* in the near future, by the way?"

IT'S GROND'S FAULT, the ship replied.

"It's no such thing," Grond retorted from the copilot's chair. "You programmed the boat. I didn't. We've *discussed* this."

"Whatever, get us closer," Brazel said. "If whoever this is is in a deep-space capable single-man rig with shields, he's probably wealthy. We *save* the wealthy around here."

The *Nameless* drew closer to the derelict ship, and Grond and Brazel watched as Namey gave them a good magnified look at the other ship in their viewscreens. It was indeed a personal transport–a tiny cruiser barely bigger than it needed to be to hold one passenger and its engine. And the engine was indeed blown–*gone* would be a better word, with only tiny scraps of metal clinging to the back of the ship. The exterior of the ship was painted a nonreflective, matte black color, with no markings or identification to be seen anywhere.

"It's a miracle they didn't blow their life support," Brazel said. "How the hell did they not lose pressurization?"

"The engine must have blown directionally," Grond said. "Lucky, lucky son of a bitch. Sabotage?"

"Only if they wanted the target to starve to death instead of blowing up," Brazel answered. "Which I guess could happen."

THE PILOT IS A MALE HUMAN. HE IS IN STASIS, Namey announced. LIFE SUPPORT SHOULD LAST ANOTHER THREE WEEKS PROVIDED NO FURTHER DAMAGE TO THE SHIP.

"He's suited up, though, right?" Brazel asked.

HE IS NOT.

"You're kidding."

I WAS INSTRUCTED NOT TO KID ANY LONGER.

"He took an intersystem trip on a one-person cruiser and he's *not suited?* Even once his engines blew, he didn't put one on? Meaning that he doesn't even have one *with him?* Lucky *and* stupid."

"Amazing how often those go together," Grond said. "Can we bring it in?"

"It'll be tricky," Brazel said. The cruiser was far too small to dock with, since the *Nameless* sported a traditional airlock but the cruiser was too small for one. There was a hard canopy over the pilot's head that would swing up on a hinge so that the pilot could climb into and out of the ship. The *Nameless* had a cargo manipulating arm, though...

"Namey, can we grab the whole boat and put it in the cargo bay?"

POSSIBLE. THE CARGO BAY WILL HAVE TO BE PREPPED FOR DEPRESSURIZATION. IT HAS BEEN A WHILE SINCE THAT WAS LAST DONE. IT WILL TAKE A WHILE.

Grond groaned. Prepping the cargo bay for depressurization meant that every single object that was in the bay—most of which he had just moved—would have to be either moved out of the bay entirely or carefully secured against the loss of atmosphere when the cargo bay doors were opened. Namey was right that this hadn't been done in a while. With both of them working as fast as they could, it would be most of a day's work to do the job right. It would be hours of work just to do it *sloppily.*

"Answer the distress call," Brazel said. "See if the ship starts waking him up right away or if we're going to have to do it. Grond, can you think of any way to get him aboard without spending the next few hours moving furniture?"

"None that don't involve hurting him," Grond said. The other pilot would survive a few minutes of hard vacuum, especially if he was in stasis when Grond pulled him out of his ship, but he wasn't going to come through unscathed. "This would be a lot easier if he'd bothered to bring a goddamn envirosuit with him. Who even *does* that?"

"He'll have some stories to tell us, that's for sure," Brazel agreed. "But we gotta get him out alive first. We can shake him down for a story and a reward afterwards."

"Lucky, lucky son of a bitch," Grond repeated, heading for the cargo bay. Their day had just gotten much busier.

They chose "quick and sloppy," and with Asper's help had the cargo bay more or less locked down in five or so hours of continuous work. Brazel and Grond worked together well in situations like this. Brazel was detail-oriented and there was very little in the bay that Grond couldn't move by himself. Between the two of them, everything of value or portable was safely locked down. Asper split the difference between the two of them, sometimes helping Brazel with directing Grond's lifting and sometimes providing muscle alongside the halfogre.

"Here's how this works," Brazel said. "You go put on an envirosuit. Magnetize the boots. I'm gonna grab his ship and then open the doors. Problem is with something that big you'll probably need to guide it into the bay, so I'm gonna have to cut gravity. You're strong, but you're not *that* strong."

"I'm tempted to say *try me*," Grond said, heading for his envirosuit.

"I'm tempted to do it," Brazel said, "but I need you walking and not *hobbling* when we figure out where we're going next. There's already a good chunk of a day gone and we haven't even woken this halfwit joyrider up yet."

"I'll be good," Grond said. "Let's do this."

The operation went as smoothly as could be hoped, Grond carefully guiding the weightless cruiser into the center of the cargo bay and securing it in place before Brazel closed the bay doors and reestablished atmosphere and gravity. A few moments later, Grond felt the ship reenter tunnelspace and Brazel and Asper joined him.

Grond was staring at the ship's pilot through his viewport, a quizzical look on his face.

"What?" Brazel asked. He looked through the canopy. The pilot was dressed all in black, wearing an opaque interface helmet common to this style of ship. There was little about him that looked notable.

"Something has occurred to me," the halfogre said.

"And that would be?"

"That your average one-person cruiser is not exactly designed to be opened from the outside once it's sealed itself to hard vacuum," he said. "Getting this guy out of the can he's locked himself into might be a little bit more complicated than we thought it was going to be."

Brazel laughed.

"We can't just burn our way in?"

"Could," Grond said. "But that thing's supposed to withstand reentry. I don't know if I have a torch that'll melt through it anytime soon. At least not without cooking the poor fellow that we just wasted several hours to save."

"So, what, we just leave him in there until his life support wakes him up?"

"It won't be the first time we've had a corpsicle in the cargo hold," Grond said. "They're just usually clients." There was no real risk of the life support running out, since his ship would figure out he was in atmosphere again soon enough.

Brazel shrugged. "Fine, whatever. Just, like, leave him a note on the dashboard or something, so he doesn't try and rob us blind when he wakes up. Not like we don't have a job to do." He turned to leave.

"Take a look at this engine," Grond said. "How do you read the damage?"

Brazel looked at the engine, which took up–or, at least, *had* taken up–about two-thirds of the cruiser's length. Had the engine still been attached, fitting the ship into the cargo bay would have been impossible.

"I think you were right," Brazel said after a few moments. "Look at how the pieces that are still attached are bent. They're curled *outwards*, toward the cockpit. There was something explosive wedged in right behind the pilot, it looks like, and it exploded *away* from him. So, a directed bomb, like a claymore or something like that. Designed to blow the engine to bits and leave the occupant alive. Sabotage."

"So either he was supposed to die *slowly* in space or somebody else was supposed to pick him up and we got there first," Grond rumbled. "I do love it when we do a good deed and it mixes us up in somebody else's bullshit."

"I think I can get him out," Asper said.

"How?" Brazel asked.

"You won't like the answer, I suspect," xe answered.

"Magic? How is magic going to help here?"

"You say that as if you know anything about my capabilities," Asper said, putting xir hands on the canopy. "Watch."

Asper closed xir eyes, lips forming words but no sound escaping from them. A yellow glow emanated from xir hands and encompassed the ship. Grond and Brazel covered their eyes as the glow increased in brightness. The entire ship shone like a small sun and Brazel and Grond both heard a distinct *click*.

Grond opened his eyes. Asper waved a hand theatrically and the canopy swung upward. The pilot didn't move.

Grond stepped onto what was left of the wing of the ship and pulled the pilot out. He still didn't react. He was completely dead weight.

"Hey, look at this," he said.

The helmet the pilot was wearing had somehow attached itself to him. Four thick needles–two on each side–had extended from the sides of the helmet deep into his neck.

"That's ... not normal, right?" Grond asked. "I've never worn one of these things before, but they don't *stick themselves to you*, do they?"

"Not that I've ever seen," Brazel said. "Let's get him to the medbay."

Calling what the Nameless offered a "medbay" was overstating the case a bit. "Medical closet" was probably a bit more accurate. They had a bed that flipped down out of the wall to put him on, and even strap him to if necessary, a precaution they took. Brazel attached a few sensors to the man's chest.

"What's going on here, Namey?"

PROCESSING, the ship answered. The three of them waited while the diagnosis package did its work. CORRECTION. THIS MAN IS NOT IN STASIS AS IT IS TYPICALLY UNDERSTOOD. HE IS PARALYZED AND HALLUCINATING. THE HELMET HAS INJECTED HIM WITH A VARIETY OF PSYCHOACTIVE DRUGS.

"The fuck? Seriously?" Grond asked. "He did that on purpose?"

JUDGING FROM WHAT I AM DETECTING IN HIS SYSTEM, I SUSPECT NOT. I HAVE DIFFICULTY BELIEVING HE IS ENJOYING WHAT IS HAPPENING TO HIM RIGHT NOW.

"What should we do about it?"

SIMPLY BREAKING THE NEEDLES WILL STOP THE DELIVERY OF THE DRUGS. I WOULD SUGGEST BREAKING ALL FOUR AT THE SAME TIME IN CASE THE HELMET HAS SOME SORT OF FAILSAFE.

Brazel left for a moment and came back with two pairs of wire cutters.

"These ought to be strong enough. You do one side, I do the other?"

"Sounds good," Grond said. He took two of the cutters from Brazel.

"On three," Brazel said. "One ... two ... *three*."

The pair snapped through the needles. Grond pulled the stubs out of the man's skin and carefully pulled the helmet from his head.

And then jumped back in surprise as Haakoro sat up and screamed.

NINETEEN

Watching a battle from orbit was surprisingly satisfying. It was difficult to see from here which side was winning, but the mere fact that the battle was taking place was more than sufficient. This battle had been going on for more than a day, and the city, whatever it was, was slowly being reduced to rubble. Soon enough there would be nothing on Khkk worth defending at all.

Unless the Benevolence interfered. Which, with luck, would be very soon, and certainly before too many more of their engineers were lost in battle. Both sides were using weapons that the Benevolence had paid to have developed. The simple fact that the war was progressing so quickly and efficiently was testament itself to the efficacy of the Khkks' work.

"Got some news for you."

He turned away from the viewscreen. It was all being recorded anyway. If anything especially impressive happened during the interruption he could watch it again as many times as he wished.

"Go ahead."

"The Benevolence sent some mercs after Roashan. They musta just hired whoever was in the area. They did some damage, but not enough. Roashan jumped away."

He nodded. "Only the first battle. There will be more."

"The signal came from one other place before it showed up on Roashan, though. You're never gonna believe where it was."

A smile. "Tell me."

"Arradon. It was on *Arradon*."

"Arradon."

"You heard me."

"That is ... remarkable. Have you passed this information on to anyone yet?"

"Nah. Just found out myself. I figured you'd wanna know first."

"Oh, I do. When was the last time you were on Arradon, old friend?"

Deep, guttural laughter. "I think you know the answer to that as well as I do."

"Do you fancy a return trip, by any chance?"

"I could use a vacation."

"As could I. Let us go see how Arradon has changed in our absence."

He turned away from the fighting. As exciting as it might be to watch a battle, participating in one was so much better.

"Namey, do find my wife, please, would you?" Haakoro had lapsed back into unconsciousness after screaming his throat raw for a few seconds. Brazel and Grond had taken the opportunity to tighten the restraints on their makeshift hospital bed.

The three of them heard the *click* as the *Nameless* established a comm channel to Arradon.

"Don't really have time, Brazel," Rhundi said. "You would *not* believe the bullshit I am putting up with right now."

"I think I have an idea," Brazel said. "I'm guessing Haakoro escaped?"

"Please tell me how the hell you know that," she said.

"He's *here*," Brazel said. "He ... stole a ship, I'm guessing? Which means you probably need to fire somebody? And then he lost his entire engine. And his helmet attacked him. I'm not really clear on the details, and he hasn't woken up yet."

"How in the ... where are you two again?" Rhundi tried to do the math in her head to figure out how long ago Haakoro had managed to escape and gave up.

"That's the amazing part. We're nowhere, basically," Brazel said. "Technically I think we're still in dwarfspace, but not any part of dwarfspace that's actually *near* anything. We're looking for Remember."

"How do you look for Remember?"

"You wait for her to find you, apparently. That's what she told us last time. She'd find us if we needed her. She didn't seem to want a lot of follow-up questions."

Rhundi opened her mouth to protest, then closed it again. *Worry about that later.* "Listen, I was about to comm you anyway. You figure out what to do with Haakoro. We've got our own problems over here..."

Talking quickly, she explained what she'd done with Irtuus-bon and the children.

"You sent the troll off to take care of our kids."

"I sent *our kids* off with a security team, and told *them* to take care of the *troll*," she said. "And I'm losing who knows how much money trying to clear all of the short-termers at least out of the resort, since I don't especially want them killed if the Benevolence come calling, and I don't really want to *tell* them that, so most of my time over the last day or so has involved coming up with creative and easily-reversible ways to *screw up our plumbing*. You would not *believe* how angry the goblins are with me right now."

"Nobody noticed their missing ship?"

That brought her up short. "No. Did it look expensive?"

"Hard to say. The entire goddamn engine was missing."

File that away with the rest of the stuff we have to worry about later. "If he killed a client, you're keeping him alive until *I* have a chance to kill him. Understood?"

"Yep. Do the kids have a destination?"

"Not especially, but I told Darsi to head for Taralon if and when they needed a resupply." Taralon, a terrestrial moon orbiting a gas giant on the other side of gnomespace, was a notorious hideout for pirates and villains. Rhundi was good friends with half of the residents and the other half owed her favors or money. Ironically, it was probably one of the safest places in the galaxy for their kids.

"Works for me. I think we're gonna wake up your little escapee here soon. I'll keep you posted. Stay safe, okay?"

"Always," she said, signing off.

⊰⬢⊱

"This is all very unexpected," Brazel said. "Namey, do we have some smelling salts around here? Or something we can inject him with?"

PROBABLY, the ship said.

Asper slapped Haakoro twice. He stirred, groaning again.

"Or we could just do that," Grond said. Haakoro's eyes opened, slowly, fluttering closed a few times. Grond leaned in and waited, his face centimeters away from Haakoro's, his eyes brightening to red.

Haakoro's eyes focused. A moment later, the man processed what he was looking at. He shrieked, swearing, pulling on the restraints and trying to get away.

"Stuck, fucked, and out of luck," Grond said. "Explain. And this time *I* get to decide if you're lying."

"I thought you needed help," he said. "So I followed you."

"And how did you get the ship?"

"I had a hardlight chip in my suit. You guys didn't notice it. I turned that on in my room then went to the dock. One of your guys just *gave me* the keys to that ship."

"You just walked out, without anyone noticing. Or the security guys we had watching your room. Or the *cameras*. I find my hitting hand is itchy again."

He shrunk back. "I ... I might have had two. I used one of them to hide in."

Grond considered this. Hardlight generators were expensive as hell, and using one for invisibility was pretty much impossible.

"Lying. You had a *holo* generator for the bedroom. I can buy that. Hardlight? Bullshit. That's the *second* obvious lie you've told us in the last few days. You can't even *fit* a fucking hardlight generator into the damn bodysuit you had on. Brazel, can I hit him?"

"Sure," Brazel said. Grond cracked his knuckles. Haakoro screamed again.

"Wait," Asper said.

"What?" Grond asked. "This is the *fun* part."

"You're right, he's not telling the truth," xe said. "But I don't think he's lying, either."

"You'll have to explain that a bit more," Brazel said.

Asper put a hand out, moving Grond out of the way, then put xir other hand on Haakoro's head.

"Hold him down," xe said. "He's going to fight this. The restraints may not be enough."

Grond held Haakoro's shoulders down, and Brazel moved around the two of them to hold down his legs. Asper put both hands on his face, using xir thumbs to pull his eyelids down. Xe stared into his eyes.

"I was right," xe said.

Asper continued staring into Haakoro's eyes, chanting to xirself. A white light shone from xir eyes, connecting them to Haakoro's. The man began shaking and bucking his body, nearly escaping even Grond's grasp.

The glow extended from Haakoro's eyes down his entire body. Asper's chanting grew louder and more intense, speaking in a language neither Brazel nor Grond had ever heard. Haakoro took a deep, ragged breath, then exhaled sharply, coughing a black mist out of his lungs. Asper broke eye contact for the first time to stare at the mist, which briefly caught fire and then disappeared. Haakoro collapsed and stopped fighting.

"Give him an hour," xe said. "He will be back to normal then."

"What the hell did you just do to him?" Grond said.

"He was under a compulsion," Asper said. "Which explains how he was able to find you so easily. Or, more likely, to find the statue. I have broken the compulsion. We shall see what he genuinely remembers when he wakes up. He may have some useful information for us."

TWENTY

Sirrys ban Irtuus bon Alaamac had decided that he did not like children very much. He was both lucky and unlucky to be on a ship full of gnomish children: lucky, because gnomish children were well known to be substantially more independent at a younger age than children of other species, but unlucky because gnomes tended toward very large families, and Brazel and Rhundi had produced a very large brood indeed. He had done his best to provide the children with tasks that needed doing and that he thought they might enjoy. He'd asked a couple of them to work on inventorying their various supplies on the ship, for example, and since he had a vague notion that gnomes were fond of water he'd set several of them to mopping and keeping the floor clean. He did not believe that the children were doing their best in attending to these tasks, but was unsure about what to do with them otherwise. They seemed to be eating and sleeping on their own, and Rhundi had neglected to provide him with any sort of *list* or similar document detailing what "take care of the children" actually *meant,* so he felt that he was probably safe in attending to his own duties so long as no one was injured or starving.

It had been very difficult to restrict himself to the small amount of equipment that Rhundi had allowed him to bring. Furthermore, the ship was built for speed, not for transporting large numbers of passengers and a troll with hundreds of kilos of surveillance and codebreaking equipment along for the ride. It was crowded and loud. Their security team, at least, seemed to keep mostly to themselves, although one of them seemed to spend an excessive amount of time in the presence of the oldest Tavh're'muil child. She carried a weapon openly. Perhaps he was her trainer.

Regardless of the many small indignities of the trip, however, he *was* making progress on the encrypted Benevolence files. Whatever this Haakoro had been, or however he had managed to get ahold of them, there absolutely *was* Benevolence technology encoding those files. That was, in Irtuus-bon's estimation, virtually impossible to fake–and certainly impossible to fake to a degree that would fool *him*.

As if on cue, one of his computers pinged. He walked over to take a look. He had tried several combinations of twelve different decryption packages and icebreakers, several of which he had invented himself, and had finally seen some success: he had managed to pull a list of file names out of the morass of encryption. He looked at it carefully, scrolling through the list and memorizing the contents as they fled past him. They appeared to mostly be technical documents and blueprints. He mentally flagged a couple of them as looking useful for the decryption effort itself–it was possible that the secrets to unlocking the files were within the files themselves, and if he managed to unlock the right one first, the rest would come much more easily.

His eyes lit upon a particular cluster of files and he abruptly stopped scrolling through the list. A low whistle escaped his lips.

"Oh," he said.

He knew which files he was going to attack first, and they had nothing to do with encryption. He mentally blocked out the noise of the chattering children and the activity in the ship around him and got to work.

"I don't know how much I remember," Haakoro said.

"His memories themselves are suspect," Asper said. "The compulsion could have created them, or prevented him from recalling things that in truth happened."

"Can you fix it?" Brazel asked.

"No," Asper said. "My parent may be able to. But it is beyond my skill. Memories unrelated to the compulsion are probably unchanged, however."

"Like what happened to the ship," Grond said. "Because I'm *super* curious about that."

"That I can tell you," Haakoro said. "I talked my way into the ship at the resort. Managed to convince one of your people that I'd lost the identcard they give you to get into the hangar and then picked a ship that looked easy to steal."

Yep, Rhundi just fired someone, Brazel thought.

"It was an anti-theft device. Nastiest one I've ever seen. Blew out the engines, tossed those needles into my neck, and then started me on the drugs. Hallucinations. Felt like a month of *lectures* on *why theft was wrong*. The owner must have been the world's most vindictive rich asshole. It explained right away I was stuck out there until I starved to death."

"I don't even like you that much and I'm glad we rescued you," Grond said. "Nobody deserves that."

"So how'd you get *here?*" Brazel asked. "*We* don't even know where we're going right now. How do *you* know how to find us? Space is *big*."

"That is the compulsion," Asper said. "He is following the statue. Even with the statue in stasis, he can find it. That's how he found Arradon."

"There's *no way* to hide from a compulsion?"

"There are," Asper said. "But they require magical aid as well. If I had known he was following us I could have hidden us. He would have searched until he lost his mind, and then the compulsion would have broken."

"Man, somebody *really* doesn't like you," Grond said.

"So, that bit about the female halfogre selling you the statue and the plans..." Brazel asked.

"That's true," he said. I remember it."

"No, you don't," Grond said.

"I swear I do," Haakoro said. "I wasn't lying about that."

A dangerous look started to creep onto Grond's face. "You don't know much about halfogres, do you, son?"

"Well, no, but..."

Asper cut him off. "He's clearly not supposed to remember how he got the files or the statue. He's constructed something in his mind. It's pointless to try and convince him otherwise."

"I'm serious," Haakoro said, growing agitated. "That happened."

Grond started to argue and Asper raised a hand. "I'm sure it did," xe said. "We believe you." Xe looked at Grond. "Don't contradict him. No point." Grond shrugged.

HEY, EVERYBODY? Namey said over the speakers. WE'VE GOT A PROBLEM.

"More specific," Brazel said, heading for the cockpit. "Always more specific."

SOMETHING BIG JUST MOVED INTO SENSOR RANGE.

"How big?"

TERRIFYINGLY.

"*AGAIN with the BE MORE SPECIFIC!*" Brazel said, moving faster. Grond headed for his co-pilot's chair.

"Asper, there are crash couches in the common room. Get him strapped in. Then ... well, go wherever you want."

BLOCKSHIP SIZED.

"Get out *now*," Brazel said. "Anywhere. *Now.*"

I TRIED, Namey responded. WE ARE ALREADY WITHIN THE BLOCKSHIP'S RANGE.

"Shit," Brazel said. "How many other fighters? How fucked are we?"

EIGHT.

"Eight's too fuckin' many," Grond said. "Find someplace to hide!"

"Asper!" Brazel shouted, forgetting the comm. "You got any magic that can hide us? Anything? Namey, find a moon or an asteroid field or something!"

"Not an entire ship," Asper said.

WE ARE HUNDREDS OF THOUSANDS OF KILOMETERS FROM ANYTHING, Namey said. THERE IS NOWHERE TO HIDE. THE SPIDERSHIPS WILL BE WITHIN RANGE IN A MATTER OF MOMENTS.

"Shields? Chaff? Activate *everything.*"

MISSILE LAUNCHES DETECTED.   WE DO NOT POSSESS ANY USEFUL COUNTERMEASURES AGAINST BENEVOLENCE TARGETING TECHNOLOGY.

"What the hell do we *have?*"

"I'll do my damnedest to shoot 'em down," Grond said.

"We've had missiles shot at us before!" Brazel said. "What the hell did we do then?"

GOT HIT, MOSTLY, the ship replied. MISSILES AND SPIDERSHIPS WITHIN RANGE IN TWO MINUTES.

"There's no way out," Brazel said.

"Then we die shooting," Grond said, and opened fire into the black.

Rhundi had expected an invasion. What she got was a single capital ship, and not one anywhere near the Benevolence's weight class, either. In fact, it looked almost secondhand, like someone wealthy and important had used it for years, someone who had then upgraded to something flashier and more impressive and cast the old ship aside. It had entered the system a few hours ago, and almost lazily made its way to her resort, descending as slowly as possible. Every attempt at communication had been ignored.

She stood at their hangar, Gorrim and Tarrysh, her head of security, flanking her. Tarrysh was the toughest gnome Rhundi had ever met, standing a full head taller than her, and Rhundi was on the tall side for a gnome. Tarrysh regularly sparred with Grond, training the halfogre on how to fight creatures much smaller than him. That she had thus far escaped those sessions with no major injuries was the best testament imaginable to her abilities.

"Not Benevolence," she said. "Means we're dealing with Option Two on the plan, then. You two both clear on what to do?"

"I don't like this," Tarrysh said.

"I pay you to not like my plans," Rhundi said. "That's fine. You're going to do your job, though, right?"

"Of course I am," she responded.

"Okay. Gorrim?"

"Pretty much nobody here but the folks who won't leave," he said. "Mostly employees."

"I *told them* to go," Rhundi said.

Gorrim only shrugged. "Sometimes we don't listen to you."

"So long as everybody follows the rules," she said. "No violence unless they bring it, and then only enough to put on a good show. Nobody dies to defend this place."

"Take your own advice, boss," Tarrysh said.

"I plan to," she replied. "Get moving, both of you."

The two gnomes melted away. Rhundi thought over her options again. This was about the best set of circumstances she could have imagined. The Benevolence very well might have started with a bombing run just to soften everyone up. She'd known as soon as the capital ship had moved within visual range without opening fire that the dice were rolling in her favor.

She stood and waited, alone, as the ship landed.

A portal on the side of the ship slid open, and a ramp descended to the ground. A handful of armed soldiers stomped out of the ship and formed a loose line a few meters from her. She looked them over. They were dressed similarly enough that *soldiers* seemed like a more appropriate term than *mercenaries*, and they appeared to be fairly well armed. But the line was ragged, and a few of the soldiers were looking around, shifting their weight from foot to foot, almost impatient.

Trying to impress me, she thought. Which meant that whoever was running this crew thought they *needed* to impress her. She'd never encountered or heard of Benevolence who felt the need to worry about what anyone else thought.

Two more figures walked off the ship. One was an elf, dressed in a loose shirt and black pants made of expensive-looking, shiny cloth. Xe was—wait—

Is that a beard?

It was. The elf was *male*. And the figure behind him was an ogre.

Rhundi wasn't sure whether she should laugh or pinch herself. She'd wargamed a number of possible ways this could go, and had prepared Gorrim and Tarrysh for a number of possibilities and contingencies.

Their antagonists being people she knew had *not* been on the list of things likely to happen.

"I'll be damned," she said. "Barren. K'Shorr. You might literally be the last people in the galaxy I was expecting to see today."

"Where are they, Rhundi?" Barren asked. He actually had to put a hand on one of his soldier's shoulders and move the man out of his way to get through the line. A better-trained corps would have already had a way to make that move look more elegant. Like, say, *leaving a gap.* This crew really had been put together in a hurry.

"They?"

"Your husband and your halfogre," he said.

"Dunno," she said. "Probably off on a job somewhere. They do freelance, you know."

"Let's not lie to each other, dear," Barren said. "We scanned for life signs from orbit. You have less than five percent of the crowd I'd expect in a place like this. Either you have gotten much, *much* more ineffective since last we met or you evacuated. Which means you know exactly why I'm here."

"I don't have your statue anymore," she said. "Or your errand boy."

"I don't want the statue," Barren said. "I want *Roashan.*"

Rhundi raised an eyebrow.

"Never been there," she said. "Is that in elfspace? I don't travel too often."

Barren glanced at K'Shorr. The ogre walked over to Rhundi, towering over her. Rhundi blinked at him. She'd gotten too used to Grond, and it was easy to forget just how large a full ogre could get. This one probably came close to topping three meters, and probably outweighed Grond by fifty kilos, damn near all of it muscle.

"Thanks," she said. "Sun was in my eyes. Do you think trying to scare me will help? You've known me longer than that."

"It's not you I need to scare," Barren said.

The kick came faster than she could have imagined. She felt herself go airborne, tumbling, and lost consciousness as her head slammed into the ground.

>⟨⊙⟩<

TWENTY-ONE

They lasted ninety seconds.

Ninety seconds: a minute and a half of dodging, shouted instructions, hairpin turns, and astonishing luck–before the first missile broke through their shields. The Benevolence spiderships weren't bothering to use more than a couple of cannons each, meaning that they were more maneuverable than they would have been if they were using more firepower. The *Nameless* was listing to starboard and leaking air moments later. Grond had scored a number of direct hits on the attacking spiderships that did nothing to their shields and had managed to blow several missiles into powder before impact.

All for nothing.

The warning klaxons on the ship were overlapping and so painfully loud that Brazel shut them down.

EVACUATE, Namey said. EVACUATE NOW. Something else hit the ship, tossing Brazel out of his pilot's seat and breaking his scalp open on an instrument panel.

"Everybody drop what you're doing and get into an atmo suit," Brazel shouted over shipwide comm. "Namey ... just run. Keep us alive as best you can."

"Our escape pod isn't sized for four," Grond said. "It's gonna be crowded in there."

"I don't think it matters much," Brazel said, struggling into his suit. The *Nameless* had two spares for guests, cheap expandables meant to fit anything from a gnome to a younger ogre. Another explosion shook the boat. The lights went out.

"Namey? Still there?" Brazel asked. There was no response from the ship.

"Head for the escape pod," Grond said. "I'll be right back."

"*WHAT?*" Brazel screeched. "We don't have *time for this,* Grond!"

"Then leave without me!" the halfogre shouted. "You really think it matters much?"

"This way," Brazel said to the other two, and headed for the escape pod. Most ships the *Nameless'* size didn't have one, but theirs had doubled as a smuggling compartment in the past, and actually more or less required the ship to be falling to pieces before it was usable–the outside of the thing was laced with shaped charges designed to blow it free from the ship. If the Benevolence didn't bother scanning for life signs, they might actually mistake the pod for scrap, which was part of the idea. He threw a shelf out of the way and punched an access code into a keypad hidden in the wall of the common room. The door slid open and he shoved Asper and Haakoro inside.

"GROND! You've got thirty seconds!" he shouted, hoping their subcomms were still working and suspecting that they probably weren't.

It took the halfogre twenty-five. The boat was rocked by another enormous explosion, and Grond hit the doorway at an angle, nearly careening past it. He threw a bag and a bundle wrapped in cloth into the room, then pulled the rest of himself inside as the *Nameless'* gravity gave out and everything went weightless. As soon as he was inside Brazel slammed the lock shut then shouted to Asper, who stood at the button to blow the pod free of the ship.

"Everybody hold on to something!" the gnome shouted, and the elf pushed the button. Brazel and Grond scrambled for the seats built into the sides of the pod and strapped themselves in. Haakoro had already found his.

A series of dull thuds sounded as the explosive bolts attaching the pod to the *Nameless* detonated, then a much larger explosion as the pod tore itself free of the ship. A moment later, the escape pod was rocked by another shockwave as the spiderships blew the *Nameless* into pieces.

✺

This time, the white light came on by itself. The elf found his sight suddenly beginning to fade out and barely had time to fall into a chair before the vision overtook him completely.

He felt pain. His entire body ached. Old pain, like a broken limb that had never properly healed. He looked down at himself. He was in a child's body again, only this time the milk-white skin was mottled with bruises and scabbed-over cuts and lesions. The luxurious white robe of his last vision was gone. What little clothing he was allowed was torn into filthy rags and insufficient to hide his shame.

YOU HAVE FAILED, the voices said. They were louder, this time, and their anger was obvious.

"I have not failed," he said, pulling himself into a subservient position, his face pressed to the white floor. "I swear to you that I have not."

YOU HAVE NOT ACHIEVED YOUR GOALS. THE DISSIDENTS HAVE NOT YET BEEN BROUGHT TO HEEL.

"I only require more time," he said. "I swear to you that it will happen."

OUR PATIENCE GROWS THIN. THE GIFTS OF AZAMOEG ARE SOON TO BE WITHDRAWN FROM YOU IF THEY ARE NOT PUT TO PROPER USE.

The elf abased himself further, stretching out full-length on the ground, face down, his arms splayed out to his sides.

"I swear to you that I shall succeed," he said. "I swear on my life. I swear on my *soul.*"

YOU HAVE ALREADY SWORN ON YOUR SOUL, the voices said. WHEN NEXT WE MEET IT WILL BE EITHER IN SUCCESS OR IN FAILURE. THERE WILL BE NO FURTHER CHANCES, OUTCAST.

"Never," he said. "I sw–I promise. It shall be as I have said."

AND NOTHING LESS, the voices said. He felt a sudden, terrible pressure on his body, pushing him into the floor, and felt the nose and ribs of the little body he occupied shift and crack.

When he came back to himself, he was still screaming.

>-{⚏}-<

"*So ... uh ... now what?*" Haakoro asked. The four of them were packed into the *Nameless'* escape pod, an undersized box with walls lined with crash couches and compartments for storage. There was room to move, but not much. If they ended up having to use the couches, the ogre would have to take one and the three of them would be getting *very* friendly on the other.

"You shut the fuck up," Brazel whispered, "and we beg every higher power we can think of that they keep not noticing us." It had been five minutes since losing the *Nameless*, and as far as he could tell none of them were dead yet. Unless they were, and this was the way the afterlife punished him for a lifetime of irregular behavior. He tried to think of any ways eternal damnation might be different from being locked in a tiny space with Haakoro and came up blank.

He glanced over at the elf. Xe had ignored the couches, sitting cross-legged on the floor, xir eyes closed and lips moving. A pale golden glow emanating from xir body provided the only light in the escape pod.

"What do you think xe's doing?" he whispered to Grond.

"Xe said the *Nameless* was too big to shield from notice," the halfogre replied. "Maybe the escape pod isn't. Contacting somebody, maybe. I have no idea." He unbuckled his restraints and moved to the front of the pod, careful not to touch the elf.

"I can't get any status on the air supply without powering the pod," he said. "And the last thing we want is to go live right now. Braze, do you happen to remember the last time we recharged it?"

"It hasn't been long," he said. "If it was just the two of us, we'd be good for a week."

"And with four?" Haakoro asked.

"It gets *shorter* with every *word you say*," the gnome snapped.

The kid held up both hands, surrendering.

Grond pulled open a panel. "Plenty of food. Only other thing's fuel. And we're kinda in the middle of nowhere, so who knows how far we'll have to go to–"

Something slammed into the side of the pod, sending the halfogre drifting into the opposite wall. Asper, still sitting cross-legged on the floor, didn't react at all.

"The hell was that?"

"No idea," Brazel said. "Something else blew up out there? If they were shooting at *us* we'd be dead. They can't be shooting at each other, can they?"

"No," Grond said. "But something's going on."

Something else hit the pod again, this time throwing it into a spin. Grond swore, ricocheting off the floor and a wall before managing to pull himself back into a seated position.

"I think it might be time to risk powering up," he said. "It's better than getting battered to death."

Brazel unbuckled himself. "I got it," he said. He had always been better at zero-G maneuvering than the halfogre anyway, and at his size he did a lot less damage if he bounced off of something. He pulled himself to the pod's rudimentary cockpit and flipped a few switches, putting the pod into a low-power standby mode—which activated passive sensors and let them see through the front canopy.

The blockship and the spiderships were already gone. The escape pod floated in the middle of a debris field created by the destruction of their own ship.

"Time to go, then," Brazel said, restoring gravity and pivoting the ship around.

"Wait," Grond said, pointing at the long-range display. "What's that?"

A single blip had appeared on the display.

"They might have left somebody behind to see if we did *exactly what we were about to do*," Brazel said. "Going back to passives."

"It's closing in," Grond said. The blip was moving toward them at high speed.

"Everybody just relax," Brazel said. "Nothing we can do about it."

Asper stopped chanting, and the glow faded. The four of them sat in near-darkness, only a few dull red lights from the console penetrating the gloom.

They all felt it as the ship started pulling to starboard. The stars outside the ship started moving.

"Oh, what the *hell*," Brazel said. "Tell me that's not an inertia beam. *Please.*"

"It is an inertia beam," Asper said. The pod began rotating, bringing the distant ship into view. None of them recognized the make of the ship, a fact that did not change as the ship grew closer. One thing was clear: it was *much* bigger than them, big enough to be able to power an inertia beam in the first place, and big enough to pull them into its dock without any input from them at all. The pod continued rotating and was pulled through the field emitter that kept the air inside the ship and set down gently in a cargo bay, the canopy facing open space.

"They coulda blown us out of the sky in a boat that big," Grond said. "This has to be good news, right?"

"Depends. Does *captured* sound like an improvement?" Brazel answered.

"It sounds better than starving to death," Haakoro said.

"We weren't gonna starve to death. We had *you,*" Brazel said. "Air was always going to be the problem."

Haakoro took a moment to work that through, then wisely closed his mouth again.

Grond picked up the bag and the bundle he'd brought onto the ship. He removed a few weapons—one of Brazel's guns, Angela, and a few mid-length knives—from the bag, then put the bundle into it and stashed the entire thing in the compartment with their food supplies.

"You risked your life to save your longbow?" Brazel said.

"Angela is not just a *longbow,*" Grond said. "And yes." He looked at Asper. "I assumed you had the statue. I couldn't find it."

The elf nodded. Brazel thought about asking where xe was hiding it and decided against it.

"Where the hell are you hiding it?" Haakoro asked. Asper calmly reached behind xirself and produced the statue. Haakoro opened his mouth to continue protesting. Grond grabbed his chin and closed his mouth for him.

"That's enough for now," the halfogre said. He handed Asper and Haakoro each one of his blades.

"Those are my favorites," he said. "Try not to lose them."

He pointed at Brazel, then at the exit hatch. His body language made it clear: he would go out first, followed by Asper and Haakoro, then Brazel. He snapped his wrist and Angela flared into readiness, the energy string casting a blue glow over the room.

Brazel counted backwards from three to zero and then pulled the hatch open. Grond charged through, ready for anything.

The dock was empty. There were no other ships or pods, and no other people. There wasn't even really anyplace for anyone to hide. Their escape pod was the only object in the dock. Grond turned to look behind the pod, just in time for the doors to close over the force shield that had kept the atmosphere in place while the inertia beam dragged them inside.

"What?" he bellowed. "You want us to go looking for you?"

"I didn't really want you around at all, if you want the truth," a voice said.

Grond whirled around.

"Ah, *shit*," he said.

TWENTY-TWO

Sirrys ban Irtuus bon Alaamac was growing frustrated with the ship's comm system. He had been trying to raise his employer for nearly an hour with no luck. Neither her office nor her private quarters were responding, and Rhundi had always stubbornly refused to give him access to her private subcomm. *She* had *his*, of course, and could contact him whenever she wanted, but he was not granted the same courtesy from her. He wouldn't even mind talking to Gorrim, if the obnoxious little gnome would at least tell him where to find Rhundi.

Wait. He was on a ship with her children. Surely the Tavh're'muil children would have access to subcomm frequencies that Irtuus-bon did not—if not for their mother, then surely for their father, who rarely appeared to have anything very important to do.

He approached the eldest daughter. What was her name again? *Darsi.*

"Child," he said.

The girl had the nerve to roll her eyes at him. "My name is Darsi, Irtuus-bon," she said. "People my age don't really like being addressed as *child.*"

He nodded. This was entirely irrelevant.

"I need to contact your mother," he said. "She is not responding to any of the comm frequencies I have been provided with, and I cannot reach her secretary either. I was hoping she had provided you with additional means to contact her that I might use."

"What, you mean her subcomm?"

Irtuus-bon grated his teeth. This child would require things to be spelled out clearly to her, apparently.

"Yes. Or a direct comm to your living quarters, or to her sleeping-den. I just need to get ahold of her."

"She told us never to give those to you," Darsi said. This was true. However, Darsi suspected that under the circumstances the rules might be bent a bit. "I'll see if I can raise her, if that's good enough for you."

"That will have to be sufficient," Irtuus-bon said.

Darsi raised her mother's direct subcomm. Subcomms weren't location-dependent, but they *were* range-dependent, meaning that it wasn't a method that she thought was terribly likely to work very well. They'd been tunneling away from Arradon for several days. Even a high-powered subcomm was unlikely to be able to throw a signal that far, and the one her parents had allowed her to embed was not terribly strong.

No luck.

She tried her father. Nothing there, either. Over the next few minutes, she tried several of the same comm locations that Irtuus-bon had already attempted, hoping that Rhundi–or anyone, really–might answer a comm from *her* when they might have ignored one from the troll. She got nowhere. All of the lines timed out without any connection.

She thought for a moment. This was probably bad. The troll had likely already run through the exact same frequencies she had. Her parents' direct subcomms and their living quarters were the only ones that she had access to that he didn't, and those hadn't worked.

"I can't find her," she said.

"That is unfortunate," said Irtuus-bon, who appeared to be struggling to keep his height. "I have information that she will find very useful. It would be best to be able to give it to her."

"You could just send her the data, you know," she said.

"I would prefer to speak with her first," Irtuus-bon said. "I have my reasons."

Darsi thought for a moment. Oddly, she really didn't feel like her parents were in any trouble. She'd found herself inexplicably worried about her father any number of times in the past only to discover that he'd just narrowly pulled himself out of a scrape. She didn't feel that way this time. She looked around for Barash, her youngest sister. Barash had been known to have nightmares or sudden panic attacks in the same circumstances. Barash looked a bit frightened, but many of the younger children had spent most of the trip looking worried. There was nothing to worry about there.

Wait. She was being stupid. She knew plenty of other people on Arradon. She went and found Krin. The gnome brightened visibly as she walked toward him. The other members of the security team snickered a bit, but didn't move away at all.

"I need you to get in touch with Tarrysh," she said.

This startled him.

"What for?"

"The troll and I can't find either of my parents," she said. "I'm hoping she knows where they are."

"You know Tarrysh isn't really big on being bothered," Krin said. "Any chance she's just busy?"

"You're suggesting that my mother, Rhundi Tavh're'muil, your *boss*, is so busy that she won't take any calls from either her oldest daughter or her head researcher, both of whom she sent away from their homes so that they would be safe? You're saying this as a member of their *security team?*"

Boys could be so *dumb* sometimes.

"Okay," Krin said. "You're probably right. But I'm not gonna be the one to call her. I don't run the team. Let me talk to Lorryn." He walked back to the rest of the security team and had a word with their security chief, who argued for a moment, then shrugged and threw up her arms, no doubt as Krin used the same line of argument against her that Darsi had just used against him.

Lorryn approached Darsi. She was an older gnome, selected for her intelligence and cunning rather than strength and size, with most of her fur starting to go to grey. She'd spent most of the trip ignoring the family and Irtuus-bon entirely, spending her time and effort on keeping her security team focused on their jobs, along with occasionally spelling their pilot.

"What do you need?" she asked.

"I don't want a lot of Tarrysh's time," she said. "Just to know where at least one of my parents are. *We* need to know that too, you know. We probably ought to head straight for Taralon if they've gone missing."

Lorryn nodded once, accepting her argument. "All right," she said. "I'm supposed to check in with Tarrysh every couple of days anyway, and we're about due for that. But I talk to her, not you. I'll find out about your parents. If she needs to talk to you, I'll bring you in on the comm."

"Okay," Darsi said. That felt like she'd won.

The older gnome walked away, heading for the security team's quarters to make the comm. She was gone for no more than a few minutes. When she returned, Darsi noticed she'd armed herself.

"Your mother's been taken," she said. "You're right. We have a problem."

"*Ilana*," Brazel said. "I'll be damned."

"You couldn't have shown up two hours ago? Before the Benevolence blew up our *fucking ship?*" Grond asked.

"No," she said, not bothering to elaborate. She stared the halfogre down for a moment, a sight that was almost comical: Ilana was human, but barely half a meter taller than Brazel and as slender as a teenager. "Remember sent me. This is when I got here. She said to bring you in."

"She couldn't send the *Memento?*" Brazel asked. Remember lived, as far as he knew, on the other side of the galaxy. It was far too far away to ever imagine traveling to, even in tunnelspace. The last time they had met her, she had brought them to her with a teleporter, technology that Brazel was still half-convinced was impossible. The teleporter was called the *Memento,* Remember apparently being somewhat of a fan of puns.

"She sent me," Ilana said. "I'm bringing you to the *Memento.* The *Memento* will send you to her, just like last time."

Grond's lip curled in disgust.

"So ... who's this?" Haakoro asked.

"Her name's Ilana," Brazel said. "She's one of Remember's people. We had a ... uh ... *minor disagreement* the last time we met." The minor disagreement had left Ilana disarmed and unconscious on the floor in front of her employer. Brazel decided to leave that part of the story out. "This is Haakoro. The elf is Asper."

"I know who you are," she said. "Come on, we don't have a lot of time." She led them to quarters on the ship, putting Brazel and Grond together and giving Haakoro and Asper their own, separate bunks. She then excused herself, citing a need to find out where to meet the *Memento*.

"I hate it when they do this to us," Brazel said, eyeing the bunks. They were much too large for him and much too small for Grond.

"It's only for a little while," Grond said. "You'll be fine. I'm the one who has to break my spine if I want to sleep."

"Hopefully it won't be for long. Who knows where the *Memento* is right now."

Grond nodded. "Listen, Braze, about the ship..."

The gnome held up a hand. "Not right now. We'll worry about that later."

"But—"

"I mean it, Grond," Brazel said, taking a sharper tone of voice than the halfogre was used to hearing. "We worry about the boat when we have time to worry about the boat."

"Have it your way," Grond said. "I'm gonna go get our stuff from the pod and then see if I can fit into the showers on this thing." He left the room, the door sliding shut behind him.

"I have a damage report," the dwarf said.

"Proceed," Overmorrow said. Xe sat on the floor, legs crossed in a meditative pose. Xe had been maintaining that pose since Roashan had jumped into tunnelspace to flee the Benevolence assault. Truthfully, there was little to do. Overmorrow was not an engineer or a mechanic and would not have been terribly useful in calculating the damage done by the mercenaries to Roashan's complicated and overlapping systems.

"It's surprisingly minimal," the dwarf replied. "The biggest problem was the damage to the field emitter. One of our ship bays is going to have to be closed for a few days to repair that. We lost about a dozen people. Everything else is minor or just cosmetic. We have three prisoners. All three are injured, one badly, but they'll survive."

"Have the dead been identified?"

"Ours, or–"

"Ours," Overmorrow said. "I don't care about theirs."

"Most of them," the dwarf answered. "Two are–well, two are going to be more difficult, and in all the chaos we haven't had a lot of time to figure out who's missing and who fled on their own."

"Do what you can, and send me a list of the deceased. We will remember them."

The dwarf nodded, making a note.

"How did they get that close to us?"

"Valid identity codes," the dwarf answered. "Everything they had checked out. There was no warning until they started shooting."

"Any idea how they got those valid identity codes?"

"We're working on that," she replied, "but it seems most likely that the mercenaries were provided the codes by the Benevolence somehow. They were almost all human mercs, no evidence that there's anybody that we've worked with before."

"That is not a good sign," Overmorrow replied.

"It's not, no. Do you want to talk to the prisoners?"

"In a bit," xe said. "Do you happen to know where we are heading right now?"

The dwarf appeared taken aback. "I don't, actually," she admitted. *She wouldn't,* Overmorrow thought. It was entirely possible that no one did other than the navigators, and random chance played a significant role as to where Roashan went when the station jumped under duress. It was all part of the secrecy necessary to keep them out of the hands of the Benevolence. It would probably be necessary to go directly to the navigators to get an answer.

"My apologies," Overmorrow replied. "That would be outside your sphere of influence, I suspect. Have security informed that the prisoners are to be kept reasonably comfortable but under close guard. Continue to work to repair the damage with all possible speed, and convey my personal thanks to your team."

"Everyone's saying it would have been much worse if the halfogre and the gnome hadn't been on board," the dwarf added. "The two of them and Asper drove off half the invasion by themselves, I hear."

Overmorrow nodded. Xe was well aware of Asper's abilities, and Brazel and Grond had proven to be impressively capable themselves. The dwarf let herself out.

Overmorrow forced xirself to be still and mentally reached out to Asper. Xe received a confusing jumble of sensations in response. There had been danger, but it had receded, and strong uncertainty and anxiety about the future was present but Asper was controlling it. Overmorrow sent a whisper of reassurance and pulled back from their connection, choosing to let Asper handle xir own problems.

It was time to decide what to do next.

TWENTY-THREE

"Not in front of the kids," Darsi snapped, grabbing the surprised Lorryn by her elbow and pulling her back into the room she'd just come from. "What in blazes does *taken* mean?"

"First of all, young lady—"

Darsi's eyes flashed. "Don't you dare *young lady* me right now. Neither of us has time for it."

Lorryn laughed.

"I'm being funny?"

"You're being your *mother*," she said. "Or maybe that's your dad, since you just insulted me without any real thought to the consequences."

"Marvel at my development later," she said, a smile creeping onto her face anyway. "Right now just tell me what happened."

"The resort's fine," Lorryn said. "And as far as anyone knows, your mother is too. They cleared the resort for the same reason they sent you away: they were expecting an attack. It never came. One ship landed. An elf and an ogre got off. The ogre knocked your mother out and they took her away."

"They didn't *follow?*" Darsi asked.

"They tried. Tarrysh was breathing *fire* when I called. Your mother had locked down the security team's ships with a voice override. It didn't expire until an hour or so ago, but by then they were *gone*."

Darsi brightened.

"This is good news?"

"It means she's fine," Darsi said. "I don't know what she's got planned, but she's got something planned and she's fine."

"Good to know," Lorryn said. "What are *we* going to do? Since you're in charge now, of course."

"Mom said we should head to Taralon if anything bad happened. I think this probably still qualifies even if we're not worried about her. So we just need to inform the pilot–"

Lorryn visibly shuddered, then looked around, alarm on her face.

"What?"

"The ship just dropped out of tunnelspace. We don't have any reason to–"

The relative quiet of the ship shattered as alarms began sounding everywhere.

"Shit," said Lorryn. "I'm in charge again. No arguing. Get you and your siblings' asses into a secure room and strapped to something and do it *now*."

Darsi turned and bolted away to collect her brothers and sisters. Lorryn signaled to her security team to follow them and to secure the troll, then headed for the cockpit.

"Status report," she said.

The pilot only pointed.

Lorryn's jaw dropped.

"Oh, *shit*."

Rhundi awoke in a cell. On the *floor* in a cell, which seemed needlessly insulting. She took a few moments before opening her eyes, breathing steadily and listening carefully, trying to pick up any sounds or scents of anyone else in the room. One thing was certain: the place *smelled* terrible, of body odors and fluids from more species than she could count.

Not much *blood*, though, so she probably wasn't in a torture chamber. After convincing herself she was alone in the room she sat up and looked around. She was on someone's boat. She could feel the engine thrumming through the floor, which was a metal grate partially covered with some sort of cheap rubberized mat. Her fur was damp. She didn't especially want to know what with. There was a bench set into a wall that she could use for sitting or sleeping, but it was sized for humans. She'd have to climb to get onto it. Surprisingly, neither her feet nor her hands were bound.

Typical, she thought. The room had no windows and wherever the door was, it was flush with the wall. There were no toilet facilities, which was probably why the room had a grated floor and stunk of urine. *A bit barbaric, but not torture*, she thought. She was meant to get out of the room at some point. They had put her here to soften her up and break her will, not to leave her to die.

She checked her subcomms, not expecting any luck, and got none. Everything was still implanted properly but they'd been either dampened or deactivated. *No surprises there.* She was still wearing the same clothes she'd had on when K'Shorr had knocked her out. She'd had a couple of smaller weapons concealed on her but those were both gone. She'd had a belt on, too. That was missing too.

Okay, then. K'Shorr had kicked her in the chest, just at her breastbone. She stood up and stretched, checking to see if any bones were broken. They weren't. Other than quite a bit of lingering soreness and a big lump on the back of her head where she'd hit the ground, she was basically fine. She thought about the implications of that for a moment. The ogre had been a pitfighter for as long as he'd been alive. He had trained *Grond*. Rhundi was certain that he could have broken her neck with a kick a few centimeters higher, or aimed his foot a few centimeters to the right or the left and broken some ribs or a collarbone. He hadn't. She mentally upgraded her status even further. Not only did her captors not intend to kill her, they didn't seem to really want her *hurt*.

"I'm practically a guest," she said.

She climbed onto the bench and stretched out. With no one in the room and no visible cameras or ways to contact anyone else, there was little to do but try to catch up on sleep. You never knew when you were going to have a chance to get more.

The Memento hung in space, silent and impossibly large, a portal opening in the side to admit Ilana's ship. Brazel still couldn't fathom the sheer scale of the thing. He'd landed ships on smaller *planetoids* before–had, in fact, had smaller planetoids *thrown* at him before–and the *Memento* was entirely artificial.

"What I'd do to get access to her bank accounts," he muttered to himself. He and Grond had handed the *Nameless'* sensor logs over to Rhundi after encountering the giant teleporter the first time, and she'd passed them along to her engineering crew. It had taken only an hour for a member of their team to summon the courage to accuse Brazel and Grond of faking the sensor data somehow. The *Memento*, apparently, was both physically *and* economically impossible.

And yet there it was. Ilana's ship moved into the center of the giant sphere and landed a few minutes later.

He went and found Grond.

"You felt the ship land. We're here."

"And so we are," Brazel answered. "You're not going to try and kill Remember again, are you?"

"Not planning on it," Grond said. "I figure I got enough enemies right now."

"And you like winning your fights," Brazel said. Remember had rather handily humiliated the halfogre last time.

"And I like winning my fights. Sure. You ready?"

"I am," he said, standing up and stretching. "Not like I packed a bag before the boat got blown up."

Grond opened his mouth to respond. The gnome held up a finger.

"Still not the time. Later."

Grond closed his mouth again. About half of him wanted to start a roaring argument with his partner. The rest recognized that Brazel was probably right, even if he was being an asshole about it. The two of them left the ship, joining Haakoro, Asper and Ilana outside.

"You coming with us?" Grond said to Ilana.

"No," she said. "Just on pickup duty. You got everything off my ship?"

"Everything but the escape pod," Grond said. "And I don't think we want that anymore." He glanced at Brazel, who shrugged.

"Good luck, then," Ilana said, turning away.

"You're not waiting for us?"

"I'm not," she said over her shoulder. "Remember said she'd take care of you. And I don't especially want to be around you if I don't have to." She entered her ship without another word.

"I remember her being friendlier," Grond said, looking Brazel's way. The gnome shrugged again, then headed for the teleporter without speaking.

"You two haven't done this before," Grond said. "I hope you're not modest. Remember has a bad habit of stealing all your stuff on the way through the teleporter. The first time Brazel and I used it we came through stark naked on the other side."

Asper looked impassive. Haakoro turned bright red, then looked at the elf and giggled.

"You're kidding," Grond said.

"Let me guess. You've never seen an elf naked before," Asper said.

"Nope," Haakoro said.

"I hope the experience is illuminating for you, then," Asper replied.

There was a table outside the teleporter itself, which hung in the precise center of the hollow sphere of the *Memento*. There were four glasses on the table, filled with a blue fluid. Brazel was already halfway through his by the time the rest of them arrived.

"Drink up," Grond said. "It'll make the trip itself a lot easier."

The four of them downed their drinks, Haakoro's nose wrinkling at the taste. The entrance to the portal slid open on its own, and they filed in. The inside of the room was featureless, the walls and floor covered with a black, cushioned substance.

"Lay down," Grond told Haakoro and Asper. "If you've got anything with you, I'd put it next to you, too, rather than keeping it attached to your body." He pulled Angela off his back and set her carefully on the floor next to him along with the rest of his weaponry. Haakoro looked around for a moment and sprawled out on his side of the room. Asper sat on the floor cross-legged, the backs of xir hands lightly resting on xir knees.

There was a wet sound as the black material oozed over the doorway, sealing the room shut.

"Get ready," Grond said.

A moment later, the material expanded into the room, filling it completely, and there was a tremendous sound as the four of them were flung across the galaxy.

※{☉}※

"I am angry," Overmorrow said.

The elf sat in xir quarters, speaking into a stationwide comm. Xe rarely had reason to address all of Roashan at once, but when xe did it generally brought all activity at the station to a standstill.

"We have had hard losses today. Our base on 9013LV has been overrun, and civilian losses run to the thousands. Roashan itself has been attacked, and several of our own who were warm with life yesterday lie cold today. But we do not bend to our sorrows. We are warriors, and warriors are grown used to loss."

Xe paused for a moment, letting the sound of xir breathing pass over the comm.

"It is time for the Benevolence to experience loss as well. We have fought them for generations, and in that time we have prevented their spread in our lands and our stars. But we have not pushed them back. We have not *beaten* them. We have, at best, stood in their way."

"Right now, there are beings fighting to resist the Benevolence. There is war and death in ogrespace, as the Benevolence's allies scheme and attempt to go around us where once they might have simply fought through. And they are succeeding. Our partners and our friends are dying on Khkk as we speak."

Overmorrow paused again, letting xir consciousness expand to fill the ship. Xe felt fear and trepidation, but also bravery and strength. And xe did *not* feel rebellion or betrayal. The people of Roashan were standing together.

"We have lost one planet today. We shall not lose a second. I call on Roashan: We shall travel to Khkk and we shall join the battle there. We shall fight against the Benevolence's allies, and if the Benevolence themselves arrive we shall fight them as well. The Benevolence shall not gain *one single meter* of new territory while I live."

"We depart for Khkk in one half hour. Those of you who are uncertain of your devotion to our cause have that time to take your belongings and leave. No one will try and stop you, and none shall criticize your decision. The rest of us should prepare for battle. The Noble Opposition goes to war today!"

As xe closed the connection, xe heard cheers echoing from every corner of the station.

Overmorrow had xir people with xir. Now all that was needed was to keep them alive.

TWENTY-FOUR

"Ow," *Grond said to no one in particular.* His head ached abominably. The pain wasn't as bad as the first time he'd used Remember's teleporter but it was still far from a pleasant experience. His vision cleared a bit, and he realized something: he was *still dressed.* Angela sat next to him, right where he'd left her.

He sat up and looked around. Asper and Brazel were both on their feet and dressed. Haakoro was still unconscious, sprawled out on the floor. He was the only one whose possessions and clothing had not made the trip with him.

"Whaddaya know," Grond said. "Remember's got a sense of humor."

"Kinda surprised she let *you* through," Brazel said.

"Guess she forgave me for last time," Grond replied. "What do we do with him?"

"Carry him with us," Asper said. "Remember would not have brought him across if she did not feel he belonged here."

Grond lifted the unconscious man off the floor, draping him across his shoulders.

"There'd better be a robe for him in there," the halfogre said.

The door squelched back open. The last time Brazel and Grond had been through, it had opened into what looked like an opulent lobby. This time it delivered them to the bridge of a capital ship. Just like last time, there was a small table next to the door with a box on it. Grond opened the box, which contained a robe for Haakoro. The halfogre set the man on the ground and covered him with the robe.

"I'm not dressing him," he said. None of the other three argued.

The bridge was a hotbed of activity, with beings of several different species moving about purposefully and a low buzz of background noise from staff going about their business. Nothing the size of a capital ship had a transparent canopy, but this one had the next best thing, with a huge holographic display running across the front portion of the bridge. They were within visual range of a reddish-brown terrestrial moon orbiting close to an enormous yellow gas giant. Brazel thought it looked familiar.

No one took any particular notice of the four of them, who stood awkwardly at the exit from the teleporter for a moment.

"This is new," Brazel said.

No one answered.

"Tempted to shoot something and see if they notice us," Grond said a few moments later.

"Please don't," a voice said from above them. They looked up to see a 'bot hovering toward them. "Lady Remember is aware of your presence and your inconvenience. She asks that you follow me."

"I would like to hear the words *apologizes for*," Grond said.

"Apologizes for," the bot replied, floating away.

Brazel snorted.

"That is *not* what I meant," Grond said.

"I think it is the best you can expect, however," Asper said. This time xe picked Haakoro up, first wrapping him in his robe and then slinging him over xir shoulder, only showing the smallest bit of strain under the man's weight.

"Shouldn't he be awake by now?" Grond asked.

"He will awaken when Remember wishes him to, I suspect," Asper answered. The three of them followed the 'bot, which led them around the perimeter of the bridge and then into a corridor. They entered a simple meeting room, featuring a table with a holoprojector and, rather incongruously, a cot. Asper tossed Haakoro off xir shoulder and onto the cot.

"The Lady will be with you momentarily," the bot said, flying off. Everyone took a seat.

They waited only a short time before Lady Remember swept into the room.

The Lady looked much as she had the last time Brazel and Grond had seen her, her silver-white hair gathered in a loose topknot and flowing down her back, clad in a billowing robe with deep sleeves that concealed her figure almost entirely. Her hands, as they almost always were, were clasped behind her back. She took a seat at the head of the table.

"I understand you have something for me," she said.

Asper glanced at Brazel, who nodded. Xe produced the statue and placed it in front of Remember, who looked at it carefully, leaning forward and examining it closely without touching it. The statue had returned to its dormant form, looking once again like a simple sphere on top of a wood base.

"Is it back in stasis?" Brazel asked. "I don't hear the humming anymore."

"It is," Asper said.

"That may be dispelled," Remember said.

"The signal will let them home in on us," Brazel said.

"That is my intention," Remember responded. "As it happens, we are travelling to them."

Grond and Brazel sat up straighter in their seats.

"I'm not sure I like that idea," Grond said.

Remember scraped a long fingernail over the top of the statue, which opened up and unfolded its arms again.

"If I were to touch this now," she said, "it would allow me a connection directly to the Benevolence. They use these to communicate with each other as well as with their underlings who are not themselves part of the Benevolence. That is how this particular statue has been tuned. It is set to communicate with only a few individuals, and not as a general-purpose communicator. I admit I am very curious to see who it is tuned for."

"It brought the Benevolence to two different planets and to Roashan as well," Asper said. "It is certainly communicating with *someone*."

"But only once in force," Remember said. "And once, truly, not at all. Those were mercenaries who attacked Roashan, not Benevolence. The battle would have been much harder otherwise."

"How do you know all of this?" Asper asked.

"It is my privilege to know many things," Remember replied, "and my job."

"I think the phrase you used last time was *Learn to live with ambiguity,*" Brazel said.

Remember merely nodded.

"Are you going to try and use the device?" Asper asked.

"I am considering it," Remember replied. "But not now. We have other things to discuss first." She activated a button at her seat and the holoprojector on the table came alive, showing a map of the galaxy. A portion of the map was tinged blue in color: Benevolence space.

"Here is our current location," she said, and a yellow spot began glowing brightly on the map.

"We're ... wait. So we *are* near Khkk." Brazel said.

"We are," Remember confirmed. "The Noble Opposition has certain interests on Khkk. So do the Benevolence. And so, as it happens, do *I*. The Benevolence are finally looking to make a move into ogrespace, and they have chosen Khkk as their starting point. They must be stopped."

"I think it's time that we got paid and left now," Brazel said. "I lost my ship and right now I don't know where my family is. We got hired to do a simple snatch-and-deliver job and now you're talking about *stopping the Benevolence*. At least two of those words don't belong in the same sentence together, *especially* when you're involving *me*."

The gnome stood up.

"Come on, Grond. We're leaving."

Grond didn't move.

"We, uh, don't really have anywhere to *go*, Brazel. Or any way to get there."

"Bullshit. Remember's *really* proud of throwing around how wealthy she is. Fuck the pay. I want a *ship*," Brazel said. "And enough fuel to get me the hell away from whatever the hell insane-ass plan you're putting together. I'm done with this. The rest of you can go get killed on your own time. We're *leaving*, and if we have to steal something to do it we're going to."

Remember raised an eye. Haakoro snored.

"And you can keep *that* asshole away from me for the rest of forever, too," he snarled. "I ever see him again, I'm putting holes in him."

"I have something to show you," Remember said, standing up. "Come with me." She turned and left the room, not waiting for the gnome to agree.

Brazel glared at Grond.

"What?"

"You know I hate it when people cut off a rant."

"And that's *my* fault?"

"I need someone to glare at," Brazel pouted. "You're nearby."

"Something makes me think she's probably not waiting out there," Grond said. "We may as well go with her."

Brazel swore under his breath and followed Remember out the door.

"Go with them," Asper said. "I'll stay here with Haakoro."

"Not sure if I should thank you or argue with you," Grond said. "But somebody ought to keep Braze from doing anything too stupid." He left as well, heading after his partner.

The door sliding open woke Rhundi up from a fitful, wary sleep. She rolled onto her side, glaring disdainfully as Barren and K'Shorr walked into the room.

"I bet you like the old-style doors better," she said. "No way to dramatically kick open a slider."

"Shut up," K'Shorr said.

"And if I say 'make me'?"

"I'll rip your jaw off." *But you haven't yet*, she thought. She moved her gaze from the ogre, who had had to duck to get into the room, to the elf. He threw a pair of cheap-looking electrorestraints at her and waited while she put them on.

"What can I do for you, Barren?"

"I am actually not sure *what* you can do for me, Rhundi," he replied. "It seems that I am having to do everything for *myself* lately. Wipe out the Malevolence's weapon dealers on Khkk. Wipe out the Malevolence *themselves*, when they come running to defend their friends. And the ... *precious* little bonus of *finally* being able to even the scales with you and the halfogre on top of everything else. I am having a *splendid* time."

"Glad to see you happy," she said. "You look a little worse for wear from the last time I saw you, honestly." Which was a taunt, but was also *true*. K'Shorr looked as dangerous as ever, but Barren looked ill and thin compared to the last time she'd laid eyes on him, and he hadn't been in good shape then either. His beard and hair was unkempt and poorly groomed, his clothes ill-fitting and somewhat threadbare.

"Soon to be rectified," he said. "Come with us, please."

Rhundi stood up, stretching her limbs and gesturing for Barren to lead the way. The giant ogre followed behind her as Barren walked to the ship's bridge. She spent the walk carefully examining the layout of the ship. It seemed a perfectly ordinary design for a capital ship, if a bit ragged and poorly maintained. Barren had clearly acquired the ship used.

I bet I could find my way around in here without much trouble, she thought. The design was fairly standardized. If the builders had offered much in the way of customization the original owners hadn't had the money to pay for much of it. She didn't see nearly as many people as she would have expected for a ship of this size, either. As she walked, she quietly stretched her arms and legs, working feeling back into them that had been lost in several hours of lying on hard metal.

They passed through a common crew area on the way to the bridge. The mercenaries who had failed to impress her earlier failed to impress her again as their captain walked through their space. Not a one stood or saluted. At one point Barren actually slowed down as someone walked in front of him. *No discipline*, she thought. *Means no devotion either*. This crew wasn't going to be too helpful in the event of actual trouble unless they saw the money that they stood to earn beforehand.

Eventually they reached the bridge, which was no more impressive than the rest of the boat had been. The holoscreen stretching across the front of the bridge was practically staticky, and Rhundi thought she could see some spots where it was actually losing the image from the ground. They were in orbit around an orange-red planetoid, mostly land mass with a scattering of blue veins in between the continents, wet areas too small to call oceans. Whatever this rock was, it was exceptionally dry. There was only a skeleton crew on the bridge, probably the bare minimum needed to keep the ship aloft.

So, what's happening here? she thought. *Is this budget? Can't afford a crew? Or can he just not keep people with him?* The Barren she'd known would never have put up with any of this. Everything about his operation was shabby. He'd gone terribly downhill. It was a wonder K'Shorr was still with him.

"So what are we looking at?" she asked.

"You don't recognize it?" Barren said.

"You may recall the bit where I asked what it was," Rhundi replied. "And I didn't say *Oh, that's where I grew up,* or something similar."

K'Shorr growled, his eyes glowing red. Barren only smiled.

"A small foolishness, I admit," he answered. "Welcome to Khkk. If you wait long enough, you may be here to watch it die."

"Melodramatic," she said. "I thought you guys wanted them working for you?"

Barren shrugged, still smiling sardonically. "I don't especially care, to tell the truth. I am trying to lure your Malevolence friends here so that they can be destroyed. I suspect my plan has worked. What the Benevolence does with the place afterward is up to them. The war was never more than a distraction."

"And what's your reward for all this?"

For a moment, Barren didn't say anything. His shoulders slumped, and he let out a sigh.

"I may ... return *home.*"

"Home. Got it," Rhundi said. A moment later, she finished picking the lock on her electrorestraints.

"Gotta go now," she said.

She spun on one heel and slammed her bound hands into K'Shorr's groin, simultaneously twisting and snapping open the restraints. The electric charge triggered, a safeguard that was supposed to immobilize the wearer so that he or she could be recaptured.

Unfortunately for K'Shorr, the electric charge went directly into *him* instead. Somewhat more fortunately, the restraints were set to "gnome" and not to "ogre." The big brute shrieked, a higher-pitched sound than any adult male ogre ought to have been able to make, and hit the floor in a heap. Rhundi jumped over him, kicking him in the face in the process, and fled.

TWENTY-FIVE

Remember did not say a single word as she led Brazel and Grond most of the way across what was proving to be an impressively large ship. A fair portion of the trip was by a lift, and Grond was shifting his weight awkwardly from foot to foot and fidgeting with his clothes as a reaction to the angry, silent atmosphere. Brazel simply glared, and Remember acted as if neither of them was there at all.

Eventually, they reached the ship's main hangar bay. Remember stopped outside, turning to the two of them and finally speaking.

"I have three things to show you," she said. "The first is in here." She placed her hand on a recessed panel and a door slid open.

Grond's eyes tripled in size and his jaw dropped open.

"It's ... it's *beautiful*," he said.

"You may take what you feel you may need," Remember said.

Grond rushed inside. Brazel stayed put.

"This is the second time you've effectively *bribed* my partner, you know," he said curtly. "The first time it was books. This is even *less* fair."

Remember had let them into the armory. The room was clean and white, lit with soft, warm light like an expensive suite in Rhundi's resort. That was where the similarities ended, however, as the room was lined with shelves and wall racks, every centimeter of which was covered with weapons: blades, blunt weapons, energy and projectile weapons, and explosives. Oh, *so many* explosives, from grenades to missile launchers and everything in between. Brazel could hear Grond *cackling* as the halfogre explored the collection.

"No one said I had to be fair," Remember responded. "And I mean that *literally*. No one has *ever* said that to me. And you are correct. You have earned your pay, and the Noble Opposition is in no real position to pay you at the moment."

"I'll take your weapons," Brazel said. "But don't expect me to thank you for it."

Remember merely nodded, and Brazel followed Grond into the armory. It was nearly twenty minutes before the halfogre agreed to leave, carrying enough weaponry to make even him strain under the weight. Brazel wore a simple bandolier with a few small guns attached, and a few more things concealed under his clothes.

"Now what?" the gnome asked.

"The next decision is yours alone to make," Remember said, and led them into the actual hangar.

"Pick one," she said.

This time, Brazel's eyes widened. There were easily fifty ships of every type and description in the bay, ranging from larger, bulkier cargo transports to smaller one- or two-man fighters to genuine warships.

"So which two are sized for gnomes?" he said.

"My technicians will retrofit any ship you like," she said. "The cockpit or the bridge can be rebuilt to your satisfaction. It should take no more than a day."

"Any ship I want, huh?" he said.

"Any ship you want," she replied.

"I don't suppose the *Nameless* is hiding in a corner somewhere."

Remember did not respond. Brazel looked at Grond for a long moment, then walked out into the hangar to explore. Grond waited, following his partner at a distance. The gnome took his time, pausing before several of the ships before seeming to select one, stopping in front of it and staring at it for a few minutes.

Grond examined the ship. Its basic outlines were those of a cargo ship: perhaps seventy-five meters long, with a snub-nosed cockpit to the front rather than to the side as the *Nameless'* had been. The body of the ship swept back from there to a long, rectangular storage bay, followed by the engines, which looked impressive. The main airlock and the storage bay cargo door both opened from the port side. It looked both faster and leaner than the *Nameless* had been, with a bit more space to boot.

That wasn't the biggest upgrade, though: this ship had a *ton* more weaponry. The *Nameless* had been able to scrap when necessary but was never meant to be a fighter. This one, on the other hand, was *clearly* designed as a battleship despite the large amount of room for cargo. *Maybe a troop transport originally,* he thought, but designed to insert warriors and vehicles into hot zones, meaning that it needed armament. No doubt the shields were a vast improvement over the *Nameless'* as well.

"I don't know if I like the paint job," Grond said. The ship was styled in wild swaths of red and gold, with the occasional silver or black highlight. He'd never seen anything quite like it.

"Stands out, don't she?" Brazel said. "Too flamboyant for a smuggler's ship. But we can fix that."

"More easily than you think," Remember said. Brazel started visibly at her voice. Neither he nor Grond had heard her approach them. "The colors are actually part of the identity package. The ship can alter them on command. You can cloak yourself from visual scans as well. The ship is virtually invisible in space if you make it black."

"I like it," Brazel answered. "I want to see the inside."

"The ship will open for you," Remember said. Brazel walked to the side cargo door and placed his hand on a reader. The bay doors opened up slowly, revealing the boat's interior. He disappeared inside.

"Your engineers are gonna ogre-size my parts of the thing too, right?" Grond said.

"This particular ship actually has a copilot's seat in the cockpit," Remember said. "I will make certain they are sized appropriately, and I will have your quarters adjusted as well. It should take no more than an hour."

"What about the AI?"

Remember raised an eyebrow. "Military-grade. Most of the ship is former Benevolence technology, actually.

Nonetheless, I suspect you will find the AI ... inadequate to your needs." Then, smiling: "It is easily enough replaced."

"That's good to know," Grond said.

They waited in silence until Brazel finally exited the ship.

"It'll do," he said.

"That's all?" Grond said. "It'll *do*?"

"Go pick a bunk and find someplace to stow your new toys," Brazel said. "We're leaving as soon as we can get this thing fueled up and the pilot and co-pilot seats swapped out. I can make do with my quarters without their techs screwing with them. Asper can stay or come with us. It's up to xir. Haakoro is Remember's problem now."

He crossed his arms and glared at Remember, who did not return the look. "How quick can your people finish this up?"

"You are too hasty," Remember said. "I said I had *three* things to show you. This is but the second. You may find yourself reconsidering once you see the third. The ship is yours. I have already signaled my crew to begin work. They should be here in a moment if you wish to oversee them. I suggest, however, that you come with me."

"Just let me drop the guns off," Grond said. They really were starting to get heavy.

Cameras, Rhundi thought as she fled down a corridor. If this were her boat they'd be everywhere, and there would be a few nanoclouds stored in strategic locations for when she needed them. But this wasn't her boat, and she didn't think Barren had been terribly careful about upkeep.

No point worrying about whether she was wrong or not. If they found her, she'd need to fight, and if they didn't find her, she'd probably have to fight sooner or later anyway.

So: first, *distance*. Second, *weapon*.

Or a hiding spot. That would do too. She looked around. These types of ships tended to come with their own cleaning systems. 'Bots, little ones, that ... *there*.

A grate, floor-height, that would be just about the right size to let a cleaner 'bot move throughout the ship. Or a *gnome*, if that gnome didn't have a problem with small spaces. Perfect.

Rhundi pulled the grate open, taking a moment to marvel at her luck that it didn't lock when the 'bots weren't using it, and crawled inside, easing the grate closed behind her. One problem: The 'bots weren't going to need light to see, so once she got more than a few meters into the system, she was going to be blind. That was still a lot better than being loose in the corridors, though. She felt vibrations as large feet–more than a couple of pairs, it sounded like–stomped down the hallway past her. *Good.* They'd figure out where she'd gone sooner or later, but she had plenty of time to wreak havoc between now and then.

She reached a T. She took a moment and stayed still, listening and smelling in both directions. One of them smelled slightly more strongly of cleaning fluids than the other. She went that way, crawling on her hands and knees, hoping that the passageway didn't narrow any further. She kept moving deeper, making a few more turns, always heading toward the scent of cleaning products.

There was a buzzing, clattering sound from in front of her. She froze. A few moments later, a pair of red lights appeared in her field of vision.

Shit. There was a cleaning 'bot, headed *somewhere*. And that somewhere was currently right toward her. There wasn't room for both of them in the tunnel.

The lights grew bigger as the 'bot zipped toward her. It slowed to a stop a meter or so in front of her face, then beeped at her inquisitively.

"Go away," she hissed. "Go back where you came from."

It beeped again, then backed up a meter or two. There were a series of mechanical clicks and buzzes.

Oh, hell, what's it doing?

The clicks and buzzes were replaced with a whirring sound. The little 'bot advanced toward her.

It thinks I'm an obstruction in the passage. Which means...

It was a cleaning 'bot. The damned thing was trying to *clear* her.

Rhundi quickly considered backing up to see if she could coax the 'bot into turning around a corner and rejected the idea. She couldn't see well enough as it was, and didn't want to leave the 'bot tunnels by accident.

Please be using brushes, she thought, and punched the 'bot. The thing emitted a surprisingly animal-like squeal and backed away, increasing its speed as Rhundi followed it. *Good.* It had some sort of self-preservation code built in somewhere. No doubt enough of these things had been deliberately kicked over the years that the manufacturers had seen a point in programming them to avoid threats. Pulling herself through the tunnel as fast as she could, she rounded a corner just in time to see the little 'bot exit through another grate into a larger room beyond.

She sniffed the air again. The smell of cleaning fluids was much stronger here. *Perfect.* The 'bot had led her exactly where she wanted to go. She pushed the grate open slowly, listening carefully for any signs of biological life in the room. Nothing, and likely no AI smart enough to notice she was in there. She looked around. The room she'd emerged into was basically a large storage closet, one wall lined with cabinet-like charging stations for cleaning 'bots and the rest of the room filled with vats of various cleaning compounds that the 'bots used while performing their duties. A handful of 'bots sped into and out of the room through three other access tunnels–though none, she noted, through the one she'd used. Perhaps the 'bots had temporarily blacklisted it. There was a touchscreen set into one wall.

"Let this be a programming kiosk," she murmured, flipping the display on.

It was a programming kiosk. She spent a few minutes learning the interface, then managed to call up schematics of the entire ship. As she'd suspected, the little 'bots could get basically anywhere they wanted through the access tunnels built into the walls.

She listened at the room's one door for a few minutes. There likely wasn't much reason for anyone to come in here, at least not until K'Shorr and Barren exhausted all the other places they might find her. She didn't hear anyone moving beyond the door, and decided not to bother trying to lock it closed. She'd just do her best to keep her ears open.

Aren't I just the luckiest today. She hadn't escaped from kidnappers *that* many times in her life, and most of those times she'd been on land and not in space, but she was pretty sure this was the most fun she was ever going to have doing it.

TWENTY-SIX

"Ow," Haakoro said. "My head hurts."

"Perhaps your brain is trying to escape," Asper said. The elf was picking idly at xir fingernails with one of Grond's knives.

"Funny," he replied. "Where are my clothes?"

"Left behind at the teleporter. I'm told Remember's robes are impressively comfortable, though."

Haakoro looked down at himself. "Yeah, I suppose. Where are the other two?"

"Gone with Remember," Asper replied. "They left me to keep an eye on you."

Haakoro stood up. "Who the *hell* decided I needed to be taken care of? I'm getting tired of you guys treating me like a child."

"Assume I was simply not invited to follow them, then," Asper said. "If that will make you feel better."

"I'm good at things, you know," Haakoro said. "I had my own ship. I was a freelancer. I did *jobs* for people. Made good money. Then I decide to go to Khkk for a while and everything goes straight to shit."

"It could be worse," Asper said. "You've passed up any number of opportunities to be killed in the past several days. You do seem to be astonishingly lucky."

"Yeah," Haakoro said. "Always have. But I used to be able to ... I don't know, *use it* for stuff. Not just getting me deeper and deeper into trouble. My luck's gone bad on me."

Asper nodded, clearly tiring of the conversation.

There was a soft knock at the door. An elf entered, carrying a box.

"Your effects," the elf said to Haakoro. "Please change. The Lady Remember has requested both of you come with me."

"What about the statue?" Asper asked. It was still sitting on the table, back in dormant form.

"Bring it with you," the elf said. "But do it quickly. The Lady is not accustomed to being kept waiting."

"Wait outside," Haakoro said as Asper picked the statue up. "You already got one look for free. I'm charging if you want any more."

Every so often, Grond found himself wishing that he worked with people whose legs were somewhere closer in length to his own. This was absolutely one of those times, as Remember strolled though the corridors of her ship at a businesslike clip and Brazel stubbornly took his time. The gnome was deliberately being obstinate, but Brazel moving at *normal* speed still forced Grond to slow down a lot of the time, and he was moving at something far less than normal speed at the moment. Trying to keep both of them in view was rapidly becoming annoying.

The only question was which of them to get angry at, and getting angry at Remember never seemed like a terribly good idea.

"Braze," the halfogre said, slowing and letting the gnome catch up with him. "This is ridiculous. You're getting what you want. Can we move this along?"

The gnome only glared, not altering his pace at all.

"I've picked you up and put you over my shoulder before," Grond said, trying to hit *I'm about halfway serious right now so please don't make me do this* in his tone and not sure if he was succeeding.

"Bluffing," was all the response he got.

"So you feel like getting lost in this ship? She's not gonna wait for us up there."

"If I get lost I'll just start stealing stuff," he said. "She'll send a 'bot."

"Most of the time when she sends 'bots they have guns on them."

"Once. And if I remember right it was *you* being inhospitable that time, not me."

The 'bot appeared a moment later. It did not have any guns.

"Lady Remember has requested that you increase your rate of movement," the 'bot chirped.

Brazel got as far as "Lady Remember can..." before Grond clamped a hand over his snout.

"We're coming," the halfogre said. "Give us a moment."

The 'bot floated annoyingly in the air in front of them, just out of Grond's reach, as the halfogre struggled with his partner. It tilted itself slightly to the side, managing to look almost quizzical, and Grond could hear a series of clicks and beeps as the thing either made a decision or quickly communicated with some other AI entity elsewhere in the ship.

"I have been requested to provide audio from your destination," said the 'bot.

Brazel looked disgusted for a moment, then nodded.

A moment later, he let Grond pick him up as the big halfogre sprinted after Remember, the 'bot straining to keep ahead of them.

Rhundi watched as the last of her cleaning 'bots rolled out of the supply room. She'd made a few modifications to a large number of them and sent them to strategic locations on the ship. It remained to be seen whether they were going to come in handy for her or not. She looked around. She hadn't found any way to access any cams through the computer console in the room, so she was still basically blind. She was still in a secluded part of the ship, which was an advantage, but she'd heard feet tromping through the corridors around her. They were stepping up the search. It was time to move. And find a weapon. Luckily, she'd been able to identify a couple of rooms that were almost certainly being used for storage–they were marked as low-priority for the 'bots and in out-of-the-way parts of the ship.

Hopefully she'd be able to find weapons in there rather than having to take them away from one of the people on the ship.

Only question was how to get there. She could try and make the trip through the access tunnels, but if someone overheard her while she was in there she'd have nowhere to go to escape. If she moved through the boat itself she at least had a chance to flee or fight anyone hunting for her. In the tunnel, all it was going to take was a gun fired around a corner or a grenade rolled toward her and she'd be done for.

Corridors, then. She stared at the map for another moment, making sure she knew the route and had a couple of escape paths in mind. She memorized the cleaning 'bots tunnels while she was at it, in case she had to duck back into them at some point.

Rhundi took one more look around for a weapon. There simply wasn't anything useful–at least, nothing that she hadn't already repurposed somehow. She'd hoped for a toolbox and hadn't found one. She stashed a portable control unit for the cleaning 'bots in a pocket.

"No point wasting time," she said, and listened carefully at the door. Nothing. She slid it open and headed toward the first of the rooms she'd identified, listening carefully and also scanning for the rather distinctive smell of ogre. The halls smelled mostly of humans. This was probably a good thing. She figured she could handle one human easily enough: two, if she got the drop on them. Any larger group than that and she'd have to run and hide.

She heard footsteps coming toward her from up ahead, where the corridor hit an intersection. She slid into an open room and waited. The room was full of bunks, but looked unused. The boat wasn't anywhere near to full capacity. She put a couple of them in between her and the door and got low to the ground. A few moments later a group of three walked past the doorway. She waited and listened as they moved farther away, then went back into the hallway.

Lucky. Still.

She saw no one else during the few minutes it took her to find the first storage closet. Unfortunately for her, it was locked. And the lock wasn't mechanical, which meant she couldn't pick it. It was a palm lock. She knew a few tricks for fooling palm locks, but they all relied on her having hands the same size and shape as the people who were supposed to be using it. There was no easy way to trick a palm lock into thinking a gnome's hand belonged to a big.

All the garbage on this ship, and THIS is where they shell out extra money, she thought.   On the other hand, if she managed to get inside the room, there was probably something good in there if they'd bothered to go to the trouble to lock it up.

Second choice was the tunnels. Maybe those wouldn't be locked. They certainly wouldn't be palm-locked. Worst that could happen would be a proximity sensor on the 'bots themselves to get them into the room, and she had ways around that. The nearest entrance was down the corridor a bit.

She caught a whiff of ogre on the air.

Of course. She turned away from the intersection and quickly picked a mechanical lock to get into the room next to the storage closet. This one was a private berth. And the bed was suspiciously oversized. And the room *reeked* of ogre.

You've got to be kidding me. She'd found K'Shorr's quarters. Which made the palm-locked compartment next to the room make a bit more sense. The ogre likely kept his gear in there and there was no way any human on the boat was getting past a palm-lock keyed to an ogre.

Much less a gnome.

She hurriedly looked around the room and then dove under the bed. The place was almost empty of furniture. There was a wardrobe against a wall and a chair and that was about it. The floor and walls were bare, the ceiling a simple metal grate that had probably been raised hurriedly for its oversized occupant. K'Shorr apparently wasn't big on personal effects. At least the bed was big enough that there was plenty of room to hide underneath it. Otherwise, she'd be inside the closet.

She turned around, facing the door, and then her blood chilled as she realized she'd left it open. *Fuck.*

She waited.

Nothing happened. She strained her ears to pick up any sounds from the big ogre moving toward her.

Nothing.

And then it hit her. She hadn't picked up on K'Shorr's scent because he was coming toward her. She'd been *standing next to his quarters.* The hallway outside of his room was going to smell like ogre *all the time.*

He probably wasn't anywhere near her. She'd been worried for no reason at all.

"Hopefully that'll be the last dumb thing I do today," she muttered to herself, coming out from under the bed. She still needed to figure out how to break into his storage room.

After that, it would be time to move on to the fun stuff.

Grond watched his partner's foul mood fall away as if it had never been there, as the gnome buried himself in a pile of his squealing, laughing children. Darsi stood off to the side, watching and waiting for the younger kids to be done with their father.

"How the hell did *you* get here?" the halfogre asked, snatching the girl up off the ground to give her a hug and then carefully putting her back down again.

"The ship just sorta popped up in front of us," Darsi answered. "Came out of nowhere, set off proximity alarms all over the ship. Remember knew exactly where we were and where to find us. I can't imagine how."

"You'll find that you get used to that," Grond answered. "Knowing what she's not supposed to is sort of her thing."

Darsi shrugged. "Anyway, it grabbed us in an inertia beam and just held us there, and then one of Remember's people came over the comm and told us what was going on. It took a while to convince Lorryn it was a good idea. I had to tell her you've met Remember before. Hopefully Dad's not going to be mad about that."

"I doubt it," Grond said. "It's not like she wouldn't have figured it out eventually. The story's kind of blown once they physically drag you onto Remember's ship with an inertia beam. Is everybody else okay?"

"Yeah," she said. "Irtuus-bon and the rest of the crew are over there," she said, pointing toward another part of the room. They were in a large common area for the crew, one that appeared to have been hurriedly re-accessorized to be able to accommodate and entertain a large number of gnomish children.

The adults and a few other figures sat together off in a corner. "They're fine, but Remember's 'bots said she wanted us to see Dad first."

"Have you actually met her yet?"

"Not yet," she said. "One elven steward that met us at the door and a bunch of 'bots."

"What else have you noticed?"

Darsi scowled. "Everything?"

"Everything," Grond replied. He straightened up to his full height and crossed his arms in front of his chest.

The girl closed her eyes, thinking. "Seven minute walk from where the ship is docked, but that was trailing all the kids with us, so I can probably run it in two or three. No trams, so right now we're somewhere close to the exterior port side of the boat. Occasional obvious security bubbles at intersections of corridors and in larger rooms means that there's cameras everywhere and they want us to know it. We walked past twelve personnel on the way here: ten humans, two elves, plus the elf steward who was guiding us. Six males and four females, which is a little off-balance for gnomes but probably pretty typical for a human crew. No one obviously carrying a weapon, but we passed by three security 'bots armed to the teeth, and the crew walks like they're used to carrying, so they may be issued something easily concealed."

She stopped, looking at Grond. The halfogre raised an eyebrow.

Darsi rolled her eyes.

"*Fine.* No obvious military or national insignias anywhere and the crew isn't really in any sort of uniform, although they're all pretty conservatively dressed. Clear implication is that this is a private vessel, but it's *enormous* for something not owned by a governmental agency or maybe one of the bigger interplanetary corporations. We certainly couldn't afford anything like it, and there's probably not more than two or three shipyards in gnomespace that could have built it."

"Why gnomespace?"

"Bigs tend to forget we exist, and while the thing is probably pretty deeply customized it's a bit too organic-looking from the outside to be dwarven work. But the whole ship is dual-use and all of the control panels and such are accessible by someone our size. They're using live virtual wall panels where the control space can be dragged down to gnome height at a touch rather than a fixed pad that might be too high for gnomes or too short for a human. None of the doors have knobs. They're all active. Stuff like that."

"You just made an assumption."

She thought for a moment.

"All of the ship that I've seen. I said *the whole ship*. It could be that they just put us in a gnome-friendly section, which happens to be conveniently located to the ship bay. Better?"

"Attagirl," Grond said. "Proud of you."

"I need to talk to Dad without the rest of the family around," she said. "How long do I give him before we dig him out of there?"

Grond glanced over at Brazel, who was still surrounded by the horde of his children. "Another couple of minutes. We've had a rough day. Almost died. And we lost the ship."

Darsi sucked at her teeth. "You're kidding. *Please tell me you're kidding*. He loved that ship."

"Got a new one already, for whatever that's worth. Remember gave him a present."

"Are you guys okay? I mean, hurt or anything?"

"Nah," Grond said. "Everybody's sore and pissed off, but even the elf and the human came through okay. Although I notice they're not in here. You know what Remember did with them?"

"They're over there with the crew, I think," Darsi said. "They brought an elf and a human through here a few minutes ago." Grond looked again, and this time picked out Asper, determinedly ignoring everyone else and meditating cross-legged on the floor. He didn't see Haakoro. The man was likely sprawled out on a couch somewhere facing away from the halfogre.

"Heard from your mom?"

"No. That's one of the things I need to talk to Dad about." Grond raised an eyebrow, and the girl waved him off. "She's fine. Just ... kidnapped a little."

Grond nodded. "Ah. No big deal, then."

"No."

There was a chorus of wails and complaints as Brazel disentangled himself from the rest of his children and joined Grond and Darsi.

"You two are conspiring. There must be bad news."

"I'm sorry about the ship, Daddy," Darsi said.

"Boat," Brazel corrected. "And you only call me Daddy when you want something. Don't be that kid."

"I'm still sorry."

Brazel shrugged, dismissing the mistake. "What's happened to your mother?"

"Kidnapped. I don't know a lot of details. You'll have to talk to Lorryn. She might know more. All I know is that an elf and an ogre took her and–"

"An *elf* and an *ogre*," Grond said, his tone silencing the girl. He had suddenly gone very still.

Darsi took a stop back, almost involuntarily. "Yeah. Grond, what–"

"We need Remember. Right now," Grond said, addressing the comment to the air over their heads. A deep red spark shone in his eyes. "I know you hear me. *Right now.*"

A panel in the ceiling slid open and a security 'bot dropped out.

"The Lady Remember grants you audience," it said. "Follow me."

"Get the ship's crew and Asper. Tell Haakoro to stay here," Brazel said to his daughter. "And tell Hazel she's in charge until we come back. You're coming with us."

INTERLUDE 3

Then

Grond gritted his teeth, biting off a scream as he popped his shoulder back into place. He tested his range of motion—painful, but it would do—and turned his attention to his wounds. He had a laceration along his side that would want stitches, and it felt like he might have lost another chunk of his ear. His whole left side would be a mass of bruises for a day or two. At least it didn't feel like anything was broken. He ran his tongue over his teeth. None of those broken, either. One of his lips was split and swollen, but that would heal up quickly enough.

"That wasn't bad," K'Shorr said, unlocking the cell Grond had been put into and letting himself in.

"Four on one. *Not bad* is about the best I can expect," Grond said. "How many of them died?"

"One ought to make it. One's questionable. The other two I imagine you know."

"Yeah." He'd broken an elf's neck, and punched a human in the chest hard enough that he thought he'd spotted a few bits of lung tissue on his spiked gladiator's gloves after the hit. He didn't expect that either of those two were still breathing.

K'Shorr tossed Grond a spool of surgical thread and a needle. The ogre caught them, breaking open the sterile package the needle was in and starting to stitch up the hole in his side.

"We still can't afford wound gel? That fight should have earned Barren some decent coin."

"I have no idea what he can afford," K'Shorr said. "I know who he ain't spending it on."

The ogre nodded. It was a marvel he was even still alive. Barren, for whatever reason, didn't seem to want Grond's blood on his hands, but didn't have any objection to someone else—or groups of someone elses—doing the job for him. Grond had been fighting in the pits for Barren for years, ever since the elf had been cast out. In all that time he'd only really lost one fight, and the victor had rather pointedly refused to end the battle with a kill. Barren hadn't let him eat for a week after that. Grond suspected K'Shorr had intervened to keep the elf from simply starving him to death. His skin was scarred enough by now that the hardened tissue almost counted as armor. He'd started letting K'Shorr tattoo him whenever he won a fight. At least that way he had some control over how his skin looked.

"How long until the next one?" he asked. *Please let it be at least a week.* His shoulder alone warranted at least three days and possibly some actual medical attention.

"Barren hasn't said," K'Shorr said. "But I'd imagine you're in for a long couple of days."

Grond looked around. He'd slept in worse places. "Are they feeding me?"

"Shit, I don't know," K'Shorr snapped. "You have any other requests, *boss?*"

Grond quickly lowered his eyes, not responding to the taunt. K'Shorr, unlike Barren, actually appeared to thrive in their reduced circumstances over the past years, and there were days he was almost friendly. Grond always had to be careful to not take it for granted.

"K'Shorr."

Barren stood outside the cell. The elf looked a bit sickly— then again, he nearly always looked at least a *bit* off since the thing with Eremite had happened. He'd lost weight, and his threadbare clothes hung on him. His lack of attention to his dress mystified Grond. The elf had been very concerned with his appearance before, and the ogre was sure that his fights had to be winning *some* money. There were days that Barren was barely better dressed than Grond was, and Grond was a *slave.*

K'Shorr looked up. "What do you need, boss?"

"I need you to accompany me. We have business to conduct," the elf said, collapsing into a coughing fit upon finishing the sentence.

"He coming with us?"

"No. Leave him here," the elf said. "We'll be back for him soon enough."

K'Shorr nodded.

"I'll try and get something sent back for you," he said quietly. "If only because I don't need your ass getting killed in your next fight because we were starving you. But I wouldn't hold my breath waiting. They don't exactly have high standards for customer service around here."

I don't think I'm actually a customer, Grond thought. Livestock usually got fed on time. After all, it was easier to sell if it was healthy.

The pair left, the cell door clanging shut behind them.

⤐⫷⫸

He was left alone long enough to get some sleep. He was awakened by someone knocking on the bars of his cage. He cracked an eye open, wincing—that side of his face had some bruising too—and saw a small shape standing in the shadows by his cage.

"If you're not here to feed me, you shouldn't have woken me up," he said. "And I don't smell food." Except—*wait*—that wasn't true. He *did* smell food. Meat, specifically.

"I can tell you're not a gnome," the shape said, and Grond opened both eyes. He'd seen gnomes in the crowds at his fights from time to time, but hadn't ever spoken with one. This one was a male, around exactly half his height. His fur was as blond as Grond had ever seen on a gnome. All the ones Grond had seen had tended toward darker colors. He was wearing what looked like basic work clothes made of sturdy materials, with spots and smears of oil or *something* scattered all over him.

Blood? Nah. There was none on his fur, and Grond figured he'd not had time to wash his hands if he'd just killed someone.

"You got something for me?"

"You trust me enough to eat it?" the gnome asked, revealing a slab of grilled meat and some kind of vegetable paste. The meat smelled delicious. The vegetable paste ... well, was food. "I figure you can eat while we talk."

So he doesn't work here. This was interesting.

"I'm in a cell. Anyone who wants to kill me can just shoot me through the bars. If that's poisoned, you must enjoy wasting your time," the ogre said.

The gnome pushed the plate through a slot in the cell. "I'm Snider," he said, and that was all he got out before Grond grabbed him through the bars and lifted him off his feet.

"Plenty of folk like wasting their time," Grond said, holding the gnome a meter off the ground. He took a moment to be grateful he'd used his good arm by reflex. He doubted he'd be able to hold the gnome off the ground with the other one for very long. "I hope your chef is talented, because if this doesn't taste right I'm not putting you down."

The gnome looked like he was trying to shrug, so Grond quickly dipped the meat in the vegetable paste and took a bite, chewing slowly. His eyes fluttered a bit at the taste, and he dropped the gnome. He tried to make it gentle.

"Don't care if it's poisoned," he said. "It's good. *Really* good. Talk."

"Your boss is meeting with some important people right now," Snider said.

"Don't have a boss," Grond said around a mouthful of food.

"Fine, your *owner* and somebody else's boss," he said. "And my boss, too. Either way, they're meeting right now. And they're putting a deal together. For a *lot* of money. And *my* boss ... well, let's say maybe my boss doesn't like that deal very much. And wants a different deal. So I got a question for you: how much d'you like Barren?"

Grond grew very still, and stopped chewing.

"You asking me to throw a fight?"

"Only thing I asked you was how much you liked your owner," the gnome said.

"I'm not sure I like this conversation," Grond said. It wouldn't be the first time that either Barren or K'Shorr had tried to catch him in a scheme. Not at all. He still remembered which of his scars were from the last time it had happened.

"I get it," the gnome said. "You're not stupid. This could be a setup. Or it could be a *chance.*"

"A chance for *what?*" Grond asked. "Your boss to get rich? *You* to get rich? I got a *steak*. And a nice little side of fearing for my life. For all I know Barren's got this place wired. I'm not helping you, Snider. Or your boss. Somebody goes into the pit with me, I beat them until they can't fight anymore. Sometimes they live through it. Sometimes they don't. That's *all* you're getting from me. I *might* not kill all your guys."

"Freedom," Snider said. "Listen, this fight's not gonna be like your others. You need to—"

"I don't even know what freedom *is*," Grond interrupted. "How do I know it's better than this? It's not like I have *job skills*. I beat people. That's what I'm for."

He shoved the rest of the plate back through the slot, suddenly not in the mood for food any longer. *Fuck Barren.* This was probably a setup anyway.

"I'm gonna do what I've got to do. And right now I need some sleep. Fuck off."

He laid down on the bench in his cell, his back to the bars. Snider didn't say anything else, and after a while he heard the gnome leave.

One way or another, this isn't going to work out very well.

The fight was three days later. He spent nearly all of the time in between in his cell, only getting about an hour or so a day outside. "Outside" didn't mean much. Wherever they were, its atmosphere wasn't conducive to breathing and staying alive for long—it was okay for short periods of time, if you didn't mind a burning feeling in your lungs until you passed out—but most of the residents stayed underground all the time. He didn't even know what region of space they were in, much less the name of the planet. "Outside" basically just meant out of his cell, where there was at least room to stretch his legs.

Ogrespace, he realized. He *had* to be in ogrespace. He could just barely reach the ceiling if he stood on his toes, and he was *underground*. There was no other race that would bother giving them a ceiling height that high if they didn't have to. Not if they were underground.

He wondered how close he was to home, then fought the thought off. Tromaxis had been home once. No longer.

"So do I get any kind of warning about what's coming?" he asked.

"Just this," K'Shorr said, handing him a helmet. The helmet was made of some sort of polymer and had an opaque visor.

"I assume I don't have to keep it on," he said.

"Nope. But you'll wear it until you're in the pit," K'Shorr said. "Once the fight starts you can do whatever you want."

"First blood?" It was never first blood.

"Kill," K'Shorr said. "You know better."

Grond put the helmet on, and let K'Shorr lead him from the cell.

This wasn't the same pit they'd been in before. He could tell that much even with the helmet on, just from the way the roars were echoing about the space. First of all, there were a *lot* more people watching this fight, and it sounded like the pit he was in was a lot larger as well. The floor, or at least the part of it he was standing on, was sand. He preferred to fight on sand. It soaked up blood and didn't get slippery, and could be used to blind an opponent in a pinch. Of course, bashing his opponent's head into a sandy floor didn't result in a kill as often as stone did, but he had other ways to do that.

He'd been given no weapons. Not even his gloves, which were usually the minimum he was provided with. This could be good news or very, very bad. It could mean that there would be weapons in the pit somewhere. It could mean that everyone was unarmed, which he felt was probably to his advantage. Or it could mean that he was the unarmed one, which would be a problem.

He rolled his shoulders, feeling carefully for any lingering pain. It felt okay. He'd have to favor that side, but it wouldn't be a real handicap.

An announcer started speaking. He didn't bother listening. The helmet muffled the sound anyway, and it wasn't like the place was set up to pump sound into the pits. The announcer wasn't there for him.

It did mean the fight was starting soon, though. He bent his knees slightly and listened, waiting for the tone that would signal the start of the fight and cut him loose to do what needed to be done.

A few moments later, he heard it. He whipped the helmet off his head.

Oh, that's bad.

He dove to the right as a flurry of projectile shots missed him entirely and thudded into the wall behind him. He'd only gotten a glimpse of the person with the rifle—it was too big to be anything but an ogre, but wearing armor from head to toe. He landed behind a broken piece of stonework, pulling his knees up and taking a second to glance around. The pit looked to be about ten meters wide, roughly circular, with moderate amounts of cover everywhere, most of it taller than he was. It looked as if someone had wrecked most of a small building and thrown it down here. The pit was practically a maze. Plenty of room to hide, but plenty of room for *them* to hide, too.

There were at least four. The ogre in the armor, who had the gun, and three others, all smaller. Elves or humans, too big to be gnomes or dwarves. He waited a moment, listening to see if there would be more shots. Nothing happened.

I can't be that lucky. There was a chance that the ogre had wasted all his bullets in one quick burst, hoping to take him out before the fight even started, but it didn't seem likely.

He had to move, one way or another. He continued in the direction his dive had taken him in, crawling around the perimeter of the pit, keeping his good shoulder in front. He kept the helmet. The ogre was nowhere to be seen. The crowd's roaring and screaming was deafening, so he didn't have to worry about being quiet. Just unseen.

One of the smaller ones found him first. He had a sword, and Grond was able to block the swing with the helmet, knocking his—no, *xir*, it was an elf—swing wide and giving Grond a clear shot at xir face. Grond punched the elf once, breaking xir nose, then grabbed a handful of face and slammed the elf's head into the nearest piece of stonework. The elf's skull cracked like overripe fruit. The cheers from the crowd were a physical force beating down on him.

One down. He took the sword. Shorter than he'd like, but it would do.   He continued along the perimeter, his senses straining, trying to spot the others before they found him.

This didn't make any sense. The crowds were here to see a battle. But there was too much cover. There was no way most of the crowd could even *see* him right now. He risked a glance up. There was a lattice a few meters over his head that was covered with cameras. They were watching on screens, then. But what was the point of that? Why not just set it up so that they could watch the fight? Unless—

Unless the fight wasn't the point.

He heard Snider's voice. *This fight isn't gonna be like your others.* And that elf hadn't put up much of a fight. He'd won fights quickly plenty of times, but that swing had gone *so* poorly—

"I'm supposed to be hunting them," he mumbled to himself. That's why the one had had a *gun.*

The odds weren't stacked against him. They were stacked against the *other three.*

He stood up straight, striding toward the center of the pit. He caught sight of one of the two smaller combatants, who *turned and ran* when he saw Grond coming.

The one with the rifle was standing in the center of the arena. He was *facing the wrong way.*

"Hey," Grond shouted.

The other ogre turned, brought his rifle up to his shoulder, and fired.

And missed Grond by two meters.

What the hell.

He threw his helmet, hitting the other ogre squarely in the face, and closed the distance between the two of them in an eyeblink. He tore the rifle out of his hands, breaking the stock open to clear the ammunition from it and then swinging it like a club, hitting the ogre in the back of the head and putting him on the ground.

He dropped the rifle, placing a foot on the other ogre's armored chest and taking his helmet off.

It was a *kid.* Barely even big enough to fit in the armor. And he was *terrified*, tears running down his cheeks and snot

running from his nose. *I didn't know ogres this age even* could
cry. "What the fuck is this?" he asked the kid.

"P—please," was all he said. "Don't kill me."

"What the fuck is this?" he said again, this time louder and
to the entire arena. He looked around. He'd just given the other
two a perfect opportunity to take a shot at him and they were
nowhere to be seen. Which meant that they weren't coming out
at all.

"I'm done," he said, putting a boot in the kid's armored ribs.
"I'm not killing him. The fight's over."

This time, the bullet didn't miss. His back exploded, and
the world went away.

TWENTY-SEVEN

"*This ... is exactly what I wanted,*" Rhundi said to herself. She'd managed to squeeze through the cleaner 'bot tunnels to get into the storage room, and it was everything she'd hoped for in life.

K'Shorr brought *a lot* of hardware with him when he went on vacation. The room was crammed with weapons and explosives–hanging on the walls, sitting on shelves, and in cases and crates stacked in the corners. Unfortunately, most of it was ogre-sized, meaning that even the smallest guns were still massively oversized for her. She found a dagger that would pass for a sword in a pinch, but it wouldn't do her any good against more than one enemy or at a distance. She grabbed an assortment of grenades, loading them onto a belt that she was able to wear as a bandolier.

There has to be something around here, she thought. *Something he took as a trophy, if nothing else.* Eventually she settled on an energy pistol that was just a *bit* too big. Conveniently, the thing was fully loaded and used fairly common ammunition packs. She attached several of them to the bandolier.

Okay. Armed. Now what? She contemplated the room for a few minutes and then started using her control unit to retask one of the cleaning 'bots to the storage room.

She got her answer a moment later. That was *definitely* the sound of boots outside. Large, heavy boots. She briefly considered making for the 'bot tunnel and rejected the idea just as quickly. She was carrying a lot of kit with her now and the tunnels were already tight enough. She put the control unit away and slid behind a stack of crates just as the door opened.

She couldn't see around the crates, but from the swearing and the stomping it *had* to be K'Shorr in the room, and he sounded like he'd brought a couple of minions with him as well. She heard a few different pairs of feet. The minions were staying quiet, and K'Shorr was mumbling and swearing to himself in a dangerously low tone. She heard a few guns clatter to the ground from one of the shelves. A moment later, the stack of crates in front of her rocked a bit as the ogre kicked whatever it was out of his way.

"Here, take these," the ogre said, finally speaking at a volume Rhundi could hear. "And I don't give a fuck what the elf says. You find her, you shoot her *first* and then you find us. If I find her with you and she's alive I'll kill the whole lot of you. I catch you without a weapon on the ship again and you're getting tossed out an airlock. We clear?"

Sounds of movement from the men. *They're saluting*, she thought.

"Go, goddammit," he said. "Every meter of the ship until you find her."

She heard footsteps as the men left. Then one of them stopped.

"Uh, sir?" a male voice said.

"Was I not fucking clear enough?" K'Shorr said.

"Well, uh, you, uh ... you said *every meter*," the man said. "There's room in there for a gnome to hide."

"Oh, you *son of a bitch*," Rhundi said under her breath.

"So you're saying she got into my gun closet? My *locked* gun closet?"

"You said she was clever," the man said. "Maybe ... maybe there's another way in."

"There's *not* another way in," K'Shorr said. "Quit stalling."

At exactly that moment, the cleaning 'bot noisily moved the grate out of the way and rolled into the room.

Rhundi risked a peek around the side of the box. K'Shorr and the mercenary were both staring at the little 'bot. K'Shorr looked enraged. The look on the merc's face was an odd combination of self-satisfaction and pure terror that Rhundi wasn't sure she'd ever seen before.

"The grates. The *fucking service tunnels,*" the ogre said. "God *damn* it. The bitch could be *anywhere.*" He stomped the little 'bot flat, causing the mercenary to flinch. "Fine, genius, check out the rest of the room, and after that go see if we have any little pointy-eared elf shits on this ship that are small enough to crawl through those things. It's sure as hell not gonna be you or me." He stomped off, and the mercenary moved into the closet. Rhundi heard him pawing through some of the crates.

I'm not in there, she thought. Was the idiot *stealing?* She was willing to bet that K'Shorr had a good idea of the exact inventory in the room. This was not a good idea. She listened to the human continuing to rummage around in the room. *Just be patient.* Sooner or later he'd either find her or get bored and leave, and there was no point in making any sudden moves until then. She found an angle that would let her watch the man, who took an ornate-looking gun case down from a higher shelf, opening it to reveal a matched set of antique projectile pistols. He took one out, admiring it for a moment, and then dropped it back into the case and continued his search.

She stiffened as he bumped the crates she was hiding behind. He pulled one down and put it on the floor, trying unsuccessfully to open it. "Locked," she heard him mumble. "Figures."

The man stood up and went for another crate. This time he made eye contact with Rhundi.

"Hi," she said, and stabbed him in the neck.

He collapsed, pulling the blade from her hand and knocking over a few of the crates. She climbed over the pile and yanked the blade from his neck, dodging the gout of blood that fountained out of the wound after the blade. She considered trying to hide the body, then rejected the idea. There was already too much blood in the room, and it was immediately visible from the door.

Time to find a new place to hide. She quickly cleaned the blood off of her blade, then tapped the door console and left the room, letting the door slide shut behind her. She briefly considered putting a shot into the palm lock on the outside, then thought better of it and slammed an elbow into it instead. The panel shattered.

Good luck getting back in there again. There was probably some sort of override for precisely this sort of situation, but it would slow K'Shorr down if he wanted to go back to reload. *And piss him off, too,* she thought, smiling at the idea.

Something hot and bright flew past her face, singeing her fur. She heard it impact the wall behind her. *Shit.* She turned and opened fire down the hallway, diving out of the way. *If they'd been smart enough to use a volley instead of trying for a headshot, I'd be dead.*

There were two of them, about ten meters away. She didn't think she'd hit anything either, though.

A few moments later, two more mercenaries emerged from the other direction. She took a few shots at them too, forcing them to take cover, then fled into K'Shorr's quarters, looking around for anything large enough to hide behind. She considered the wardrobe and going back under the bed, then rejected both ideas as too obvious.

Damn it. She needed at least a few more minutes for all of her 'bots to get into position. She needed to find a way to buy those minutes. K'Shorr hadn't had *that* much time to get out of earshot. She had to find somewhere to hide, and fast.

She looked around the room again, and smiled.

TWENTY-EIGHT

"Did you already know about this?" Grond demanded. Remember had had them brought directly back to the bridge. Several members of the crew turned around and stared at the halfogre, shocked by his tone.

"About Barren and K'Shorr? Yes," Remember said. "And if we had discussed it before now nothing would have changed from how things currently stand. I said I had interests on Khkk. Your former owner and his associate have been trying to work from the shadows on Khkk for months now."

"Are these the people who screwed with my head?" Haakoro asked.

"I think I said something about him staying behind with the rest of the children," Brazel said. Remember waved him off.

"Haakoro is as much my guest as you are, gnome. Save your violence for those who deserve it. There will be plenty of opportunities in the very near future." Remember spotted Lorryn in the crowd, pointing at her. "Perhaps your security chief should fill you in on what happened."

Lorryn, startled at being singled out by Remember, stammered through a description of the events at the resort.

"I ... I think she's fine, Dad," Darsi said. "I can't imagine—"

"She's fine," Brazel snapped. "Those two idiots couldn't keep Rhundi locked up if their lives depended on it."

"Their lives *do* depend on it," Grond added. His eyes were still glowing a muted red.

"But that doesn't mean that we don't need to find her," Brazel finished.

"And you will," Remember said. "In fact, I intend to lead you directly to her. But it is better for all of us if you are properly prepared for that encounter, and not acting rashly. There are, if you recall, other lives and other interests involved here."

"None that I care about," Brazel said.

Remember nodded. "Nonetheless," she said. "The Benevolence are preparing to descend upon Khkk in force, and the forces that are already warring there are causing much carnage. The Noble Opposition are on their way, and will join the fray soon."

Asper reacted to this, raising an eyebrow and crossing xir arms.

"This war must be ended. The Benevolence *must not* be allowed to take Khkk," Remember continued. "We must stop them here."

"Why?" Brazel asked. "The Benevolence control *half the galaxy.* Khkk is in the *middle of nowhere.* Why is one little desert moon so important? So they've got some weapons manufacturers. They can't be moved somewhere else? The Benevolence are going to have a *hell of a time* moving against the ogres. This rock's in ogre territory and *they* haven't bothered to colonize it yet. What's the problem?"

Remember fixed Brazel with a stare. "That is not for you to know at this time."

"Oh, bullshit," Brazel said, not backing down. "That worked when you were paying us. You're not paying us right now. We're in until we've got Rhundi back and we can get clear. That's it."

Remember stared at Brazel for a long moment.

"Fine," she said. "The part of the conflict on Khkk that we are concerned about is here." As she spoke, a large holomap of Khkk appeared above their heads. The map quickly zoomed in to a specific location, a walled compound surrounding an immense, three-sided pyramid.

"That is where the Noble Opposition forces on Khkk are based," Asper said.

"It is. This place is called the Sanctum of the Sphere. It is very, very old, nearly as ancient as civilization on Khkk itself. And it has been abandoned by the Khkks for generations. It is considered taboo. They do not go there or even go near it."

"Which is why we found it to be a good location for our operations," Asper added. "It was considered highly unlikely that anyone would find us there."

Remember continued. "Something is happening on Khkk, something that I myself do not understand. Nearly the entire surface is in conflict at this time. Nearly *everyone* is at war with *someone*. Old conflicts thought suppressed or forgotten for generations have flared back into hot wars. Borders settled for hundreds of years are suddenly in dispute again. Khkk has been relatively peaceful, especially for a system in ogrespace, for as long as almost anyone in this room has been alive. Even the Benevolence presence on the moon has been minimal. They have *never* expressed any more than the most cursory interest in Khkk until very recently. All of this starting with the two of you stealing a box."

Remember looked at Grond and Brazel again.

"Do you have any idea why the train, why *that exact* train at *that exact* time, was attacked?"

"Not a clue," Brazel said. "We figured it was a coincidence."

"It must have been. And yet it cannot have been," Remember said. "We know now that Barren and K'Shorr were ultimately behind the ... *extra items* that were found, and many events since. But it does *not* follow to me that they were involved in the attack on the train, or the carnage that has followed. Something else is at work here. I know not what. And that ... concerns me deeply."

"What does that have to do with us?" Brazel asked.

"Perhaps nothing. Perhaps everything," Remember said, and Brazel scoffed loudly. "Yet your enemies orbit Khkk over this very spot. It may be that there is something at the Sanctum that has been causing this disruption. A taboo powerful enough to keep a culture away from a place for generations is not something that should be taken lightly. There is *something* about the Sanctum of the Sphere that made generations of Khkks treat it as a holy place, and later generations treat it as anathema.

Even now, there is no *battle* around the Sanctum. The Khkks have surrounded it. The Noble Opposition forces are simply being *besieged*."

"You guys don't have ships? How come they can't just make a break for it?" Grond asked.

"Much of the travel to the Sanctum was overland, by design," Asper said. "It was thought that that would be less noticeable than a sudden increase in out-of-system ships landing in what was supposed to be the middle of nowhere. Like much of Khkk, the Sanctum is surrounded by desert, rock, and scrub. It is easy to get lost in."

"A few have managed to escape," Remember said. "Others have been blown from the sky as soon as they reached a safe distance from the Sanctum. The Khkks have the capability to reduce the entire compound to molten glass in short order, should they wish to do so, and I doubt the Opposition forces would be able to hold out long in the face of a concerted assault on their position. That such an assault has not happened suggests that the Khkks have *chosen* not to."

Brazel rubbed his eyes, suddenly looking very tired. "So what's so important about all of this, then? Why even hide the stuff in the first place? What was the *point* of this entire mess?"

"I may have ... some light to shed on this," Irtuus-bon said, entering the conversation for the first time. The troll was at his full height, holding a portable datapad in one hand.

Remember, for once, looked faintly startled. "Explain," she said.

Irtuus-bon tapped a couple of icons on his screen. "You have holographic capacity on this bridge, yes? I need access to it," he said. Remember nodded at a crew member, who fiddled with a console for a moment and then nodded at the troll. Irtuus-bon did something else with his tablet, and a large map was projected in front of them.

"Here we are," Irtuus-bon said, and a spot on the map began glowing. "We are ... *technically* in ogrespace, although not a well-patrolled or influential part of ogrespace. He manipulated his tablet again, and a region of space began glowing.

"This is the heart of Benevolence territory, in what was once elfspace," he continued. Another gesture, and the map zoomed sickeningly until a hologram of an enormous, icicle-shaped capital ship manifested above their heads.

"This is the *Testament*," Irtuus-bon said.

"We've seen holos of the *Testament* before," Brazel said. "I'm sure Remember has been *on* the thing before."

"You do not understand," Irtuus-bon said. "These are *complete plans* of the *Testament*. Every deck. Every room. Every weld and every *wire*. Every weapon. There are notes on troop complements, on weapons batteries, on the range of the ship. This is *everything you could possibly want to know* about the *Testament*. I could not have asked for a more complete set of plans. It even includes information on the composition of the outer armor. And of the *shields*."

A complicated waveform appeared in place of the *Testament* plans. Everyone within sight who had ever flown a ship in combat recognized a shield composition diagram when they saw one.

There was a moment of perfect, shocked silence on the deck, and then everyone began shouting at once.

Irtuus-bon was taken aback by the reaction. He stepped away from everyone, trembling a bit and slightly shrinking in size.

Asper lifted a hand and whispered something, and the din was instantly cut off. "My apologies," xe said. "Do I understand what you are suggesting here? That we have found a way to nullify the shielding on the *Testament?* That the *Benevolence*'s flagship is actually *vulnerable?*"

"The calculations could be completed by a novice at any engineering academy, given some time," Irtuus-bon said, returning to his previous dimensions. "They took me ten minutes."

Brazel started trying to talk, but no sound came out. He gestured angrily at Asper, who made a motion with xir hand, dispelling the silence.

"Do the plans have any information about the spiderships? There's no point in attacking the flagship if it vomits a thousand of those things at you when you're half a parsec away."

"It does," Irtuus-bon said. "The shields are a common design throughout the Benevolence fleet. They are simply much more powerful on the *Testament*. Even at the proper frequencies you would only be able to remove a small portion of the shielding at once. It would have to be a precise, targeted strike. Still, with the plans, I have already determined what the most effective place to attack would be. I believe that if these plans are accurate, we should be able to cripple the *Testament*, or perhaps destroy it entirely, with an attack force of sufficient size."

"What are we waiting for?" Haakoro said. "Put me in a ship! I want in on this."

"The plans are a hoax," the troll said, and this time Asper let the shouting go on for a few minutes. Remember finally halted the shouting herself, clapping her hands for quiet in an oddly effective fashion.

"Explain," was all she said.

The troll took a deep breath, staring at the ground as he spoke. "I have ... studied the Benevolence for a very long time. And trolls are ... a long-lived species, as a rule. I am already aware of a number of particular details about the *Testament* and its capabilities. And in many ways, the details on these plans match what I have already learned. But in many other ways, they do *not*. And that is why I am concerned. The encryption on this data pad was difficult to crack, but I *cracked* it. By *myself*. And, if the truth be told, I do not feel that it was challenging *enough*. And the opportunities that these data present are ... *too* perfect, especially for files whose provenance is suspect. We know that ... *someone* ... inserted false memories into this young man's head–"

"I'm *not* lying," Haakoro insisted.

"It barely matters if you are telling the truth," Irtuus-bon said. "What matters is that ... I *do not believe you*. And I do not. You did not buy these files from some mysterious, unknown informant. You were *given* them, and your memories modified to provide an explanation. I do ... *not* believe you. And I do not believe these files. This is a trap. The Benevolence hope to draw us out, in a grand attack on the crown jewel of their power. They know that we would not dare attempt such a thing with a small force. They hope to bring out the full weight of the Noble Opposition against them, to be crushed there once and for all. And once that is done, they can begin to play the remaining races against one another, as they have done in the past, and none are left to resist them. We should ... *erase* this information, and forget we ever found it. It is untrue. It is poison. It will destroy us all."

This time, the silence in the room was natural.

TWENTY-NINE

"I'm not going in there," Almuz den Ahsaar said. He had joined up with Barren's people for three hots and a cot, not to get killed by a goddamn *tiny*. "Call the ogre. Just tell him we've got her cornered."

"Why the hell not?" asked his search partner. Almuz thought his name might be Simon. The man didn't talk much, and Almuz hadn't been terribly happy to be partnered with him to go through the ship. "Let's just go kill her like we were supposed to. We might end up with a reward if we kill her ourselves."

"That's *blood*," Almuz said, pointing at some smears on the floor next to the locked entrance to K'Shorr's gun closet. "Which means she killed one of us already. Isn't gnome blood green or something?"

"I think it's red like ours," maybe-Simon said. "And I think you're an asshole. You stay out here. We'll go kill her." Maybe-Simon gestured to two other mercs that Almuz barely recognized, one of whom hung back with him while the other shrugged and went into the room.

"Do we even *have* a direct comm to K'Shorr?" Almuz asked. "He said to let him know if we found anything but it's not like he gave us his *card* or something. I swear, this job gets worse and worse every day."

"I don't," the other man said. "We could just tell the bridge."

The sound of two shots echoed into the hallway. Moments later, there were two thuds. After that, silence.

"Fuck me," Almuz said. "I'm *not* going in there."

"Let's call the bridge," the other man said. He backed away, having a quiet subvocalized comm conversation with someone.

"We're ordered to move in," he said. "K'Shorr's on his way. They say if we're not in the room when K'Shorr gets here we're going to regret it."

"Fuck *that*," Almuz said. "I got shit to *do*. I don't feel like getting killed today."

"And *I* don't feel like pissing off an ogre. Come on, dammit, let's go."

Goddammit. Almuz checked his ammo level, which was annoyingly fine. He gestured toward the door with his gun. "You go first. Enjoy the glory."

The other man spat on the floor in front of Almuz and then slowly crept into the room, his gun at the ready. Almuz followed at what felt like a safe distance. The room was bare, featuring nothing more than an oversized bed and a freestanding wardrobe, with a nearly unused chair sitting in a corner, almost as an afterthought. The room wasn't used much. And it smelled funny.

There were two bodies on the floor. Both had a single burn wound to the head from an energy pistol.

"Under the bed?"

"Dunno," Almuz said. "Either under the bed or in the wardrobe."

The other man fired several shots into the wardrobe, then dropped flat on the floor and repeated the action into the space under the bed.

"You better hope K'Shorr's not keeping anything important in there," Almuz said.

"He isn't," came a deep voice from behind him. "Good thinking. Both of you. You check under the bed and you–" this time, pointing at Almuz–"get the closet open. She's in one of them." The giant ogre strode across the room and shoved the chair over, showing only empty space behind it.

"Nothing under here," the mercenary said.

"Must be in there, then," Almuz said. He tore the door open, revealing ... nothing. A few items of clothing, some with fresh burn marks on them. No body. No blood.

"You sure she came in here?" K'Shorr said.

"She was *shooting at us*, and then she ducked in here," Almuz said. "There's no way she got out. *Somebody* shot these guys." He looked back into the hallway.

When he turned back into the room, there was a gun in his face. The gun was upside-down. So was the gnome holding it.

Shit, she was dangling from the *ceiling*.

I didn't know gnomes could climb, he thought, holding his hands up and mouthing *don't kill me*. The gnome looked at him quizzically, then beckoned him into the room. K'Shorr was tearing his bed to pieces just a few meters away. Neither of the two of them were looking their way.

Almuz took a deep breath and took another step into the room, just underneath where she was hanging. The gnome planted a hand on the top of his head and then somehow swung herself onto his back.

"Back out of the room," she said quietly into his ear. "And expect to get your ass knocked out a few seconds later. You make a sound, I'll kill you like the other two."

He did what he was told. K'Shorr was in full rage, and Almuz watched the other merc take a punch to the chin. The man hit the wall, his neck not at all at a normal angle.

"Thanks," he heard her say, and then a blinding pain in his head as the world went black.

They emerged from tunnelspace into relative calm. Initial long-range scans showed no ships of any consequence. Whatever was going on on Khkk, it didn't involve a deep-space fleet just yet.

"Open the hangar bays," Overmorrow commanded. "Everyone who isn't already on their own boat should be at battle stations." Xe opened a shipwide comm. "Do what seems best once you are on your own. We have no battle commander. I assume the majority of you with atmosphere-capable ships will join the land battle. Roashan will remain in orbit to guard against Benevolence incursion. The best of luck to all of you. If you are to die today, make it a good death."

Hangar shields dropped and doors opened across Roashan. Dozens of spaceships, ranging in size from harmless-looking single-passenger craft to a handful of battle cruisers, poured out of the station. The cloud of ships hung in space around the Malevolence station before some critical mass was achieved and they began moving off toward Khkk, still several minutes away at in-system speeds.

"Find them something to shoot when they get there," Overmorrow said. Roashan's bridge was mostly staffed by dwarves, a few of whom were poring over holomaps of Khkk's surface.

"The part of the fight we're concerned about is here," Smashes-the-Stars said, enlarging a portion of the map and highlighting a corner of Khkk's largest continent. "We have a base at this location, a temple the locals call the Sanctum of the Sphere."

"I am familiar with it," Overmorrow replied.

"This is where most of our people are. There's some manufacturing there, mostly Khkk weapons engineers who we've been able to persuade over to our side and we haven't been able to get off-world yet, and our own support staff. We thought no one would ever notice us there. Most of the Khkks treat the place like it's cursed."

"Yet they do not mind attacking it to drive us out," Overmorrow said. "What of the rest of these conflicts?"

"Most of what's taking place on Khkk doesn't even have anything to *do* with us," Smashes-the-Stars said. "The initial spark was because of us, yeah, but after that it was like the entire planet was looking for an *excuse* to go to war with itself. The conflict's worldwide by now. The Khkks have ethnic groups and nationalities just like humanoids. Any group of bugs on Khkk that was angry at any other has basically gone directly to open force by now. There is open genocide taking place on three different continents. I've never heard of anything like it."

"Then we deal with our portion of it first," Overmorrow decided. "Once our people are safe, we see if we can assist anywhere else. The Benevolence are unlikely to concern themselves overmuch with regional disputes."

"There's a capital ship in orbit around Khkk," one of the dwarves said. "It's an older ship, not Benevolence, and it's not involved in the fighting yet. Should we contact them?"

"Leave them alone," Overmorrow said. "For now. But keep a close eye on them."

The Noble Opposition fleet sped silently through space, eager to join the battle.

"There's our answer, then," Brazel said. "No hope, no point. The whole thing was a trap. So I'm back to where we were a bit ago: I'm going to go collect my wife, and then come back to get my kids, and then we're done here. With all of you."

The gnome looked around, daring anyone to argue with him.

"We have to try," Haakoro said.

"We *don't* have to try," Brazel said. "Were you not listening? The troll says the data is fake. That means charging off to save the world is going to get all of us killed."

"Hell, I'm not even sure I *want* to be the guys who blew up the *Testament*," Grond added. "If there's a better way to paint a target on your back, I don't know what it is. Let's say you survived the attack. Are you still alive six months later? I kinda doubt it."

"I'm telling you, I can *do* this. I'm *lucky.* I always have been. Somebody's gotta do the right thing," Haakoro said. "The Benevolence are evil."

"To *you,*" Brazel retorted. "They've left gnomespace alone."

"They blew up your ship," Haakoro replied.

"I blame *you* for that," Brazel said. "Thanks for reminding me." The edge in his voice could cut glass. Even Haakoro caught his tone, and lowered his gaze, unable to make eye contact with the gnome any longer.

"Enough," Asper said. "My parent is leading an attack to preserve Opposition forces on Khkk right now. Your wife is on a ship in orbit around Khkk. Our paths will stay aligned long enough. The *Testament* is not even in-system at the moment. This argument may be had later."

"Agreed," Remember said. "We will support the Noble Opposition ourselves. Brazel and Grond will do as they wish. Your family will be safe here until your return." She turned to Irtuus-bon.

"You are certain that the data Haakoro brought is false?"

"As certain as I can be," Irtuus-bon replied. "I have been ... wrong before. I do not think I am now."

"If you will, please share what you have with my people," Remember said. "We will look through it as well. Perhaps the Benevolence inadvertently included a scrap of useful detail that you have overlooked. It seems unlikely that it is *all* useless." Irtuus-bon gave Remember a slight bow, then left with one of her crew members.

"One more thing, first," Brazel said. "Get me to a holoscreen. I need to start a fight with somebody."

THIRTY

"*What do you mean* you haven't found her yet?" Barren seethed. "A few minutes ago two of your idiots were insisting they had her pinned in *your quarters*. How did you lose her?"

"She's good," K'Shorr responded evenly. "And these idiots you've staffed this boat with aren't. I gotta be honest, boss, picking her up wasn't your best move. Shoulda killed her on the spot."

"A mistake I won't make again," Barren said. "Perhaps I *do* have to do everything myself. I will find her, and–"

His ship-to-ship comm began blinking, distracting him from his rant. He opened the connection, irritated by the distraction.

"Identify yourself," he snapped. "I have little time for intrusions at the moment."

"You know who the fuck I am," the voice on the other end said. A moment later, the holoscreen resolved itself into the shape of a gnome in a rather dapper pilot's outfit. "And I don't care what you think you have time for. I want to talk to Rhundi. Go get her."

"I'll do no such thing," Barren hissed. "If you ever want to see her again, you'll–"

"Right. Okay. You don't have a goddamn *thing*," Brazel said. "Go ahead. You've got Rhundi? Produce her. Shove a camera in her face. Hell, shoot her right on-screen if you've actually got her. I'll wait. If she's not smart enough to be able to get away from you I'm divorcing her anyway."

"You're actually *daring* me to kill your family?" Barren said, his face registering mild shock. "I can't believe–"

"Shut up," Brazel interrupted. "Shut your stupid mouth *right now*. You don't have her. Rhundi's not stupid enough that you could hold on to her for long, and if you had her, you'd be parading her in front of a camera. She's *loose* right now, isn't she? And you're trying to do your damnedest to get control of the situation back. *Fuck* you, Barren. If you wanted a hostage, you should have kidnapped one of my *kids*, you *idiot*."

Barren's eyes blazed, his mouth working, but no sound came across the holocomm.

"That's what I thought. I'll tell you what. *You've* got until we get to Khkk to hand your ship over to my wife and command whatever shred of Benevolence forces will listen to you to stand down and leave town. If that doesn't happen, Barren, I *promise you* that I will be there when you die, assuming my wife doesn't get to you first. We clear? Good."

Brazel ended the comm. There was scattered applause from the gnomes in the room.

"You didn't wait for him to say yes," Grond said. "That was rather rude of you."

"Don't care," Brazel said.

"And so much for the element of surprise," Grond said.

"Don't care about that either," he said. "I want this over. I'm tired and I'm done and I want this over. Hopefully we can get it done without killing a bunch of people. Although, if we can't, I'm not sure I care about that either."

"Fine," Grond said. He turned to everyone else. "Who's coming with us?"

"I'm coming," Darsi said.

"No, you aren't," Brazel and Grond said in unison. No one dared to laugh. The gnome girl opened her mouth to protest.

"Not the time, sweetheart," Grond said. She looked at him for a moment, then held up her hands, surrendering.

"Fine. I'll keep everybody here calm."

"Asper?"

"I believe I will accompany the two of you," xe said. "Unless the lady Remember has another ship she is willing to part with for me."

Remember nodded. "What I have is at your disposal."

"Stick with us," Grond said. "We could probably use the backup."

Asper nodded. "And Haakoro?"

Everyone looked around. Haakoro was gone.

"He was here a minute ago," Darsi said.

"He's gone off to sulk," Brazel said. "Find him later. Lorryn, you and your people are on guard duty. Stay here with the kids. We'll comm you when we have Rhundi."

"We are *literally soldiers*, Brazel," Lorryn protested. "We belong out there."

"You are *literally* my wife's employees," Brazel retorted. "And you are guarding her children from *and* among people who I trust much, much less than I trust you. We can handle whatever fighting there happens to be. You're here as a line of last defense. Hell, we probably ought to just send you *home–*"

"Not without Mom," Darsi interrupted. "No."

Brazel shrugged. "You're probably safer here than in tunnelspace anyway. Last thing we need is you running into a blockship."

"Let's get this over with," Grond rumbled.

"Fine," Brazel said. "Everybody who's leaving grab whatever they need. We're launching as soon as my cockpit's ready in the new ship."

"It should be ready by now," Remember said. "I will send word ahead."

>‑{⊡}‑<

"That's it," Barren said. "Move the crew to somewhere centralized and seal them in. We'll *vent the atmosphere* on the rest of the ship. She can hide forever. Let's see how good she is at finding her own *air*."

The elf glared at the members of the crew still on the bridge with him, clearly expecting someone to jump to execute his order. No one moved. Finally, a crew engineer raised her hand tentatively and spoke up.

"Sir, the ... the ship doesn't really work like that, sir. The ventilation system, I mean. You can't just *vent* the *entire ship*."

Barren approached the engineer, a young human whose name he couldn't remember. "Figure it *out*, or I'll start by asphyxiating *you* just to prove the concept works. I don't even care about the crew that much. They're worthless. *Find a way to kill Rhundi Tavh're'muil*."

The engineer gulped and turned back to her console.

Precisely two seconds later, explosions sounded from every corner of the ship. One was directly underneath the engineer's console, riddling her body with shrapnel and flinging her across the bridge.

"The fuck was *that?*" K'Shorr shouted. "Are we under attack?"

"Everyone remain calm. You are not under attack," came a voice over shipwide comm. Barren's eyes widened. The voice was familiar.

"Find her. Shut her *up*," he seethed.

"I ... I can't," an officer said, frantically working with his console. "She's blown our connection to comms. I'm surprised we can even *hear* her."

"Hi, Barren!" came Rhundi's voice again. "You're probably frothing at the mouth right now. I've blown holes in about a dozen places on your ship. You'll find you've lost control of *all sorts* of shipwide systems. Those cleaning 'bots go *everywhere*, and you'd be amazed at what you can make out of detergent. You're going to land on Khkk now and let the first person you find who looks like they're in charge arrest you. Or I'll detonate a dozen more bombs, and this time they'll blow the ship apart."

"She wouldn't dare," Barren said to no one in particular. "She's on the ship! She's—"

"This is probably the part where you're saying I'm not going to blow myself up," Rhundi said. "You're correct! I'm riiiiight by the escape pods. Guess how many are left? And guess how many I need?"

"The damage to the ship is extensive, sir," the officer said. "We're going to be on the ground soon no matter what happens. The only question is whether we *land* or *fall*."

Rhundi continued, more than a bit of amusement in her voice. "And, hey, if you're just along for the paycheck, do me a favor and lock yourself in your quarters. I *know* Barren's not paying you enough to risk your life. And I'm the only one who knows where the rest of the bombs are. Just wait for the ship to land, and then go about your way. That is, if you can avoid getting killed in the war he started down there. Good luck."

K'Shorr started laughing.

"Told you she was good, boss," he said. "I mean, I'm gonna find the furry little bitch and kill the fuck out of her, but you gotta appreciate the craftsmanship."

"Land the fucking ship," Barren said. "I'll show you where. I'm going to make her regret this."

The elf snarled, a trickle of blood from a bitten lip running down his chin.

"I'll make *all of them* regret this."

Overmorrow watched as gouts of flame erupted and boiled off into space from several points on the hull of the capital ship on the viewscreen.

"Did we do that?" xe asked.

"No," Smashes-the-Stars responded. "Looks like it's happening internally. Saboteurs, maybe? Shall we assist them?"

"Not unless they ask for it," Overmorrow said. "Continue to monitor the situation."

Xe felt a gentle touch in the back of xir mind, as Asper reached out to xir.

I am here.

We are on our way, Asper sent. *The halfogre and the gnome intend to follow the capital ship before you to the ground. I will rejoin you as soon as I can. Be safe.*

Of course, Overmorrow replied. *Battle well, my child. We will both end this day blooded. Earn yours well.*

Xe felt Asper let go, and returned xir attention to the people around xir.

"Multiple contacts at the edge of the system," Smashes-the-Stars said. "It's the Benevolence. They're here. And ... there are a LOT of them."

"Let them come," Overmorrow answered. "What will happen is written already."

"If you've seen the script, I'd love a look," the dwarf replied. "Not all of us are as in touch with the universe as you are."

Overmorrow smiled. "Warn everyone. It won't be long."

"There they are," Brazel said, watching the long-range viewscreen. "The Benevolence are here. A couple of capital ships. Who knows how many spiderships." There was no denying it: The new ship handled like a dream and despite the rush job the captain's seat was not only perfectly sized for him but was easily the most comfortable chair he'd ever sat in. Unfortunately, what the ship had in creature comforts was more than outweighed by its drawbacks.

TWO HUNDRED AND TWELVE, the ship's AI intoned. Brazel considered naming the AI "Drawback" and then rejected the idea. AND AN UNKNOWN NUMBER STILL HOUSED WITHIN THE CAPITAL SHIPS THEMSELVES.

"No one asked you," Brazel said. The new AI had a deep, mechanical voice. He decided that he didn't like it very much.

I RECOMMEND CEDING FULL CONTROL TO SHIP SYSTEMS AT THIS TIME, CAPTAIN, the AI continued.

Brazel glared at the nearest viewscreen, then felt silly about it and found a speaker to glare at instead. "And why would I do that?"

LIVING BEINGS ARE INFERIOR PILOTS. YOU HAVE A MUCH GREATER CHANCE OF SURVIVING THE COMING ENGAGEMENT WITH MY PILOTING THAN WITHOUT IT.

"Four minutes out," Grond said. "They'll intercept us before we get to Khkk unless this thing can go faster."

"Letting machines do the thinking for them is Benevolence work, thanks," Brazel said to the ship. "I'll fly myself."

I STRENUOUSLY PROTEST.

"I strenuously give no fucks. And change your voice to something less annoying."

THIS IS MY SOLE VOICE IMPRINT, CAPTAIN.

"Grond, do something about the AI," Brazel said. "I don't give a fuck what."

"Shooting's my job anyway," the halfogre said. "You just *fly* the thing."

ATTACK PROTOCOLS ARE ALSO FULLY AUTOMATIC, the ship said.

"Pull the fucking brainbox," Brazel said. "And throw it into something that will melt it."

MY PERFORMANCE WILL BE SIGNIFICANTLY DEGRADED IF AI FUNCTIONS ARE DISCONNECTED.

"There's *got* to be an off button around here somewhere," Brazel said, as the halfogre got out of his copilot's seat and headed for the engine room.

"Gimme a minute," Grond said. "Be right back. Try not to get blown up before then. Benevolence will be within range in ... oh, two minutes."

"Hurry," Brazel said. "Don't wanna hog all the fun."

Brazel's subcomm buzzed in his ear. He recognized the signal.

Holy shit.

"Rhundi?"

"Hi!"

"You have *really* pissed Barren off, dear. I assume you've gotten off the ship already?"

"Yeah. One problem, though? I'm sort of on an escape pod and the thing handles like ... well, like an escape pod. I'm less piloting than in a controlled fall. And he's been orbiting over what looks like a hotspot for a while. You up to a combat rescue?"

BENEVOLENCE FORCES IN CONTACT RANGE IN ONE MINUTE.

"Can you find a way to make yourself invisible in between now and then? Hopefully they're going to be too busy to shoot down escape pods." Something was nagging at him. "Wait, isn't *Barren* chasing you?"

"I sorta took out most of his guns. Long story. You'll love it."

"Okay, well, we're about to get busy here. I'll comm you when we're on the ground."

"Stay alive, okay?"

"You too, love." He closed the connection, watching a brace of spiderships heading for the fleet of Malevolence ships in the distance. Thus far, none had bothered to pay much attention to them. Then again, he hadn't given them a reason to yet.

"All right, ship," Brazel said. "Remember said you're a warship. Time to prove it."

He accelerated to combat speed, bringing the ship's shields to full power and taking aim at the rearmost spidership. *I've never actually deliberately opened fire on Benevolence before,* he thought. *Every time he'd encountered them in the past his first and sole impulse had been to run.* *Hopefully Remember wasn't lying about this boat's capabilities.*

Then, feeling odd, he corrected his own thought.

Ship.

He opened fire on the spidership, bolts of flame ripping from the warship and raking along the target's flank. He took out several maneuvering arms, and the ship spiraled away, bursting into a cloud of nanoparticles when a stray missile from another ship hit it.

"That's something," he said, taking aim at another spidership. *My first Benevolence kill.*

He felt a jolt as the ship suddenly slowed down, the inertia throwing him forward in his seat despite the dampers and his restraints. The lights in the cockpit dimmed and a loud buzzing sound filled the ship.

"Um."

That's not good.

"*GROND!*" Brazel shouted. "Did you do that? We're sorta involved in a whole *thing* up here!"

"You told me to pull the brainbox!" the halfogre roared back. Brazel could hear his partner's footsteps as Grond raced back to the copilot's seat behind him. "I replaced it!"

"With *what?*" Brazel asked. "You just happen to have another one *with you* or something? I wasn't serious about replacing the goddamned brainbox! I just wanted you to see if you could make the thing shut up!"

"Replacing the brainbox is one way to make the ship shut up," Grond said calmly, buckling himself into his seat.

The control surfaces in front of Brazel started flickering as the AI rebooted. Three spiderships disengaged themselves from the group in front of them, pivoting rapidly in space and reorienting toward their new ship.

"I am *not* getting fucking shot down *twice in one day,*" Brazel yelled, trying to force the ship into a dive. It responded, but sluggishly. The shields looked like they were still up, though. At least *that* was something. The first volley of shots from the spiderships missed or glanced off. The second round of explosives *didn't*, and the ship rocked.

"You see a damage report anywhere?" Brazel shouted.

"Maybe we should have read the manual," Grond said. The halfogre was *smiling*.

WE'RE FINE, a familiar voice said. SHIELDS AT NINETY-SIX PERCENT. WAIT. WE WERE DYING A FEW MINUTES AGO. WHY ARE WE NOT DEAD? THIS HAD BETTER NOT BE THE AFTERLIFE.

"Wha—" Brazel sputtered. "*Namey?*"

"Namey," Grond said. The damned halfogre was *beaming*.

I'M NOT ME, Namey said.

"Save the existential crisis, please," Grond said. "You're still a boat. Adjust."

Grond somehow could *feel* the boat taking a moment to get a grip.

I HAVE GUNS, Namey said. He sounded quite pleased with this development.

"One or two," Grond said. "Which maybe you want to start using soon?"

I HAVE *LOTS* OF GUNS, Namey said. I'VE ALWAYS WANTED GUNS. YOU NEVER GOT ME ANY REAL GUNS BEFORE.

"YES! You have guns!" Brazel screeched. "Now *shoot something* with them!"

WE AREN'T RUNNING? WE USUALLY RUN WHEN THIS HAPPENS.

"We'll *explain later*, dammit!" Brazel shot a look at Grond. Grond read his partner's mind: *By "we," I mean "you."*

The *Nameless* cackled as it dove into combat against the Benevolence forces.

><⊂⊃>◄

THIRTY-ONE

Haakoro had been in tunnelspace for ten minutes when it occurred to him that he had no idea what he was doing. He knew, vaguely, where Benevolence-dominated space was. He knew he was headed in mostly the right direction. And he knew that the sleek needleship he'd stolen from Remember's docks had plenty of fuel and was easily the fastest thing he'd ever flown. He briefly considered just changing course and heading off for ... well, *anywhere*.

No. I can do this, he thought. The sector of Benevolence space the troll had highlighted seemed pretty specific. The needleship appeared to be of elvish make, meaning that he probably wouldn't stick out or attract too much attention when he got there. And he was pretty sure, given the amount of time the trip would take, that he could adjust the single, powerful energy cannon on the needleship until it would cut through the Benevolence shield design he'd seen. He'd done his best to memorize it while Irtuus-bon was displaying it. He had to trust in his own luck. He always had, and until recently the practice had done him well.

And then he was off to save the galaxy. With a needleship–a long, narrow single-passenger craft that seemed to be half engine and half cannon–he'd only need a few shots, if he could get through the fields.

"I'm going to change everything," he said to himself, and began working on reproducing the shield diagram.

>{⊞}<

From the command deck on Roashan, Overmorrow watched xir people die. The Benevolence forces were too many, the networked spiderships too coordinated for xir small fleet to make much headway against them. Here or there, a spidership caught in a crossfire or overlapping explosions was destroyed, but despite their optimism at the start of the battle the Malevolence were losing badly. Overmorrow felt each death, and also felt it when pilots took flight and jumped to tunnelspace rather than fall to the inevitable.

The station's defenses were mostly automated, the patchwork of overlapping shielding technologies and Roashan's asymmetrical, cobbled-together shape making a computerized solution simply easier. Nearly every gun on the station, however, was controlled by living intelligence.

Unless xe needed it to be otherwise.

"Prep Roashan to assault the capital ships," Overmorrow commanded. "Pull everyone away from their stations and to a place of ... relative safety. We attack as soon as the station is ready. Until then, keep us alive and *hold them off.*"

"This may not be the best set of circumstances for that," Smashes-the-Stars said. "It was meant to be a last resort—"

"You do not believe we are in a position of last resort?" Overmorrow said placidly. "Perhaps you are viewing a different battle than the one I see."

Smashes-the-Stars nodded, took a deep breath, and executed the command.

From outside the station, all of Roashan's exterior and interior lights suddenly went dim. The entire station began to slowly rotate, changing orientation so that the flat side of the disc faced the battle. Nearby spiderships broke away from chasing down and destroying individual Malevolence fighters to challenge the huge space station, but its shields were powerful enough that their attacks were simply brushed off.

And then the entire station slowly began to bend, a long, ragged seam opening between the dozens of different parts Roashan had been assembled from, and folded itself behind its central drive. The drive itself was transforming as well, elongating, the emitter focusing and shrinking to only a few meters wide.

Overmorrow felt Asper in xir mind.

I said I was nearby. What are you doing?

What needs to be done, Overmorrow replied. *Remain with the halfogre and the gnome. Assist them in their tasks. I will see you again soon enough, child.*

Overmorrow felt a moment of purest panic from Asper, then just as quickly a feeling of regret and acceptance as xir child accepted what xe had said. Xe felt a whisper, a touch, and then nothing, as Asper focused on the task at hand.

"Attack the capital ships," Overmorrow commanded. "Fire at will."

Rhundi watched, strapped into a crash seat, as the escape pod tumbled toward the surface of Khkk. Tumbled far too fast, in fact. The escape pod hadn't been specifically targeted but the guidance systems had been damaged by a stray shot and she was in far less control of the descent than she wanted to be. The crash seat would protect her, but she was falling directly into what was supposedly an active war zone and she very much hoped to land in one of the *less* active parts.

What she saw didn't look good. Malevolence forces–at least, she *hoped* those were the Mals–had holed up in a walled compound the size of a small town, dotted with squat, cube-shaped buildings. At the center of the compound stood an immense three-sided pyramid that towered over the buildings around it. Amazingly, at least from a distance, the pyramid didn't appear to have a scratch on it. In fact, the entire compound appeared mostly unscathed, although the walls looked like they'd taken a lot of abuse.

The opposition, whoever they actually *were*, had the town under siege. It was completely surrounded by a troop encampment that looked to be at least half a kilometer thick, set just far enough away from the walls that range was likely an issue for those inside. Surprisingly, she saw no signs of heavy artillery or mechanized transports. Surely as well known as Khkk was for weapons design, someone had invented something that could wipe this compound from the surface. A siege seemed downright old-fashioned.

Something's making them careful, she thought, right before the escape pod took another hit, sending her directly toward enemy lines. She closed her eyes, thinking of her family, and tried to sink as deeply into the crash seat as she could. The trick in these things was always to *relax,* and let the seat do its job. This would be her fourth crash-landing. The first time she'd involuntarily stiffened her legs to brace herself and broken one of them.

The second two were Brazel's fault, she thought, smiling, and then the pod slammed into the ground.

It was a few minutes before she could convince herself she was still alive. She tested her limbs, slowly, checking her fingers and toes for pain, then moving on to her arms, legs, and finally her neck.

Alive. Hell, uninjured. Mental note: buy the company that makes these things.

Next step was getting out of the pod. The thing had two doors on opposite sides and a few explosive bolts that would blow the whole pod in half if necessary. She was hoping to not have to use those. If there was any way to get out of the pod without attracting any more attention than she did slamming into the ground, she was going to use it.

One of the doors was on the side the pod had landed on. The second pointed in the right direction. She disentangled herself from the chair and leapt for the release. The door popped open.

A few dozen oversized insects with large weapons were standing outside the door.

"Oh, shit," Rhundi said, then raised her arms in surrender.

Barren received no warning at all, a blinding white pain striking him between the eyes, the surprise and pain dropping him straight to the deck of his crippled ship. He felt the floor fall away, replaced by a shining radiance and a tremendous feeling of pressure and heat from all directions. The symbol slammed into the backs of his eyes, seared into his brain: the oval eye, eight-armed.

The voices were all. The voices were everything, male, female, old, young, human, elf, dwarf, ogre, others that he could make no sense of at all. They had but one thing in common: they were all fearsome in their implacable anger, and they spoke as one.

YOU HAVE *FAILED*, SLAVE.

Barren tried to speak, to reply, but could not. There was no air in the room to pull into his lungs, only the terrible pressure. He could feel his ribs cracking.

YOU SHALL DIE TODAY. YOU HAVE FAILED US. YOU FORCE US TO DO OURSELVES WHAT YOU CLAIMED YOU WOULD ACCOMPLISH.

He pushed with his arms, trying to stand, to at *least* raise his face from the floor, panic and agony flooding his muscles in equal amounts. He felt one of the bones in his left forearm give way with a *crunch*, and gave up. He coughed, violently, a fine spray of blood spewing from his mouth. His screams were silent, but impossible to suppress.

YOUR LIFE ENDS, SLAVE. YOUR GIFTS WILL BE SUNDERED, YOUR NAME BROKEN, YOUR MEMORY STRICKEN FROM OUR COMMUNION.

Forgive, he thought frantically, hoping they could hear him.

WE DO NOT FORGIVE. END YOUR OWN LIFE BEFORE WE REACH YOU.

In an instant, the light turned to darkness and the heat to cold. Barren was face down on the floor. His wounds were still there. His chest was burned as if with a powerful acid, his skin melted like candle wax, an eight-armed scar left behind.

He drew breath into his lungs, feeling as if he had not done so in hours, and screamed raggedly. He felt something give in his throat, cutting his shrieks short. He could feel his broken ribs digging into him, and his left arm twisted horribly.

The ogre was there, picking him up from the floor, carrying him away from the bridge. He could hear K'Shorr's words, but could make no sense of them. There was only the pain, and the sound of his screams.

>—{⬭}—<

THIRTY-TWO

Grond, possibly for the first time in his life, let out an elated whoop.

"Never make that sound again," Brazel said.

"Fuck that, this is *fun*," the halfogre said. This boat Remember had given them was a *much* more impressive piece of technology than either of them had realized, and while they weren't exactly flying rings around the spiderships, they were *holding their own*, and that was something that had never happened before. With Brazel handling the flying, Grond handling the primary guns from the copilot's chair, and Asper manning a belly turret, they'd taken out six spiderships since the battle started. In all his years working with Brazel, he'd never even *heard* of someone having that kind of success against active Benevolence. Not once.

I am going to get so many free drinks out of this, he thought. *Assuming I survive.*

WHAT THE HELL IS GOING ON OVER THERE?

"More specific," Brazel snapped. "Trying to not die here." He threw the *Nameless* into a sharp spin and dove down toward Khkk, forcing two pursuing spiderships to dodge out of each other's way.

ROASHAN.

"Seven!" Grond shouted happily as he splattered another spidership, saving a Mal pilot whose ship was listing badly and leaking something into space. He looked away from his targeting software to see what Namey was talking about.

Roashan had ... *transformed.* Formerly a patchwork, vaguely amoeboid circle, the station had split itself in half and folded backwards, now looking for all the world like an immense sniper's rifle.

He felt a brief pulse of emotion. It didn't feel like his own.

"Asper?" he commed. "Was that you?"

"My apologies," the elf responded. "I was ... speaking with my parent. I did not mean to allow that to overflow."

"What's going on?" he asked, and then the universe erupted in fire.

Grond blinked, trying to clear the stars from his eyes. "Are we hit?"

ROASHAN IS FIRING ON THE CAPITAL SHIPS, Namey said. THE AMOUNT OF FIREPOWER THE STATION IS GENERATING IS TREMENDOUS.

The spiderships pursuing them broke away, and each and every one of them turned toward Roashan, which was pouring energy into the closer of the two Benevolence capital ships. Grond and Brazel watched as the beam, itself wider than a spidership, at first glanced off the capital ship's shields, then either found the frequency or overcame the shields and burned an enormous hole into the ship. The beam wavered, flicking up and around, cutting the huge ship nearly in half. A few seconds later, it silently blew apart, the shockwave damaging the second capital ship, which suddenly had to deal with hundreds of tons of shrapnel impacting on its shields.

"How the hell long have they been able to do *that?*" Brazel shouted.

"It is the entire purpose of the station," Asper answered over the comm. "Elude the Benevolence for as long as possible, and have the power to make them regret it when escape was no longer an option. The station was a weapon, but a weapon of last resort. I doubt they have the power for a second shot. The spiderships will tear the station to pieces before it can fire again or get away. My parent sacrificed Roashan to buy xir pilots time to get away."

"We can help, can't we?" Grond said.

"No time," Brazel said. "We've got a clear path to the ground for the first time since the fight started. Let's take advantage of it. Rhundi's down there somewhere."

✦⟨⚏⟩✦

"*I don't speak insect,*" Rhundi said as a torrent of powerfully scented pheromones wafted over her. "Any chance I'm going to get lucky and find out you speak humanoid?" The good news was that the Khkks hadn't immediately opened fire— in fact, if anything they appeared to be debating what to do about her. Several of them were waving appendages at each other and making a flurry of excited-sounding noises, and Rhundi could pick up on a large part of the chemical portion of their conversation as well. Gnomes had an exceptional sense of smell, but that didn't really lend itself to being able to *understand* what the Khkks were saying to one another.

As an experiment, she started slowly lowering her hands. Several heads swiveled her way, but none of the Khkks made an aggressive move. *Okay. That's good.*

"I'm going to try and climb out of here, very slowly," she said. "I would appreciate it quite a lot if no one tried to shoot me." It occurred to her that she was still wearing several of the weapons she'd swiped from K'Shorr's closet. The Khkks either hadn't noticed or didn't care. They continued their conversation, a few of them actually moving out of the way to allow her room to get out of the escape pod.

She climbed out, then raised her hands again, squinting against the bright sun and trying to get a clear view of her surroundings without being too obvious about it. Not for the first time, she cursed being short. The Khkks were a bit shorter than she was, but there were so many of them that she couldn't see much of what was around her.

She turned around and gasped, getting her first good view of the pyramid structure behind her. It was *much* taller than she'd realized while she was falling out of orbit, and from the ground it was beautiful enough to make her breath catch in her chest. It looked like it was made of spun glass, multicolored, catching the bright daytime Khkk sun and sparkling in the sky. It looked too delicate to be even a fraction as tall as it was.

One of the Khkks prodded her in the shoulder. She turned toward it quickly, trying to suppress the reflex to move her hands toward her guns.

The Khkk raised an appendage and pointed toward the structure.

"It's amazing," Rhundi said.

The insect pointed again. She turned, and realized that the Khkks between her and the pyramid had all moved away. They actually wanted her to go *toward it*.

"You're not besieging this thing, are you?" she asked. "You're protecting it. From the Benevolence."

A flush of pheromone scents, and a gesture that looked very much like a nod.

"And you want me to ... what? Go to the compound around it?"

Another burst of the same scent, and several more gestures toward the pyramid. *The temple*, she thought. The Khkks were treating the structure like it was sacred. *That doesn't explain why they want me in there. They've got to be aware that the place is occupied right now.*

She'd figure that one out when she was around people she was biologically adapted to communicate with.

"Okay," she said. "Off I go." She turned and started walking, listening carefully to see if any of the Khkks were following her. The structure looked to be a kilometer or so away from her. It was awfully hot outside, but not so bad that she'd have to worry about water for a bit.

I just hope I can find a way in, she thought.

"*You're gonna explain that, I hope,*" K'Shorr said. The giant ogre had proven surprisingly gentle, carrying Barren to the ship's medical station and laying him down on a bed. "I've got the docs on the way. You'll be all right."

Barren tried to shove him away, catching a scream in his teeth as he used his broken arm.

"No time," he spat out. "Is the ship on the ground yet?"

"Getting there," K'Shorr said. "When I carried you off the bridge they said they'd gotten our descent under control. Should just be a couple of minutes."

"They'll fight us," Barren said. "Destroy them. Destroy *all* of them."

"Sure," K'Shorr said. The gnome had killed the bridge's ability to accurately aim much of anything, but he didn't see any reason to remind Barren of that. And he'd gotten the distinct impression that *under control* had meant something along the lines of "not actively crashing."

"The Benevolence have ... abandoned us," Barren said, coughing up blood. "We have but one chance to regain their favor. When we land, you must get me inside the Sanctum. Do whatever you need to do."

"You're the boss," K'Shorr said. A medic entered the small medbay, and K'Shorr waved the man over as Barren passed out again and his head fell back against the pillow.

"He needs to be able to walk," K'Shorr said. "Set the arm and whatever else you notice is broken. Pump him full of painkillers if you need to. Strap him down first, we're crashing. I'll be back in a few minutes."

The medic just stared at him, the slightest hint of defiance on the man's face.

K'Shorr sighed deeply, then grabbed the medic by his shirt and lifted him off the ground, putting them eye-to-eye.

"Lemme make somethin' fucking clear here," he growled, his eyes shining red and coloring the man's face. "I'm going to go and pick up as many killing tools as I can *carry*. If I come back here, and he's dead, or you're not in the room *actively* tending to him, I'm going to make killing the *fuck* out of you my first priority. I will have *nothing else to do* on this useless rock other than to cause you an incredible amount of pain until I let you die. If I come back and he's fixed, as far as I'm concerned you can *have* what's left of the ship. We understand each other here?"

The man, struggling to breathe a bit, nodded. Or tried to. It looked like it might have been a nod.

K'Shorr dropped him. The man collapsed to the floor, his legs going out from underneath him. K'Shorr smelled urine.

"Not kidding about the crashing thing. I'm not sure why the alarms aren't going off. She may have blown those too. So work fast."

The ogre turned and left, making a mental inventory of exactly what he wanted to bring with him. He had a feeling that Barren wouldn't be paying him for much longer, and had a checklist of lives he needed to end before he had to find another job.

Starting with Rhundi Tavh're'muil.

INTERLUDE 4

Then

Grond awoke to pain. His legs, his shoulders, his arms, his *chest*. He had broken teeth and a mouth full of blood. His vision was blurry, and the bright light was painful. His lungs were on fire.

I'm outside. He was outdoors, and as he looked around he realized it was worse than that. He was naked, and tied up on the ground. His hands were bound in front of him, and his feet tied together.

Someone slapped him. His teeth rattled in his mouth and he looked around wildly, trying to make his eyes focus enough to find the source of the agony. A hand grabbed his jaw, intensifying the pain.

"You stupid bastard," K'Shorr said, his eyes glowing red. The ogre had a breathing mask on, his voice magnified through speakers. "All you had to do was win that fight. *All you had to do.* And it shoulda been the *easiest thing ever.* There wasn't a one of them that should have even been in the fucking *pit* with you. But no. Had to go and *think for yourself.* You have *any* idea how much money you just cost Barren? How much money you just cost *me?*"

Grond tried to speak and failed.

"Don't bother," K'Shorr said. "I don't give a damn what you have to say. Got told to make an *example* of you. Came up with a real good way to do it, too."

The ogre rolled him over, and Grond felt something cold being shoved in between his elbows and his back. Then a horrible tearing pain in his shoulders, as he was lifted off the ground by the bar. He scrabbled for purchase with his feet, finding only a small ledge that he could stand on with his toes. There was no way he would be able to hold his weight for long, and his lungs were already straining to keep breath in them.

Then a line of ice was drawn with a sharp blade below his waist, and a searing pull that went deep into his viscera, and he blacked out again.

"*Gods,*" Snider said. "They *crucified* him."

"More than that," the other gnome said. "They halved him." She pointed.

"Maybe we ought to just let him die," Snider said. "It already took too long to snatch the rest of the kids. And how long did we have to wait for K'Shorr to leave? He's gotta be—"

"He's breathing," she said. "Cut him down. Cut him down *now.*"

The two of them worked in frantic silence for a few minutes, Snider using a microtorch to cut through the post that was holding the bloodied halfogre in the air. Eventually the post gave way, and he hit the ground with a crash. They worked quickly, severing the ropes and freeing his arms.

"If he's alive, he's coming with us," she said. "Comm the ship."

Snider shrugged. "Send the *Incandescent,*" he said into the comm. "Rhundi and I need a pickup."

THIRTY-THREE

"It is time for us to go," Smashes-the-Stars said. In one sense, they'd gotten incredibly lucky–the single blast that Roashan had managed had crippled one capital ship and caused substantial damage to the other. Some of the spiderships had left the battle to return to the capital ship, and most of the Mal pilots had leapt to tunnelspace by now. The rest were too dumb or too stubborn to flee. Or their ships were too crippled to make the jump. She tried not to think about those.

The rest of the spiderships, possibly orphaned by the destruction of the first capital ship, were tearing Roashan to pieces.

"Not until the rest of our people are safe," Overmorrow said. "The shields will hold."

"The shields are *already* collapsing, Overmorrow," Smashes-the-Stars said. The dwarf briefly considered the possibility that she'd have to knock Overmorrow unconscious to get xir to abandon ship. "Virtually everyone on Roashan is in position to evacuate as soon as you give the order. The rest are all *also stubborn assholes* and won't go until you do." She looked around for something heavy. She'd never seen anyone sneak up on Overmorrow before, but hell if she wasn't going to *try*. The elf would have to turn xir back sometime.

Overmorrow's shoulders drooped, and Smashes-the-Stars felt a wave of relief as xe reached out and let the remaining Malevolence on Roashan know that it was time to go.

"Start the countdown," Overmorrow said. "Two minutes. That should be enough time."

"I'm not sure we *have* two minutes," Smashes-the-Stars said, but she did as she was told. The station shook as more of the shields failed. She checked a damage report. They had just lost a quarter of the station.

"Then we will have to hurry," Overmorrow said. "Let's go."

A roar from the sky nearly knocked Rhundi flat. She looked up to see a familiar sight: Barren's ship, descending at what looked like an unhealthy rate of speed, heading directly for the compound that she'd been sent toward. A cry went up from the Khkks, and fire erupted from the ground–both outside and inside the walls–toward the ship.

"Oh, no," she said. *How much of their weaponry did I take out?* She was pretty sure that targeting had been disabled, but they would still have–

Dozens of tiny specks detached themselves from the bottom of the ship and ignited, speeding toward the ground.

Explosives. Simple, dumb *bombs*. They still had their bombs.

And they were going to land *far* too close to her for comfort. She looked around for cover: there was none. If there had ever been any of the rock formations that were so common on Khkk near the pyramid, they'd long since been quarried or removed. There was *nowhere* to hide. She hit the ground, curling into a ball and covering her head.

Then the bombs struck, and the world erupted in light and sound. She felt a wave of heat pass over her, and waited until the sound of shattered rock hitting the ground stopped before daring to look around.

I guess I don't have to worry about how I get in anymore, she thought. The bombs had blown a hole in the wall around the pyramid that had to be thirty meters wide, and while the ship was listing badly it looked like it was at least *technically* going to "land" inside the compound. The Khkks who had survived the bombing run looked uncertain about what to do, anger about the violation of their space warring with their taboo about getting any closer than they already were.

Her subcomm pinged.

"Brazel?"

"You okay? That didn't look good."

She let out a deep breath that she hadn't realized she was holding. "I'm fine, but I think Barren and K'Shorr are on the surface. They just crashed their ship into that compound."

"It's called the Sanctum of the Sphere. Remember told us all about it. We're coming to get you."

"Meet me inside," she said.

She could *feel* her husband getting ready to argue with her.

"This isn't our fight," he said.

"I'm *making it* our fight," she said. "Try not to get shot down by the Khkks. Do you think Barren and K'Shorr are heading for the pyramid?"

"The Sanctum," Brazel said. "And probably. Remember said it's important, but she's not sure why. We think they know something we don't."

"Wonderful," Rhundi said, picking up her pace. "Well, I haven't thrown myself into danger in a while. Let's do this."

"You have thrown yourself into danger *multiple times today*," Brazel said. "What the fuck are you talking about?"

"You're cutting out," Rhundi said. "See you on the ground."

※{⊕}※

"I am not cutting out," Brazel said.

"Rhundi lies a lot," Grond observed. "Have you ever noticed that?"

"It's the foundation of our marriage in a lot of ways," the gnome mused. "You see anywhere down there that actually looks like a landing pad?"

EVASIVE MANEUVERS, Namey said. THEY'RE SHOOTING AT US. Brazel felt the ship spin and juke, avoiding fire from the ground

"Didn't Remember say this thing had some sort of camouflage mode?" Brazel asked.

I DON'T THINK—OOH! I DO! Namey said. ENGAGING.

The fire from the ground didn't stop, but it got significantly sparser as the *Nameless* matched the color of the sky and continued evasive maneuvers.

THERE IS A LANDING AREA INSIDE THE COMPOUND, the boat said. SHALL WE ATTEMPT TO PICK RHUNDI UP BEFORE WE LAND?

"She said not to," Brazel said. "'*See you on the ground.*' Her exact words. Land. We'll figure the rest out from there."

DESCENDING, the ship confirmed, rather unnecessarily.

"Glad to know you still like the sound of your own voice," Brazel griped.

There was a pained groan from the back of the ship, and the sound of a body hitting the floor.

"Asper," Grond said, vaulting out of his seat.

He found the elf a few meters outside the cockpit, unconscious, xir breathing shallow.

"What the hell happened?" Brazel said. "Namey, is there anybody onboard other than us?"

NO, the *Nameless* responded. XE LEFT THE GUNNERY STATION ABRUPTLY AND WAS ON XIR WAY TO THE COCKPIT. NOTHING HAPPENED THAT I AM AWARE OF.

Grond crouched to pick Asper up.   The elf coughed, awakening.

"Overmorrow..." xe said.

"What happened to Overmorrow?" Brazel said.

"I do not know," the elf said, xir eyes still rolling a bit. "A wave of pain and regret, and now nothing. I ... I cannot feel my parent any longer."

ROASHAN HAS BEEN DESTROYED, the *Nameless* said. JUST A MOMENT AGO.   I AM SCANNING FOR LIFE SIGNS IN THE AREA. EVERYTHING APPEARS TO BE BENEVOLENCE. THE EXPLOSION APPEARS TO HAVE DESTROYED A NUMBER OF SPIDERSHIPS. THE REST APPEAR TO BE RETREATING AT THIS TIME.

"They'll be back," Brazel said. "Bet on it."

"So what do you think?" Grond asked. "Is Overmorrow ... what, injured? Dead?"

"I ... I truly cannot tell," Asper said. The elf took a deep breath, stretching xir arms and legs. "I have never felt anything like that before. I cannot find xir. But I am not always able to. Overmorrow may be unconscious or perhaps in tunnelspace."

Asper struggled to xir feet.

"There is nothing to be done about it now," the elf said. "We have a job to do. How long until we're on the ground?"

MOMENTS, the *Nameless* confirmed.

"Are you sure you want to come with us?" Grond said. "You were *unconscious* a minute ago."

"I am fine," Asper said. "If my parent has died today, we shall avenge xir. If xe lives still, we will meet again. This is not yet over."

The crash took K'Shorr by surprise, knocking the ogre off his feet and utterly wrecking the careful layout of his armory. He growled, looking for a particular case, one that held a pair of pistols that he kept around for sentimental reasons. He'd already had to blow the door open just to get *into* the armory, since the gnome had wrecked the locking mechanism.

"I do *not* have time for this shit," he mumbled, when his eyes finally fell upon the pistols. They were out of the case, tossed into a corner by the combined forces of the rough landing and, no doubt, the flying door. He picked them both up and holstered them, then quickly scavenged a number of blades and some explosives from the wreckage of the room. One way or another, he'd have to return to the ship to recover more of his guns. There was quite a bit in this room that he wasn't interested in leaving around for what was left of the crew or the Khkks to scavenge.

The crew. Were they brave enough to try and steal from him? Most of them no doubt were fleeing the ship as fast as they could. He snarled at the thought, then activated a mine and left it just inside the door.

If I can't take my shit with me I'll be damned if I let anyone else have it, he thought.

He made his way back to the medbay, where he found Barren standing over the dead body of the medic.

"Not exactly grateful of ya, boss," he said.

"He hit his head," Barren said.

"Sure," K'Shorr agreed. *Not that I care.* "What's next?"

"Help me off this ship," Barren said. His left arm was encased in a cast and bound tightly to his body, and it looked as if the medic had wrapped his ribs as well. The horrid scar on his chest had already bled through the gauze. "And get me inside the Sanctum. Once that happens, I don't care. You are ... *released* from any obligations you ever had to me once I'm inside. I suggest you get off the surface as quickly as you can."

"Can you walk?"

"Well enough," Barren said. "We may encounter some resistance along the way. Destroy them."

"What I do best," the ogre said, leading the elf out of the medbay.

The two neither saw nor heard a single living member of the crew as they made their way out of the ship. They encountered a few scattered bodies, some clearly killed by the crash and others that appeared to have been killed by other crew members. There had been some scores settled once the ship hit the ground, apparently. The first airlock they reached had been left open.

"Stay here," K'Shorr told Barren. "I'll see if it's safe."

The ogre edged his way to the door and looked around. There had clearly been a brief battle outside, and it looked as if his crew had gotten the worst of it. He stayed still for a moment, looking for movement, and neither saw nor heard any. Their path to the Sanctum looked clear. The giant pyramid was several hundred meters away, but it dominated the horizon. From his position, still slightly underneath a large part of the ship's bulk, he couldn't even see the sky.

He rolled his neck, hearing the joints pop, then shouldered one of his pistols and walked out of the airlock. *Go ahead, take a shot at me.*

Nothing.

"Weird," he said. "Where the hell is everybody?"

"Fled," said Barren, exiting the ship behind him. "Those who remained behind here were not warriors. I would guess that these–" the elf disgustedly shoved a crewmember's body out of his way with a foot–"killed a few defenders themselves before being killed. And then the survivors left. They will not impede us."

The elf walked out in front of K'Shorr, limping badly but still moving under his own power.

"Whatever you say," K'Shorr said, and followed his employer toward the Sanctum.

THIRTY-FOUR

The Nameless made it to the landing pad without incident. The camouflage mode likely wouldn't be terribly useful in deep space, where target identification was done with AI assistance, but for fooling anything using eyes it was a really impressive trick.

THERE ARE SCATTERED LIFE SIGNS THROUGHOUT THE SETTLEMENT, Namey said.

"Get in touch with everybody you can," Brazel said. "Let's get them out of here before the Benevolence falls back on our heads. Grond, you and I head for the Sanctum. Asper, are you coming with us or do you want to stay here and see if you can coordinate an evacuation?"

The elf considered. "I shall remain," xe said. "There are likely injured among our people as well. I will bring back as many as I can."

"Boat's pretty big," Brazel said. "Ought to be room for everybody. See if you can get ahold of Rhundi, too, or at least send some help her way. Namey, do whatever Asper wants until we get back, unless xe tries to steal you."

DEFINE STEAL, the ship said.

"I'll leave it up to you," Brazel said. "Grond, you ready?"

"Just gotta hit up my quarters," the halfogre said. "Meet you outside?"

The gnome nodded, heading for the airlock.

When Grond emerged from the ship a few minutes later, the halfogre was prepared for battle in a way that Brazel had rarely seen before. The gnome was willing to bet that the amount of armament the halfogre was carrying constituted a good percentage of his body weight.

"You cannot *possibly* think you need all that," Brazel said.

"I like to be prepared," Grond said. "You know this."

"You ought to prepare with some *armor*," Brazel said. "I don't know what you have against the stuff."

"Slows me down," Grond said.

"And two hundred kilos of weapons don't?"

"It's cardio," the halfogre said, adjusting his cloak. Other than a breechclout under a wide utility belt and his gladiator's gloves, the cloak was the only clothing he had on. Everything else was supporting something lethal.

"And if we need to be *quiet?*"

Grond adjusted something at his belt, and the world went silent.

"One of Remember's toys?" Brazel tried to say, but no sound came out.

"Yep," Grond said, dropping the effect. "I don't think it lasts all that long, but it's built into the cloak. This one's way better than my old one."

"And yet you brought Angela with you. You old sentimentalist, you."

"Of course," the halfogre said, snapping his sniper's longbow into ready mode. "Best weapon on the planet."

"You could have told me about the brainbox, you know."

"I *tried*," Grond said, the smile back on his face. "Like *four* times. You were too busy being an asshole to let me tell you."

"That's called *mourning*," the gnome said.

"Nice of you to admit it," Grond replied. "Let's go find Rhundi and kill a couple of people."

"Sounds like a great idea," Brazel said. The two of them headed for the Sanctum of the Sphere.

"*This is where we part*," Barren said. He and K'Shorr had entered the Sanctum of the Sphere through a broad, open entryway, and they stood before a modern-looking lift ringed by a low fence. The lift went underground.

The ogre looked at him quizzically.

"You're kidding me, right? You're half-dead. Where are you planning on going?"

"Down *there*," Barren said, finding a control panel for the lift and bringing the system online. "You may stay here. Execute the gnomes if you get a chance, or do a better job of killing the halfogre than the last time you tried. After that, you may do whatever you like."

"You're kidding," K'Shorr said again.

Barren looked directly at K'Shorr with eyes filled with pain and blood. "I have no energy left for such things. Goodbye, K'Shorr."

The elf stepped onto the lift, which lowered him into the depths underneath the Sanctum. K'Shorr shrugged. He would wait, if that was what Barren wanted.

Barren reviewed the ritual in his head, trying to block out the pain as the lift descended. Twice his knees buckled underneath him, and the second time he allowed himself to fall. There was no room for pride any longer. He would crawl to his death if that was what he needed to do. Perhaps, finally, the Scouring God would recognize his penitence.

At one point in his life, he had desired to be a priest of Azamoeg. Now he wished only to not be rejected by him. He had done everything he could. The Noble Opposition was being torn to pieces in the skies above Khkk, and the destructive force he was about to unleash would do the rest. For this he had sacrificed his health. For this, he had had the compulsion placed on the boy and set in motion the chain of events that had brought all of them to this horrid bug-infested planet.

For nothing, it seemed. The lift finally reached the ground, and Barren painfully climbed to his feet and staggered off the platform. The gnome woman would find a way past K'Shorr. He was certain. He needed to be some distance away when she reached the caverns underneath the surface. He kicked at the control surface for the lift, shattering it and nearly losing his balance in the process. Delaying his pursuers seemed like a good idea.

He looked around. The caves under the planet were almost beautiful. Phosphorescent mold lent a yellow glow to the caves, which towered overhead, supported by the occasional natural column. The ground under his feet was oddly soft to the touch, and lent his tired feet some energy of their own as he moved what he hoped was a safe distance from the lift.

He knelt on the ground, shaking out a thin knife from inside one sleeve. He cut the bindings holding his broken arm to his chest, shrieking in pain when the limb fell free. He cut the cast off as well, lacerating his forearm badly in the process.

Oh well. That was happening soon enough anyway.

He put the knife down in front of him and reached inside his robes again, producing a small statue. A quick press of a tiny switch activated it, and he pressed his hand down upon it. The world started to go white, but he fought the communication. He did not want to stay with the Benevolence. He wanted only to send them a message.

You told me I should end my life. I will obey that command, but in my own way.

He felt anger from the other side of the connection and forced his hand off the sphere, breaking off their communication. He closed his eyes and began to chant. A red light began to shine from his body, and a sigil was burned into the ground around him: The symbol of Azamoeg, eight sinuous legs and an eye.

He picked up the knife and continued his ritual.

The Scouring God would be summoned, and he would wipe this entire miserable world from existence.

Rhundi watched as Barren and K'Shorr entered the pyramid. Amazingly, the Sanctum didn't actually appear to have a *door*. The structure was wide open at the base, a twenty-five meter wide entryway allowing anyone and everyone inside. She crept toward the entrance, keeping low and assuming that K'Shorr at least was probably smart enough to be looking behind the two of them every now and again.

"You guys down here yet?" she said over comm.

"On our way," Brazel said. "We're heading toward the Sanctum from the north. Where are you?"

Rhundi checked the sun. "West side, I think. Do you two see an entrance from your side?"

"No," Brazel said. They were approaching it from one of the pyramid's flat sides. The farthest point of the three-sided triangle pointed south.

Just the one, then, or two on opposite sides. "Go to the east side," she said. "See if there's a way in back there. There's a huge pavilion over here leading straight in, but the damn thing's too big to see if it goes all the way through. If there's no entrance on the east side, come back around. Let me know once you know. Is Asper with you?"

"No," Brazel said. "Xe's looking for xir people and getting them back to the *Nameless.*"

"The *Nameless* doesn't have room for that many people."

"New *Nameless,*" Brazel said. "Long story. Tell you later."

"Got it," Rhundi said. "Stay safe."

"Always," Brazel said, and clicked off.

A few more minutes of careful creeping around had her within a few dozen meters of the Sanctum. The pyramid was so high at this point that she literally couldn't see the top of it, and the light reflecting off and through the semitransparent walls eliminated any chance of shadows to sneak through if she wanted to get closer. She hugged the side of a building and lowered herself carefully to the ground, watching the entry pavilion, looking for any sign of movement within.

Hearing movement *behind* her was the last thing she expected. She flipped over on her back, pistol in hand, startling the young human who was approaching her. He jumped back, hands in the air.

"Asper sent me! I'm with Asper!" he said, trying to keep his voice down and not doing a very good job.

"How the hell does *Asper* know where to find me?" she asked.

"You know how the elves are," the man said. "Xe's contacting everyone xe can who's still in the compound. Xe let us know to assist any gnomes or halfogres we found. You're a gnome, right? Is your name Rhundi?" Rhundi couldn't tell if the man was being serious or not. He smelled and looked scared, but he didn't immediately strike her as an idiot.

"Look, I can give you xir comm frequency if you want. Just don't *shoot* me."

Rhundi thought carefully. The man wasn't dressed like one of Barren and K'Shorr's mercenaries, and she could come up with no good reason that he might know her name. Barren and K'Shorr hadn't had time to set up a trap.

Fine. "So how are you planning on helping me?"

"There's another way into the Sanctum," the man said. "Underground. If you're trying to avoid the two who went in there a few minutes ago, it'll get you in without them noticing you."

Rhundi thought about this for a moment. There was no way that Barren and K'Shorr would be expecting an ambush to come from *in front* of them.

"Lead the way," she said.

"I feel like the last time you had us invading an abandoned temple it didn't work out too well," Grond said.

"Shut up," Brazel responded. "Khkk probably doesn't even *have* snakes."

The two of them had reached the eastern side of the Sanctum of the Sphere and had discovered that that side also featured a wide entryway. If anything, this appeared to be the *front* door. It soared to thirty meters from the ground and was wide enough to park a medium-sized spacecraft in. Grond peered around the corner to look inside the structure. The entire interior was open, stretching up to the peak high in the distance.

"He's in there," Grond said.

"Which *he?*" Brazel asked.

"K'Shorr," Grond said. There was no sign of Barren. The ogre stood guard by what looked to be either an open-air lift or a staircase heading underground. A railing that would probably be chest-high on a human but looked comically low next to K'Shorr surrounded it. It looked curiously modern compared to the rest of the structure, and was made of simple steel rather than the glass-like material the rest of the pyramid was built from.

"So shoot him," Brazel said. "What's that fancy longbow for if you're not gonna use it?"

Grond considered for a moment, then put Angela on the ground.

"Grond." Brazel said. The gnome had a note of alarm in his voice.

He shrugged off the utilicloak, then pulled off his belt and bandoliers, leaving the rest of his weaponry next to Angela.

"*Grond,*" Brazel repeated. "We do *not* have time for ogre honor shit right now."

"No honor involved," Grond said. "Just history." He left the gloves on his hands, cracking his knuckles and striding out into the center of the temple.

K'Shorr turned toward Grond, pointing both of his guns at him.

"Freeze," he said.

"Don't think so," Grond said.

"I'm gonna fucking *kill you*, Grond," K'Shorr said. "Have I ever lied to you before? Why would I start today?"

"Maybe," the halfogre replied. "But not with those, and not like that." He stood barely three meters away from K'Shorr, his eyes shining red, nearly matching the ogre's deep crimson in intensity. Brazel stood behind him, whistling quietly to himself. K'Shorr watched the two for a moment, then shrugged and holstered his guns.

"Where's Barren, K'Shorr?" Grond asked.

"Down there somewhere," the ogre replied. "I don't even know what the hell he's doing. And, y'know, I think he *fired* me before he went down there? After all our time together. You're interrupting me. I was pondering my *future*."

"Five minutes of grunting noises and pain, followed by death," Grond said.

K'Shorr stared at Grond and Brazel, then laughed. He unbuckled his belt, letting both of his holsters drop to the ground. "Fuck it, halfogre. Let's see how much you learned. I bet you last a minute before I halve your ass *again*." He raised his hands and curled them into fists, knuckles cracking.

There was a bang. A large hole appeared between K'shorr's eyes. He took a single step toward Grond, then crumpled to the ground, a terribly surprised expression on his face.

"Did that stupid bastard seriously just *forget I was here?*" Brazel asked, putting his gun away.

"Think so," Grond said, picking K'shorr's weapons up and kicking the ogre viciously in the head. "Funny part is, he always thought I should have cheated more often. Guess I learned my lesson after all."

"*Who* learned a lesson?" Brazel said. "I was the one who shot him. It wasn't like you *signaled* me or anything."

"Yeah, but I *wanted* you to. That counts."

"Good enough, I suppose," Brazel said. "Let's find Barren."

"Just a minute," Grond said. "You were right. Shoulda just brought my stuff with me." He went and recovered his weapons.

THIRTY-FIVE

"So what is this place, anyway?" Rhundi asked. The man's name was Colyn. He'd been based on Khkk for close to four standard months. He'd led her away from the Sanctum and into one of the smaller buildings around it. The building, which was built from mud bricks, had concealed a stairwell that opened into a surprisingly high-tech manufacturing floor. A smooth tunnel cut into the rock led them further underground. They had been able to take a tram for what seemed like several kilometers at a steep angle and had walked perhaps another half klick. She had no idea how deep underground she was any longer.

"We thought the Sanctuary was just a tower at first," Colyn said. "The two you were following are heading down a stairwell. That was covered and buried when we got here. We were trying to expand the base by going underground, since we didn't want to be too visible from the surface or from orbit. One of our excavation machines managed to dig the floor out from underneath itself. It was awful—the fall killed a couple of our guys—but we *found* something down there. There's ... a cave network, or *something*, you'll have to see it. Once the machines found the caves, we looked at the tower more closely. The entrance had been buried and plugged. We got curious and pulled the plug out."

"Well, I see no way *that* could have backfired. The thing's called the Sanctum of the Sphere," Rhundi said. "It's a pyramid. Did you ever find the *sphere*?"

"Like I said, you'll see," Colyn said.

The sound of low chanting became audible from ahead of them. Colyn and Rhundi froze.

"This is where you go back to Asper," Rhundi said. "Don't wait for me. Just go."

"Are you sure? I could–"

Spare me from human males, she thought. "You can go *find the elf,* and get onto *my ship,* where you're *safe.* I'll handle things from here, unless there's something else I need to know about what's in front of me."

"We don't know *anything* about what's in front of you," Colyn said, sounding slightly insulted. "Good luck, I guess." He turned and left, leaving Rhundi alone in the tunnel.

She crept ahead, trying to stay as quiet as she could. She made it several meters before realizing that the artificial lighting that had been illuminating the tunnel had ended. There was a yellow glow coming from in front of her, where the tunnel abruptly opened into empty space. Someone had attached a simple ladder to the lip of the tunnel. *He wasn't kidding. The excavators would have just fallen through.*

She could still hear the chanting, coming from somewhere off to her right, but couldn't see the source. She climbed down the ladder, which stretched ten or fifteen meters before reaching the ground. She looked around.

The crater from the broken excavator was not far from the foot of the ladder. The Malevolence workers had removed the machine and the bodies, but the scars remained on the floor. Several deep cracks in the surface spiraled out jaggedly from the impact point. She shined a light into one of them. It went far deeper than she felt like it ought to.

Odd, she thought.

The rest of the cavern was mind-boggling.

The floor looked like grey stone, but had a slight amount of give to it. It was nearly perfectly smooth, and stretched out in all directions around her. Above her, bioluminescent mold shone on the cave roof. Every fifty meters or so a wide column stretched from the floor to the ceiling. The columns were made of the same material as the floor.

She could see to the *horizon.* The "cave structure" appeared to go on *forever.* The entire place smelled dusty, stale, as if nothing alive had been down here for centuries.

"Sanctum of the Sphere," she said. "The *entire moon* is the sphere." How far underground *was* she? The Khkks had tunnel systems. Grond had dug his way into one when the Khkks had first attacked the train he was on. The moon had *canyons,* too. She suddenly remembered a detail from her initial research about Khkk that its few seas and lakes were thought to be abnormally shallow. *Does this thing extend under the surface of the whole world?*

What the hell have we gotten ourselves into?

The chanting continued from somewhere far ahead of her. She jogged toward it. The floor was ... *springy?*

Yes. Springy. Just a little bit. It was quieter to run on than she expected it to be, too. Given the shape and size of this place, her footsteps should have echoed for kilometers. All she heard was the chanting. Her feet were nearly silent.

After a few minutes of running, her husband's voice in her subcomm spoiled the quiet.

"Rhundi."

She stopped. "What?"

"Ssh. Look up."

She looked up. In the distance in front of her, the roof suddenly swooped upward into a hollow cylinder that soared toward the surface. A huge spiral staircase ringed the cylinder. Brazel and Grond were crouched at the end of the stairs, just before it left the column to hang in empty space. Another ladder extended from the staircase to the floor. The halfogre was blinking a handheld signal light at her. She waved to show she'd spotted them.

"What's that chanting? Can you see Barren and K'Shorr?"

Grond pointed. The yellow glow from the mold was omnipresent throughout the caves, but Rhundi thought she could see a reddish glow in the distance. It wasn't bright enough to pick out any details.

"Get down here," she said. "If that's them, we should go after them together." She couldn't shake the idea that Barren still had something planned. Moving silently, Grond and Brazel descended the rest of the way to the cave floor.

"I can't believe Barren even survived the climb," Rhundi said. "He wasn't in very good shape the last time I saw him."

Grond pointed at a spot on the floor. Rhundi could just make out a circular object. "Some sort of lift," he said. "Barren *rode* down, and then wrecked the damn thing. Brazel and I got to walk. Something else I get to kick his ass for."

"Just *his* ass?"

"K'Shorr's dead," Grond said. He showed her the pistols at his waist. Rhundi's eyes widened slightly.

"I hope it hurt," she said.

"Actually, probably not," Brazel said. "Tell ya later. Let's get Barren."

As if on cue, the chanting stopped, and the vague red glow brightened and intensified, its glare filling the cavern.

"That can't be good," Rhundi said. The three of them charged toward the light.

Barren knelt on the floor, surrounded by an enormous sigil: a single, glowing eye, with four long, twisted tentacles protruding from either side. The elf's wrists were bleeding freely. A whirling nimbus of red and white light surrounded him. He had his head thrown back, his arms outstretched, blood dripping down onto the sigil. He held a long, twisted knife in one hand. His other arm, badly broken, hung at a sickening angle from his elbow. If he felt any pain at all from it, it didn't show.

Grond, Brazel and Rhundi all opened fire at once, their shots harmlessly being absorbed by the light.

"Shit," Grond said. "What do we do?"

"Grenade," Rhundi said, snatching one off Grond's belt and throwing it at Barren. The grenade simply evaporated upon hitting the light.

"We've seen that symbol before," Brazel said. "And it didn't end well for *anyone*. We should leave right now." He tried to open a comm to Asper, then to the *Nameless*. Nothing. *We're too far underground*, he thought.

"We can't just *leave* him down here," Rhundi said.

"We don't have a *choice*," Brazel said. "You think any of us can get through that field?"

"Only one way to find out," Grond said.

⸭⟨ᴏᴏ⟩⸭

Asper stood in the cockpit of the Nameless and stretched xir senses as far as xe could, searching for any more living beings within the compound surrounding the Sanctum. The elf sensed nothing but the fear of the people xe had already rescued. Most of the refugees were humanoids, but there was a fair number of allied Khkks among them. Their fear was alien, but still recognizable.

ASPER? said the *Nameless* over the comm.

"Go ahead," xe said.

SOMETHING IS HAPPENING IN ORBIT OVER THE MOON. AN ENERGY DISCHARGE OF SOME KIND. THE SOURCE IS UNKNOWN.

"Show me," Asper said, and the *Nameless* activated a holographic display. Xe could see a single point of immensely bright light, hanging in the sky a few kilometers over the tip of the Sanctum. It was almost as if a second sun had decided to appear in Khkk's sky. The point flared, growing in size.

"I need to see that with my own eyes," Asper said. "Don't go anywhere." Xe raced back outside the ship, looking up at the anomaly, hanging in the distance high overhead. A moment of concentration sharpened the elf's vision, screening out some of the light from the anomaly and allowing xir to see finer details within it.

Something inside the anomaly moved.

What was that?

Something started to come out of the ball of light. A long, sinuous shape, followed by several more, emerged from the anomaly and flailed around blindly.

"Ship, can you see that?" Asper asked.

MY SENSORS SEE NOTHING OTHER THAN THE PORTAL, the *Nameless* reported. BUT THE PORTAL IS GROWING.

That was bad.

That was *very* bad.

"Azamoeg," Asper said. Wherever Brazel and Grond were, the two of them had failed. Xe tried again to reach out to the two of them specifically, wherever they were, and could not find them.

"Prepare to leave," Asper commanded the ship. "We're taking who we have with us. We don't have time to wait."

THAT IS STEALING, the *Nameless* responded. I WAS CLEARLY ORDERED TO NOT ALLOW MYSELF TO BE STOLEN.

"It's not stealing if your owners are *dead*," Asper retorted. "We have to *go*, or we're going to *join* them." The elf boarded the ship through the open cargo door, shoving refugees out of xir way as xe bolted for the cockpit.

Asper arrived just in time to witness the explosion, as a bolt of light shot down from the heavens to strike the Sanctum of the Sphere.

And the Sanctum *shattered*.

The roar of sound was overwhelming, and Asper fell to xir knees, both hands clasped over xir ears. Xe could feel, but not see, the refugees being deafened elsewhere in the ship.

"Take off," xe pleaded. "Take off *now*."

ACKNOWLEDGED, the *Nameless* responded, and lifted off Khkk's surface, his shields flickering as they absorbed the impacts of uncountable thousands of tiny pieces of shattered glass.

>{⊡}<

THIRTY-SIX

Grond was only a meter or two away from Barren's shield when the blast came. He was blown head over heels, landing on his back several meters away, dazed and startled. Rhundi and Brazel were knocked flat.

The halfogre staggered to his feet, still not entirely sure what was happening. Barren's shield was gone, the ground around him cracked open. Grond reached for Angela at her usual place at his back, couldn't find her, and then staggered toward the elf anyway.

Barren stared at his hands, the glow entirely gone from the sigil around him. The sigil itself slowly faded away as Grond watched.

"Rejected," the elf moaned. "He is gone. I was not even worthy of *death*." He held the knife loosely in one hand, as if he barely considered the halfogre a threat any longer.

"Who's gone?" Grond said. The elf was hard to hear, his voice nearly drowned out by a ringing in Grond's ears. And, oddly, a dull roar. The ogre shook his head. He'd been hit in the head plenty of times. It had never led to *roaring*.

Beyond Barren, he could see Rhundi and Brazel shaking their heads, slowly climbing to their feet.

"Everything," Barren said, lifting his head to look at the halfogre. The elf's eyes were filled with blood. "Everyone. Gone." Tears rolled down his cheeks, staining his thin beard a soft pink color.

Grond found one of K'Shorr's pistols at his waist. He fumbled it out of its holster and pointed it at the elf.

"You're coming with us," he said unsteadily.

"Never," the elf said, and slashed his throat. Grond watched, dully, as Barren collapsed, dying in a pool of his own blood. The roaring in his ears grew louder.

"I was not expecting that," Rhundi said.

"Leave him here to rot," Brazel said. "Let's go. It's a long climb back to the surface."

"Does anyone else hear that?" Grond asked. "Is that the—"

The rest of his question was lost in the cacophony of millions of pieces of shattered glass tumbling into the cavern. The three dropped to the floor again, covering their heads. Grond crawled over to Brazel and Rhundi, covering the two of them with his utilicloak. The avalanche of shrapnel continued for several minutes, smaller pieces bouncing off the cloak, the sound drowning out speech and thought.

Eventually, the din subsided. The air was thick with dust, and all three were coughing.

"There's a tunnel," Rhundi said when she recovered. "It's how I got in. We can try that way." The spiral staircase that Brazel and Grond had used was destroyed, torn away by the mass of the broken Sanctum.

Grond nodded, not trusting his ability to speak yet. He held up a finger, looking around for something. Brazel read the look on his partner's face and began searching as well, eventually discovering Angela a few yards beyond where Grond had been thrown by the blast. The halfogre nodded again, a thankful look on his face, and hung the longbow back in her holster on his back.

Rhundi pointed out the way to the exit. The three of them turned, leaving Barren's thin, broken corpse behind.

The Nameless picked up speed as it exited Khkk's atmosphere. Asper cleared xir head, sending a brief pulse of reassurance to the panicked refugees in the cargo hold.

"Stay away from the anomaly," xe said. "But keep it on the viewscreen. In the *visual spectrum*, not sensors. Use cameras."

I DO NOT UNDERSTAND, the ship responded.

"There is something inside the anomaly," Asper said. "Your sensors can't see it."

The boat beeped an acknowledgment and an image of the anomaly appeared on the viewscreen. Asper watched as one of Azamoeg's long tentacles swept through a spidership that had gotten too close, smashing the fighter into scrap metal. The battle around Khkk was over, every ship that still survived fleeing for safety, ignoring each other.

"If Azamoeg comes through that portal, he'll scour the entire planet," Asper said. "Contact everyone on our side who is not already in tunnelspace. Send them to Remember's ship." *I do not know what else I can do,* the elf thought.

TRANSMITTING COORDINATES. SHALL I SHOOT AT THE ANOMALY? I WANT TO USE MY GUNS MORE.

"Absolutely *do not do that*," Asper said. The tentacles continued to flail about, finding nothing else within reach to smash. And then an amazing thing happened: They began *withdrawing*, pulling back inside the glowing portal.

The anomaly flared once more, the light's intensity forcing Asper to shade xir eyes, and then disappeared, the ghost in the elf's retinas the only evidence it had been there at all.

IT'S JUST GONE, the *Nameless* said. THERE IS NO TRACE OF THE ANOMALY LEFT AT ALL. NO RESIDUAL ENERGY SIGNAL OF ANY KIND. CAN WE GO BACK NOW?

"Do you really think that they could have survived that?" Asper asked.

BRAZEL AND GROND HAVE SURVIVED WORSE THAN THIS, the ship responded. AND RHUNDI HAS SURVIVED WORSE THAN EITHER OF THEM.

"There are a number of individuals on this ship in serious need of medical attention," xe said. "I cannot see how spending time searching for our missing friends is more important than getting people who we *know* are alive to safety."

I WAS TOLD TO NOT LET YOU STEAL ME, the *Nameless* repeated. I THINK YOU ARE TRYING TO STEAL ME AGAIN. The *Nameless* took control of itself and dove back toward Khkk's surface. With its active camouflage turned on, it was unlikely that the Khkks would be able to see the ship from the ground, but it became clear quickly that none of them were bothering to look. Between Barren's bombing run and the explosion of the Sanctum, most of the settlement had been flattened. The Khkk army that had surrounded it was scattered, many of them fleeing.

"This doesn't look promising," Asper said.

WE WILL KEEP LOOKING UNTIL I RUN OUT OF FUEL, the *Nameless* said.

Ten minutes later, they picked up a comm signal from Grond.

"*The wars have not ended,*" Remember said. "Khkk remains in as much conflict as it was in before we arrived."

"We never thought we were going to end it," Brazel said. "Whatever that was, we didn't cause it."

"Are you not curious?" she answered.

"No," the gnome said, cutting Remember off. "Not a bit. The job's over. I'll accept the new ship as payment. I've got my whole family back together. I don't see the point of further curiosity."

"Many of my people continue to call Khkk home," Asper said. "We owe it to them to at least rescue whoever we can." The elf looked at Remember. "With your permission, I would like to use your ship as a base while we evacuate everyone else we can. After that, we will locate another cell of the Noble Opposition and rejoin them."

Remember glanced at Grond, who shrugged.

"What is mine is yours," she said. "I believe we will remain here for a while longer as well."

"I admit I'm still curious too," Rhundi said. She sat on the floor on a comfortable oversized cushion, most of her younger children competing with each other to find ways to lie on top of their mother. Darsi and the older children sat nearby. "There's something very odd about that place. The 'sphere' the pyramid was named after? I think it was the *entire center of the moon.*"

"Fascinating," Remember said. "Are you certain?"

"It certainly looked like it," Rhundi answered. "The caves went off to the horizon in every direction. It may not be the *whole* world, but they're pretty extensive."

"It must have been an enormous undertaking," Remember said. "Perhaps some culture before the Khkks carved it."

"That's the weird part," Brazel said. "I don't think it was carved. It *wasn't rock*. The floor had a little bit of give to it. Running on it, you'd bounce a little bit."

Remember raised an eyebrow. Irtuus-bon, standing nearby, went through at least three different shapes and sizes in a matter of moments.

"What?" Brazel and Grond asked simultaneously.

The troll went digging through his things, looking frantically for something. He eventually found a datapad. He spent a few moments accessing something and then presented it, without comment, to Brazel. The gnome took the pad and looked at the information on the screen.

"What's a dragon?" he said.

>⟨⊞⟩<

THIRTY-SEVEN

Haakoro exited tunnelspace with his fingers crossed, hoping beyond hope that he'd picked the right spot. Working the calculations to properly calibrate the needleship's gun had tired him, and he had simply trusted to his luck and picked a sector that he thought might be close to the one the troll had pointed out. If he needed to spend a few days or weeks searching, well, it wasn't as if he had anything more important to do.

It wasn't as if *anyone* had anything more important to do.

His stolen ship emerged from tunnelspace into a far more populated area than he'd expected, joining a flow of other ships coming into the sector in more or less the same direction. He activated the ship's sensors, scanning the area around him.

He was *surrounded* by Benevolence. Everything nearby was transmitting Benevolence identity codes. Dozens of spiderships flew nearby in what almost looked like a leisurely fashion, and he saw models of ships he'd never even seen pictures of before.

Several thousand kilometers in front of him, the largest ship he'd ever seen floated silently in space.

The *Testament*. He'd *found* it.

"I am the luckiest son of a bitch who ever lived," he said.

He had barely begun accelerating when the spiderships around him opened fire.

⋊⊙⋉

THIRTY-EIGHT

Deep underground, under millions of tons of rock, the broken body of an elf lay still on the ground. The body sat in a pool of blood, strangely still liquid despite the dusty, dry air and the passage of time.

In the silent chamber, the body of the elf twitched once, as the sound of a single sharp snap echoed. A tiny crack, the width of a finger, opened in the ground underneath it.

The elf's blood drained away into the depths of the Sphere.

THE END
June 6, 2014
January 16, 2015

THANK YOU

for reading *The Sanctum of the Sphere*.

If you enjoyed this book, please leave a review for it at the book review site of your choice.

ABOUT LUTHER M. SILER

Luther Siler was born in 1976. He lives in northern Indiana with his wife, three-year-old son, a dog and two cats. In his spare time he works at a middle school.

He only occasionally refers to himself in the third person, and writing this is making him slightly uncomfortable. He is also god-awful at smiling for pictures.

Luther Siler's blog: http://www.infinitefreetime.com

Follow Luther @nfinitefreetime on Twitter.

ALSO BY LUTHER M. SILER

SKYLIGHTS

Available in print and digitally.

August 15, 2022: the Tycho, the most advanced interplanetary craft ever designed by the human race, launches from Earth on an expedition to Mars. The Tycho carries four passengers, soon to be the most famous people in human history.

February 19, 2023: The Tycho loses all communication with Earth while orbiting Mars. After weeks of determined attempts to reestablish contact, the Tycho is declared lost.

2027: Journalist Gabriel Southern receives a message from a mysterious caller: "Mars." Ezekiel ben Zahav isn't talking, but he wants Southern to accompany him for something-- and he's dangling enough money under his nose to make any amount of hardship worth it.

SKYLIGHTS is the story of the second human expedition to Mars. Their mission: to find out what happened to the first.

Read on for an excerpt: the prologue to SKYLIGHTS.

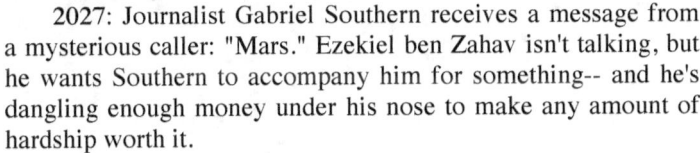

Flashbulb memory, they call it. It's when you remember exactly where you were when you first discovered something or saw something happen.

If you're younger than me, which a lot of you probably are, then your first flashbulb memory is probably related to terrorism somehow. Anybody in, say, their early thirties or older probably remembers exactly where they were on September 11, 2001. A little younger than that and your first flashbulb memory is probably one of the bombings in Chicago in 2018.

I was six years old when the space shuttle *Challenger* exploded. It was January 29, 1986, at exactly eleven thirty-nine in the morning. I was in first grade. For some reason-- I could look this up if I wanted, I suppose, but my first-grade self didn't know, so I'm not going to bother-- NASA had decided that it would be great if they put a schoolteacher on the Space Shuttle. Her name was Christa McAuliffe, and she'd been a middle school teacher, her students not a lot older than I was at the time.

There was a ton of publicity about her presence on the shuttle. Come to think of it, that might have been the reason that NASA put her there in the first place. Every single kid in my school was watching the flight launch on television. The *Challenger* took off, and we all clapped. Seventy-three seconds later, an O-ring failed on the shuttle's right Solid Rocket Booster. There was a little puff of smoke from the side of the ship.

Some of us were still clapping.

I remember noticing it and wondering, for the split second that I had, what had happened. And then the *Challenger,* with me and millions of other people around the country watching, silently blew apart. There were a few seconds of shocked silence in the room, and then every kid in the class-- every one in the building, probably-- started crying at once.

You know what? Writing that just now, I wondered what my teacher must have done afterwards. I can't even remember her name. I can remember the wood surface on my desk, because I dug my fingers into it so hard that day that they scratched it and I got splinters. I can remember the wood-grain on the television set they had us watching. I can remember being surprised that Rachel Douglas, the biggest butthead in the entire first grade, was crying as hard as I was. But I can't remember a single thing that our teacher did to try and bring everybody back to sanity after watching that happen. That's how flashbulb memories work; you'll remember the event itself forever, but that doesn't mean you'll remember anything else that happened around it.

Seventeen years and two days later, it happened again. This time, it was the shuttle *Columbia,* and I was twenty-four and no longer sitting in a classroom. In fact, when the *Columbia* was falling apart in the morning sky over Texas, I was stuck in traffic and late to work. I found out about it about ten minutes after I got in, when the smarmy dope from the office next door made some sort of comment about it to me. We had the Internet by then-- yes, there was Internet back then, although I think we might have still been calling it the World Wide Web-- and I saw the entire thing on CNN's Web site. This time there weren't any tears, just a dull sort of ache in the pit of my stomach. I spent the rest of the day on the computer, chasing down eyewitness reports and trying to devour whatever little bits of actual news managed to leak out. It was funny; I hadn't spent much time thinking about space flight since the first grade, but suddenly the families of the men and women on that shuttle were all I could think about.

I was working for the *Indianapolis Star* at the time, splitting my time between a biweekly column in the science section and general reporting on local news for the rest of the paper. It was a good job; I was happy enough, and making enough money, but I wanted something different from my life.

I decided to write a book.

A year later, I'd completed *Nothing to Bury: the Martyrs of the Space Race*, a look at the lives of the astronauts who had died on the *Challenger* and the *Columbia*, as well as a host of other lives lost in the pursuit of space, and a look at the culture of NASA in between the two disasters. I was pretty proud of it as a piece of work; I wasn't expecting it to necessarily sell well to the general public, but it was a good piece of writing. It did better than I'd expected, enough that I've been able to be comfortable with freelance writing since then. I'm still working for news sites and some of the few print papers that are left, mind you, but I can pick my own assignments and do my own reporting now as opposed to having people assign my projects.

You know where this is going, don't you? I imagine you do.

On August 15, 2022, after years of technical and political delays, the space shuttle *Tycho*, carrying four astronauts, launched on a six-month journey to Mars. They were to remain in orbit around Mars for thirty days, during which they would land on the planet's surface for the first time in human history, then to return to Earth. The run-up to the launch was the biggest public relations bonanza NASA had ever seen. Everything just *stopped* the day the *Tycho* launched. It was just like it had been for the *Challenger,* only times a hundred. They just weren't as good at hype in the eighties, I guess.

I was watching at home, with a couple of friends-- I actually had a little party for the launch. I didn't realize how tense I was until I looked at my hands afterwards. There were furrows in my palms from my fingernails. Then the shuttle took off, soaring into a perfectly blue sky, and I held my breath for a few moments.

The launch went off without a hitch, though, and pictures of the *Tycho* blanketed every website and print doc on the planet over the next few days. For the next six months, everyone was obsessed with Mars. The astronauts provided regular updates on what they were doing. You could get daily blink messages from them if you wanted to, and progress along their flight path was updated live on a map running at the top of CNN.com for the entire duration of the trip. Those six months, I'm convinced, inspired a whole generation of new astronauts, astrophysicists, and pilots. I've never in my life seen America more excited about science. It was amazing.

And then, on February 19th, 2023, when the long voyage was finally over, we... well, we don't actually know what happened. The *Tycho* was supposed to aerobrake into orbit around Mars, stay in orbit for a day or two, and then the astronauts were going to leave the ship to descend to the planet's surface in a lander. They were going to stay on the surface for two weeks or so, doing experiments, exploring the Martian surface, and making history.

There wasn't anything resembling photo evidence, not good evidence at least-- NASA had been sending a steady diet of pictures and video from cameras affixed to the outside of the *Tycho* for months, but they failed at the same time as the audio feed. But we were getting audio beamed back from inside the cabin. Right up until the point where the flight commander, a decorated Marine pilot by the name of Alondra Gallegos, spoke the last words that the *Tycho* sent back to Earth.

"Is that..." was all she said.

After that, nothing. No sound, no signals, no big explosion to be played on the news over and over again. Just nothing at all, and what started off as mild concern slowly morphed, over the next few days, weeks, months, into the certainty that, somehow, the ship had been lost. There was hope for a while that there had just been some sort of global communications failure, that the *Tycho* was still out there but had lost the ability to talk to us. Sadly, those hopes didn't make much sense in reality-- the *Tycho's* communication capabilities were among the simplest systems on the ship, something a talented twelve-year-old would have been able to repair, *and* there was a redundant backup system. Anything catastrophic enough to have completely crippled the ship's ability to talk would have caused fatal damage to the rest of the ship as well. We just couldn't figure out what. Conventional wisdom eventually decided there had been some sort of asteroid or meteorite impact, something like that.

There was no flashbulb moment for the *Tycho*. The families of the four people lost on that mission-- Alondra Gallegos, Harrison Brown, Kassius Newsome, and Ai-Li Wu-- will never be able to move on. Many of them are convinced that their family members are still out there somewhere. There was no national mourning like there was for the *Challenger* and the *Columbia*. It was as if, after three high-profile ship losses, this time the country just wanted to forget about it.

I got a few calls for interviews after the *Tycho* lost contact, and a few more a few months later, once NASA officially stopped trying to reestablish contact with the ship. I turned them all down, though; I didn't want to base any more of my career on profiting from the deaths of people more heroic and important than I was. I didn't want to write about space any more.

Little did I know.